Kissing Toads

Jemma Harvey is a freelance journalist and author of *Wishful Thinking*. She lives and writes in Brighton.

Praise for Jemma Harvey's *Wishful Thinking*

'A fuzzy, feel-good summer romp' *Woman's Own*

Also available by Jemma Harvey

Wishful Thinking

Kissing Toads

Jemma Harvey

arrow books

Published in the United Kingdom by Arrow Books in 2006

1 3 5 7 9 10 8 6 4 2

The Ra
20 Vauxhall

Random House .... (Pty) Limited
20 Alfred Street, Milsons Point, Sydney
New South Wales 2061, Australia

Random House New Zealand Limited
18 Poland Road, Glenfield
Auckland 10, New Zealand

Random House (Pty) Limited
Isle of Houghton, Corner of Boundary Road & Carse O'Gowrie
Houghton 2198, South Africa

Random House Group Limited Reg. No. 954009

www.randomhouse.co.uk

A CIP catalogue record for this book
is available from the British Library

Papers used by Random House
are natural, recyclable products made from wood grown in
sustainable forests. The manufacturing processes conform to
the environmental regulations of the country of origin

ISBN 9780099469148 (from Jan 2007)
ISBN 0099469146

Typeset by Palimpsest Book Production Limited,
Grangemouth, Stirlingshire
Printed and bound in Great Britain by
Cox & Wyman Ltd, Reading, Berkshire

Chapter 1:
Committing Sooty

Ruth

It is a truth universally acknowledged that a single woman in possession of an adequate income must be in want of a life.

I woke up to singledom on the sort of grey November morning that would make the most carefree and cheerful person feel like hitting the Prozac. I don't know if there are any statistics on it – probably, because there always are – but I'm sure most suicides happen in the dark months, when the days are short and gloomy and the nights seem to be taking over, and the magazines tell you the party season is under way but you haven't been invited, and there's nothing to look forward to but the chill, damp, endless south-of-England winter, too cold for fun yet not cold enough for snow . . . And when you add abrupt, unexpected, gut-churning, heart-aching singledom on top of that, it wasn't surprising I lay in bed considering possible short cuts out of this world. Gas is traditional, but my cooker is electric, and I had no idea how to electrocute myself and a strong suspicion I would make a mess of it if I tried, upsetting everybody else by short-circuiting the whole building. There was always the overdose, only I wasn't sure what of; so few pills are potentially lethal these days. Aspirin can ruin your liver without actually killing you, and apart from that all I had in the cupboard was multivitamins, birth control pills, and Imodium (death by constipation?). It was very selfish of the chemical companies, I thought, keeping people alive in this way – probably so they could make a fortune selling all the would-be suicides anti-depressants. Exploitation of a vulnerable minority; perhaps we could do a piece on it . . .

That's how you think, after years in TV journalism. You can't help it. One moment you're contemplating killing yourself, and the next it's become an item on the show.

The show . . .

Thoughts of suicide faded into a grimmer reality. I would have to leave my job.

I'd been working on *Dick Ramsay: Behind the News* for nearly seven years. I'd come as a bright young thing of twenty-six, starting as an assistant to the assistants and graduating to full-on assistant, and at thirty-two I knew I was almost past my professional sell-by date. There were lots of other bright young things, possibly brighter and certainly younger, queuing up to take my place in the assistant stakes. I should have been a proper producer by now, but it would have meant moving to another show, and I'd stayed and stayed – because of Kyle. Kyle Muldoon, the on-screen talent with his tough-guy exterior and caramel-soft centre, who had been half of my life, or perhaps more than half, for the past six years. I'd gone with him on some assignments and waited for his return from others, worried about him, welcomed him, sobered him or put him to bed, boosted his ego, soothed his tantrums. It hadn't been a perfect relationship, but what is? He'd stood me up, let me down, wriggled out of weekends with my parents, got embarrassingly drunk at friends' weddings and those few dinner parties I could persuade him to attend. It didn't matter. I loved him.

And now his caramel heart had melted for someone else, all in an instant, and he was out of my life for good. I couldn't stay with the show, go on working with him – that would mean constant anguish and humiliation. I'd have to leave. Now. Under the tidal wave of my misery, imminent joblessness and career disintegration began to appear almost desirable, a necessary part of the doom that confronted me. I was single; I might as well be unemployed to complete the picture. To all intents and purposes my life was over. Time to get up, send the relevant emails, tie up the loose ends.

I reached for the telephone, then my specs, so I could see what I was saying.

'Delphi?' I was addressing, not the Greek oracle, but my best friend, Delphinium Dacres.

Yes, *that* Delphinium Dacres. The glamour girl of TV gardening shows. It's a long story, but she really is my best friend. We grew up together.

'For God's sake,' she said. 'It's *before nine o'clock* on a Saturday morning . . .'

'Friday.'

'Are you sure?'

'Sure.'

'You at work?'

'No, and I'm not going to be.'

Finally, the best-friend antennae began to twitch. 'What's wrong?'

'I've split up with Kyle.'

'You do that all the time. It never lasts. If I thought it was for real, I'd be cheering.'

Delphinium disapproved of Kyle for all sorts of reasons, starting with the casual way he treated me. She thinks men are supposed to worship and obey. Most of hers do.

'Cheer,' I said. 'This is it. For real.'

3

'You sound awful.' Her tone was modulating into genuine concern. 'What's he done?'

'Got married.'

'*What??*'

We met in a coffee bar later that morning. By then, I'd already emailed my excuses for the day and my resignation for the future to Dick Ramsay and the producer. Somehow, it had taken the edge off my suicide plans, leaving me grey and empty and suffering. Delphinium, when she saw me, didn't cheer. True friends don't cheer at your distress, even if, in principle, they welcome the cause, and Delphinium is my truest friend.

In the business, she isn't popular; the up-and-coming ones very rarely are. They're too hungry, too pushy, too undeserving of their fortune to go down well with those who have been elbowed out of their way or who have to submit to their professional whims. Those who make it to the top of the heap can afford to relax and be generous, earning the regard of gushing subordinates who want to curry fame and favour. But Delphinium is still on the upward ladder. She doesn't have enemies: it's just that most people dislike her. According to her detractors, she has a Barbie-doll body and brains to match; for the rest, she's got big features on a small face (except for her nose, which she had reduced), peach-perfect skin and lots of three-tone streaky blonde hair. Her style of dressing varies dramatically depending on her mood: that day she was wearing four-inch platform boots, bumsqueezer cropped jeans, bumfreezer jacket trimmed with dead bunny. 'Rabbit is okay,' she declared at my murmur of criticism. 'There are far too many of them eating up the countryside. Killing rabbits is eco-friendly.' I forbore to mention that the rabbit she was wearing had probably been bred for the purpose and had never had the chance to mess up its fur running around in the wild. I felt too low to argue about serious issues.

We were sitting at a corner table which should have been out of earshot of the café's other clientele. Unfortunately, Delphi has a carrying voice and no concept of discretion, though she's uninterested in any gossip that concerns those outside her social and professional circle. It's probably one of the side effects of egotism. She ordered a regular latte with skimmed milk, no sugar, and no biscuit-on-the-side; I ordered a double espresso with extra caffeine to give me the oomph to get back to suicide.

'You look terrible,' she said. 'Tell me everything.'

'You know Kyle's been in Eastern Europe doing that sex-trade investigation?'

'Not another one?'

'The producer loves them. Beautiful girls kidnapped, raped, and forced into prostitution – the public never get tired of it.' I'm not usually this cynical – well, not *quite* – but, as you may have gathered, I wasn't having a good day. 'I was supposed to be on location with him but I had to do the follow-up on corruption in Doncaster, so they sent Judi instead.' Judi was one of several assistant-assistants aiming to scramble past me on the ladder of success. Now, she would have a clear rung.

So to speak.

'Don't tell me he's married *her*!' Delphi exclaimed, appalled. 'Not Jude the Obscure!' Delphi rarely reads a book, but she knows the titles.

'Of course not. He met a girl out there – he said he had to marry her, it was the only way he could get her out of the country, protect her from the local mafia. Her father's unemployed, in hock to the gangsters, her mother works twelve hours a day in a sweatshop. They don't know what happened to the sister but she was last heard of in Vienna. Kyle gave me a whole sob story.' And I'd swallowed it – whole. Kyle knew exactly how to get to his audience, and there were so many stories like that out there, true stories, stories to wring your heart. Well, my heart had been wrung, in the end.

'I'll bet he did.' Delphi would have scowled if she hadn't had Botox injected between her eyebrows.

'He assured me the marriage was strictly cosmetic, she'd only be staying at his place for a few weeks. Then I ran into someone from the drama department who told me this girl's an actress, a real one – she starred in some foreign film that won an award – and she wanted to come to London as a career move. So I went round to Kyle's flat, and Tatyana came out of the bedroom wearing nothing but his shirt like someone in an old movie, and I felt so stupid, so *stupid* . . .' I broke off, knuckling my mouth like a child, horrified to find myself fighting tears. Pain is bad enough; humiliation makes it infinitely worse. 'He said he was glad I found out 'cos it saved him the trouble of telling me. He said he's really in love with her. He said . . . sorry. Just *sorry*.'

'Arsehole,' Delphi said comprehensively. 'What's she like?'

'Oh, you know. A dark Scarlett Johansson with a dash of Ingrid Bergman. Just your average Eastern European stunner.'

'Yuk,' Delphi said. 'I hate those Slavonic types. There are hordes of them coming over here. It goes to show we have to do something about the immigration problem.'

Delphinium has no truck with political correctness. She would happily screen out female immigrants on the grounds of youth and beauty, and the way I felt then, I almost agreed with her.

'Still, they go off when they're forty,' she went on, trying to cheer me up. 'One moment they're all cheekbones and flawless skin and the next they're wrinkled old peasants in headscarves. It happens practically overnight.'

'Tatyana's twenty-two.'

'Bugger.'

There was a despondent silence. At least, it was despondent on my part; Delphi was obviously thinking.

'You've got to be positive,' she announced. 'It's a good thing for you: you'll realise that in the end. He was always messing you around – cancelling dates or rolling up at two in the morning pissed out of his brain. He never took you out for intimate dinners or sent you flowers or—'

'He sent me flowers on my last birthday!'

'That was only because he forgot to buy you a present. Anyway, they were *chrysanthemums*. There's nothing romantic about chrysanthemums. They're the kind of flowers you send your grandmother. Don't interrupt. The point is, you've got to move on. Find yourself a nice guy who'll adore you and make a fuss of you. It's a pain you'll still be seeing Kyle at work—'

'No I won't,' I said. 'I've quit.'

'*Quit?* How quit?'

'I sent my resignation in by email this morning. I can't go on working with Kyle. It would kill me.' I suppose I was exaggerating, but not much.

'You can't do that! This is your *job*. Worse still, it's your *career*. If anyone has to leave, it should be him. He's behaved like an utter bastard, and now you're committing sooty—'

'Sooty?'

'Like those Indian women. Throwing yourself on a bonfire and turning into a heap of black ash. Sooty.'

'Okay . . .'

'I'm not saying you shouldn't make a change – it would be a great idea, you need to move up as well as on – but you *never* leave a job until you've got another one lined up. It's like with men. Sort out the new one before you ditch the old. Roo, darling, sometimes you're . . . you're *deliberately* hopeless.'

My name is Ruth – Ruth Harker – but Delphinium's called me Roo since childhood, hence the Winnie-the-Pooh spelling. A lot of people pick it up from her.

'I know,' I said. 'No job, no man. Total sooty.'

'We have to do something,' Delphi said. 'We don't want people to think you're suicidal.'

'I *am* suicidal.'

'Yes, but we don't want people to think so. We have to do something *quickly*.'

My heart quailed – a curious verb, when you come to think of it, since a quail is a small game bird with fiddly little bones that make eating it awkward. Of course, quails are very shy, prone to hide from people with shotguns, which would explain the verb. Anyway, my heart contemplated Delphi, thinking as if it were a small bird looking down the twin barrels of a twelve-bore, and scurried out of sight into the undergrowth.

When we were children, it was always Delphi who thought of things. It was Delphi who thought of dosing the au pair with a cocktail made from brandy, vodka, cointreau, aquavite and a dozen pounded-up aspirin so she would fall asleep and we could run away to Hollywood. Fortunately, Ilse tipped it down the sink after one sip. It was Delphi who disguised her pony by painting it with black spots so we could be high-waymen and hold up the Master of the Hunt's vintage Jaguar. My dad's income didn't run to ponies, but I was allowed to ride pillion. It was Delphi, aged twelve, who went into the local jeweller's and asked to look at diamond engagement rings, in order to steal one for her elopement with Ben Garvin. Ben was seventeen at the time and only hazily aware of her existence, though he came to notice her a good deal more later on. Delphi the child lived in a world of glamorous make-believe, devoid of scruple and out of touch with reality; whenever she thought of something, it was always the precursor to trouble, usually involving me. I checked trains and planes to Hollywood, fell off the back of the pony in mid-hold-up, distracted the shop assistant in the jeweller's with a sudden attack of stomach cramp. I was both terrified at being dragged into adventure and ecstatic because I was able to help. Delphi was my playmate, my soulmate, closer than a sister, if I had had a sister – twin cherries on a single stem and all that. Bonds forged in the furnace of childhood never wear out.

The problem was, as an adult Delphi hadn't changed much. She wanted to be a star, beautiful and rich and successful, and at thirty-four she had made it. But she still existed on a slightly different plane from everyone else, believing she could bend the universe around her, push and pummel events into the shape she desired. The scary part was that sometimes it worked. Failures and disasters were brushed aside; her ebullient mind bounced on to the next project, the next objective, with a sort of resilient optimism I could never match. Occasionally, I suspected the bounces soared over deep gulfs of subconscious trauma – like when she was ten, and her father left, or nineteen, when Ben finally walked out of her life – but the gulfs remained unplumbed, even with me. For Delphi, tragedy was a lost earring, or arriving at a party to find Carol Vorderman was wearing the same dress ('I mean, *Carol Vorderman* – sooo embarrassing. I could have laughed it off if only it had been Liz or Paris . . .'). But she always entered into my very different tragedies with an enthusiasm that was both comforting and panic-making. If she was a Barbie, she was Bossy Barbie, Benevolent Barbie, Jane-Austen's-Emma Barbie. And unlike Emma Wodehouse, no goofing and no gaffes disturbed her faith in her own omniscience and enterprise.

She sipped her latte, discovered it was cold (her own fault

for lingering), and summoned a waitress to complain and order another. The waitress looked sullen, but Delphi didn't notice.

'I've got an idea,' she announced. 'But don't get your hopes up yet. I have to check it out.'

My hopes were incapable of getting up, even with Viagra, though I didn't say so. 'What sort of an idea?' I said with misgiving.

'A job idea. Look, cancel your resignation—'

'I can't do that.'

'Yes you can. Tell them . . . tell them you had PMT, it was a typing error, you sent it by mistake – whatever. They won't want to lose you – you're much too indispensable.'

'I wish that were true. In any case, I've resigned, and that's that. I don't ever want to go back.'

'Look,' Delphi said with the laboured patience of someone addressing an idiot child, 'you cancel your resignation, they welcome you back with open arms, *then* you leave. Not in a huff but to go to a new and much better job which will have your rivals gnashing their teeth with envy and your bosses realising *exactly* what they've lost. It's much better for your image, and your image needs a boost right now.'

I grimaced. 'I don't *have* an image.'

'*Everyone* has an image,' Delphi insisted.

I didn't withdraw my resignation, of course; it was probably a good idea, but I'd left it too late. It was too late the moment I sent it. Neither the producer nor Dick Ramsay begged for my return on bended knee; they simply made regretful noises, and, in the producer's case, said things like: 'Been expecting it for some time. Shame to lose you, but you're getting in a rut here. You've got your career to think of. Off to higher things, huh?' He'd obviously missed the gossip about Kyle and me which I knew was doing the rounds, and I didn't fill him in. I said I wanted a break first and left the rest to conjecture.

I had to go into work for the next few weeks, but most of the time I managed to avoid Kyle. If we were in meetings together, I didn't talk and he didn't listen, leaving most of the communication to others. On one occasion, he trapped me at my desk, hitching one buttock up on the corner and exuding good intentions and the fumes of Dutch courage from lunchtime in the pub. His jaw was unshaven, his jeans unwashed, his sweatshirt sweaty. The awful thing was, I still found him sexy, despite what he had done to me. I kept remembering the way his voice went gravelly when he was aroused, and the rough insistence of his hands, and the beery taste of his kisses. I could understand why people get so angry after a split-up, unnecessarily angry, even long after – anger sweeps away the ingrained response, the sweet tension in the body, the softening of the heart. But I couldn't bring the anger back; I suppose I'm not the type. I just clenched inwardly, freezing out my own feelings.

'I think you've done the right thing,' he said, sounding suspiciously like the producer. 'You need to move on. You've been bogged down here for too long: I was holding you back.' *What?* 'You're a great girl, Roo: I want you to know that. I really wish you luck.'

He spoke as if he were making a generous gesture to someone who had jilted him, rather than vice versa. I stared at him, confused, outraged, stunned by his twisted world view. Then the anger came back.

'If you had any . . . any decency,' I said, 'you'd be the one leaving. You cheated me and lied to me and let me down – and now I'm out of a job. I had to quit because of you. So don't you *dare* wish me luck. It's so fake – so—'

11

'If you're going to take it like that . . .' He looked nonplussed and mildly huffy.

'How else am I meant to take it?'

'Look, it was hardly a serious affair, you and me. We didn't live together, we didn't get engaged—'

'It was six years,' I said, trying to stifle the fresh hurt as every word stabbed. *Hardly a serious affair* . . . 'Your clothes are in my wardrobe, your razor's in my bathroom –' that was probably why he hadn't shaved – 'your CDs are in my living room, your porn mags are under my bed. I'll send it all back, okay? Just leave me alone.'

I piled the lot into a dustbin bag the next day and left it at the office. I didn't care who saw, especially when *Leather Fantasy* fell out.

'You're supposed to cut the crotch out of his trousers,' Delphi said when I told her. 'It's traditional. And stamp on the CDs.' I hadn't mentioned the porn mags. Sometimes, Delphi can be quite easily shocked.

'I was trying to do dignity,' I explained.

'Dignity is fine in the right place,' Delphi said, 'but you need to assert yourself. Kyle walked all over you from day one. You ought to have gone out in style.'

'Yes, but whose style?' I sighed. 'This *is* my style. Not a bang but a whimper. Other people do clothes-slashing and deliver horse manure to the office. It's just not me. Anyway, I don't see why I should imitate everyone else.'

Unexpectedly, Delphi hugged me. 'We could think of something original,' she suggested after a pause. 'Something no one's done before. Set a new fashion in revenge. Spike his drink and when he's unconscious give him a really stupid haircut, or—'

'Been done,' I said.

'By whom?'

12

'Delilah.'

'That's in the *Bible*.' Delphi was mildly scornful. 'Nobody reads *that*.'

'It isn't original. Anyhow, I don't want revenge. I want . . . I want to stop hurting. I want to stop feeling as if my whole future is grey and empty. I want . . .'

'You want another man,' said Delphinium, bouncing over pain and loss, on to the next object.

I wasn't sure she was right. Kyle Muldoon had become a part of me, and I was afraid no other man could take his place.

On my last Friday, they gave me a leaving party. I wanted to slink away unnoticed, like an injured animal crawling into a burrow to lick its wounds, but no one on *Behind the News* was ready to miss an opportunity to get drunk. In any case, nowadays you're not supposed to lick your wounds in private: you're supposed to flaunt them in public and tell not just friends but strangers every detail of your suffering. Clever psychologists call this Achieving Closure and disregard the cost to your auditors, who collapse with exotic foreign symptoms like *ennui* and *Schadenfreude*. I didn't intend to talk about anything, but I couldn't get out of the piss-up.

Of course, it wasn't really a *party*: no canapés or paper hats and only a couple of rounds of free drinks to get the ball rolling. It was held in a neo-gothic bar in Soho called Nick's Cave with glittery spiders' webs on the walls and lurid green cocktails with ice cubes shaped like skulls. I arrived to find about half a dozen people waiting, all of whom assured me how much they'd miss me, even though two of them worked for another show and barely knew my name. A Serpent's Kiss was pressed into my hand: it looked and tasted like lavatory cleaner. *Cheap* lavatory cleaner. I sipped it nervously. There was no sign of Kyle.

Dick Ramsay turned up late, already drunk. For those of you who don't watch investigative TV, he's a former news anchorman with an OBE, a toupee and a booze problem, two of which were in evidence that night, one causing lopsided hair, the other lopsided vision. He bought a bottle of champagne, put his arm round me and told me how invaluable I'd been and how difficult I would be to replace. Then he told me about my replacement. 'Smart girl – brunette – great legs – Cheryl? Cherie? Very bright, very clued-up, good with people.' So much for being invaluable. Cheryl/Cherie was relatively new in the line-up of assistants – I couldn't recall her right name even when I was sober – and had made an impression on the men by wearing very short skirts (favourable) and on the women by having perfect hair (unfavourable). Her personality, if any, had passed me by completely. I realised to my horror that I was becoming bitter and cynical, infected by the petty jealousies of media life, and decided on a wave of something like relief that the producer was right, Kyle was right, it was time I got out. I polished off the Serpent's Kiss with the resolute air of Socrates swigging hemlock and moved on to champagne.

At least, I reflected, Cheryl/Cherie had the decency not to come that evening. Then I saw her, lurking in a corner, distinguishable by her outthrust legs and the scantiness of her dress which, at the beginning of December, must constitute a health hazard – to others if not to her. Glancing round, I saw various familiar faces gathering in the green-tinted gloom of the Cave. Someone placed another cocktail at my elbow. In the poor light, its colour appeared suspiciously close to purple. A Screaming Mandrake, I was informed. I drank it down. What the hell. By way of variety, it tasted like oven cleaner.

Nit-pickers might point out that it's unlikely I've ever drunk either oven or lavatory cleaner. Not knowingly, anyway. That is mere quibbling. Anyone who has ever cleaned their loo –

or failed to clean their oven – knows what I mean. Combine the smell, the colour, the location, the germ-zapping, grease-dissolving acidity, add alcohol, and *voilà*! The killer cocktail. I could feel it strip my stomach lining while my friendly bacteria expired in droves.

I'd finished the Screaming Mandrake and was partway down an aptly-named Goblet of Fire when Kyle arrived. There was a fleeting, treacherous second when I was pleased to see him, when I thought he might have come to say something – anything – that might turn the misery of my situation inside out. I was drunk, and hope, as always, triumphed over experience. Then I saw the girl trailing from his left hand – the girl I'd last seen dressed only in a shirt – now wearing an ensemble of ripped frills and tousled hair which merely served to enhance her general flawlessness. My stomach plunged so violently I actually felt sick. I was vaguely aware of eyes swivelling in my direction, and suddenly my former colleagues seemed like a ravening mob, avid for my humiliation. Then someone squeezed my arm – Dick Ramsay, of all people, surveying me with bleary kindness, murmuring something supportive. I didn't catch the words, but it didn't matter; I got the meaning. He might be an old soak who would make a pass at anyone remotely female and who had slagged off three wives, five leading politicians, and about twenty close friends in his memoirs, but, I thought confusedly, he was a good person *underneath*. Tears started, but I blinked them back. It occurred to me I was even drunker than Dick.

Across the room Kyle caught my eye and gave me a cheery wave. Yuk. I forced a smile; I don't know why. I suppose because you do in these circumstances; you have to maintain a facade of politeness and amiability for pride's sake, for the benefit of the audience. I've never been much good at pride, but I made the effort.

15

In due course Kyle came over and I was formally introduced to Tatyana, Taty for short, presumably to match the frills. She gave me a distant, slightly wary greeting which told me everything I needed to know about how Kyle had explained my initial reaction. It had been a casual affair, I'd taken it too seriously: the bunny-boiler syndrome. A film that was intended to discourage male infidelity actually provided them with a useful label for any ex angry at her maltreatment. Taty obviously thought of me as a potential stalker and tried to edge away without letting go of Kyle's hand – I could see the strain in their mutual grip. But Kyle was determined to show everyone that he was cool, I was cool, we were both totally cool about everything, and any rumours of his bad behaviour had been grossly exaggerated.

I played along. For pride's sake. Or merely to avoid embarrassment. I retained just enough sobriety for that.

'We've had some good times, haven't we?' Kyle was saying (cheerily). 'Remember Kosovo, when that sniper shot at us?' In fact the target had been at least two hundred yards away, and the sniper in question had missed, but who was I to spoil the Muldoon legend? He continued with more improbable reminiscences before expanding them to include Dick, recalling an awards ceremony when Kyle was a rookie and the two of them had got smashed with Sir Robin Day. It was a story I'd heard often, but now, apparently, I'd been added to the cast list, even though the incident had happened well before the start of my TV career. But I didn't argue. I was concentrating on staying sane.

At some stage Kyle, at his most lavish, ordered a round of drinks (it was a gesture he tended to avoid unless he could put it on expenses), and I found myself confronted with the Cave's pièce de résistance, a Slayer Special – about five kinds of alcohol with a range of additives, producing a garish rainbow of green shading through orange to scarlet and crimson. I sucked on the straw as if it were a milkshake. Kyle was still being cheery while Dick's clasp on my arm had progressed from comforting to alarmingly affectionate. Then the producer clapped for silence, someone switched off the music, and I realised to my horror that he was going to make a speech.

I tried to blend into the sofa cushions while he launched into a eulogy that wouldn't have sounded out of place at my funeral – what a great person I was, a terrific team player, pouring oil on the troubled waters of high-stress TV reportage, etc. etc. At the end everyone clapped and, at Kyle's instigation, sang 'For She's a Jolly Good Fellow'. I ached to drown him in his own hypocrisy. Then came the leaving present. Automatically, I pulled off the wrapping paper. It was a set of six cut-crystal wine glasses, expensive-looking and very beautiful – if you like cut-crystal. (I don't.) But I knew where I'd seen them before. Kyle had picked them up on the cheap during an earlier trip to Eastern Europe as a wedding present for a couple who'd split up a week before the ceremony. The glassware had been hanging around his flat for months – did he think I wouldn't remember?

I gulped down my milkshake, battered by alternate waves of emotion and inebriation. The room was spinning slightly, in slow motion, and the music was back on, hammering at walls, ceiling, eardrums. Kyle leaned over to whisper to Taty (or possibly, in view of the noise level, to shout in her ear). She pulled his face towards her and kissed him, a tongue job, as blatantly hurtful to me as a spit in the eye. They got up to leave. She dived towards the Ladies, finally releasing his hand in the process. He bent over and, lips still wet from hers, began to kiss me too. My mouth fell open in shock – there was tongue contact – he pulled back, grinning, pleased with himself, as if the kiss had been an act of real generosity, a kindness to the girl he had just dumped.

My pride, such as it was, went by the board. I don't remember picking up the box of cut-crystal, only the crunch of breaking glass as it hit the floor at – and partly on – Kyle's feet. Toes must have been crushed; I saw his face tighten in sudden pain. The music should've stopped – there should've been a frozen silence, but of course there wasn't. I was hazily conscious of people staring, uncertain what had happened. I stumbled to the door with Dick Ramsay and the producer hurrying in my wake.

Outside, I threw up on the pavement, in several colours of the rainbow.

Delphinium

When Roo didn't phone the morning after her leaving party, I knew something awful had happened. I'd been expecting her call from ten a.m., perhaps even nine-thirty, since Roo does the early-rising thing, and when I hadn't heard by midday, and all I could get was her answering machine, I had this terrific sense of foreboding. Or maybe I mean afterboding, since whatever it was must've happened already. Some people say I'm insensitive, but actually I'm very telepathic with my friends, except, of course, when they bore me.

I'd had the bodings about Roo, on and off, from the moment she got mixed up with Kyle Muldoon. Kyle is the kind of undesirable guy whom too many women consider madly desirable: sweaty armpits, scruffy clothes, body hair, lots of male charismo and machisma and the attitude problem of a gorilla with an attitude problem. He was always turning up late for dates or not at all, embarrassing her in front of her friends, taking her for granted, shagging around on the side (I couldn't prove that but I just *knew*, on account of being tele-pathic). I had a guy like that once, when I was a teenager – only not quite so sweaty and with less body hair, because, well, I had Taste, even as a teenager – but once was more than enough. You make a mistake, you learn, you move on, but Roo didn't learn, or *wouldn't* learn – she got hooked on her mistakes, going for the same type over and over again. With Kyle, she said it was love. 'No it isn't,' I said. 'It's just lust that's got out of hand.' But she only smiled and shook her head, and after that I kept the bodings to myself. Mostly, anyway.

When you care about someone, like your best friend, you'd do anything to stop them being hurt, but if they're as obstinate as Roo, and set on a suicide course, there's nothing you *can* do. Except be there. Roo's a very gentle person but she has this stubborn streak, especially when it comes to the wrong men. There was Micky Treherne when she was at university, and Lee Harrison at school, though fortunately neither of them lasted long. I'd had hopes of Robert Clifton. She went out with him for over a year, and he was just getting ready to propose when she finished it.

'Why?' I said – a cry from the heart. 'He's well off, he's good-looking –' well, quite – 'and he adores you. *Why?*'

'It doesn't work for me in bed.'

'Use your imagination!'

'I can't.'

And that was that. Roo's an imaginative person in some ways, honestly, but when it came to sex, she couldn't replace Robert with, say, a swarthy pirate with a cutlass behind each ear, or Tarzan in a bulging loincloth, or a whole queue of barbarian raiders in ripped sheepskin and codpieces with metal studs. In bed, she was stuck with reality. How sad is *that*?

Anyway, I was all set to Be There the morning after Roo's leaving party, but she wasn't calling, she wasn't answering, and I didn't like it at all. When I'd done my face, fixed my hair, changed my mind about my outfit – you never know when you're going to run into the paparazzi – I left the house, grabbed a taxi and raced round to her place. I'd rung three times before she opened the door, looking worse than awful.

'My God,' she said carefully, as if speaking too loud or moving too fast might cause the top of her head to fall off. 'Come in. My God.'

'You look worse than awful,' I said.

Roo doesn't suit hangovers. She's medium height and medium slim, with the kind of fair skin that bruises easily when nothing's happened to bruise it, and soft dark hair that goes feathery at the ends. She's pretty in an old-fashioned way that would appeal to men's protective instincts if they still had any. That day, there were smudges under her eyes from exhaustion and residual mascara, her complexion was raw oyster and her hair looked as if she'd been sick in it. (She had.) Even her specs were bleary. I sat her down, tried to work out the coffee machine, gave up and made instant. While she drank it, Roo told me about the previous evening.

'Dick Ramsay brought me home,' she said. 'He kissed me, even though I must have tasted of sick, and I remember I straightened his toupee, and told him he was a really wonderful human being – God, I was drunk – and he said we must do this again some time, only probably not the part where I vomit. Then he left.'

'Sure? I mean . . . he didn't, like, *stay* . . . ?'

'Of course not!' Indignation revived her.

'Well, you think he's a wonderful human being, and you're on the rebound, and he's famous,' I pointed out.

'I *don't* think he's a wonderful human being, I just *said* I thought he was a wonderful human being. And I'm not going to rebound on to anyone yet, if ever. And—'

'I know. You don't care about him being famous.' I'm resigned to Roo's impracticality by now. Almost.

'I'm single,' Roo went on dejectedly. 'It isn't bad to be single. I'm going to be single and like it.'

'You're *always* single,' I said. 'You're so single, you're even single when you're attached. Look at you and Kyle. You never did couple things. He was never bloody there.'

'We had sex,' Roo said. 'That's a couple thing. Sometimes, anyway.'

'You're always focusing on sex. Being a couple is about a lot more than that. Alex and I do all sorts of things together.'

Alex Russo is my boyfriend. We'd been together two years and we'd just set a date for the wedding, but I didn't think this was a good moment to tell Roo, even though I wanted her to be my maid of honour. Alex is incredibly desirable from every angle. He has a mews house where I live with him most of the time (I keep my own place for emergencies), the right background (third generation rich and second generation posh), the right clothes, the right accent, the right friends. He's got one Italian grandfather and one Persian (Iranian, actually, but Persian sounds more romantic), a genetic mix which means he's stunningly handsome: jet-black hair, creamy gold skin, classic profile. A friend at Armani wanted him to do some modelling, but he couldn't be bothered. He has a production company which doesn't produce very much yet, and is always just about to make a big film, which means he spends lots of time hanging out with actors who are going to be in it. He isn't famous in his own right but he moves in a cloud of distant fame, the rubbed-off kind that comes when your mother's second marriage features in *Tatler* and your father owns a winning horse at Ascot and your sister does time in the Priory with the daughter of a rock star. He's twenty-nine (five years younger than me), prefers wine to beer, shaves regularly, and has only a tepid interest in football. (He's mad about cricket, but nobody's perfect.) We look beautiful together. I was already fantasising about the wedding photos, and whether we should sell them to *Hello!* or *OK!*

'There's only one Alex,' Roo said with a curiously inscrutable expression on her face.

'Yes, but there are lots of great guys out there,' I said untruthfully, wanting to be positive. 'It's just that you always turn them down.'

In fact, the supply of decent single men is very limited; I'm not quite sure why. It isn't as if we've had a major war to wipe them out. Everybody knows the First World War produced a generation of lesbian spinsters because half the guys were dead, but that's ancient history. Nowadays, according to a friend of mine who's a pop psychologist, men are all so shattered by female emancipation they've retreated into their shells, becoming geeks, nerds, recluses, and, in extreme cases, serial killers with mother complexes. They have poor social skills and shrinking levels of testosterone – and it's all our fault.

Frankly, I'm not sure about this psychology stuff.

It just goes to prove what I told Roo before: never drop one guy until you've got another lined up. Forget all that 'best to be off with the old love before you're on with the new' garbage. There was some French singer – I think her name was Pilaff – who always made a point of starting her next affair *before* she'd finished the previous one. And she sang about having no regrets, which goes to show she got it right. (*Je ne regrette rien*, which means *I don't regret nothing*. Not very good grammar, but the French can't help it: they're foreign.) Being single isn't a lifestyle choice, whatever your guru says: it's just desperate. I haven't been single since I was thirteen.

I've made periodic efforts to dredge up eligible single men for Roo over the years, but that's when her stubborn streak comes into play. I sometimes suspect that as soon as she senses I approve of the guy she loses interest. So there was no point in fixing her up with someone – even if I could think of someone to fix her up with – unless I was very, very subtle. Better to concentrate on the job issue.

I didn't want to promise anything until I was absolutely sure it was in the bag, but I dropped a few hints which I hoped would cheer her up. Roo didn't look particularly cheered – she was obviously determined to wallow in gloom – but you can't go on being miserable indefinitely, it's too boring, and with luck a little reluctant optimism would kick in later. I left her with the newspapers, which were so depressing they were bound to brighten her day. Roo is the sort of person who reads about famines and massacres in Africa or somewhere and feels ashamed of trivial stuff like agonising over her love life. Me, I expect I'm a coward but I'd rather not read about horrors, especially at breakfast. I mean, it's great if you can do something – like *Ground Force* revamped Nelson Mandela's garden – but mostly you just feel so helpless, because Africa's a long way away, and no matter how much money you give there are always more famines and more massacres, and nothing ever seems to change. I don't do the papers, but if I did I'd rather read about celebs having affairs, because that doesn't make you feel helpless or guilty, and there's always a chance of hearing about your friends.

Anyway, when I went Roo hugged me very hard, and I said she should come to a party with me and Alex that evening, whether she liked it or not, because staying in with a DVD and a bag of tortilla chips would only make her feel worse. Then I walked down the road deep in thought, so absorbed in my plans for Roo's future that I forgot to hail a taxi for at least ten minutes.

Roo and I go way back. The Harkers lived in the village – Little Pygford – while we had the big house out on the edge, with stables and paddocks and dogs and a huge rambling garden. After my father left, Mummy immersed herself in exotic shrubs, rockeries and compost heaps, becoming plumper and earthier as the relationship deepened, until she had a rustic complexion and sun-dried hair and was famed for her expertise with hardy perennials throughout the gardening world. My sister Pansy and I had already been saddled with bizarre floral names, though it could have been much worse: her other favourites included snapdragons, clematis and saxifrage. She wasn't exactly an affectionate parent – she preferred flowers to children – but she was vaguely kind and generous to everybody, and when Mrs Harker died of cancer Roo was semi-adopted into our household. 'Three kids are no more trouble than two,' Mummy said, which was true for her, though probably not for the au pairs. (We got through dozens.) Geoff Harker was an engineer who went away a lot, building bridges and flyovers in countries that were roadless and bridgeless, and during his absences Roo stayed with us. When Daddy left, less than a year later, she became part of the family.

There's no point in saying much about my father because since he debunked he hasn't really featured in my life. He was dark and disreputable, in a classy sort of way, and very, very charming, and for ten years I was his little princess, until he left his wife for someone else's and went to live in the South of France. I wrote to him a few months later, when we had an address to write to, saying I'd saved my pocket money for the ferry and would sneak away to join him. He wrote back, quite briefly, telling me it wasn't a good idea and I should stay with my mummy, and maybe I could come for a visit when I was a bit older. After that he barely wrote at all. The visit I dreamed of never happened, and even Christmas cards stopped, though sometimes I imagined they were intercepted, by my mother or, more likely, the woman who had stolen him from me.

Three years ago I was making a programme on a garden near Antibes and I went to see him. His second wife had died long before, booze I think, and he was living in the villa she had bequeathed to him, a pink and white spun-sugar house with vines over the terrace and a view that just about made it to the sea. We lunched on the terrace, beside the view, waited on by an adoring housekeeper; he looked older, sort of smaller, the way people do when you see them through grown-up eyes, but the same, the same smile, the same charm. I'd dressed and made up very carefully, looking ultra-glamorous, basking in my new stardom. Suddenly this girl came running up the steps – about seventeen, no make-up, short, dark hair, big French pout, tatty jeans. 'This is my daughter,' Daddy said, as if I wasn't, or didn't count. 'My darling Natalie.'

It's just as well we don't carry guns in Europe, because if I'd had one, I'd have shot her on sight.

He was all over her, ruffling her short hair, swapping smiles and whispers, like I was a distant acquaintance given a privileged glimpse of their happiness. I felt overdressed, overmade-up, *old*. All he remembered of me was a few improbable anecdotes; she'd spent her whole life with him, and until that moment I didn't even know she existed. She was clearly the most important thing in his world, and he hadn't mentioned her to Mummy or me, not because *she* didn't matter, but because *we* didn't. We'd been brushed aside and all but forgotten. Roo says that's how some people deal with pain, but just then I didn't care. I couldn't even be angry. I felt as if my insides had been emptied out and a thin veneer of my Self was desperately hanging on, trying to appear unaffected and totally cool about everything.

We'd been looking at a photo of Pansy which Daddy had found in an English society magazine when Natalie showed up. 'Is this your sister? Of course, I haven't seen her since she was a baby . . .' At the time Pansy had her hair cropped and dyed black; she didn't really look like Natalie, but there was, I suppose, a resemblance of style if not content. Anyway, Daddy was glancing from the pictured daughter to the one who was present, comparing them, excluding me, except as an audience, saying: 'She's not as pretty as my Nat, is she?' like I was meant to agree. I'm not Pansy's biggest fan but suddenly I felt hot all through.

'Pan's a supermodel,' I said. 'She's ravishing. She took Paris fashion week by storm.'

Pansy isn't a supermodel. She'd done a bit of modelling in Paris that year for a designer friend who's into eco-couture, attracting attention from the British press because of the green angle and because she's my sister. But hearing him compare her in that disparaging way with his pouty Eurobrat made my blood boil.

I don't think he noticed. He's the sort of person who doesn't notice unpleasant things. I left a bit later, though I had to sit in the car for a while before I could drive, I was shaking so badly.

So much for my dad. These days, my immediate family is just Mummy, who prefers flowers, Pan, a sisterly pain in the bum, and Roo.

No wonder I love Roo best of all.

My plans for her future had taken longer than I'd wished to get off the ground because the person I needed to talk to, Major John Beard-Trenchard, was away until the following week. I'd called him on his mobile, explained the situation, and fixed up lunch, but he was playing golf in the Caribbean and visiting exotic gardens and couldn't be induced to come home early. (When I say *in the Caribbean*, I don't mean literally, since golf happens on golf courses, but, on the other hand, the balls seem to shoot off anywhere, frequently into water, so it could have been literal after all. Boring game, anyway.)

I'd better take a moment to explain how the Major comes into this.

He really was in the army, somewhere back in the year dot (he still tends to stand in that rigid military way, as if he's got a musket up his backside, though it could be stiffness in the joints), but plants have always been his real love: he brought horticulture to television in the early days when the only other gardening programme was Bill and Ben. Nowadays he holds directorships and sits on Boards, and has his own company, Persiflage Productions, specialising in all things rural. He's an old friend of my mother's (horticultural types invariably are); rumour has it she once saved his life, or his reputation, or whatever. Something to do with begonias. He produced *Earth Works*, the series which kick-started my career. Apparently he was discussing it over lunch with Mummy, saying he needed a female sidekick for Mortimer Sparrow to give it a bit of glamour, and she suggested me. I was acting at the time, resting between jobs, so I accepted the offer, though I wasn't really that keen. Any child of Mummy's can't help knowing about gardening, but I had no intention of digging, or weeding, or getting my hands dirty. (Fortunately, you have researchers to do all that.) Anyway, by the end of a year I was getting more fan mail than Morty and I left to present *Gilding the Lily*, which focused on the gardens of the rich and famous.

This gave me a lot more scope to develop my image, wafting between banks of flowers in designer dresses, which I didn't have to pay for because I was going to wear them on television, and hanging out with A-list stars. Fame, as everyone knows, is catching – a bit like measles – and I caught it. I'm not much good at maths, but this is the kind of equation I can handle: the total famousness of any given group of famous people is more than the sum total of their fame. Or something. I became a star in my own right and *Gilding the Lily* ran and ran, until it ran itself out of prime time and into an afternoon slot, at which point I left. Julian, my agent, says it's essential to quit while you're ahead, and not to get stuck in the dead zone between two and six when the only people who watch are OAPs, on the dole, or chronically ill. Of course, for a TV personality, *not* being on TV, even for one season, can be the kiss of death, but overexposure is equally fatal. Too much of one face on the small screen and viewers get 'face fatigue'. Remember that guy with the big mouth and the cockney accent who used to be on *all the time*? And the woman with the flick and the gravitas? One moment they're there, and then they're gone. In the trade, we call them the Disappeared. And the worst of it is, *you can't even remember their names* . . . But I wasn't worried. I wanted the chance to get back to acting, though Julian said I shouldn't diversify. (Sometimes, I'm afraid he thinks I'm a one-talent girl, which is rubbish.) I'd been talking about a role in a new period drama for the BBC when Crusty called. Crusty is Pan's name for the Major, Crusty Beardstandard. She says he's one of those crusty old men who are all heart underneath. He was making a new series – six episodes – all on one garden. A garden, apparently, that hadn't been properly gardened for centuries, and existed in a state of nature round a castle in Scotland recently acquired by a friend of his.

'What friend?' I asked warily. Crusty's friends are a mixed bag.

'God,' said the Major.

'I beg your pardon?'

'God.'

GOD????

GOD!!!!

Not . . . surely not . . . *the* God? Hot God, otherwise Godfrey Jakes, the ultimate veteran rock star. Sixties rebel, seventies superstar, eighties alcoholic, nineties comeback kid, millennium icon. You know his story – who doesn't? It's like the stories of all the other rock stars rolled into one. Critics say he should have died, it would have been more in keeping with his image, but instead he lived on, giving endless farewell concerts, updating his wives every season. He'd started as Hot God and the Fallen Angels, then moved on, going solo, going mega – shooting up, snorting up, trashing cars and hotel rooms, spawning headlines like 'HOT GOD HELLRAISER' and 'AMERICAN BIBLE-BASHERS BAN GOD'. A kiss-and-tell feature a few years back had only put a gloss on the halo, claiming 'GOD'S ROD STILL HOT'. He'd taken a liability name like Godfrey and abbreviated it into his biggest asset. Never mind his music: the guy was a PR genius.

Lately, I'd read he was doing the recluse act, which only works if you are a HUGE star. Otherwise people just ignore you.

Now, apparently, he was into gardening.

'He's really keen on it,' Crusty said. 'Been boning up on every-thing. Wants to get involved. I took him to meet Jennie.'

Crusty took Hot God to meet my *mother*? Naturally, she's a big fan – she's got a stack of his old albums a yard high – but the idea was still shocking, even embarrassing. Caviar and mashed potato. Glitz and grits. Had he been bored, or merely patronising? Had she blushed and gushed – Mummy, whose face is too weatherbeaten to blush and who only ever gushes over plants? Unthinkable.

Of course, they *are* nearly the same age. Come to think of it, he must be older . . .

'I thought you might like to present,' Crusty went on. 'Jennie said you were at a loose end.'

I am *not* at a loose end. I'm a star. Stars don't do loose ends. They have things in the pipeline, exciting new projects, people angling for their time and attention. But Crusty is of the old school, as they say. He just isn't clued up.

But never in a million years was I going to turn down the chance to work on Hot God's briar patch.

Unfortunately, he also wanted Mortimer Sparrow, the housewives' pin-up, he of the faux-rustique accent and relaxative manner. I wasn't eager for the reunion. Morty is an inveterate bum-patter and tit-fondler who, when I started on *Earth Works*, had thought he could jump on me just because we were colleagues. I didn't need him, didn't fancy him, and said so, which hadn't helped our professional relationship. How someone as cool as Hot God could admire Morty . . . Which just goes to show that even superstars can be as dumb as ordinary people, only on a bigger scale.

I had protested at the inclusion of Morty but had to give in, so I sort of felt Crusty owed me a favour. Not that I would put it like that, naturally. I do tact, whatever people may say. But the designated producer was due to bunk off on maternity leave at the crucial moment, and the Major hadn't appointed a replacement yet. It wasn't Roo's field, but what she really needed was a complete change of scene.

Sometimes, things just come together. Fate taking a hand. I felt this was one of those times.

Roo spent the week after her departure from *Behind the News* going back into the office to pick up things she had left behind (five times), having lunch with people who might be useful but weren't (three times), and getting incredibly depressed (all the time). I took her to my health club and to a theatrical party with Alex, but at the former she tried to drown herself in the jacuzzi and at the latter she spent the whole evening talking to the only gay guy there. Shakespeare once said something about how you should grapple your friends to your soul with hoops of steel (sounds a bit like bondage to me), but my hoops were beginning to show the rust. Meanwhile, Crusty Beardstandard got back to England on Saturday, had tea with my mother on Sunday (I'd already enlisted her support for Roo), and on Monday I met with him at the Rip-Off Café.

I chose the Rip-Off because I know Crusty likes it, though I don't. It has scenic views over the river, glass and steel minimalist décor and film-starlet waitresses. The food is as minimalist as the décor and very, very expensive – a single plover's egg with a stick of asparagus, or one raviolo parcel drizzled with a sauce so subtle it has virtually no flavour at all. You know the kind of thing. They once served me a *fritto misto* which included two langoustines battered *in the shell*. How the hell was I supposed to eat that? Peel off the batter, get the langoustine *out* of the shell, then reunite the two? (I sent it back.) I go to the Rip-Off quite often, naturally, because it's very trendy, but I still don't think much of it. Of course, it's frightfully good for your figure, because the portions are so small.

Crusty was there before me, drinking prosecco. He's known in television as a Character and he looks the part, on account of the upright carriage mentioned earlier, a hint of Edwardian side-whisker, and that solid portliness that comes from a lifetime of good lunches, probably followed by port. Only the well-off become portly; the poor just get fat, usually on junk food, but portliness implies high-priced high living (and port). Crusty also has the resulting cerise complexion, set off by his white hair and currently deepened to a sort of beetroot-bronze by the Caribbean sun.

As soon as we'd ordered I began to explain about Roo. I hadn't been sure what to say about the Kyle affair, but I had to give him her reasons for dumping *Behind the News* and, anyway, Crusty is awfully chivalrous, despite decades in television.

'She wasted years on that show because of Kyle,' I said. 'She effectively put her career on hold to work with him, and now he's married this slapper out of the blue and she's left high and dry. *He* should be the one to quit, but of course she did, because she's so honourable.'

Honourable is a good word to use with Crusty. It presses all the ex-army buttons.

'Poor child,' he said. 'I seem to remember meeting her at your mother's place . . . ten, twelve years ago? Quiet little thing, rather pretty. Nice manners.'

'That's her.' Well, she *does* have nice manners, except for the lapse with the cut crystal, which I totally approved. I don't like cut crystal either.

'Trouble is, it'll be a tough job, dealing with . . . well, a lot of difficult people.' Surely he didn't mean *me*? 'People who won't necessarily get along. A nice girl like her, she mightn't have the thick skin, the requisite resilience . . .'

'Roo does tough,' I insisted. 'She's worked on location in war zones, with guerrillas shooting at her.' More or less. 'And she's naturally diplomatic. She'll be really good with Hot God.'

'Jennie spoke highly of her,' the Major conceded. 'She said your Roo's one of a kind.'

'She is,' I averred, dropping my voice to do sincerity. I mean, I *was* sincere, but on television you learn it isn't enough to feel emotion – you have to *sound* as if you feel it. And I *am* a proper actress. I do *all* the emotions. What was it Dorothy Parker said? The whole gamut from A to B.

'Better see her,' said Crusty.

We were home and dry. I knew he'd love Roo.

Chapter 2:
The Road to Dunblair

Ruth

How do you tell your best friend you don't want to work with her?

When we were kids, and Delphinium decided she was going to be a star, I was variously cast as her agent, her assistant, her social secretary – sidekick, confidante, whatever. I was thrilled to be included in her life on a long-term basis, but deep down I knew I had to go my own way. How far her career choices influenced mine I don't know. Delphi wanted fame and fortune at any price and television was the obvious route; I didn't have her hunger for stardom, but there's no doubt her ambition, and her belief that every goal was attainable, had its effect on me. When at sixteen I told my father I was going to work in the news media, he was nervous, considering it beyond my range, but to Delphi and her family any endeavour was possible. She and Pan took my future success for granted, and even Jennifer Dacres was carelessly supportive, saying whatever was necessary to allay my father's fears. My dreams of supreme producerdom had shrunk over the years as such dreams do, but they had never included a switch from covering the big issues to the world of TV gardening – and I had never, ever contemplated producing Delphi. I love her, but she's a spoiled egotist who sees life from a single viewpoint and thinks that giving an inch means losing a mile. I knew instinctively that she was every producer's nightmare.

I couldn't possibly say so.

'I know nothing about gardening,' I said, hedging.

(Sorry about the pun. It was unintentional. Horticultural puns spring up like – well – weeds.)

'You don't actually have to garden, stupid,' Delphi said impatiently. 'Good God, you don't imagine I do, do you? Only think what it would do to my nails. We have dogsbodies for all that – researchers, runners, that's what they do. You're a producer: you just produce. It'll be the same as *Behind the News* only you'll be in charge, nobody will be trying to kill you, and there'll be no Kyle Muldoon. And instead of a refugee camp in Africa or a brothel in Budapest we'll be staying in a fabulous castle in Scotland and hanging out with the most famous rock star of all time. What more do you want?'

I not only hedged, I fenced. I walled. I built small balustrades and ducked behind them.

'It's just . . . I've got the chance of something with News 24. I have a contact there . . .'

'*News 24*? No one watches that!'

'I do.'

'Yes, but you're not a typical viewer. Typical viewers watch soaps because their own lives are so boring, and gardening shows because they never garden, and cooking shows because they never cook, and reality TV because it's completely unreal. Everyone knows that.' She was, of course, perfectly right. 'Nobody *watches* the news. They just have it on.'

I didn't argue.

'It's a wonderful opportunity . . . I'm so grateful . . . but . . .'

'You're determined to be difficult,' Delphi concluded. 'It's because you don't want to accept favours, isn't it? I know you're always having scruples about things. If someone offered you a diamond necklace worth a hundred thousand pounds you'd probably turn it down because you didn't approve of conditions in the diamond mines. Look, you can't afford to have scruples in television. And I'm not doing you a favour: you'll be doing me one. I'm being totally selfish about this. I'd much rather work with you than anyone else.'

Oh shit.

'Maybe Major Beard-Trenchard won't like me,' I suggested hopefully.

'Of course he will,' Delphi said.

Major Beard-Trenchard did like me, alas. I liked him, too. I knew I'd met him years before, but I had only a hazy recollection of a flourishing moustache on a large pink face; memory had exaggerated the moustache, though not much. He was, as Delphi had told me, a Character – there aren't that many left in television nowadays – one of the old school, probably Eton, though the ex-Etonians I've come across from the younger generation are mostly arrogant rich kids adorning assorted merchant banks. Anyway, Crusty Beardstandard – I couldn't help thinking of him as Pan's nickname – was courteous rather than merely polite, thoughtful, kindly, faintly avuncular. I don't know what Delphi had told him, but he evidently considered the job mine already, and his principal concern appeared to be whether I would be happy in it, and if there was anything more he could do to look after me. Senior executives do not normally treat producers as if they are fragile beings in need of TLC, and I would have been darkly suspicious of whatever Delphi might have told him if I hadn't realised that this would be Crusty's customary attitude to any female in his employ. However, since his company is pretty successful he must expect high standards in return, and instead of saying the job wasn't really what I wanted I found myself assuring him I could handle it.

Afterwards, I clung to the hope that News 24 would come up trumps. I hadn't signed anything yet with Persiflage Productions and there was still time to back down if something else developed, but my back-up funds were limited and I needed work (and pay) as soon as possible. That's how life goes: you make your grand dramatic gesture, and then you're stuck with the more mundane consequences, like how to eat and pay the mortgage. Delphi has a grandparental trust fund to take her through a lean period, but my family weren't trust fund material. Time passed, and I waited by the phone in vain, succumbing to idiotic fantasies that my next caller might be Kyle, not News 24, telling me he'd made a mistake, was getting an instant divorce, wanted to be with me again. In the event, I didn't hear from either of them. The telephone is the ultimate watched pot: it never boils (or rings). Ever. I finally called the BBC myself, to be greeted with ums and ahs and murmurs of cutbacks. No job. I thought about suicide all over again, but it was no good: the prospect of working with my dearest friend might be scary, but it didn't drive me to wrist-slashing despair. I rang the Major's PA and braced myself.

I didn't even hint to Delphi, of course. Under the rhino hide necessary for media stardom, the effortless arrogance, the self-assurance, the bouncing ball of her optimism, I've always sensed hidden insecurity, a deep-seated vein of sensitivity – in short, the usual junk we all carry around. I haven't ever seen much evidence of it, but I know it's there. When I confessed to having taken the job she bubbled over with enthusiasm and self-satisfaction, insisting on a champagne lunch because we had so much to celebrate. 'We'll put it on expenses,' she concluded.

Oh God.

'No we won't,' I said. 'Crusty would fire me before I've even started, and he'd be perfectly justified.'

'Darling, I *always* put things on expenses. So does he. When did you get to be so stuffy?'

'When I accepted the position you pulled strings to get for me,' I responded unhappily.

'Look, it's quite all right. Ask Crusty if you don't believe me, though I must say—'

'*No.*' If I didn't assert my authority now, I never would.

'You told me Kyle used to put everything on expenses.'

'Not when I could stop him.' As a mere assistant, my powers had been limited, but I was determined to take my new responsibilities seriously.

Delphi agreed to pay for lunch, pained rather than grudging, an injured innocent labouring under the stigma of unjust accusation. But she'd forgotten about it before the starters arrived.

'We have *lots* to celebrate,' she declared. 'I've been wanting to tell you, only you were so miserable about Kyle I didn't think it was tactful. Alex and I have got a date.'

'What kind of a date? You've been dating for years – I mean, you live together. You don't need a date.'

'A date for the *wedding*! Honestly, Roo . . .'

'Oh . . . That's wonderful. That's absolutely terrific. When?'

'Next summer – when I finish the series. Of course, we've been vaguely engaged for ages, but he's bought me a ring now. I wore it last week and you didn't even notice.'

She was right. I'm not awfully observant at the best of times, and times lately hadn't been the best. I admired the ring, a chartreuse diamond of impressive dimensions in a modern setting. Alex had very good taste.

'He has, hasn't he?' Delphi glowed contentedly. Half the clientele of the Ivy could probably see the aura. Of her glow, not the ring. 'Actually, I chose it, but he agreed with me. I want you to be my maid of honour. I'll have a couple of sweet little girls – Alex has some nieces who'll do – but you're the important one.'

'Do I have to? I look awful in frilly dresses.'

'No frills, I promise. This is *me*, remember? We've always said we'd be maid of honour for each other, ever since we were kids. Roo . . . you are pleased for me, aren't you?'

'Yes, of course.' Her flicker of anxiety, indicative of those hidden sensibilities, touched me with guilt, and I injected real warmth into my voice. She was genuinely happy, and I was being picky and ungenerous.

'You do like him?'

'Very much. He's adorable.'

This was true. Alex *is* adorable – he's adorable like an Andrex puppy or a small child. You want to cuddle but not shag him. At least, that was my reaction. Evidently Delphi felt differently. And he had always been a near-perfect boyfriend, remembering her birthday (I suspected she took care to remind him) and even mine, squiring her to all the right social occasions, bringing her flowers after any tiff (Delphi and Alex didn't row, they only tiffed), giving her surprise presents of things she didn't want, like Perspex jewellery and soft toys. They'd been drifting towards marriage since they met, when Delphi ticked off his various qualities on some private check-list in her head. She'd moved into his mews house within four months, redecorated it in her own image, done her best to charm his parents, his three sisters, and any partners of same. Spoilt, indolent and sweet-natured, Alex seemed only too happy to let her run his life. They had the sort of successful, stress-free relationship that all the rule books advocate. It was just . . .

It was just that I didn't think it was love.

Three-quarters of the way down the Bolly, I said so. In a roundabout way. Vestiges of diplomacy remained to me.

'You do love him, don't you?'

'Of course I do!' Delphi's eyes widened at the imputation. 'I wouldn't *dream* of marrying without love. Alex is fantastically handsome – he's charming, he loves *me* to bits. How could I not love him back?'

Lorelei Lee, I thought, recalling Monroe in *Gentlemen Prefer Blondes*. But Delphi wasn't a platinum-haired gold-digger who'd hooked a compliant millionaire. Delphi had subtle streaks and deep-seated veins – or something.

I really shouldn't have champagne at lunchtime.

'It's only . . .' I floundered, 'you never seem to get upset about him, or worry if he's late to meet you, or think he fancies other women.'

'Alex only fancies me,' Delphi sighed blissfully. 'He's so good like that.'

'But when we were teenagers, and you were keen on Ben—'

'Ben Garvin,' she retorted tartly, 'was a mistake. I *learnt* from that. That's your trouble, Roo: you never learn. You keep doing the same old thing over and over again. If you'd only learn from the Kyle business, you could meet Mr Right and get married and live happily ever after, like me. It's like someone or other said – before you get your prince you have to kiss an awful lot of toads. Ben was one of the toads, Alex is—'

'A frog?'

'Alex is *my* prince.' Delphi swept minor niggles aside. 'You're still stuck in toad mode. You've got to start thinking princes.'

Maybe she was right. She looked happy – radiantly happy, serenely confident of the future. Who was I to quibble because Alex never made her miserable?

'We've got to start planning the wedding,' she went on. 'It's going to be mega. I was thinking a castle, like Madonna and the McCartneys. Maybe Hot God would lend me his? I had considered Brighton Pavilion, because that would be *amazing*, but apparently *anybody* can get married there, so obviously it won't do. Alex wants us to use his father's place in Wiltshire – it's huge, about twenty bedrooms and acres of garden – but I told him you can't get married in your own home, it's so naff. And then there's the dress. I want it to be *totally* over the top, but tasteful. How about Stella – or John Galliano?'

Evidently Alex's perfections were to be set aside for more important matters.

'Who did Posh use?' I murmured wickedly.

Delphi all but blenched. '*I* don't model myself on Victoria Beckham,' she said. 'I don't follow; I lead. Which reminds me, once I'm married I'm going to broaden my professional horizons. I think it's time I became a lifestyle guru . . .'

According to T.S. Eliot, J. Alfred Prufrock measured out his life in coffee spoons. Lately, I seemed to be measuring mine in champagne corks. A few days after my celebration with Delphi, Crusty invited both of us to lunch to discuss the show. The location moved from the Ivy to the Garrick, with its pictures of legendary thespians like Ellen Terry and Sarah Bernhardt, its misogynistic rules (we weren't allowed in the main dining room), its modest Euro-English cuisine. Working on *Behind the News* hadn't involved glamour-lunching; socialising usually happened in pubs and bars, the sleazier the better. I'd generally avoided drinking during the day and when Crusty ordered Krug as a matter of course I asked timidly for mineral water. (My glass got filled anyway.)

'Sensible girl,' Crusty said approvingly. 'But don't worry,

champagne isn't a *real* drink. I always think it's a lot like Perrier, only nicer.'

He drank it like Perrier, I noticed.

The working title of the series had changed several times, as is the way with titles. *God's Scottish Paradise*, *Redesigning Eden* and *The Rock Star and the Rockery* had given way to *Dunblair: Quest for a Garden* (the castle was called Dunblair) and now, Crusty informed us, *The Lost Maze of Dunblair*.

'They grew maize?' Delphi demanded, at sea.

'He means maze as in Hampton Court,' I hazarded.

'Exactly.' Crusty beamed further approval at me, which would have been embarrassing if Delphi had paid any attention. 'Dunblair was originally the property of the McGoogles, an old Scottish family going back to the time of Hadrian, or thereabouts.'

I could see Delphi opening her mouth to ask about Adrian and murmured *sotto voce*, 'Chap with the wall.'

'Some time in the sixteenth century the incumbent McGoogle planted a maze, asserting, according to local tradition, that when it was grown high enough to hide him, he would marry.'

'Why?' Delphi interjected.

'Probably wanted to put off getting married,' I suggested, a little thoughtlessly. 'Any excuse. Besides, folklore is like that. When the first apple ripens on the tree planted yesterday the queen will be with child. That sort of thing.'

'Anyway, the Laird was quite old before the hedge outgrew him – he was a tall man – and he took as his bride a girl young enough to be his granddaughter. Unfortunately, her heart was given to Another.' Crusty clearly favoured the old-fashioned cliché – I could hear the capital letter. 'She trysted with her lover in the secrecy of the maze, until one night her husband caught them there and slew them both in his jealous fury. After that it was said to be haunted; several people who wandered into it were never seen again. Bonnie Prince Charlie hid there from the British, although this time it was the soldiers sent to search for him who disappeared.'

'Convenient,' I remarked.

'It's a wonderful romantic story,' Delphi enthused.

'There's more. In the Victorian era there was a laird called Alasdair McGoogle who came into his inheritance at an early age. He was handsome and popular with his tenants, so everyone was upset when instead of the wife chosen for him by his family he married an English girl. However, on their wedding day the whole district was invited, and there was drinking, dancing and games far into the night. Some say the bride ran into the maze to tease her husband or hide from him, others that she was decoyed there by her rival, but she never came out, nor was her body ever found. Alasdair was so distraught he razed the hedges to the ground and ordered all copies of the plans destroyed, so the maze could never be planted again. Then he went to Africa, died of a fever, and was succeeded by a long-lost cousin.'

'He dunnit,' I said promptly. 'The cousin.'

'The rival girlfriend,' Delphi said. 'And I bet she married the cousin in the end.'

'Actually, I believe she did,' Crusty conceded. 'But there's no way of finding out what really happened. However, HG –' presumably Hot God – 'thinks he may have found a surviving plan of the maze at the back of an old painting. It's in a poor state of preservation, but it may be recoverable. His idea is to bring in full-grown hedges and restore the maze to its original glory.'

'What about the ghosts?' I asked.

'HG is calling in a psychic researcher.'

'Oh God,' Delphi said. 'Not one of those people who

wander round picking up sinister vibes, and saying they feel a supernatural chill when everyone knows the central heating doesn't work?'

'I'm afraid so.' Under the moustache, Crusty smiled ruefully. 'But we're also getting a serious historian on the case – Nigel Willoughby-Purchiss, you must have heard of him – and we're considering incorporating some dramatic re-enactment into the programmes.'

Delphi looked dubious – she was losing too much of the limelight. Then her expression brightened. 'I could do that,' she said. 'After all, I *am* an actress. I could play the vanished wife.'

'Which one?' I said, wondering if she would appropriate both.

'The English one. I don't do accents.'

'That sounds like a great idea,' Crusty said, looking unfazed. It occurred to me that with Delphi acting as well as presenting he would have one less person to pay. Maybe he was more devious than I'd expected.

We went on to discuss further aspects of the maze and the mystery, while I panicked inwardly, seeing my job growing several new heads, like the Lernean Hydra after pruning. (That's the mythical monster, not a plant.) At the end of the meal Crusty paid with a card. 'It'll all go on expenses for the show,' he told me.

Damn.

'Who's Nigel Willoughby-Purchiss?' Delphi demanded when we were alone.

'He's the latest TV historian.' She didn't watch educational programmes, naturally. 'Did a series recently on the Minoans. Young men with pecs running round the ruins of Knossos half naked. It got quite good reviews, at least from gay critics.'

'Is he good-looking?' Delphi enquired hopefully. Possibly she thought he might be a prospect for me. 'Some of those academic types are.'

'It depends. If you admire men with no chin and a long twitchy nose like a shrew . . .'

'They shouldn't allow people like that on television,' Delphi said. 'It puts off the viewers.'

'He's got character,' I said for the sake of argument. 'And brains.'

Delphi treated the remark with the contempt she felt it deserved.

Actually, what he had was the right kind of name. Names are hugely important in the media: it's the first – sometimes the only – part of you people see, whether in the newspapers or in the credits: it's the part that hangs around when your face has gone. For off-the-wall yoof TV you want to dye your hair purple and call yourself something like Pollenta Le Vain, but for shows appealing to an upmarket intellectual audience you need a posh forename like Piers, Simon or Hugh (preferably spelt Huw), and a really memorable double-barrelled surname. Something like Firmly-Knittingstall, or Teabag Multistori, or Mountflummery-Massiveturd. The sort of name that nobody could possibly make up and nobody will ever forget. A name that says immediately what a unique person you are. In the name stakes, Nigel Willoughby-Purchiss had a head start.

The job I had taken as a soft option seemed to be offering me a plethora of new challenges, whether I wanted them or not. Not only working with Delphinium and Crusty, expenses and all, a temperamental rock star, and a larger crew than I was accustomed to, but now actors (more temperament) a fashionable historian (academic temperament), a professional psychic (sensitive temperament) and a bevy of ghosts. When I got home and dosed my champagne headache with Nurofen it occurred to me I hadn't thought of Kyle for at least three hours. If nothing else, my new producership was likely to keep me far too busy to miss him in the foreseeable future. Thanks to Delphi, I thought.

On a wave of remorse I told myself I should be happy for her and Alex. Just because love made me wretched, swinging between extremes of ecstasy and anguish, didn't mean it had that effect on everyone else. For Delphi, the course of true love really *did* run smooth. Next summer, she would marry her prince while I wept pleasurably in her train.

Provided I wasn't dolled up in taffeta frills or lilac chiffon, of course.

Delphinium

One of the things everybody knows about a career in the media is that it involves a lot of lunches. There are business lunches (plenty of those, especially in the run-up to a new series), and friendly lunches (occasionally), and look-at-me lunches where you lunch with the right people in the right places in order to be seen. You can combine the being-seen element with either of the other two by simply choosing suitable restaurants, like the Ivy and the Rip-Off Café, even if you're not being seen with anyone significant. But with the Hot God show and my own wedding in the offing I felt I was due for a proper look-at-me lunch, so I went to Skittles with my celebrity best friend, Brie de Meaux. Skittles is the newest, trendiest, hottest, coolest, hippest, hoppest restaurant in town, and may well remain so for at least a month. The prices are so high they cause the edges of your plate to curl up, and the cuisine is in the latest mode, concerted Euro-Asiatic fusion, or con-fusion, involving things like Deep Egg, Windy Sausages, Prawn Blisters and Blood Ice. (The last item sounds like a sculpture by Marc Quinn, but is, I think, something to do with oranges.) The knack is to be seen eating there at the right time (now), to mention nonchalantly in the hearing of several journalists that you have been doing so for at least a year (even though it's only been open a few weeks), and to shake the dust of the place from your feet before it's discovered by city suits and the vulgar herd. Brie and I both know how to play that game, and I spotted two society columnists rubber-necking from tables at the side as soon as we went in. Good.

Roo is my *real* best friend, of course, but Brie is my official best friend, the one I dish up for interviews and colour supplements when I need a high-profile supporting act. She's a former glamour model who's trying to turn respectable with minor acting roles (she can't act), a pop record (she can't sing) and glittering appearances at any event where celebs can appear and glitter. Her real name is Jilly Evans; she chose Brie de Meaux because she'd seen it somewhere and thought that as it was French it must be classy. By the time she found out what it meant it was too late, but in fact it's worked well for her. Having a name that looks familiar before you've even started always helps. To look at she's very pretty, with a café-au-lait complexion from a Pakistani grandmother, sea-green eyes and blonde hair recently turned brunette to enhance her new image. She's not as tall as me and used to have all-over curves, but as her career advanced her boobs got bigger and her hips and thighs got smaller, until now she looks like two melons on a stick. Even though she wants to be Taken Seriously, she can't bring herself to have a reduction.

She had just emerged triumphant from *Celebrity Murder Island*, where viewers had voted her a particularly gory death after she seduced the fiancée of a TV property dealer. The lesbian touch was a stroke of genius, giving her a sort of credibility with the liberal left while spawning male erotic fantasies everywhere. In Skittles those members of the hoi polloi who had been able to get in gawped at us, while lesser lights from the media smiled and nodded as if we were mates, even though we weren't. I let Brie enjoy her moment of glory. After all, lesbian sex in a tropical paradise on prime-time TV was, so to speak, a mere splash in the fan compared with a garden makeover for Hot God lasting six forty-five minute episodes, and a forthcoming marriage to feature lavishly in *Hello!* or *OK!* Brie was reputedly much engaged but hadn't come near marriage except for an aberration with a plumber when she was fifteen, which didn't count.

We studied the menu in mutual incomprehension and chose at random, since to betray ignorance and ask for subtitles would be fatal. Brie suffers from several eating disorders and has days when she'll touch nothing except salad and spa water, and days when she'll pig out on four courses with extra chips, depending on which disorder is in the ascendant at the time. That day, it turned out, she was on something called the Hodgkins diet, which involved only eating food of certain colours at specified meals. 'Today it's red,' she announced. 'Tomato, red peppers, lollo rosso, red meat, red fish.'

'What if that stuff you ordered isn't red?' I asked.

'I'll just pick out the bits that are. Anyway, there was carpaccio of tuna in there somewhere. Tuna's red.'

'No, it's not. It's a sort of mauvy brown,' I argued.

'That counts as red.'

Which only goes to prove my private theory that all diets are just eating disorders in a more controlled form.

When the starters arrived Brie duly picked out the red bits, with disastrous results, since some of them were raw chilli. Once she had drunk about a bottle of water, recovered, complained, ordered something else instead – a tiny cup of pale pink froth which was apparently salmon cappuccino – we were at last able to settle down to serious conversation. Inevitably, Brie wanted to talk about *Celebrity Murder Island*, boring on at some length about the ageing children's TV presenter who had been elected sole survivor. Interestingly, she didn't mention her lesbian girlfriend at all.

So I did.

'How is Morgana? Are you still seeing her?'

'Shit no. That was just for the cameras.' As I'd guessed. 'Off the record, she was awful. One of those arty Islington types. I'd have much preferred her boyfriend, only he wasn't there.'

'Was the sex good?' I knew ears were twitching at every adjacent table.

Brie shuddered. 'Don't ask. I mean, I thought it would be, because women are supposed to know what other women like, right? Our bodies all work the same. The kissing was okay, but her tits were so small I could feel the ribs underneath and she had a bush like a wire brush. She wanted me to go down on her and she didn't even have the consideration to shave. It was disgusting.'

'Did you?'

'Only for a minute or two. Cunnilingus is bloody difficult. Give me dick any day – it's so much easier to get at.'

By now, the ears had stopped twitching and were extended on stalks. Brie, I knew, was perfectly well aware of that.

'It just goes to show,' I said, 'how wonderful men are.'

'Finding the clit, you mean? Well, yes . . . *if* they manage it, which lots of them don't. How's Alex in that department?'

'Gifted,' I said, which wasn't precisely true. Alex can *find* the clit but he's never really figured out what to do with it when he gets there. It doesn't matter much – I can handle it myself.

'By the way,' I added, casually, 'we're getting married. We've set a date.'

Brie said things like 'Wow!' and 'Fantastic!', turned pale green over my ring, and eventually asked 'When?'

'Oh – in the summer, when I've finished the new series. Organising things is going to be difficult: I'll be on location at the castle all the time while we're shooting. They're going to do some historical re-enactment scenes, so I'll have a chance to act as well.' Brie had recently been turned down for a part in a period film, so I knew that would make her even greener. I like her very much – in a social sort of way – but I wasn't going to let her think she was the star in our friendship.

'The castle?' she queried.

'Didn't I tell you? We're doing a garden makeover at this place in Scotland, Dunblair Castle. For *God*. You know – Hot God. I gather I'll be staying with him for the duration of the series.'

Brie said 'Wow!' again, more than once. 'How did you land that one?' she demanded unwisely.

'Hot God asked for me,' I lied airily. There are times when it's obligatory to lie. I wasn't going to say that the executive producer was a friend of my mother, and the person Hot God had really asked for was Mortimer Sparrow. Apart from the need to upstage *Celebrity Murder Island*, there were those stalking ears to consider.

(Hot God should be grateful to me. Did he *really* want people to know he was a fan of Morty?)

'Is he going to appear in the programme?' Brie persisted. 'I mean, he hasn't been filmed for years, and last time one of the paparazzi got into the grounds of that castle he was torn to pieces by Rottweilers.'

'Of course he's appearing,' I said, concluding, with authority, 'He wants to get involved in the whole makeover process – replant the maze, that sort of thing.'

'He grows *maize* in the garden?'

'M-A-Z-E. As in Hampton Court.'

Brie looked blank. She had obviously never been to Hampton Court.

'I hear he's got, like, really fat,' she went on. 'Positively obese. Like Brando when he got older. I expect that's why he doesn't want to be photographed.'

'I'll let you know,' I said sweetly.

'Is Alex going?'

'No.'

'Won't he mind being left out of the party?'

Brie and Alex don't get on. He says he hates silicon, her looks are *ordinaire*, her personality is even more *ordinaire*, she's self-

centred, insincere and on the make. She says he's a spoilt little rich
kid, too pretty to be hetero, self-centred, insincere, and would be on
the make if he wasn't too lazy. You get the picture.

'I'll arrange for him to visit sometimes,' I said.

'Don't you worry,' she said, 'leaving him alone for so long?'

For answer, I just smiled and flashed my chartreuse diamond. As
I turned my hand, it took the glow from the nearest wall lamps and
transformed it into a thousand splinters of starlight. So there.

We weren't due to start shooting until March, since before that the
ground would be too frozen for digging and Hot God would be spending the winter on his private island somewhere in the South Pacific.
Roo got some temporary work for one of the digital channels on the
sort of stocking-filler show which you can only bear to watch if you've
had half your brain removed. She was struggling valiantly against
depression, but with a daily grind of karaoke kittens, a haunted laundrette, and an old woman forced to live in a shoe, her stiff upper lip
was beginning to wobble.

'I can stand it,' she said palely. 'It's all part of life's rich pageant.'

'So is mass murder, and Manchester, and McDonald's,' I retorted.
'That doesn't mean you want to have anything to do with them.'

I took her to the *Celebrity Murder Island* Christmas party by way
of light relief. Alex wouldn't come with me, partly because he didn't
want to hang out with Brie, partly because he was attending a fringe
event to meet a young genius who had just written a wonderful screenplay, or was about to write a wonderful screenplay, and together they
would make the film of the century. I had heard it all before, but I
didn't say so. It's very important Alex thinks he's doing something
positive even if he isn't. Roo turned up for the party with no make-
up on (she said she'd had to leave home in a hurry) and a dress
she'd had about five years, which is her idea of new. If it had been
any older it would have been retro and back in fashion; as it was, it
just looked passé. I've tried to take her shopping once in a while and

buy her something gorgeous, but she says she doesn't like shopping – does she seriously expect me to believe that? – and she won't let me give her things unless it's her birthday or Christmas. It really annoys me when she starts acting proud. It's so selfish. I have this great chance to enjoy myself being generous and benevolent and she totally spoils it.

The party wasn't really a success. Being without Alex, I decided to pull the most attractive man in the room, not for sex, but just to prove that I could. This turned out to be the B-grade pop star who'd been on the island and had been elected first murder victim by the viewers, probably because they'd heard him sing. He wasn't an inspiring choice, but the only other options were the ex-children's TV presenter, an ex-small screen cop (with ex-hair), and an ex-footballer who hadn't made it as a commentator. The kind of celebs who went on *Murder Island* were all desperate to relaunch flagging careers. Anyway, just as I had the pop star cornered Brie joined us, wearing a dress that appeared to have been made in spandex and spangles for Slappers 'R Us and a perfume so sweet it smelt like something dead. Not that I wish to be critical, but she doesn't really have Taste. She proceeded to mention my engagement three times before collaring the pop star for the rest of the evening. Roo, meanwhile, was talking to Morgana, in the mistaken belief they had a lot in common.

'What's the matter?' she demanded as I dragged her away. 'She seems very nice.'

'She isn't *nice*,' I explained. 'She's chatting you up. Don't you read the tabloids?'

But of course Roo didn't.

For Christmas, we usually go home. Home as in Little Pygford, which I still think of as 'home' on a subconscious level, even though home is really me and Alex. Probably one of those Freudian things which I can never figure out. Geoff Harker used to come until he remarried, and Pan's always there, and Mummy cooks, and Pan and I argue, and it all follows a safe familiar routine. But this year I was going to the Russos – Alex's father, his current wife, assorted siblings – in the big country house where I had no intention of getting married. I didn't like leaving Roo, though she said she would be all right. After intensive doses of VivaTV, all she really wanted to do (she said) was sleep. I spent the holiday getting cosy with Alex's family, discussing wedding plans, and deciding *not* to have his two nieces as brides-maids, since they were very badly behaved and clearly had no idea what a privilege it would be to dress up like flower fairies and feature in a leading magazine. The older one used my make-up when my back was turned and I found the younger peacocking round in my shoes and my favourite evening scarf, which is handmade cobwebby lace and much too delicate to be touched by children. I pointed out to their mother that they were aspiring vandals in need of discipline, but she just said they were such darlings, they loved dressing up like grown-ups, just got a wee bit unmanageable when the nanny wasn't around. Some parents have *no* sense of responsibility. That lace scarf would have been frightfully expensive if I'd had to pay for it.

When I have children I intend to make sure their nanny teaches them to behave perfectly *all the time*, not simply when they're under her eye.

Among other things the two hooligans got a puppy for Christmas, a tiny bundle of white fluff with round dark eyes and black button nose – utterly adorable, but prone to pee and poo all over the place. Their father said the girls would have to train it themselves, which didn't augur well for the future of their carpets. Alex was very taken with it. 'It's a bichon frisee,' he told me. 'Pure pedigree: its great-grandfather (or great-great) won Crufts.' Personally, I would have given them a mongrel with plenty of Rottweiler in the hope that it would grow up and eat them.

We had dogs when I was a child, but they were Labs and retriev-ers who knew to poo in the fields when out for walks or in the garden where Mummy and the assistant gardener could clear it up. I loved them, but that was in the country. Dogs in the city require a lot of effort (Alex's sister and the brats live in Bayswater). And small dogs, though cute and attractive accessories, have to be walked and trained just like big ones.

In January, we went to stay with friends who have a ski lodge in Zermatt. I don't ski much – I'm not supposed to risk injury: no TV presenter looks good on crutches – but the weather was fabulous and I sunbathed at the bottom of the piste, moisturised and UV-screened against wrinkles and skin cancer. Alex skis well, having learned when he was in nappies, and looks good in the gear. I had some great new kit too, though I didn't intend to spoil it with overuse – tight Lycra pants and padded jacket, cream with pink ribbing. There were paparazzi around and the pictures of us both looked almost too gorgeous to be true. Snow-sports suit Alex: they add a flush to his golden skin and rumple his black hair. (I won't let him wear those woolly hats that make everyone look like a nerd.) Skiing puts him in a good mood, though he was sulking a bit about my trip to Scotland.

'You're jealous,' I said, 'because I'm going to be hanging out with the sexiest, most famous rock star of all time.'

'Of course I'm not jelly!' Alex will use these abbreviations. In every relationship, you have to compromise with the other person's irritating little habits. That's one of his. 'Anyway, they say he's got positively bloated since he came off the drugs. Like, *gross*.'

'That girl in the kiss-and-tell piece didn't mention it,' I pointed out.

'She wouldn't, would she? No one wants to admit they slept with a whale. Besides, that happened at least five years ago – it just took her ages to decide to sell her story. He's probably put the pudding on since.'

Alex always calls flab 'pudding'. If he thinks I've put on a pound or two he'll pat my thigh, or my tummy, and accuse me of 'growing pudding'. It's a bit irritating but it does make me avoid over-eating and try to go to the gym regularly.

'He's married again,' I said. 'Some model. Spanish, I think.'

'He must be absolutely rolling in it,' Alex said, with the unmistakable envy the mildly rich always feel for the filthy rich. 'Honey-money. There'll always be beautiful models queuing up to marry him, even if he's wallowing in lard and plugged full of collagen to puff up his wrinkles.'

Alex thinks he'll never be fat, never be old. His problem, of course, wasn't sexual jealousy; as Brie had said, he simply felt neglected.

'You'll have to come for a visit,' I said placatingly. 'So you can see for yourself.'

Secretly, I was feeling a bit Alexed out.

I do love him, that goes without saying, but you can have too much of anyone, no matter how beautiful they are. It's like doing one of those diets where you only eat one kind of food – bananas, or cabbage soup: after a week of it you never want to see another banana or liquidised cabbage leaf again. I'd had an intensive diet of Alex all through Christmas and skiing, hanging out with each other non-stop, and although of course I would want to see him again very soon I needed a break to appreciate him. I felt a bit guilty about it, so I determined to be extra nice to him first, not objecting when he wanted to watch awful stuff on TV (*Airport* and reality hairdressing), or ate peanut butter and Frosties for breakfast, or sat around cuddling a giant pink fur rabbit, christened Harvey, which was his long-standing security blanket. I was nice to him in bed too, doing all his favourite things, like tickling his scrotum with an ostrich feather and letting him suck my toes. (I won't list the rest: they're even more embarrassing.)

I've never really got the toe thing. We all walk around barefoot some of the time, and your soles get hard and dusty, and no matter how many pedicures you have feet are still – well, *feet*. There to be stepped on and kicked around; not major erogenous zones. Whenever Alex goes down on me, as in that far down, I worry about hygiene issues and have to go and wash them before he can resume. I don't mind not being turned on, but it's no fun when sex is actively stress-making. But I controlled myself, and let him lick away, trying not to wonder what my toes tasted like. Nothing – nothing on earth – will make me reciprocate.

(The good part is that Alex is nuts about my shoes. He's the only man I know who gets a hard-on for Jimmy Choo stilettos.)

When it comes to sex, men fall into roughly two categories. There are those who like sex the way a chocoholic likes chocolate: it's a delicious indulgence, they crave it, they savour it, but they know, for all the strength of their craving, that it isn't essential to life. And then there are the guys who fuck to live, to feel alive – the intense types for whom sex is bread to the starving. The sort who never waste time on the outer limits of your body (like your toes) but zoom straight in on the principal target areas, and have got inside your bra and twisted your knickers into a thong before you've even offered them coffee. Ben Garvin was like that – but I don't want to think about him. No point in dwelling on mistakes. When I want someone to think about there are always Viking raiders and leopard-print Tarzans and so on. Anyhow, Alex is a chocolate guy; he dips into sex like it's a box of Belgian truffles, lingering over every flavour. It's lovely to feel desired and lingered over like that, even if it *does* make things rather long-winded sometimes.

I'm supposed to be a sex symbol, and sexy women are women who like sex. You can't possibly be sexy if you don't. I read *Lady Chatterley* when I was a teenager (the dirty bits, anyway) and what struck me was how, when poor Constance wasn't getting laid, she went all wan and droopy, but when she started humping the game-keeper she became sleek and opulent again. Mind you, this is a man writing, saying that if you don't fuck you're not a Real Woman, which is what any man *would* say, though they don't usually take a whole novel. It left me with the impression that if I didn't shag regularly my tits would droop – a worry that has lurked at the back of my sex life ever since. So I make sure Alex and I do it a lot. He feels replete, my tits stay full and bouncy, and I can catch up on orgasms later, by myself.

In Scotland, I would have to go without; I flirt, but I don't do infidelity. Too risky. When you're a celebrity, there's always someone watching. But it was only for a few months. There would be chances to visit – my tits wouldn't start sagging just yet. And privately, in the inmost corner of my Self, I really was looking forward to it.

Ruth

Working for VivaTV wasn't one of the highlights of my life. In fact, if your life can have lowlights, that was it. (Or them.) Ongoing lowlights, every day. The producer was a plump, pasty-faced woman who ate too much sugar to counteract the constant fear of losing her job. She passed her stresses on to me, shouting when she didn't need to and changing her mind every ten minutes, and I, willy-nilly, passed them on to the researchers, though I tried not to. Some writer or other once said: 'Most men lead lives of quiet desperation', which may or may not be true, but of one thing I am sure: most women lead lives of vocal desperation. The studio environment seethed with it. On location, we seemed to spend too much time standing around outdoors, waiting for our prey to emerge from office or home, or filming alfresco activities like bicycling poodles, pro-celebrity streaking, and a performance artist who claimed he was turning into a tree. The winter, instead of being merely damp and chilly, was cold, with falls of rather gritty snow and the kind of wind that blows through the hollows of your bones. I had borne far worse in Eastern Europe – but in those days I had Kyle to keep me warm.

'I hear you used to work on that Dick Ramsay show,' one of the researchers said brightly. 'Isn't this a bit of a comedown?'

'I'm changing direction.' Downwards.

'Did you know Kyle Muldoon? I think he's dead sexy.'

'Dead,' I said. Dead in the water. The winter got inside me and I thought it would never get out.

Then came the day when we were covering the haunted house. Our producer was keen on hauntings; I'm not sure why. Ghosts are notoriously camera-shy so any item about the supernatural is basically an item about nothing, with extra padding and creepy music. I suppose the producer felt an item about nothing is an item where nothing can go wrong. We'd done a haunted laundrette (the spin-dryer activated itself), a haunted school (the teacher fainted after her pupils microwaved a voodoo doll), and even a haunted swimming pool (two near-drownings and a plague of frogs). After all that, a haunted house seemed a little mundane, but Dylis (the producer) assured us it was a classic specimen, not simply ghost-ridden but historic, half-timbered and incredibly photogenic. Apparently, among other manifestations, it had a poltergeist who was given to throwing things (they call them apports) like eggs and crockery, causing considerable damage and reducing the two younger children to hysteria. Dylis was so excited by this she told us she was sending a psychic researcher along to analyse the phenomena.

We arrived on a suitably stormy afternoon to find the family in residence: middle-aged dad, youthful mum, sullen teenage daughter by first marriage, two boys from second. The storm broke, causing the electricity to fail, which would have been brilliant if the camera had been rolling. (We staged a re-enactment later with someone throwing a switch.) Then the poltergeist joined in, yanking a rug from beneath the feet of our reporter, who claimed she had injured her back in the fall and would be suing for damages (she wasn't sure whom). I retreated into the kitchen for coffee with mum, refusing sugar

– just as well, because it was salt; poltergeist again – and heard with a sinking heart that the psychic researcher had arrived. Great. All I needed now was Madam Arcati with hennaed hair sensing vibrations from the otherworld.

It wasn't Madam Arcati. For one thing, the researcher was youngish (thirty-odd) and male. If anything, he looked like an elf: pointy face with high cheekbones, slanting eyebrows, ears that looked pointy even though they weren't. He had dark hair worn rather long, pale skin, leaf-green eyes. His name, he said, was Kristof Ashley. 'Call me Ash.'

'My God,' said the researcher who fancied Kyle, 'he looks like Johnny Depp,' and collapsed on the spot, remaining useless for the rest of the day.

I was not thrilled. I don't like pretty-boy types, and besides, everyone else was enraptured by him, so I felt it obligatory not to be. It was clear Ash took himself much too seriously, a major defect in anybody, particularly if they are dabbling in the para-normal. He questioned the family in detail about their ghostly experiences, and listened with evident absorption to the reporter's account of her accident, transforming her from a litigious fury to a simpering ingénue. He even examined the offending rug, for all the world like an investigator from CSI. It was what we were paying him for, but I felt my annoyance mounting. Ten to one the rug had just skidded on polished floorboards.

But he was great TV. He didn't gush, preferring the signif-icant silence to excessive speech, but when he stood in the Jacobean gloom of the drawing room, looking pensive, with what little light there was striking the planes of his cheekbones just *so*, that was all we needed. 'There is a distressed spirit here,' he pronounced at last, though the phantom, not surpris-ingly, had been quiescent. 'With a little understanding, it can be pacified. There will be no more disturbances.'

An apport came flying out of nowhere. I jumped, the sound recorder jumped, and the cameraman swore, presumably because he didn't get a shot of it, but Ash fielded it neatly, completely unperturbed.

'What was it?' I demanded, slightly shaken but determined not to show it.

'A farewell gesture.' That wasn't what I meant, and he must have known it, but he had slipped the object into his pocket. 'Before we go, I would like a private word with the older members of the family. I'll see you outside.'

We had obviously extricated all we could from the situation, so I waited by his car (a new-look VW Beetle in silver).

When he appeared, I asked: 'What was really going on in there?'

'Do you care?'

That stung. That's the worst of something like VivaTV: it deadens your reactions. He was accusing me of lacking compassion, and I felt he was right, though I had no idea what I was supposed to be compassionate about.

'Of course not,' I snapped. 'If I was a caring person, I wouldn't be in this job.'

He didn't smile. He never smiled. 'It was the girl,' he said. 'Teenage hormones. And she was jealous of the second wife and her two stepbrothers. She chose that way of expressing her feelings.'

For a minute, surprise wiped out my animosity for him. 'How did you guess?'

'The rug. She'd looped a string through a hole behind the fringe. She'd managed to pull the string out, but I saw the hole. It's an old trick.'

'And that last missile?'

'That was easy. You were all watching me, not her. She turned aside and threw it over her shoulder. She'll have done that several times, though not for the camera. The house was on her side; it's old and dimly lit. Easy.'

'If you were so sure,' I said, 'you should've exposed her when we were filming.'

His lips thinned. 'I wouldn't do that to her. If you feel I'm in breach of contract, don't pay me.'

I *really* hated him. I hated his unruffled coolth, his know-it-all superiority, his elfin cheekbones. I even hated his compassion. He'd shown me what I had become, and I didn't like it at all. And he was a bloody psychic investigator, one of the Madam Arcati brigade, a professional phoney. It was totally unfair.

'We'll pay you,' I said. 'I'll see to it. You were quite right not to . . . Just don't mention it to my producer.'

He gave a brief jerk of the head, maybe a nod. 'Worried about your job?'

I shrugged, trying to match his cool. 'My contract's short-term. By the way . . . what was it she threw? The thing you put in your pocket?' Vulgar curiosity, but I wanted to know. Otherwise it would nag at me in the bath.

'It was a pendant. A heart, in agate or jasper. I gave it back to her. I should think it was quite expensive.'

He didn't look gratified by the offering. He was probably used to poltergeists throwing hearts at him. I mumbled routine thanks, and he got into the VW and drove away, leaving me with a disagreeable feeling that I didn't really want to analyse. Let's face it, I'd made a bad impression. I'd come across as cheap, flip, cold-hearted, and though what Ash thought wasn't important, the root cause bothered me. In such a short while, had VivaTV made me one of their own? On *Behind the News* we'd covered serious issues, we'd cared. Well, *I'd* cared; I couldn't answer for Kyle any more. He'd seemed to care, at any rate, though he used to say that if you threw your heart in the ring every time sooner or later you'd break it. But that was just surface toughness, his way of coping with all the pain we saw. On VivaTV there was no pain, just the quiet desperation of people who will do anything for a moment on the small screen. Yet somehow I felt soiled by it, by the way we exploited their thirst for a little immortality. I was becoming someone I didn't like, and a phoney psychic researcher, of all people, had made me see it. So of course I didn't like *him*.

The world of glamour gardening was looking more attractive by the hour. After all, you can't exploit a plant (can you?) and a lifelong rock icon is way beyond being used by anyone.

It was only later that evening that I remembered we were going to use a psychic researcher on *The Lost Maze*. But on television, spurious experts are two a penny, and the chances of the Major picking the same one were surely small to non-existent.

Or so I hoped.

Chapter 3:
King of the Castle

Ruth

I went up to Scotland with the advance guard, to establish a
beachhead and dig ourselves in. Crusty Beardstandard was
already there, smoothing the path for his team, or possibly
smoothing the superstar for the path, I am not sure which.
My experience of makeover shows was non-existent, but I was
certain few subjects received this level of prenatal consideration: when you are dealing with a rock icon, the rules change.
I made a private resolution that *my* rules, at least, wouldn't
change at all. I wasn't going to be thrilled, I wasn't going to
be overawed. At most I might be mildly impressed if the occasion called for it. I hadn't chosen this job, it had been chosen
for me, and while it might be a big step up from VivaTV it
was several steps down from *Behind the News*, despite Dick
Ramsay's toupee. I was used to real suffering, real courage,
life in the raw. A rock star, no matter how famous or infamous,
was a lightweight to me.

Crusty picked me up at Inverness Airport in a Range Rover
from Hot God's stable and we drove west to Dunblair. A good
deal of scenery of a Scottish nature spread out or reared up
on either hand: green slopes dotted with sheep or cows, both

64

decidedly shaggy, bristling stands of fir and pine, rocky heights nudging skywards, the tallest drizzled with snow like white icing on a pointed cake. Crusty kept up a gentle flow of conversation, or rather information, as he drove, filling me in on the set-up at the castle and, I sensed, on any areas where tact and diplomacy might be required. (Most of them.) I hoped I would remember it all, but I was distracted by the passing landscape. Despite a tingle of nerves at the prospective challenges of the job, I couldn't help feeling a little as if I was going on holiday. Maybe it was the beauty of the surroundings, the luxury of being met at the airport by someone who would do the driving, the fact that I was finally escaping the clinging memories of Kyle. Ahead of me lay, not the seedy drama and hopeless tragedy of too many news stories, but more luxury in a romantic castle, and filming that would focus principally on plants. What trouble could I possibly have with a plant? I set minor worries aside and sat back to enjoy myself.

Eventually the trees parted, a sunbeam sliced down between stravaiging clouds, and we saw the mirror-flash of light on water.

'Lochnabu,' Crusty told me. 'We go through the village first, then up to Dunblair. It's at the northern tip of the lake; you'll get a view of it in a minute.'

The road swooped down towards the shore; the trees drew back. I could see more of the loch now, a silver tongue of water perhaps two and a half miles long, with a small jetty at one end where a couple of boats were moored, and, above it, on a sort of promontory, a castle. I glimpsed a sturdy tower, grey battlements, extraneous turrets, a cluster of pointy roofs. Even at this distance, it was everything a castle should be.

'It's beautiful,' I said.

'Bit of a hotch-potch,' Crusty responded. 'The oldest parts go back nearly seven hundred years, but over the centuries almost every incumbent added a turret or two in the fashion of the time. It was all rather tumbledown when HG bought it, but he's spent a fortune on restoration. Totally faithful to the original building on the outside, of course. Inside . . . well, he's installed central heating, and done a lot of work on the plumbing. Used to be pretty Victorian.'

Victorian? Victorian was good. I'd had nervous recollections of a longdrop loo I'd seen once in a medieval tower, where you sat on a hole at the top and your output splashed all the way to the bottom. The thought of Delphi's reaction to such amenities was the only thing which had kept me from voicing my fears.

'Décor's a tad . . . erratic,' Crusty was saying, on a note I identified as self-restraint. 'HG let his latest loose on some of the rooms. Spanish model, late thirties, admits to twenty-nine. Her name's Basilisa; don't call her Baz. The locals have dubbed her the Basilisk – inevitable, really – but don't use it in HG's hearing. He's left her behind on Mande Susu for the moment – that's the island – but I daresay she'll turn up some time. Doesn't like the Scottish winter. Doesn't like Scotland at all, I expect, but she'll come home to be on TV.'

'She wouldn't have acting ambitions, would she?' I enquired, my heart sinking.

'Bound to,' said Crusty. 'They always do.'

Shit. As soon as she heard about the historical re-enactment there would be two of them after the starring role. My holiday anticipation deflated like a pricked balloon. 'Oh God,' I said, forgetting to maintain my cool. 'Will we have enough beautiful heroines to go round?'

'Overegg the pudding,' Crusty suggested, with the unflappable calm which, I was beginning to guess, was the secret of his success. Most people in television are very flappable, existing on a roller coaster of neuroses. Dylis, for instance, had flapped like a banner in every breeze. 'Plenty of history out there to re-enact. What is it they say in government? Sex it up. Sure Nigel will be happy to help. Women in period costumes with lots of cleavage – did wonders for Jane Austen. Can't hurt us.' Beneath the Edwardian whiskers and old-fashioned gallantry he really was nobody's fool. I was suddenly very anxious not to let him down.

'We're going to have problems with some of these people, aren't we?' I said candidly, realising too late I sounded naïve. On location with a small team in Slovenia, Slovakia, or even Doncaster, people-problems with colleagues had been the least of my worries and temperament took second place to professionalism. Here, all too obviously, it was going to be different.

'Doesn't matter,' Crusty said with the single vision of the true obsessive. 'Only the garden matters. The dramatic stuff – that's trimmings to broaden our audience. But the garden's the star.'

'What about HG?'

'He'd agree with me,' Crusty breezed.

Ah, well. Everyone has their blind spot.

We drove through a small, rather dour-looking village, stone houses hunkered down in anticipation of bad weather, inhabitants, sheepskinned and wellied against the climate, who glared at us with the traditional hostility of natives everywhere (or possibly because they knew what was afoot and were madly curious). Then on to a twisty track, recently resurfaced, which bent this way and that to skirt ridges and duck trees. Gate posts loomed ahead, and Crusty braked while another, even more hostile, individual came and glared, though in an official sort of way. Then the gates opened and we drove the last half-mile to the castle.

Close to, the conglomeration of styles resolved themselves into Gothic Fantasy constructed on and around a solid keep of medieval origins. Bits of the keep were attractively crumbled and had been left as such; the effect was rather like a strangler fig, a parasitic tree which entwines and overgrows the host until the latter is completely smothered. Despite that, it was gorgeous, and I forgot my resolution to be only mildly impressed. This was Dunblair, not its owner. I could let myself go.

While I stood gawping, two people emerged from the castle to deal with my luggage: a sandy-haired man of thirty-five to forty with an engaging grin who proved to be the butler, and a gawky youth with acne whom I labelled as a hired lad from the village.

'Dorian Jakes,' Crusty said by way of introduction.

Oh.

Poor boy, I thought instinctively. It must be bad enough to be an awkward teenager with spots, without having an iconic celebrity dad to live up to. I smiled kindly at him – at least, I hoped it was a kind smile – causing him to drop my shoulder bag so abruptly I wondered if I'd grown vampire teeth. The butler had gone ahead, so Dorian was deputised to take me to my room, a lengthy trek during which I attempted conversation and he stuttered in reply. In a gallery which should have been hung with cobwebs and ancestral paintings, I came to a dead stop. This was evidently the Basilisk's handiwork: sheepskin rugs dyed magenta, a Dali lip sofa in cerise velvet, zebra hides on the walls.

'My God,' I said in undiplomatic horror.

Reassured by my reaction, Dorian lost his stutter. 'My stepmother did it,' he said. 'She's awful.' And, after a pause: 'She's much too young for him. It's so embarrassing. He ought to stop marrying young models and settle down with someone his own age.'

So much for living up to Dad. I'd got it wrong again. I'd underestimated the modern teenager's capacity for embarrassment.

'Perhaps she makes him happy,' I suggested tentatively.

He made a gesture somewhere between a shrug and a head-shake. 'She only married him for his money. You'd think he'd be smart enough to know that.'

'Fame,' I said. 'For some women, that's a big aphrodisiac.'

'Oh no. She couldn't *like* sex with him, could she? He's frightfully old. She just uses it to get what she wants. Actually, I think she likes boys. You know, really *young* boys. Like, she's a sort of paedophile. She came on to me once.' He shuddered at the memory.

'Did you tell your father?'

'Of course not. She said she'd tell him I was making it up, and he'd believe *her*, and I knew it was true. That's what they do, isn't it? Paedophiles? That's how they control you. Only I couldn't . . . I couldn't do it. I mean, she was all thin and bony and sort of predatory, like a praying mantis. It was disgusting.'

One smile, I thought, and it turns on a gush of confidence. Perhaps he was lonely.

'I'll bet it was,' I said warmly. 'How – how old were you?' I was picturing a child of ten or eleven confronted by a devouring Spanish lamia.

'Fourteen.' And he added: 'Before I got spots.'

'Have you tried tea tree oil?' I found myself responding.

'No . . .'

'A friend of mine uses it: he says it's pretty effective. And sun lamp treatment. That's great if you don't overdo it.'

'Yeah? Morag said there was nothing I could do. She's our housekeeper. She says we all have our crosses to bear.'

'Probably, but not at your age. You're too young for crosses. I don't know if you could get a sun lamp round here, but—'

'That's okay. I'll go online. I have all Dad's credit card details.' Whether legitimately or not, I didn't ask. 'I just didn't think . . . Dad said he had spots when he was sixteen.

He said you grow out of it in a year or two, but that's *ages* away . . .'

'Sun lamps and tea tree oil,' I said. 'It may not clear them all up, but it'll make a difference. Things have changed since your dad was a teenager.' Not 'alf.

By the time we reached my bedroom, we were best friends. 'Sorry about this,' Dorian said as I surveyed a light fitting that appeared to be made from dented tin cans and a futuristic four-poster draped in lilac chiffon and quilted in lime-green silk. 'It's Her again.' There was a definite capital letter. 'But at least the ghost doesn't come in this part of the house.'

'I'm not surprised. What kind of a ghost is it?'

A teenage poltergeist, maybe?

'The usual kind.' He was vague. 'You'll see. Look, I'd better leave you to settle in. Come down for tea about four.'

'I'll never find my way.'

'Harry'll fetch you. Harry Winkworth – he's the butler. He brought your case upstairs.' Sandy hair. Grin. Of course. 'See you later.'

'See you.'

When he had gone, I unpacked. There was far too much wardrobe space for my clothes, making me feel inadequate. Was I supposed to dress up like a *Vogue* fashion plate every evening? Well, Delphi could do that; no one would care what I wore when she was around. (Except her.) Suddenly, I found I was missing her acutely. We hadn't got together for over a week and I wanted her buoyancy, her confidence, her arrogance, her opinion of Basilisa's décor. I sent her a text – 'Dream castle. Nightmare inside. Wait till you see it' – and changed into a cashmere sweater in an attempt to smarten up for tea.

Tea was served in a drawing room largely untouched by the Basilisk effect, with a couple of stags' heads on the wall, shelves of books and CDs, Persian rugs and sofas covered in hessian and scattered with tapestry cushions. Crusty was there, with Dorian, and a square-faced, square-bodied woman with gunmetal hair who had to be Morag the housekeeper. She gave me tea and home-made shortbread biscuits of true melt-in-the-mouth consistency. She was obviously a native – she looked dour if not actively hostile – but, like Crusty, might well have a heart of gold beneath her unpromising exterior, though in the light of her views on acne and crosses I doubted it. Two more people joined us, one of whom I recognised from his TV show as Nigel Willoughby-Purchiss – the probing nose, the retreating chin, the eyes that managed to seem at once sharp and bleary, like a rat with a hangover. However, I knew he was both articulate and clever, and I determined not to hold his appearance against him. Our society is too obsessed with externals, when we should look deeper into the soul. It was not his fault that nature had given him ratty eyes and the profile of an aggressive coat hanger. I shook his hand, gazed (briefly) into his soul, and turned to his companion. My host. Hot God Jakes.

An elderly man, shorter than I'd expected – superstars tend to be short, something to do with the Napoleon complex – in shabby jeans and trainers, rolled-up sleeves showing the sinewy forearms of someone who could not only play the guitar but wrestle it to the ground. He had a leathery, rubbery sort of face with very mobile features (no Botox, then) and more than the usual complement of lines, doubtless the product of his former lifestyles. All four decades of them. Overall, he had a faintly piratical air, probably due to the eyepatch. And the long, streaky grey hair tied back with what had to be a red bandana, since no rock star would be caught dead in a hair ribbon. He greeted me with the relaxed friendliness of some-one who has been doing relaxed and friendly since he got off heroin, and I so far forgot myself as to blurt out: 'Are you all right? Your eye . . .' In all the things I had heard or read about him, no one had ever mentioned him losing an eyeball.

'Cataracts,' he said briefly.

Cataracts? A legendary rock icon couldn't possibly have cataracts. Syphilis, yes, even AIDS, hepatitis, beriberi, swamp fever – any disease that was either sleazy or exotic. But not *cataracts*.

Next thing, it would be lumbago.

'I'm so sorry,' I said, feeling gauche.

'It's still a bit red,' he explained. 'More comfortable if I block out the light. How do you like your room?'

Was he joking? 'Lovely,' I lied, thinking of the tin cans and the lilac-and-lime bed.

'My wife's taste.'

'Yes, Dorian did mention . . .'

'Did he tell you about our ghost?'

'I'm afraid I'm a bit of sceptic,' I said apologetically.

'Me too,' said HG. 'But there's no doubt we have *something* in the oldest part of the castle – a presence, an absence, the feeling of eyes on your back . . . a touch on the nape of your neck. A draught where no draught should be, the rustle of a curtain, a footstep. There are more things in heaven and earth, Horatio.'

'Does it throw things?' I asked.

'A poltergeist? Nothing so vulgar. But see for yourself.'

'Clanking chains? Skirling pipes?'

'No chains. But I think I've heard the pipes once or twice, faint and far off, when I've woken up before dawn.'

'Maybe you did,' I said. 'Some villager practising beside the loch in order to get the right atmosphere.'

'Maybe.' He smiled, deepening the lines in his cheeks. It occurred to me that in an elderly, wrinkled sort of way he was attractive. Charisma. Charm is superficial and beauty fades, but charisma only increases with time. HG had buckets of it.

Whoops! I was being thrilled, if not overawed. I tried to look at him through Dorian's eyes – an awkward father who wouldn't act his age, constantly dating women who were too young for him. Still cavorting on stage occasionally, thinking he could dance – the ultimate horror for any teenager is their seniors wriggling around to old pop songs. Put that way, a rock-star dad would be about as embarrassing as a parent could get. Hot God's pelvic lunge was famous, but, to his son, it would probably be excruciating. Mind you, at his age it might well be excruciating for him too.

The voice of Morag broke in on my thoughts. 'Ye shouldna mock the powers o' the dark,' she intoned in a superb Scottish brogue that rolled off her tongue like porridge. Sooner or later, I deduced, she's going to say: 'We're all doomed.' It was inevitable.

'Morag's very religious,' HG offered.

I'd never have guessed.

The conversation moved on to matters historical and horticultural, with Nigel Willoughby-Purchiss holding forth authoritatively on the gap between legend and fact. After dinner, I was promised a sight of the long-lost plan of the maze, carefully restored from a few lines on ageing and discoloured paper to a feasible sketch of the layout.

'It's incomplete, of course,' HG said, 'but Nigel reckons there will be clues in the terrain to help us fill in the gaps.'

'The ground will be uneven,' Nigel elucidated. 'There will be little ridges – dips, nuances – which only the trained eye can perceive.' Clearly his was the trained eye in question.

'Ye would do better tae let the ghaisties lie,' Morag remarked predictably, pausing as she tidied the tea things.

'I keep her around for the atmosphere,' HG explained when

she had left. 'I suspect she plays up to it, but that's okay. At least she provides an authentic feel of Scottish drama.'

He didn't just want the castle, I reflected, he wanted the whole package. We weren't here just to replant the garden: we were bringing Birnham Wood to high Dunsinane. (This wasn't the last time that particular metaphor would come into play.) And *Macbeth* is supposed to be unlucky. Suddenly, like Morag, I experienced definite qualms about the omens.

Before dinner, Dorian took me to check out the ghost. The oldest part of the castle boasted bare stone walls, narrow uncurtained windows, heavy oak beams plainly added as an afterthought and vaguely military wall decorations, including a moth-eaten banner and something which might have been a claymore – if a claymore was what I thought it was (a sort of chunky two-edged sword). The banner was embroidered with the arms of the McGoogles: a cow rampant – 'Lochnabu means lake of the cow,' Dorian explained knowledgeably – confronting what looked like a giant horned dachshund.

'It's a dragon,' Dorian said.

'It doesn't look very dragonish to me.'

'Either that, or it's a cross between a dog and an iguana . . .'

'What about the ghost?' I asked. 'Does it run screaming through the hall, or wash its hands in someone's blood, or what?' My mind was still running on *Macbeth*.

'It gets very cold,' Dorian said, a shade defensively.

'It's March,' I pointed out. 'There's a north wind blowing. This hall stretches far beyond the range of your father's new central heating.'

'The fire always goes out.'

I gazed at a huge chilly fireplace. 'Chimney needs sweeping? Probably draws badly. Jackdaws nesting in there somewhere, I expect. I don't know much about chimneys but I'm told jack-daws like to nest in them.'

'You get this creepy feeling . . .'

'I get a creepy feeling in *nightclubs*,' I said. Dorian was looking crestfallen, and suddenly I felt like a wet blanket. 'Sorry. I'm just not a ghost person, I suppose. Do we know whose ghost it is, and why it's meant to haunt the place?'

'Not exactly. Morag says the spirits of all those who died in the maze will sleep until it's replanted, so it can't be one of them. Of course, these old Scottish clans were always having feuds and murdering each other. It could be practically anybody.'

Myself, I can't see the *point* of being a ghost. Just hanging around the same place for hundreds of years, scaring people. I'd find better things to do with my death. Perhaps that's why I have trouble believing in them. It isn't the phenomena that fail to convince, it's the motivation.

'We're calling in a psychic researcher,' Dorian went on. 'Major Beard-Trenchard suggested someone, I think.'

'I've heard.'

'Dad says if there's a troubled soul here it should be set at rest.' Nice to know a rock icon could be as susceptible to paranormal bullshit as everyone else.

'And if Morag's right,' I said flippantly, 'when we replant the maze, we'll be up to our ears in spectres.'

Dorian managed a chortle. (You shouldn't say a boy giggles: giggles are for girls. A chortle will do.) An icy draught came from somewhere, raising the hairs on my nape. But icy draughts were to be expected in an antique castle at the tag-end of winter.

'Who's the psychic researcher?' I asked, as idly as I could. 'Some woman with purple hair and jewellery made of melon pips?'

'It's a man,' Dorian responded. 'Ashley somebody. I don't remember exactly.'

Maybe it was the icy draught which made me shiver. Suddenly, Dunblair Castle didn't seem so much fun any more.

I had known it would happen, of course. If you make a bad impression on someone, and you say to yourself, 'It doesn't matter, I'll never see him/her again,' they're absolutely guaranteed to become a major part of your life within a month or two. I had always suspected Fate was a malevolent goddess, and now I was sure of it. Worst of all, I found I wanted to show Ash that he was wrong about me – that I *do* care, I *do* have compassion – but my chances of showing compassion in the luxury castle of an ageing rock star were practically nil. At Dunblair, compassion simply wasn't in demand.

Damn Kristof Ashley. I knew a craven urge to jack the job in then and there and flee south – a reaction out of all proportion to the circumstances. I had to get a grip.

It really was awfully cold in there. And gloomy. The tin-can light fittings and magenta sheep hadn't penetrated this far. I almost regretted them.

'Can't you feel it?' Dorian said, clutching my arm. 'Like . . . this eerie chill, giving you goosebumps.'

For once, I didn't say anything cynical. There was a chill, and my geese bumped.

'Let's go,' I responded.

Delphinium

Roo met me at the airport, driving a Millennium Mini from Hot God's garage. 'It's the only normal car he's got,' she said. 'He bought it for Dorian, I gather, only he hasn't passed his test yet.'

'Who's Dorian?'

'Son. Sixteen. Not sure which wife.'

I'd been doing a little homework on Hot God, and I made a mental calculation.

'Should be the model – Tyndall Fiske. Neck and legs like a giraffe, big nose, own hair a yard long. Good-looking in an ugly sort of way. After the split she got mixed up with some cult in America living out in the middle of nowhere and growing their own vegetables and not having proper sanitation. I remember reading about it. Is Dorian like her?'

'Spots,' said Roo.

'Yuk. Must be awful for Hot God, having a son with zits. I mean, it reflects on him genetically. Roo, I'll never get all my luggage in here. Couldn't you have borrowed a bigger car?'

'Big cars make me nervous,' Roo said. 'HG offered me a cream-coloured Bentley, but I was afraid I'd scratch it.'

'Let's get this straight,' I said. 'You could've picked me up in a Bentley, and you chose a *Mini*?'

There are times when I despair of Roo.

In the end, I left two suitcases at the airport to be collected later, and crammed everything else into the back of the car. Roo complained she couldn't see out of the rear window, but, as I said, there was nothing there but a load of landscape. We drove for hours (or what seemed like hours) through more and more landscape, the kind that looks good in pictures or as background in Christmas cards. I can never figure out why some celebrities want to go and live miles from anywhere, when you can be a recluse perfectly happily on a gorgeous estate about an hour from London, and all the people who want to invade your reclusion can do it much more easily from mainline stations or after a short drive down a motorway. After all, there's no point in being a recluse if the world doesn't want to beat a path to your door, is there? Should I ever decide to take up reclusivity I shall do it somewhere civilised, like Wiltshire or Gloucestershire, out of sheer consideration for my fans and media colleagues. Which shows I'm really a very unselfish person, whatever people may say.

The castle stood beside a lake (or loch) and looked *wonderful*, like something out of Disney, all funny little towers and roofs like upside-down ice-cream cones, with a row of crumbling battlements in the middle and a big arched doorway like something in a cathedral. I was a bit disappointed there wasn't a moat, but I suppose they had the lake instead. (Of course, with his kind of money Hot God could have moved the castle somewhere more convenient, like Surrey, but not the lake.) It looked like a real Cinderella castle, and although I've met my Prince Charming I couldn't help thinking it would be a great place for Roo to put on her crystal slippers and dance with Mr Right. A sixteen-year-old with spots didn't sound a promising candidate, but there were bound to be others.

'Did you say Nigel Thingummy-Whatsit was here already?'

'Uh-huh.'

'Is he as unattractive as you said?'

'Well,' said Roo judiciously, evidently trying to be fair, 'after three or four wee drams his chin does look slightly less receding, in a poor light.'

'What's a wee dram? It sounds like some kind of Scottish loo.'

'It's a measure of whisky.'

'Horrible stuff.' I shuddered. 'It's the colour of wee, too. They'd better have champagne.'

We'd parked outside the castle and various minions appeared to take my luggage. In the lead was a man who was clearly the welcoming party: just under six foot, gingery-fair hair, grin. I don't like gingery hair: it's invariably accompanied by ginger eyelashes, and everyone knows villains in novels have ginger eyelashes. And I don't like men who grin. Sophisticated guys smile; grinners are always laddish, beer-guzzlers, football fans, too red-blooded for comfort. I knew I was leaping to conclusions – the guy couldn't help his hair, though he could help the grin. It was the kind of grin that says, *How about a quick one?*, and I don't mean a drink. I wondered who he was.

'Harry Winkworth,' Roo supplied. He shook my hand. His grip was rather too firm, almost a squeeze, though not quite.

'Hot God's PA?' I hazarded, for Roo's private ear.

'Butler.'

Butler? The *butler* was grinning at me? As it happens, I've never had a butler, but I know how they're supposed to behave. At school, Sapphira Fox-Huntley's family had a butler: he was about a hundred and wouldn't retire and her mother did all the lifting in case he hurt his back. And Alex's father has a butler at the country house, only he's Middle Eastern and looks so sinister he could be running a spy ring on the side. But I've seen period films and read a couple of Georgette Heyers, and *real* butlers are dignified, unflappable, preferably elderly, and should never show emotion. As for this Harry Winkworth person, his grin might be merely familiar rather than suggestive, but he had no business to grin at me at all. It just wasn't butlerish.

He picked up a brace of baggage in the offhand manner of

someone with serious muscle and offered to show me to my room.
I said 'Thank you' in a cool, repressive way and from the tail of my
eye I noticed he grinned again, for all the world like a bloody Cheshire
cat. Was he too yobbish to know when he was being snubbed? I
followed him into the castle, a bit disappointed that Hot God himself
wasn't there to welcome me, but, on the other hand, glad I would
have the chance to change and reapply my make-up before making
a stunning first impression.

Roo had warned me about the décor but my mind was elsewhere and it wasn't till I got to my room that I received the full
impact. Here, Mrs God had gone all folksy and ethnic. Devil masks
on the walls with malevolent expressions – not the sort of thing you
want staring at you when you're getting undressed – tasselled
spears and shields upholstered in animal skins, carved wooden
furniture with batik print cushions, an eight-foot teak giraffe lurking
in a corner. The bed had a frilled canopy with sweeping muslin
curtains, suspiciously like mosquito netting, supported by a set of
primitive female statues of the sort who have tits to the navel, huge
round bellies and buttocks like a hippo. And glancing through a half-
open door into the en suite, I saw a mural of bright green jungle
with a waterfall cascading down towards the bath taps and a leop-
ard skulking in the undergrowth.

The whole room looked as if it had been done over by *Changing
Rooms* on acid.

'I can't stay here,' I murmured faintly. 'I haven't got my malaria
pills. Isn't there somewhere a bit more . . . subdued?'

'All the ones with bathrooms have been allocated,' the butler said
cheerfully. 'This is the African Bedroom. HG thought you would like
it.'

'He did?' Well, at least he had put some thought into the accommodation chosen for me, even if he had the artistic taste of a gorilla.
Still . . .

'What are *these*?' I enquired, indicating the tit-and-bum carvings.

In my horror at the décor, I had forgotten I was supposed to be putting Winkworth in his place.

'Fertility goddesses,' he said. 'HG thought they would be in keeping with your image.'

'*What?* I'm not *fertile* – I mean, I'm not pregnant or . . . or anything, and I *don't* have a figure like an overinflated balloon!'

'You present a gardening programme. That makes you a kind of modern goddess of fertility – or at any rate of fertiliser.'

That did it. He was taking the piss, I knew he was taking the piss, he knew that I knew, but I couldn't do anything about it. I assumed an air of quiet dignity guaranteed to reduce him to the nonentity he really was.

'Thank you so much. If you would just send the maid to help me unpack . . .' I'd never needed a maid to help me unpack; I'm quite capable of unpacking myself, but in a place like this it would be fatal to show it.

'There isn't one,' the Cheshire cat said smugly. 'A couple of village girls come in and clean, but not till tomorrow. You could have Morag the housekeeper, only she's got religious mania so she'll probably disapprove of you. However, if you don't mind a jeremiad on the minimalism of your underwear . . .'

I gave him a look that would have fried an egg.

'In that case,' I said, abandoning dignity for something more forceful, 'you – *you personally* – can bring me a pot of tea, lapsang souchong, with lemon and no sugar, and two aspirin.' I glanced round the room again, wincing. 'No, a *bottle* of aspirin. And sleeping pills. Lots of sleeping pills. I'm going to have *very* bad dreams in here.'

'*Jumanji,*' he said. 'You know, that film about the jungle board game that came to life. Watch out for the giraffe: it could turn nasty.'

I turned my shoulder on him by way of dismissal and presently I heard the door shut. I unpacked hastily, noticing that several of my things needed ironing. On *Gilding the Lily* I'd had a wardrobe assistant/hairdresser/make-up artist who saw to it I looked pressed, styled and beautiful every time I appeared on camera, but here, Crusty had said, I wouldn't need one, since Hot God had such a large staff. Ha! I thought. Some staff! Did religious mania allow time for ironing?

Roo arrived at the same moment as my tea, and I sent Winkworth off to fetch a second cup, rather glad that he would (probably) have to walk a long way to get it.

I encountered Hot God for the first time that evening. We assembled in the Relatively Normal Drawing Room for pre-dinner drinks. There was no sign of the spotty Dorian, but Crusty was there, Nigel Willoughby-Purchiss, and, of course, Mortimer Sparrow, who'd arrived shortly after me. It wasn't an impressive array of male talent. Roo's a kind person and I realised her description of Nigel's charms had, if anything, erred on the side of generosity. Morty is a pin-up for middle-aged women who see him as a cosy, guy-next-door type; he has a fair, rumpled look which he thinks goes with his metier, a thickening waistline hidden under a succession of baggy jumpers and sweatshirts, a wife no one ever sees and a bad case of roving hands. He greeted me with an enthusiasm which was a mixture of lechery and hypocrisy and was then deflected by Roo, who bore up nobly while he talked to her about how famous he was, how difficult it was being famous, and how good he was at making allowances for non-famous colleagues, particularly if they were young, female and attractive. He must be really worried about his career, I thought, to be pushing himself so hard.

Hot God arrived last. It's always a shock when you meet someone like that – someone who's been in the public eye much of his life, constantly photographed at twentysomething, thirtysomething, fortysomething – and discover they've got old. Icons are supposed to be immortal, beyond the reach of wrinkles and sags. Hot God hadn't grown fat; instead, he seemed to have shrunk. His skin – his whole body – had crumpled, as if he had spent too long in the bath. Roo had warned me about the eyepatch, but he had removed it. One eye was still a bit pink and puffy, though the other retained a little of the demonic twinkle he used to show on stage. Not that I'd ever been to any of his concerts; I know his classic hits because everybody does, but that's about all. I'm not one of those people who sit listening to music for hours, or go around plugged into a Walkman looking brain-dead. I like music to be there in the background where it belongs. Of course, rock stars are something else. Rock stars are a major social asset, like royalty, as long as you don't have to listen to them play.

Anyway, it didn't matter what Hot God looked like, though I was a bit daunted when he said he didn't have champagne.

'I don't like it,' he said. 'I never did. It upsets my guts.'

Too much information. Icons aren't supposed to have guts (or cataracts). They're supposed to be made of celluloid and live for ever.

Winkworth presented me with a vodka and diet tonic; good anticipation, but it didn't excuse his attitude. I took a restorative gulp and set about fascinating my host, turning on sparkling charm in bucketloads (or whatever sparkling charm comes in). Roo had told me Dunblair was informal but I'd still dressed up a little, in a fluted skirt of jade-green velvet and a long sweater sewn with feathers whose deep V-neck showed off my cleavage and the leftovers of my ski-tan. As far as I could see, HG appeared to be appreciating both. Then a woman with the face and personality of a drystone wall intervened, wielding a glass bowl.

'The children o' the ungodly shall burrn in the fires o' heil,' she announced. 'Ha' some peanuts.'

This could only be Morag the housekeeper.

'She's a character,' HG said indulgently.

He would probably say the same of the grinning butler, I thought, my enthusiasm for rock icons cooling abruptly. In my opinion there were far too many Characters in Dunblair. Then Morty gatecrashed the conversation, and it turned to flowers.

The fact that Morty had started his career as a voice-over on paint commercials hadn't prevented him from becoming an authority on all matters horticultural. With such series as *Earth Works*, *Sparrow in the Garden* and the appallingly twee *House Sparrow* (including interior design), he had become a household name, rather like lavatory cleaner. He had done several books, mainly remarkable for large colour photographs, much deplored by my mother, who hated the modern tendency to turn a garden into an outdoor room and thought nothing should get in the way of the plants. But he hadn't had a regular slot on prime-time TV for nearly a year, and everyone knows viewers have short-term memory loss. After all that booze and drug-taking I would have expected HG to be the same, but instead they both plunged into a passionate exchange of floral chit-chat, Latin names whizzing to and fro like ping-pong balls. '*Lavandula conservatoria . . . Floribunda ponderosa . . . Gossiporia austropossum . . .*' You get the picture. My mother always says men love to get hold of a little knowledge and show it off. It's a guy thing.

I don't need to do homework. When I want to sound expert, I simply ring Mummy and ask: 'What's that awfully pretty yellow flower you've got growing down by the pond?' or 'What was that blue stuff that did so well the other winter despite three blizzards and a deep freeze in May?' and she comes up with the answers. Then I can impress the hell out of people who think I'm just a camera-friendly bimbo. Mummy may not have been great at parent–child bonding, but, when it comes to gardening expertise, she's better than a whole library of reference books.

At dinner we were joined by Russell Gander, the director, and the discussion veered to the historical re-enactment scenes, and which bits of history we were going to re-enact, and how. Should we go for a misty effect of muted colour, slow-motion movement and subtle music, or strong dialogue and dramatic action? Or both? Nigel was determined to script the scenes and Russell was equally determined to prevent him, on the grounds that no academic can write anything using words of less than four syllables. As neither could state his intention openly the discussion began to bubble with suppressed feelings, like a volcano with a plug in the cone. Both of them used phrases like, 'If I might be allowed to add . . .' and 'Let me just mention . . .' and similar ominous lines. I was sitting next to HG but he got drawn in, leaving me few opportunities for conversational sparkle. I grew increasingly pissed off, Roo looked amused, HG talked about the exploits of the McGoogles as if he had bought the ancestors with the castle, and Morty tried cheerfully and vainly to bring the subject back to himself. Nigel's nose was twitching like the nose of a shrew on the trail of whatever shrews eat, and Russell was beginning to sound trenchant, a defender digging in for a long siege. I got bored.

Here I was – romantic Scottish castle (if you excluded some of the décor), huge international rock star – bored. Bored, bored, bored. There was a moral in there somewhere, if you do morals. I don't. The awful butler caught my eye and gave me a wink. A *wink*! Who did he think he was?

I assumed an expression of suitable hauteur and forced my attention back to the table.

Later, I phoned Alex, but he was watching *Failed Celebrity Diets* and had evidently resolved to take no interest in Hot God or anything at Dunblair.

The next day the crew arrived, taking root in the village of Lochnabu and horrifying the locals by offering their teenage children spliffs and drinking the pub dry by the end of the week. Everyone was upset except, of course, the teenagers – and the pub landlord, who had never made so much money in his life. According to Roo, he made a point of looking gloomily resigned, borrowing from Morag's repertoire to declare that they must dree their weird, and the Bible bid them welcome the stranger, and give food to the hungry and drink to the thirsty, especially the latter.

'Does it?' I asked.

'I've no idea,' Roo said. 'Nor, I'm prepared to bet, has he.'

She was signing for a parcel at the time, addressed to Dorian Jakes, spots and all, who was a weekly boarder at Gordonstoun, so was only around from Friday night to Sunday. He had proved to be both gawky and geeky, expressing himself mainly in grunts and ponging faintly of nervous sweat and tea tree oil. Thinking of Morag & Co, I reflected that even rock icons have weirds to dree. Particularly if you've produced children in a careless fashion over a period of far too many marriages.

The parcel, Roo said, was a sun lamp. For the zits. I hoped it would work.

Meanwhile, Crusty, Morty and Russell (an old gardening hand who had directed *Earth Works*) were drawing up plans for the future of the grounds which HG would then criticise and discard. The cameraman filmed the castle, inside and out, in its natural state – except, of course, for any parts decorated by Basilisa Ramón. The sound recordist chain-smoked dope and had a close encounter with a ghost in a false beard who made various damaging allegations about skeletons buried in the maze and the illegal activities of past McGoogles. We suspected the landlord of the Dirk and Sporran, who knew when he was on to a guid thing. Several minions, some theirs (local lads), some ours (aspiring producers, directors and presenters), began digging, breaking up the frozen earth and uprooting unwanted vegetation. One of them found some bones, which got everybody excited, until they were identified as those of a dog which had belonged to the castle's previous owner. The camera truck, catering truck and other trucks blocked the access road and traumatised HG's security staff, accustomed to stalking the grounds in splendid isolation. The electrician blew a fuse and plunged the entire castle into darkness at five o'clock one evening.

In short, for any TV team on location, business as usual.

After an exchange of phone calls with my mother, I came up with a list of exotic plants which would thrive in the prevailing soil and climatic conditions. Crusty knew my secret, but Morty was upstaged

86

and HG hugely impressed, and my stock skyrocketed. In between, I changed my toenail polish three times, made long telephone calls planning my wedding, and refused to go on camera without a make-up artist, mainly as a matter of principle, since I'm perfectly capable of doing my own. But if you let people treat you as anything less than a star, pretty soon you won't be one.

Eventually, they imported make-up and wardrobe people to sort out hair, costumes and so on for the re-enactment scenes, so I appropriated one of those.

I realised that in order to be sure my role was substantial enough to properly showcase my talent, I would have to cultivate Nigel Wallaby-Porpoise, despite his nose. (Chin, eyes, and other features.) As resident expert he had won his point and was allowed to script the scenes, provided Russell totally rewrote the dialogue afterwards. I found him in the room he had taken over as a study, two-finger typing on his laptop.

'I hope you don't mind my interrupting,' I said, knowing he wouldn't. What chinless academic would object to being chatted up by a beautiful television star? 'I wanted to talk to you about my role as Elizabeth Courtney.'

His little face brightened, looking at once perky and pleased with himself. It was pathetic really. He actually thought I fancied him. Men, no matter how clever they are, have a major blind spot about their own sexual attractiveness. They want to go out with gorgeous women but it never occurs to them that their own gorgeousness might not match up.

'I want a chance to really get under the skin of the part,' I went on, pulling a chair up beside him, much too close. 'I think she was a great tragic heroine. I mean, she and Alasdair were so much in love. He defied everyone to marry her, he rejected the fiancée his family chose for him, and then to lose her, on their wedding night . . . you must see what a brilliant story it is. But it won't be deeply moving unless the viewers feel they know her a little first. We need plenty of scenes to show how beautiful she was, how special.'

'We-ell . . .'

I fixed wide eyes on his face. 'You do see what I mean, don't you?'

'Of course. Of course. Elizabeth *was* a rather interesting character, in fact. Her father had been in trade. That was another reason why the McGoogles didn't like her – lots of money but no class – and she had a very advanced education for a woman of her time. She wasn't a conventional beauty, but she was very sought-after because of her inheritance. They say she'd already declined a baronet and jilted the son of an Earl when Alasdair came along. Elizabeth fell violently in love with him on sight – he was extremely good-looking – and he seems to have reciprocated, though he probably had an eye on her fortune as well.'

'We won't mention that,' I said firmly. 'Or her downmarket background. We've got to show that he adored her, otherwise it won't be a tragedy when she dies. As I see it, she was this amazing free spirit, wild, unconventional, stunningly lovely, a natural aristocrat despite her birth, pursued by every man who knew her yet spurning them all for this dashing young laird from the Highlands. We need to see them meeting in England, falling in love. She follows him to Scotland, they marry in the teeth of family opposition, under the vengeful gaze of her rival, and then she vanishes for ever. Swallowed up in the . . . the labyrinthine tentacles of the monstrous maze.'

'I wouldn't say it was *monstrous*, precisely,' Nigel demurred, looking slightly bemused.

'Of course it was,' I insisted. 'I can just picture it, this giant dark *thing*, all looming black hedges and narrow paths twisting and turning, ensnaring people, *devouring* them.' I shivered, carried away by my own fantasy. For a moment I visualised it sprouting outside the castle, gloom-laden and doom-laden, like those walking trees in *Lord of the Rings*, waiting, ominously, to draw us all in. Not just a collection of pathways and hedges but a living thing with a will and purpose of its own.

'What an imagination you have!' Nigel said. 'We must talk more. I'm doing a book – factual, of course, but extrapolating from history into a more novelistic form to really bring the past to life. Something of a departure for me. I must say, I would welcome your input. You obviously have the true dramatic vision.'

I smiled sweetly. If he wanted my dramatic vision, he would be wax in my hands. And while Russell might rewrite the dialogue, the scene structure should stay – in whatever form I wanted.

'I'd love to help you,' I said. 'With the book *and* the re-enactment scenes. It would be a privilege.'

It was only when I got up to leave that I saw Winkworth lounging in the open door – butlers aren't supposed to *lounge*, for heaven's sake – having evidently heard at least part of the conversation. He stepped aside a fraction too slowly, so I had to hesitate before I swept past. There was a *knowing* look on his face which I didn't like at all. I wondered if he was going to try and throw a spanner in the works (why or how I wasn't sure), but he only gave me a slight, sardonic bow before turning back to Nigel.

'I found the drawings you wanted to look at . . .'

Having committed myself to charming Nigel, I was stuck with it. I had to endure several lectures on Elizabeth Courtney, only daughter of a self-made millionaire (cue further lecture on how much richer you had to be to achieve millionaire status in those days) who died when she was sixteen, leaving her in the wardship of her uncle. Her aunt came from higher up the social stepladder and was determined to elevate her orphaned niece still further, using what contacts she had to push Elizabeth into the upper echelons of society. Elizabeth's vast wealth and naturally elegant manners carried the day, and she became one of the most courted heiresses of her generation. The earl's son was a suitor so desirable that when she turned him down flat her aunt, said Nigel, extrapolating furiously, must have been horrified, doubtless threatening to wash her hands of her obstinate niece. A nameless laird from a family which, though ancient, was relatively impoverished would have been no substitute. It must have taken considerable courage for Elizabeth to defy her own relations (said Nigel) as well as his. And then tragedy struck, and Alasdair went off to the colonies, as they did in those days, joining his cousin in darkest Africa to do his bit for the British Empire. He bade farewell to the fiancée he had abandoned and to his mother, neither of whom he would ever see again. Lady Mary McGoogle, despite her opposition to the marriage, mourned her daughter-in-law of a single day so deeply she wore black for the rest of her life.

In darkest Africa, Alasdair formed alliances with the cream of the natives and fought battles with the less creamy ones, showing himself generally resourceful and heroic, before dying of a fever probably brought on by his broken heart. His mother looked after the Dunblair estate until her own death three years later, after which his cousin, the sole remaining heir, returned to live there. Alasdair's discarded fiancée of years before wasted no time in marrying him.

'What was *she* like?' I asked, genuinely curious.

'She was the local beauty,' Nigel said. 'An admirer wrote that her complexion rivalled that of the rose and her hair was as black as the wing of a crow.'

That didn't mean much. According to gossip at the Dirk and Sporran, gleaned by Russell and the crew, *Morag* had been a local beauty once, complexion, hair and all.

'After Alasdair deserted her,' Nigel went on, 'she wouldn't look at another man – until his cousin came to Dunblair eight years later. It may sound a little prosaic, but possibly there was a family resemblance which attracted her.'

'Perhaps she wanted to marry the castle,' I suggested, 'not the man.'

Roo, who was with me at the time – I had begged her to be my chaperone – said suddenly: 'Alasdair got rid of the maze and *then* went to darkest Africa, right?'

'Exactly,' Nigel affirmed. 'He is said to have burned the hedges himself, going round afterwards to dig up the roots. There was a statue at the centre, a bronze of the Greek god Pan, though some said it was meant to be the devil, and he had it melted down. He wanted nothing to remain.'

'It's a bit odd, isn't it?' Roo said. 'I mean, you'd think he'd have destroyed the maze because he was intending to stay and he couldn't stand to look at it. If he was planning a kind of voluntary exile, he wouldn't see it again anyway.'

'Don't you understand?' I said. 'He hated it. He blamed the maze for Elizabeth's death. It was this dark evil *thing* which had enmeshed her in its tentacles and swallowed her up. Maybe he hoped to find some trace of the body.'

'Possibly,' Nigel said, 'but he didn't. The destruction of the maze is well documented. Servants helped with all the digging and burning, and the statue was far too heavy for one man to move.'

'I still think it was a lot of trouble to take,' Roo persisted, 'when you've made up your mind to leave shortly after.'

'Maybe he *hadn't* made up his mind,' I said, using my dramatic imagination. 'Maybe he destroyed the maze, thinking this act of revenge would somehow ease his suffering, only it didn't, and he realised he would have to go away – far away – perhaps for good.'

'Here it is,' Nigel offered, indicating his laptop. 'This is my reconstruction of it, based on historical accounts and the sketch plan HG found.' The screen displayed a 3-D image with bright green hedges and a tangle of paths. Like that, it didn't look monstrous or horrifying, just a routine puzzle like something in a children's book. He swivelled the map, shot down a path, and brought us presently to the centre, where a squat god Pan stood on a plinth, leaning on a staff with a two-pronged head.

'Pan ought to have pipes, surely?' Roo said.

'No drawings of the statue survive,' Nigel explained. 'But there are a couple of references to it which describe it as holding a staff or double-pronged spear. Hence the confusion about its identity. Of course, the physical concept of the devil probably derived from the pagan god anyway. Nowadays we think of Pan as a woodland deity, mischievous but benevolent – a Puck-like figure. But he was also the god of lust and madness. I'm sure you've both seen those male fertility statues with their exaggerated genitalia. They're goat-legged too – representations of Pan. The goat and its mythical counterpart, the satyr, are both associated with unbridled lasciviousness.'

I wondered if he was leering at me; the thought of Nigel leering was definitely unpleasant – but decided not to look, just in case.

It's curious how often academics talk about sex. They start off with something serious, like a piece of history or a computerised representation of a maze, but somehow pretty soon their exposition gets around to shagging, though they think if they use big words, like lasciviousness, they can still pretend their interest is purely intellectual. I had hoped Roo being there might discourage Nigel, but we were on to overgrown dicks already.

'Of course,' Nigel continued – he was fond of prefacing statements with *of course*, demonstrating that something was obvious to *him*, though no one else was clever enough to see it – 'of course, the devil-image was originally a symbol of forbidden sex. Christianity has always been about repressing sexuality – the concept of the virgin birth, the cult of female chastity, the notion that fornication was a sin. Jesus was probably more tolerant, but when ideologues like Paul got hold of his teaching they twisted it every which way to suit their own hang-ups. The devil became a label of convenience for the evils of sex, evolving naturally from Pan, a primitive lust-god worshipped by our ancestors with mass copulation at ritual orgies and bacchanalia—'

'I thought they worshipped Bacchus at bacchanalia?' Roo interrupted. 'Binge-drinking.'

'An apt comparison. Bacchus was the wine-god, his worship a preliminary to the uncontrolled sexual activity demanded by Pan. The contemporary ladettes, out on the town, no doubt never realise they are duplicating behaviour patterns that were once part of a sacred rite. Of course—'

'Would those be box hedges?' Roo asked flatly, pointing at the screen.

'Beech,' I responded, educated by my mother. 'The soil here is too acidic for box.'

'If we replant,' Roo said, 'how on earth will we get them to grow fast enough for the end of the series?'

'We won't,' I said. 'The best we can do is import half-grown ones. You can't conjure a maze overnight. Remember how long it took the first laird before the hedges were above his head?'

'It'll be quicker with HG,' Roo said with an irrepressible giggle. 'He can't be more than five foot six.'

'*Revenons à nos moutons*,' Nigel said – which means 'return to our sheep', or, in his case, goats. 'I understand he has commissioned a modern replica of the statue to stand, once again, at the heart of the maze. It really is intensely symbolic. The convoluted paths of human relationships leading to a dark centre of venery and concupiscence.'

'What?' I whispered to Roo.

'Sex,' she translated.

You see. More sex.

'Personally, I prefer masturbation,' I announced, which shut him up for a minute or two.

'Is it really worth it?' Roo enquired later. 'I mean, all these long conversations with Nigel, just for a few more minutes in a push-up bra.'

'Sometimes,' I said, 'you have to make a few sacrifices for your career.'

That's the trouble with Roo. She never has. She's made her sacrifices for other people, like Kyle Muldoon, who didn't appreciate them. I make sacrifices for *myself*, which is much more to the point.

'We could sacrifice Nigel!' she suggested brightly.

I gave a wistful sigh. 'Look, he's boring, he's unattractive, he's a lech. But if chatting him up gets me a better chance to show what I can do as an actress it's worth it. This is prime-time TV, don't forget. I could be spotted for a film role, or at the very least a Sunday night costume drama. I heard a rumour they're casting for a new Dickens, *The Mystery of Edwin Dude*. Something like that sells all over the world. It could be my stepping stone to Hollywood. Spending time with Wannabe-Porsche is a very small price to pay.'

'*You* may be willing to pay the price,' Roo said, 'but I'm not sure I am.'

'You're my friend,' I said unanswerably. I knew she was kidding. 'Anyway, that isn't what *really* bothers me. I know it's weird, but . . .'

'But?'

'It's the maze itself. Something about it creeps me out.'

'It's your dramatic imagination,' Roo said. 'You keep seeing it as a giant octopus twining people in its tentacles. That's enough to spook anybody. Try picturing it as a load of two-foot hedges with a statue by Anthony Gormless in the middle.'

'Who?'

'The Angel of the North.'

'Shit,' I said. 'You mean the new sculpture is going to be twenty-foot high with a giant penis covered in rust?'

'Nigel will love it.'

'Has HG really commissioned from what's-his-name?'

'I don't know,' Roo said. 'He might have. International rock stars are capable of anything.'

'This business of the maze is scary enough,' I said. 'Don't make it worse. I wonder what *really* happened to Elizabeth Courtney? You know, I think we ought to find out. I feel I owe it to her.'

'You're going all Stanislavsky on me,' Roo said. 'It was too long ago. She's lost in history. All we can do is speculate.'

'I want to know the truth,' I said. 'I feel . . . I feel her spirit won't rest until we do.'

'Don't start talking like a psychic!' Roo snapped, unreasonably annoyed. 'We'll get enough of that when the researcher turns up. Next you'll be telling me you've heard the castle ghost practising the bagpipes in the wee small hours.'

'I don't believe in ghosts. But memories hang around: everyone knows that. If I really get under the skin of the part, maybe I can kind of communicate with the *memory* of Elizabeth Courtney.'

'Bollocks,' said Roo with uncharacteristic nastiness.

It occurred to me later that the castle was having a strange effect on both of us. Something was rotten in the state of Denmark, as Macbeth would have said.

Chapter 4:
Plan and Superplan

Ruth

Unlike the movies, filming for television is normally done as fast as possible. Budgets are small, crews expensive, and on a programme like *Behind the News* traumatised interviewees rarely want to go through their experiences more than once. As far as possible, you got it right the first time. According to Russell Gander, most makeover shows were the same, only without the trauma. (That came later, when people saw what the invaders had done to their homes and gardens.) But *The Lost Maze* was different. The involvement of Hot God meant far higher viewing figures and a correspondingly bigger budget, not to mention the funds he himself was pumping into the transformation. Then there was the fact that the garden covered a large area and would require nurturing over a considerable period of time. We could cheat by importing certain plants half-grown – here's one I prepared earlier, so to speak – but nature can't be hurried, and inevitably we were going to be on location for some while. As it was, a skeleton crew would have to return later in the year to film additional material.

With the inclusion of historical scenes the proceedings became even lengthier and more complicated. Hearing Delphi had taken the role of Elizabeth Courtney, Hot God expressed a desire to play the McGoogle who had first planted the maze – a viewer-friendly idea whatever the critics might make of it – but actors would have to be brought in for the other parts, and would need to be housed, fed and watered for the duration. With them would come people doing costumes and make-up (Delphi had already demanded a make-up artist before she would set face on screen), though fortunately computerised special effects would provide the period details for the background. All this should have been arranged long before, but the historical touch was a last-minute inspiration, and, in the meantime, the garden wouldn't wait.

The series was rapidly sprouting in several different directions at once, rather like bionic ground elder. (I don't know much about weeds, but as a child I remember Jennifer Dacres complaining that ground elder was the worst.) The scale of the project meant a lot of time had to be spent on planning and deciding where the maze ought to go. Morty and Nigel each had the layout of the grounds on their respective laptops, and whirled the maze from location to location like genies teleporting Aladdin's palace, arguing constantly about whether it should go here or *here*.

I'd feared my lack of horticultural expertise would hamper things, but in fact I realised it had probably influenced Crusty in my favour. It meant I could get on with organising the smooth (or, more often, bumpy) running of the project without getting into the creative squabbles that absorbed everyone else. Crusty, Morty Sparrow, Russell Gander, Nigel (from the historical angle) and HG himself all had their own ideas, many of them conflicting, and frequently issued contradictory orders to the researchers and other assistants. Trees and shrubs were exhumed which should have been left in place, rockeries were de-rocked, water features drained. Too many cooks, I thought, wondering if HG would lose patience and consign the entire series to the compost heap. And then someone would have a brainwave, or an outburst of enthusiasm, and suddenly they would all be friends again – for ten minutes or so.

Even Delphi joined in sometimes, drawing on Jennifer Dacres' know-how to come up with flowers no one else had thought of which would do well in the surroundings. Once the make-up artist had arrived we filmed her wandering round the garden, in Dolce and Gabbana jeans far too tight to allow for crouching or bending, nonchalantly passing judgement on other people's hard work. The rest of the time she set about charming Nigel to get her role in the historical scenes inflated, charming HG as a matter of principle, and trying to sort out, by telephone and email, the preliminary details of her wedding – like where it should be held, the guest list, the present list, and what religion, if any, they should subscribe to.

'Isn't Alex a Muslim?' I inquired wickedly. 'After all, if his grandfather was Persian . . .'

'His other grandfather was Italian and presumably Catholic, but they both married English women, which toned it down. Foreign genes are all very well but you shouldn't have too many of them. Alex has just enough to be really good-looking but with a nice English temperament underneath.'

'The English don't have temperament,' I said, 'do they?'

'That's what I mean. Anyhow,' Delphi went on, 'Alex was brought up C. of E. like everybody else, which is the same as having no religion at all. I did wonder about Buddhism, because Lakshmi Macallan's wedding last year was absolutely beautiful, but I don't look good in saffron.'

'That wasn't Buddhism,' I said. 'That was New Age retro-hippy bullshit. And that yellow sheath she was wearing wasn't a monk's robe, it was Ben de Lisi.'

'Galliano,' Delphi said abstractedly. 'But it was still sort of monkish.'

'Not since she had her tits done.'

Eventually, after a brief dalliance with Westminster Abbey, religion was set aside in favour of a Tudor mansion in Surrey or a castle in Kent. The castle won by a short head, or rather a long hall, large enough to accommodate several hundred guests and a ten-foot train. After that, Delphi spent most of her spare time poring over the invitation list trying to decide which celebrities to include and which to snub, and wondering how she could guarantee HG would actually be there.

As well as all the TV people, I had to deal with Hot God's household, whose attitude to the intruders was a mixture of superiority and resentment. In addition to Harry Winkworth, the butler, and the religious Morag there was the original senior gardener, Auld Andrew, his assistant, Young Andrew, a brace of local girls who came in to help with general housework, two minders, two German shepherd guard dogs, a chauffeur/handyman, and Cedric, the chef. Auld Andrew appeared to be about a hundred but was reputedly only in his sixties and had a Scots accent so thick most of his conversation was completely impenetrable, though I assumed he felt his territory was being invaded and was correspondingly bitter about it. Young Andrew was so inarticulate that his attitude, too, was impenetrable. The minders were respectively tall and lean and short and broad, imported cockneys inappropriately christened Jules and Sandy after the camp duo in the vintage radio series *Round the Horne*, their real names, I learned later, being Julian Crouch and Bob Sandford. Years of celebrity minding had inured them to media invasions, but in the event of war they would be ranged on the side of the staff. The German shepherds, Elton and Sting, were pure cream, desperately affectionate, and irresistible. ('Trained to kill,' Sandy assured me, as Sting rolled over to have his tummy tickled.) The chauffeur/handyman was another local, called something like Dougal McDougall, who lived in a tied cottage (though I wasn't sure what it was tied to) and was the only person who understood the castle's antiquated wiring system. Problems had already arisen between him and our sparks, but the mutual consumption of large quantities of malt whisky had led to détente, though it had done nothing for Dunblair's electrics. HG's renovations had been superimposed on more ancient amenities, and the net result was a high-tech, low-tech, no-tech mishmash of gurgly pipes and shorting circuits. The resident ghosts, I felt, didn't need clanking chains when there was a temperamental *son et lumière* already available.

The most difficult member of staff, however – and, if rank existed at Dunblair, the most important – was Cedric. Full name Cedric Harbottle, he came inevitably from Brighton, spoke south-coast cockney with occasional lapses into French ('The language of cooking, sweetie'), and lurked in the kitchen like Grendel in his lair. Wonderful food emerged as and when ordered, but you entered at your own risk. Unfortunately, it was a risk I felt I had to take. HG had vetoed the catering truck, saying it took up space and Cedric could handle all our requirements, but someone had to handle Cedric. I didn't think HG would be happy if his prize chef complained he was being asked to cook above and beyond the call of duty and went on strike.

Directed by Harry, I ventured nervously into the nether regions of the castle – at least, down a few steps from the rest of the ground floor – into a large room vaulted like a crypt whose huge cold fireplace was equipped with witch's cauldron and rusting spit, while more spits and antique pans adorned the walls. The effect was curiously reminiscent of the weaponry in the galleries above. In marked contrast, there was an ultramodern range with fan ovens and gas hobs, a shiny new Aga, even a microwave tucked in a corner. Cedric was chopping vegetables at racing speed with the kind of knife that could have split a hair on water. He was a skinny, brown, monkey-like creature with an ugly Puckish face and a malevolent grin, right now not in evidence. Who was it who said: 'Never trust a thin cook'?

'What d'you want?' he demanded, without looking up.

'I'm sorry to disturb you . . .'

'Then don't. Piss off and let me get on with my work.'

'Look, I know HG has asked you to cook for everyone—'

'He didn't *ask* me, he *told* me,' Cedric interrupted. 'He's the boss.'

'I realise it must be pretty inconvenient . . .' I wasn't making much headway here.

'Cooking ain't inconvenient: it's my job. Visitors are inconvenient. What *do* you want?'

'I just came to apologise for all the trouble we're giving you. Cooking for a few guests is one thing, but an entire TV circus—'

'You're one of those soft, squishy females who go through life apologising for things which aren't your fault, right? Sorry for this, sorry for that, sorry for breathing, sorry I don't drop dead. Women like you get trampled on all the time.' He had ceased chopping and fixed me with the evil black glare of someone whose ancestry is part French, part Indian, part Chinese, part *Welsh* – part any race that gives you that level of sloe-black malignance. The knife, sharp as Excalibur, was still in his hand.

'You try trampling on me,' I said, abandoning diplomacy, 'and you'll see how squishy I am.'

He flashed me a smile full of uneven teeth. 'That's better, love. Give as good as you get. It's the only way to live.'

'I expect you're right,' I said, unnerved by his abrupt volte-face. 'All the same, I find general courtesy helps too.'

The smile cracked into a laugh. '*Courtesy!* Posh word, innit? You mean *manners*. I don't do manners. Gordon Ramsay don't do manners, does he? Effing this and effing that and eff you for a rotten cook. I could've been on TV like him. I'm the best, I am. Could've found yourself working with me, couldn't you? I would've been a star if I'd had a fancy for it.'

'Why didn't you?' I asked, suppressing doubt.

'I *didn't* fancy it, did I? Smarming around with Nigella and Jamie-fucking-Oliver, having to put on my make-up to cook in and suck up to a load of celebrity morons. See, there was this friend of mine, *he* had a friend who was a producer, said I'd be great for the telly. Got the cheekbones, got the profile.' He tilted his head sideways so I could admire it. As profiles go, it went. '*And* I've got this great personality, all upfront fuck-you star quality. But I fancied this job. The boss, he's the best – biggest rocking fucker that ever was. He's the best and I'm the best, see? We're good together. I let him do his thing, he lets me do mine. It works for both of us.'

'I can see it does,' I said faintly. 'Well, I'm really glad we've cleared all that up—'

'Besides,' Cedric resumed, 'my 'eart was broke. Down south, it was. The Scots are right about them – southerners. Shallow, that's what they are. He was my man and he done me wrong. Come here to forget, didn't I?'

'You and me both,' I said before I could stop myself.

'Yeah? Here – you want a bit of cake? I done it for tea yester-day, but nobody ate any. Too busy arguing about their bloody garden. Take a piece –' he waved a tin at me – 'I do a mean ginger cake, I do.'

I nibbled a slice. It was moist, spicy, gingery. In a word, mean.

'What happened with your bloke, then?'

'He got married,' I said. 'To someone else.'

'Fucking 'ell. So did mine. Ten years together and he drops me for a fat blonde with a uterus. *I want kids*, he whines. *I wanna settle down, go straight*. Huh! He couldn't go straight if you tied him to a ruler. Ain't men all shits?'

Through a mouthful of cake, I agreed.

'How about a drink? You like port? I've got the best stuff down here – I tell 'em it's for cooking. Have a slug.' He whipped a bottle from a discreet cupboard and poured a glass for both of us. It was a little early in the day for me, but who cared?

In the interests of good relations with the staff . . .

'To your ex and mine!' Cedric raised his glass. 'May their new wives give 'em the clap, may their balls shrivel like pickled walnuts, may their todgers drop off and—'

'Excuse me,' said a cool – a *very* cool – voice somewhere behind me. 'I'm looking for the producer.'

It was, of course, Kristof Ashley.

It's the sort of thing that happens in stories, but only because it happens in real life too. Art imitates Life, Life imitates Art – the vicious circle goes on and on. If there's someone you don't want to see, they're bound to make an entrance at the worst possible moment. The psychic researcher was rapidly becoming a sort of recurring bogeyman for me, as ill-timed and unwelcome as one of his own phantoms. There I was, sitting in the kitchen, swigging port at barely five o'clock with a questionable eccentric whose dental work was worthy of an orc, whatever the calibre of his profile. And knowing Ash, he'd caught every word of that toast. Yet again, my compassion wasn't showing.

'That's me,' I said. 'Again. Hi.'

Ash evidently hadn't been told whom to expect.

'Oh,' he said. 'It's you. Hello. Again.'

'A beautiful stranger.' Ash's elfin looks were having their inevitable effect on Cedric. 'Only not so strange to you, right? This ain't your ex, is it?'

'Of course not!'

'Glad to hear it. Sit down, love –' this to Ash – 'have a port. We're drinking to the men who broke our 'earts – may they rot! You got an ex like that to drink to? Nah, you're the sort what does the exing, anyone can see that. I only hope you ain't a lying, cheating bastard like my Neville, or the creep who dumped angel here.' I *wished* he wouldn't go on about my being dumped. It was bad enough knowing I lacked compassion without looking completely pathetic as well. 'Look into my eyes. Fucking allspice! I take it all back. If you're a liar, baby, you can lie to me any time.'

Ash looked only mildly startled. Presumably he was as blasé about advances from gay chefs as he was about besotted poltergeists. He leaned back in the chair, stretching out his legs and accepting the proffered glass of port, though he didn't drink it.

Cedric fetched a sigh which was probably intended to be soulful but sounded more like lustful. 'So what's your job on the telly team?' he asked. 'Bet you're on camera – they wouldn't want to waste that face behind the scenes.'

'I'm a psychic researcher,' Ash explained. 'I'm not a TV person; I just give expert advice. Most of my work's quite different.'

'Like what?' I inquired, politely curious.

'I lecture, write for a magazine on paranormal science, that sort of thing. I've done a couple of books. I also get called in to investigate supernatural phenomena.'

'A ghost-buster!' Cedric and I said almost simultaneously.

Ash's lip didn't even twitch. 'I've heard that one a dozen times. This week.'

'Do you come across many real ghosts,' I asked, attempting to take him seriously (and failing), 'or are they all fake?'

'It depends what you mean by fake,' he said, taking himself seriously enough for both of us. 'The ghosts are so often inside people, manifestations of their subconscious. Deep-seated unhappiness, suppressed trauma, forgotten fragments of memory – all these can show themselves as ghosts, creeping out of the dark places in the mind to cause freak behaviour patterns, the physical and metaphysical stigmata of the soul.'

It sounded like bullshit to me, but perhaps that was just the long words.

'Bit of a psycho, aren't you?' Cedric said smartly.

'I beg your pardon?'

'Psycho. Person what pokes around in people's heads. Like Freud and that. Psychoanalyst.'

'Ah . . .' For once, Ash looked nonplussed.

'What do you expect to find here?' I persisted. 'Human ghosts, or . . . ghostly ones?'

'I don't know,' he said. 'I've yet to learn the nature of the phenomena.'

'Well,' I said, 'there are plenty of icy draughts, creaking floorboards, unexplained drops in temperature. But then, it's an old building.'

For the first time that I could recall, he smiled. It was an unexpectedly attractive smile. Or rather, in view of his elfin good looks, an expectedly attractive one. 'Old buildings always carry their own atmosphere and special effects,' he said. 'The phantoms of the past can live on in many ways. A lot depends on how you define a ghost.'

'Meaning?' For all my scepticism, I was becoming sincerely interested.

'I mentioned atmosphere. A house absorbs a certain resonance from incidents that have occurred there. You must have noticed how even a new place can feel instantly welcoming or inexplicably depressing – the legacy of the people who've lived there. I remember many years ago visiting an old manor with my aunt, a very down-to-earth, matter-of-fact sort of person. She became uncomfortable as soon as we went in. After about fifteen minutes she was so pale and faint she declared she would have to leave. She knew nothing of the manor's history, but in the Victorian age it had been an orphanage where the children had been treated with notorious cruelty, probably sexually abused. They'd dug up several small skeletons in one of the cellars. That was a classic case of an "atmosphere" ghost, and my aunt, though she didn't know it, was what some people call a sensitive. Atmospheric ghosts are fairly common, though rarely so potent. Very few phantoms pop up as an apparition draped in a sheet, moaning round the corridors at midnight. Apparitions are pretty unusual.'

'Have you ever seen one?' I asked.

'No,' Ash said. 'But I've met people who have. Normally very young children, or the old, or the sick. I sometimes think you have to be close to death, at one end of life or the other, in order to acquire that kind of specialised vision.'

'Young children are close to birth, not death.'

'But what comes before birth? I see our whole existence as a period of life that intervenes between two phases of unlife. Birth and death are not enduring states, merely forms of transition.'

'Bloody philosopher, aren't you?' said Cedric, who was obviously feeling left out.

'It goes with the territory.' Ash sipped his drink, more, I suspected, for politeness's sake than anything else.

I was feeling slightly woozy. My lunch break had disappeared in routine chaos and the port was very strong.

'I saw a ghost once,' Cedric offered. 'When I was a kid. Me

mum took me to see round this stately 'ome, don't remember the name. I got bored, wandered off, the way kids do, and suddenly I was in this little room all by myself, and there was a funny old biddy in a long dress all bunched up behind –' ('A bustle,' I supplied –) 'bending over a desk. Think I spoke to her, but she didn't say nothing, didn't even look at me. Then people came calling for me, and I turned round, and when I turned back she'd gone. I asked me mum, "Where's the funny old lady?", and I remember the guide going all pale and shushing me, but they never told me who she was, or what she was doing. I only realised she was a ghost years later.'

'How old were you?' Ash said.

'Dunno. Six. Seven.'

'Sounds fairly typical,' Ash concluded. 'As I said, children see things other people don't, though they're usually even younger at the time.'

'Might of been,' Cedric said. 'Four or five, maybe. Ain't never seen anything here, mind, though the castle's supposed to have more spooks than a Stephen King graveyard. And there's this here haunted maze they're always on about. You going ghost-hunting in the garden, then?'

'I'll look around,' Ash said. 'That's what I'm here for.' He turned to me. 'Perhaps we should . . . ?'

'Yes, of course.' I stood up, too quickly, and nearly over-balanced. Damn the port. 'Have they given you a room?'

'Mm.'

'Hope it's haunted!' Cedric said with a cackle. 'Don't want to disappoint you, do we?'

'It's . . . purple,' Ash said with visible restraint.

'That'll be the Basilisk,' Cedric said. 'Boss's wife, see? She done the place over herself. I love it – totally OTT – but can't stand *her*. Don't know if you do prayer, but you might want to take it up, just to pray she don't come home. It ain't the dead that cause the trouble here, believe me: it's the living.'

'It always is,' said Ash.

As we left the kitchen, I decided I was starting to feel more comfortable with him. Perhaps it was the drink. Or the way he'd said: 'It's . . . purple.' Or the absence of Cedric, who, despite a certain goblin charm, was someone you wanted to take in small doses, at least to begin with. I talked to him about the show, and the history of the maze, and the castle and its inmates. Not surprisingly, I discovered he was being employed by HG rather than us, though at the Major's recommendation.

'I'm to liaise with you,' he said, sounding non-committal. I inferred he didn't like the idea, and started feeling paranoid again.

'I understood you were going to contribute to the programme?'

'If appropriate, yes. But I'm not under your orders. If you were planning any dramatic exposés of the dark side of human nature . . .'

'I wasn't planning anything,' I snapped, suddenly hurt. 'My job keeps me too busy for that. All I want to do is get the series made before any of the egos involved decide to murder each other.'

The smile flickered again. 'Okay.'

'Okay, then.'

It seemed to be a ceasefire, if not precisely détente.

We'd been at Dunblair nearly three weeks, though it seemed like a year, and Easter was almost upon us. Dorian was back from school, pink-faced from early trials with the sun lamp, the crew were bunking off for the holiday, and Crusty suggested Russell and I repair to London to audition actors for the lesser historical roles. Delphi declared she too was heading home, to be measured for her wedding dress, and, as an afterthought, to spend some time with Alex. She had finally chosen a designer, Maddalena Cascara, niece of the legendary 'Lucky' Luciano Cascara and inheritor of both his label and his vast and slightly dubious fortune. They had already had several hours' worth of telephone calls to discuss details like length of train, depth of cleavage, and the exact shade of white to set off Delphi's St Tropez tan. 'Of course you're going to London,' she said to me. 'You have to come with me to Maddalena's. We need to talk about bridesmaids' dresses too. I've decided I'm going to have you and Brie; *definitely* no cute kids, not after Christmas. I'd rather have just you, really, but one bridesmaid looks so sad, like you've only got one friend.'

'What about Pan?' I suggested.

'She's an inch taller than me,' Delphi said. 'It's *fatal* to have taller bridesmaids. Either they look gawky, or the bride gets upstaged. Anyway, she's into alternative fashion at the moment. I'm not having a bridesmaid in grunge. Maddalena's in London over Easter so I fixed up for us to have a consultation on the Saturday and we can do a follow-up on Tuesday.'

'I'll be busy doing auditions . . .'

'Don't be frivolous,' Delphi said. 'This is *important*.'

Ash and Nigel were both staying at the castle, one to pursue his historical researches, the other to absorb atmosphere. Assorted minions were going to get ahead with those elements of gardening that were too dull to film at length – digging out weeds and so on – personally supervised by HG, with Crusty and Mortimer Sparrow to help, guide and advise. Dorian, I discovered, offered qualified approval of his father's latest enthusiasm: he clearly considered gardening a suitable pastime for an elderly man.

'It's better than giving any more concerts,' he confided,

having invited me up to his lair to admire his Internet connection. 'He's sixty-seven – *sixty-seven!* – and he goes on stage in tight leather trousers, prancing about and wriggling his crotch. Honestly, it's *awful*. Some of the critics write horrible things about him: "Not so much vintage as antique", "Time God went to heaven" – that sort of stuff.' There was evidently a protective aspect to Dorian's embarrassment. 'I like it when he just stays quietly here, pottering round the garden.'

'What about bringing us lot in?' I asked. 'Wasn't that taking pottering a bit far?'

'I wasn't sure to begin with . . . but I like *you*. I like you very much.'

I blinked. 'Th-thank you.'

'D'you want to see my website? I invented this game, it's a kind of whodunnit, set in the castle.' More three-dimensional plans pivoted in front of me. 'I got over six thousand hits last year. The images aren't good enough, but I'm improving them all the time. That's what I'm going to do when I leave school. Dad wants me to go to uni but I don't see the point. I can do all the graphics without that.'

'You might have fun at university,' I said. Dorian was plainly much brighter than his Gordonstoun education would have led me to presume.

'I have fun here,' Dorian said, focusing on the computer console with the dedication of a true geek.

There was no answer to that.

We left on Thursday morning, driven to the airport by Jules, who was the person available at the time. Staff duties were flexible at Dunblair, and Dougal McDougall was away visiting his daughter in Aberdeen. Elton and Sting decided to come too, piling into the Bentley with Delphi, Russell and me – and the luggage Delphi considered essential for a short trip home, which filled the boot and overflowed into the back seat. ('I'm taking clothes home to bring back different ones,' Delphi explained patiently. 'I can't wear the *same things* every day.') Russell was in the front seat with Jules, Delphi and I were in the back, hemmed in with assorted hand baggage and exuberant dogs. It was a big car, but not big enough. Fortunately, Delphi was brought up with large dogs and merely shoved Elton on to the floor when he began to moult on her coat, ordering him to *sit!* in a tone of voice honed with childhood practice. Elton obediently sat, mainly on my feet, while Sting hogged my share of the seat. 'They really are *beautiful*,' Delphi cooed.

Crusty was there to see us off.

'When you get back,' he said, 'it's down to the real work. Want to get the historical bits filmed as soon as possible, then we can concentrate on the garden. Call me with the cast list. Nobody high-profile, it's too expensive and we've got enough stars already. Don't need great actors here, just competent ones. It's prime-time TV so there'll be plenty of candidates. Russell knows which agencies I use.'

I nodded, trying to look efficient. I'd hardly ever dealt with actors before, but I didn't intend to say so.

'Good hunting,' Crusty said, and we drove off.

Delphinium

At the mews, I got a welcome home I hadn't expected. A ball of white fluff leaped at me, barked, bounced up and down several times, then shot round the room like a turbocharged powder-puff before assaulting the dangling strap on one of my bags. When more or less stationary, the fluffball looked suspiciously like the puppy Alex's nieces had been given for Christmas.

'What's that?' I said accusingly.

I like dogs. Elton and Sting are ravishingly beautiful, besides being a pair of big soppies, but they're a major responsibility. And London isn't a dog-friendly environment. I like horses too, but I wouldn't want one in the house.

'This is Fenny,' Alex said blithely. 'You remember him? At Christmas? The girls found him a bit too much for them, so I said we'd have him. Isn't he a popsy?'

'I thought he was a bichon frisee.'

Alex ignored this, scooping up the puppy and allowing it to lick his face.

'Is he house-trained?' I demanded.

'Nearly,' Alex said ominously.

'What did you say his name was?'

'Fenny. Short for Fenris. It comes out of some book or other. I thought we could change it for something more suitable, like Snowy or Tin-Tin or—'

'Dogmatix?' I quipped. Alex is a great reader of comic books, which he calls graphic novels. Early in our relationship I'd read a couple, just to please him, but happily we'd long got beyond that stage.

'The problem is, he already answers to Fenny. I rang the dog psychologist but she said it's too late to try anything new. The change of parent is destabilising enough; another name could really traumatise him. Bichons are awfully sensitive.'

So am I, I thought. 'Put him down for a minute. Aren't you pleased to see *me*?'

'Of course we are. Isn't Fenny pleased to meet his new mummy?'

'I'm not his *mummy*,' I said. 'I'm his . . . his mistress.'

Alex giggled.

I gave up. 'Can you bring my bags up? The cab driver left them downstairs.' And, as I walked into the bedroom: 'This place is a mess. What's happened to Anna Maria? Is she off sick?' Anna Maria's the maid who comes in twice a week to tidy up after Alex; having been spoiled rotten all his life, he's incapable of putting anything away himself. She's from somewhere in Eastern Europe, probably illegal, and a treasure.

'She left,' Alex said. 'She objected to darling Fenny — can you believe that? Still, we didn't want the ugly old cow, did we?' This to the dog, who whiffled into Alex's shoulder.

'She *left*?' Anna Maria was my maid, whom I'd brought with me when I'd moved into the mews. Good cleaners are gold dust. I'd rather have lost my second-best pearls. 'Alex, how *could* you? You don't let a maid like that just *leave*. What happened?'

'It was her choice,' Alex said petulantly. 'I didn't fire her or anything. She said she was going, and went.'

'Why?'

'Just because poor Fenny had a little accident on the Bokhara, and I asked her to clean it up . . . After all, cleaning up is her job.'

Aha.

'I thought you said he was house-trained?'

The time had come for a tantrum, and I threw one. I screamed, Alex yelled, the puppy barked. (A yell is half an octave down from a scream; *no one* can match my volume when I'm angry.) Things deteriorated still further when Alex declared we were upsetting the dog, and broke off shouting to console him. When I'd screamed myself out we made it up, retiring to the bedroom for some chocolate sex, though even that failed when Fenny tried to join in. He crawled under the duvet and nuzzled his way up to Alex's groin, attempting to boldly lick where no dog had licked before. The resultant misunderstanding made me laugh away the rest of my bad temper, but Alex, for the first time, was seriously put out with his pet, and tossed Fenny out of the bed with such violence the row nearly started all over again, only with Alex and me switching roles.

It wasn't a promising beginning. Absence is supposed to make the heart grow fonder, and I'd imagined returning to find my fiancé at his most beautiful and adoring, hugging me passionately and telling me how much he'd missed me. Instead, I was upstaged by a dog. In the heat of the moment I came within a millimetre of calling off the wedding, but of course I couldn't, not when it had been leaked to all the papers. I spent the afternoon on the line to Anna Maria, offering her a fortune to return and promising to train the dog myself. In between, I taught Fenny to sit by pushing his bottom on to the floor after the appropriate command and giving him a piece of ham when he stayed put. He was bright, and caught on quickly. Pointing to a pool of wee or a squiggle of crap and telling him off in my severest voice, which is pretty severe, clearly got through to his little doggy brain, but he was less sure how to process the information. That would take time. 'You've got till Sunday,' I told him, 'or I'll have you made into mittens.'

There was no proper dog food in the house, not even any biscuits – Alex had been feeding him on cold chicken and chocolate buttons

– so I had to go out and buy some, dragging Alex along to educate him about what puppies eat. A paparazzo lurking near Waitrose got a shot of us in mid-squabble, which *really* pissed me off.

Then Alex said we couldn't go out to dinner because poor Fenny hated being left alone for any length of time. My last fantasy of romantic intimacy went by the board as we ordered a takeaway from Cecconi's and sat down in front of *101 Dalmatians 2* – 'Fenny will love it, won't you, popsicle?' – while I tried to discuss wedding plans. Alex said yes to everything including the Buddhist option, until I brought up having Brie as my second bridesmaid.

'She's a lezzie,' he said. 'I'm not getting married with a lezzie going down the aisle behind us.'

'She isn't *really*,' I said. 'Anyway, lesbians are cool. It'll just make the whole wedding even trendier. Honestly, Alex, you sound like some frightful yob from the BP.'

You know what I mean. That *Britain for the British* party who're always going around waving Union Jacks and beating up Asians and seriously embarrassing the Queen.

'People might think you and she—'

'So what if they do? The Bohemian thing would be good for my image. Besides, *you* think lesbians are sexy. All guys do.'

'I think pink fur underwear is sexy,' Alex retorted, 'but I'm not wearing it at my wedding.' He has this thing about underwear. He'll even wear my thongs – he says it brings him closer to me – but I don't like it since it stretches them out of shape.

'Look, I want two bridesmaids, and she's my official best friend. She's very high-profile right now—'

'I don't care. I can't stand her. She's pushy and common and dumb and her tits are fake—'

'*Of course* her tits are fake: it goes with the job. Anyhow, everyone has fake tits nowadays.' Except me. 'You've only met her two or three times. Give her a chance. After all, you're having that awful Darius Fitzlightly as your best man, and *I* can't stand *him*. He's got two convictions for cocaine-dealing and he would have gone to prison for forging his ex's signature on a cheque if his dad hadn't bailed him out. If I can put up with him, the least you can do is get to know Brie before you condemn her.'

I'm a much stronger person than Alex, and in the end he agreed to a bonding session, just the three of us. I intended to make sure it was in the kind of club where celebrities would come up to Brie and fuss over her, since I knew Alex would be impressed by that. I also committed Roo to babysitting the dog, confident she wouldn't let me down.

The next morning, I rang to tell her so.

'Fenris?' she echoed. 'Alex has a poodle called *Fenris*?'

'He's not a poodle, he's a bichon. He doesn't have a silly haircut. D'you know what Fenris means?'

'He was a giant wolf in Nordic legend,' Roo explained on a note of suppressed laughter. 'He bit off the hand of the god Tyr.'

'They had a god called Tyre? You're making that up.'

'Nope. Tyr was the god of war. Fenris was so ferocious he had to be chained up with a magic chain. They said he would break free on the Day of Doom.'

'Those bloody kids. Saddling a puppy with a name like that. It's a hell of a lot for a bichon to live up to.'

'Satire?' Roo suggested.

'They're too young for satire. Probably just stupid.'

'Maybe they thought he'd grow bigger,' Roo said. 'A *lot* bigger.'

She wasn't keen on puppysitting, but I wheedled and eventually she agreed.

It was Brie who proved to be the stumbling block. When I rang her mobile, she was in Capri. A weekend at a health spa, she explained. 'There are these amazing baths, and they cover you in mud and exfoliate everything and give you massages. They're putting warm stones on my chakras right now. One of the Roman emperors used to come here – Tiberius I think they said – and we all know how fit the Romans were.'

'He went to Capri,' I said, 'but I don't think it was for his health.'

Alex had a point, I reflected. Brie was dumb. I might not know about Nordic wolves, but I knew about Tiberius on Capri.

I would have to think of some other way to end hostilities between her and Alex.

On Saturday morning, Roo and I went to see Maddalena Cascara. Her Bond Street boutique contained about three items of clothing and five assistants, including an incredibly glamorous black guy who did nothing but open and close the door. We were shown upstairs to a private apartment especially for celebrity fittings, where Maddalena herself welcomed us in a swirl of lurid silk and waist-length bronze hair. It didn't suit her, but when you are that rich and well-connected you can go beyond fashion into the realm of eccentricity, and bad taste is mysteriously transformed into unique personal style. Particularly if people suspect you have the contacts to get your critics strangled in dark alleyways. She bristled with mascara, gleamed with lip gloss, and had the kind of killer tan you can only get if you start sunbathing in nappies. Somewhere underneath was the short, rather dumpy Calabrian peasant of her genes, but no one ever said so. Her PR claimed she was thirty-two, which might have been true if PRs were capable of telling the truth. Killer tans are very ageing.

A minion opened champagne while we air-kissed and I introduced Roo.

'Brie de Meaux's going to be my other bridesmaid,' I said, 'but she couldn't make it. She'll look okay whatever style we choose. The important thing is that the dress looks really fantastic on Roo.'

Maddalena promptly seized her by the shoulders, twirled her round, then cupped her face between fingers with two-inch gilded nails. '*Bellissima*!' she declared, predictably. 'The face is the mirror of the soul. You have *una cuore gentile* – a gentle heart. It shines from your eyes. I will dress you to show this – your sweetness, your gentleness. You will follow Delphinium up the aisle like an angel behind a goddess.'

'I'm not gentle or sweet,' Roo said, horrified. 'I've worked in television for years.'

Maddalena paid no attention, appropriating a champagne flute and thrusting some sketches at me with the flourish of a silken sleeve. I saw a dress which clung and flared and flowed, combining the medieval look with enough touches of indecency to grab the headlines. In front the skirt was cut away and scooped up just off centre to show plenty of leg, while the strapless bodice scalloped low over my breasts and chiffon sleeves fell off the shoulder. Behind, the dress stretched out into a train, embroidered with a vast design of art nouveau flowers. No doubt, Maddalena was a genius.

'Heavy silk,' she said. 'Warm white, I think, not cream or oyster. Everyone does oyster. You have the complexion to wear white. The flowers will be in iridescent pastels, like a rainbow. When you split the white light, you have *tutti i colori*. So it will be with this dress. There is profound philosophy behind my art.'

'What about the veil?' I said, ignoring philosophy. 'I must have a veil.'

'Of course. We will match it to the sleeves. It will be as gossamer, a spider's web – a wisp of air, a drift of mist. It will come to a point and be weighted with a single pearl . . . *there*.' She tapped a nail on one of the drawings. 'I will make you a bride the world will talk of for a month – a year. A fashion landmark.'

'Fabulous,' I said.

'It's a bit over the top,' Roo murmured.

'Exactly. I *want* over the top. Otherwise you're just trapped between the virgin and the meringue.'

'More like an exploding pavlova,' Roo muttered, but fortunately Maddalena didn't hear her.

'I *like* it,' I hissed.

'Sorry,' said Roo. 'You know you'll look great whatever you wear.'

Which was nice, if not quite the answer I wanted.

We moved on to discussion of the dress for Roo (and Brie). Maddalena sat drawing rapidly on a large sketch-pad, peeling off a sheet every time the result wasn't to her satisfaction. A line here, a line there – rip – discard – start again. The effect was impressive even if the final version lacked detail or definition. 'We want to echo the lines of the bride's dress, but simplify,' Maddalena announced. 'Less cleavage, no leg, the same sleeves, though not so long. *Per colore*, we take the rainbow from the flowerdesign, but deepen it. Blue, mauve, pistachio, *rosa*. A single orchid motif embroidered down the back of the skirt – a colour contrast for the chiffon. It will be *meraviglioso*. You will see. A goddess in silk and starlight; an angel in rainbow flowers.'

'Two angels,' Roo reminded her.

'Brie won't be very angelic,' I said, 'even in one of your dresses.'

'I design for *you*,' Maddalena told Roo. 'Brie de Meaux, she is pretty, but that is all. I have seen her clothes. She has no *stilo*, no class. I dress her as I dress a doll. With you, I dress your soul.'

'Th-thank you,' Roo stammered, clearly unnerved. Knowing Roo, she preferred to keep her soul out of sight, but Maddalena had a point. You should dress for your inner self, not just your outward appearance.

We refilled our champagne and turned the subject to shoes and jewellery, then to general wedding matters. Maddalena held forth with all the authority of someone who has already notched up two or three marriages. 'They did not last long,' she admitted. 'Being married, it is very boring. I am not, you understand, *molto domestica*. But the wedding – ah, the wedding is romantic, magnificent. I had wonderful weddings. When a man ask me to marry him, always I say yes – for the sake of the wedding. I cannot resist. To wear a beautiful dress, to go to a church, a synagogue, a mosque and swear eternal fidelity, to be the centre of attention, princess for a day – ah, how can any woman say no to that?'

'If I ever get married,' Roo remarked afterwards as we sat down

Jemma Harvey

to a late lunch, 'I'll wear jeans, if only to prove I'm doing it for love, not romance. Not that my marrying is very likely just at the moment. If at all.'

I sensed the spectre of Kyle at the table, and determined to exorcise it. 'You will,' I said. 'And don't you *dare* wear jeans. I'm supposed to be your bridesmaid too, remember? Fair's fair.'

'You may have a long wait,' said Roo.

Unselfishly, I abandoned wedding talk to get back to the series and how the auditions were going for the minor roles. I was concerned about who would play Alasdair McGoogle, my on-screen lover. 'If there's no chemistry between us,' I pointed out, 'the whole thing simply won't work. I can't appear opposite a total nonentity. I need a guy with charisma.'

'Charisma costs money,' Roo said. 'Crusty's tightening the budget on this one.'

'Orlando Bloom,' I mused. 'I know, too famous – but someone like that. Someone really gorgeous, whom I can actually fancy.'

'Orlando Bloom,' Roo murmured. 'I'll bear it in mind.'

Back at the mews, Alex had bought me an Easter Egg. It was two feet long, sashed in pink, nestled in a silk-lined basket and surrounded by miniature eggs in matching bows. It was a lovely lavish gesture even though I discovered later he had used my credit card to pay for it, since he was up to the limit on his own. Eating it would totally ruin my figure, but I had no intention of doing so. I would show it off to my friends and then donate it to any children who came to hand.

Romance, I felt, was back on the menu. Since I'd arranged for Roo to puppysit, Alex and I were able to go out to dinner, starting with drinks in the Sanderson Bar and eating at the Wolseley where we could bump into lots of C-list friends and everyone could see how idyllically happy we were. I told Alex all about the castle and how sweet HG was, especially to me, and having to be charming to Nigel and the importance of the historical re-enactment for my career. He got interested and forgot to sulk about being left out, contenting himself with being mildly peevish each time HG's name came up.

'You know lots of actors,' I said. 'Can you think of someone really gorgeous to play Alasdair, the guy who's in love with me?'

'*I'm* the most gorgeous man you know,' Alex pouted.

'Well, someone *nearly* as gorgeous as you,' I said tactfully. 'I've got to be madly in love with him, too, and if he isn't gorgeous it won't be believable.'

'There's Jace,' Alex said, referring to his friend Jason Knight, who's good-looking but chronically out of work. 'He's resting.'

'He's always resting,' I pointed out. 'He's spent practically his entire career resting. I thought he was working behind the bar at the Groucho?'

'There's nothing wrong with that,' Alex said. 'Lots of successful people have worked at the Groucho. Sienna Guillory was a waitress there.'

'I daresay, but it's not exactly acting.'

'He's been in lots of stuff,' Alex said. 'He did a commercial for electric razors only last year, and he was in that open-air production of *The Dream* with me for charity – Shakespeare in the Park. You remember. Everyone said his Bottom was amazing.'

'It was before I met you,' I reminded him. When men get into long-term relationships they tend to forget things like when it started and your first date and just assume you've always been there. Which is sweet, in a way.

'I was Lysander and what's-her-name from *EastEnders* was Titania,' Alex reminisced. 'The critics were horrid about her but we made a fortune for famine relief – some country in Africa – only what's-her-name insisted on presenting the cheque to the vice-president personally, and he did a bunk with it to the South of France.'

'That's always happening with aid,' I said wisely. Myself, I don't know why they can't simply bulk-buy something really fattening, like

Mars Bars, and just drop them on the villages. That way nobody would get a chance to embezzle the money, and Mars Bars don't go off, so it wouldn't matter that they don't have fridges. I sometimes think these aid people must be really impractical.

Of course, the chocolate would go a bit sticky in the heat, but if you were starving I don't think you'd be picky about that.

Alex was still going on about Jace's amazing Bottom and his own moment of glory as Lysander. He's done a bit of acting but it's too much like hard work – 'Imagine being stuck in a show running six months in the West End when you want to go to St Trop or Mustique' – and he prefers to be one of the movers and shakers, with projects in the pipeline and lots of expensive lunches. That doesn't interfere with his life so much. I was thinking about that and half listening to him chatter when I had my brainwave. Or rather, the first part of my brainwave. The second part came later.

'*You* could do it!' I said. 'You could play Alasdair McGoogle!' Alex hasn't exactly got charisma but he's so beautiful he doesn't need it. And he'd look fantastic in period clothes.

Pity it was the Victorians and not something more dashing.

'I don't look Scottish,' he objected, obviously attracted by the idea but determined not to show it. 'They're all ginger and hairy.'

'Not *all* of them. Anyway, Alasdair was frightfully handsome, so he can't have been. It'll be *perfect*. We'll look wonderful on screen together and it'll be fantastic PR for our wedding. I'll talk to Roo about it as soon as we get home.'

'I can't leave Fenny.' Alex was evidently panicking at the notion of a real job, even one this glamorous, but I'd made up my mind.

'You can bring him with you.' I was very nearly sure Elton and Sting wouldn't eat him.

'I don't know . . . Will there be sex scenes?'

'Not on a gardening programme. Even if there were, wouldn't you rather I did them with you than somebody else?'

To my annoyance, Alex didn't look convinced about that.

'HG's going to be in it too,' I said. 'He's playing the laird who planted the lost maze. You'll be his descendant.'

That did it. Alex's face lit up, though he took care to stay cool. 'I suppose it might be fun . . .'

We'd been planning to drop in on Chinawhite later, but I wanted to see Roo and tell her my brainwave so we went straight home. Fenny raced three times round the room and leaped up and down like a fluffy yo-yo by way of greeting. He was adorable, especially when Roo confirmed that he'd peed on the newspaper and done a poo when she'd walked him round the mews, which she'd scooped up in a bag and popped in a bin. As we were saddled with a dog in London I was determined we were going to be environmental about it. Being in a gardening programme it's very important to be conscientious about all that eco stuff.

When I explained my idea I could tell she was pleased, though of course she couldn't commit herself without Crusty's say-so. 'I'm not sure,' she temporised. 'Alex may be a bit dark. I've seen a picture of Alasdair and he had light brown hair.'

'Minor details,' I said largely. 'The important thing is that Alex is stunning. I'll talk to Crusty myself.'

We opened a bottle of champagne in anticipation of success and drank to Alex's and my future as great lovers on the small screen. Then we drank to our wedding, to the bridesmaid, to Maddalena's designs – and somewhere towards the bottom of the bottle the second half of my brainwave kicked in.

'Brie!' I cried. 'We need someone to play the local girl Alasdair rejected. How about Brie de Meaux?'

It was a stroke of genius. Roo seemed unenthused – I didn't blame her; Brie isn't much of an actress – but the more I thought about my idea, the better I liked it. As I said to Roo, it wasn't a demanding role: all Brie had to do was stand around looking deserted. She would have few lines, if any (the spotlight would be on me) but we could call it a Special Guest Appearance, like Jordan on *Footballers' Wives*, and it would bring us an audience who normally got no further than Page 3. 'She won't do it,' Roo said, but I knew she was wrong. Brie would never be able to resist the lure of Dunblair and HG, not to mention the chance to appear in a show that would be watched by millions and might give her public image some much-needed gravitarse. I'd be doing her a favour, which gave me a lovely warm benevolent feeling. (It also meant she'd owe me one, which could come in handy some time.) And it would provide me with the perfect opportunity to build bridges between her and Alex so she could walk up the aisle in my wake.

I telephoned Crusty on Sunday morning. Despite Roo's reservations, he went for it immediately.

'Sounds like a good idea,' he said. 'Won't be able to pay them much of a fee, though. Spent most of the budget on you! Still, if you think they'd be prepared to appear anyway – jump on board for the fun of the ride, you might say . . .'

'Of course they will,' I said. Alex would come because of me, Brie because she pounced on every second of possible TV exposure in a panic that it might get away. 'I'll talk to them now.'

Alex grumbled a bit, but only because of his ego.

'Look, if you really don't fancy the idea, forget it,' I said as a clincher. 'We'll find someone else. I know things like that don't matter to you, but most actors would be queuing up for the chance to stay with Hot God. Not to mention the possibility of a screen kiss with me.'

I know I wasn't being very subtle, but Alex is a man: subtlety tends to pass him by.

'Suppose I should do it,' he said. 'For your sake. Although I still think that a minimal fee isn't enough . . .'

'No, no. If you're not keen it really isn't important. Roo says there's a guy from some fringe production at the Bush who'd be ideal – major sex appeal, definitely going places, just needs a few cameos to boost his career. Apparently he's half Scots too.'

Alex bristled. 'I said I'd do it, okay? I simply feel the payment should, you know, reflect my talent and the level of my contribution.'

'Artistically,' I said loftily and untruthfully, 'mere money is irrelevant. It's participation that counts.'

I knew I'd won. Five minutes later, he was packing.

Brie made even more difficulties, but she's a celeb, in a D-list sort of way, so making difficulties is obligatory. Underneath, I knew she would never let slip an opportunity like this, and she knew that I knew, and I knew she knew I knew, but I was very, very diplomatic and took care not to show it.

She was in the middle of colonic irrigation when I called.

'This is wonderful,' she declared. 'Honestly, Delphi, you should try it. I feel, like, totally purified. I bet the ancient Romans had this.'

I'd asked Roo about Tiberius, and she'd confirmed that he was a bisexual sex maniac and cross-dresser with psychopathic tendencies and a taste for paedophilia on the side. Colonic irrigation didn't get a look-in.

'I'm sure they did,' I said, and proceeded to explain my brainwave, keeping to myself the fact that it came from me and dangling it like an offhand carrot in front of a temperamental donkey.

'Sounds quite fun,' Brie said nonchalantly. 'But I'd want serious money. Like somebody or other once said, I don't put my clothes on for less than ten grand a day.'

In view of her career history, that remark was a bit ambidextrous, but I let it go.

'That's what I told them,' I responded promptly. 'I said, she'll never do it. The thing is, this whole historical re-enactment business has been put together at the last minute and there isn't much slack in the budget. After all, HG's appearing for nothing – he's so famous we could never afford to pay him anyway! Don't worry, I'll say you weren't interested. I promised to mention it to you, but . . .'

'Hold on. I didn't say *definitely* . . . I mean, it could be quite a laugh, really. The castle and Hot God and everything. I've got this film role coming up –' like hell – 'but there are no dates yet, so I'm free for a bit. I suppose it's kind of like doing a charity thing. I *could* look at it that way.'

'Absolutely,' I said. 'You're doing your bit for the restoration of our national heritage.'

'I haven't made up my mind yet.'

We faffed about for a bit longer, then Brie said she would consult her agent and get back to me. As I cut the call, I allowed myself a gleeful smirk. I knew she'd taken the bait. Everything was working out the way I'd planned . . .

(Who was it who kept saying that? Oh yes – the evil Emperor in *Star Wars* . . .)

It was Easter Sunday, and I'd decided to take my egg to Great Ormond Street Children's Hospital. With any luck, someone would leak my generosity to the press. (I wouldn't do it myself: that would be crass.) I wasn't pleased when I discovered Alex had already started eating it. I couldn't present a ward full of sick children with a half-eaten Easter egg, and there were no shops open to buy a replacement. To annoy Alex, I spent much of the day training Fenny to get in touch with his inner Rottweiler, and respond to the command *kill!* by violently attacking a rubber ball.

Chapter 5: Past Imperfect

Ruth

I wasn't at all happy with the inclusion of Alex Russo and Brie de Meaux in the Dunblair project. Alex read the part well enough and looked impossibly handsome, in an extremely un-Gaelic way, but I knew he had the attention span of a delinquent child and an equally limited capacity for hard work – should any be required. As for Brie, she was a smart bimbo who'd capitalised on her looks to launch a precarious career, and was now established tabloid fodder. She probably couldn't act, which didn't matter much as very little was necessary for her role, but it meant another overgrown ego on the loose and we already had too many of those. I'd met her several times with Delphi, but as I was neither male nor well-known I had no claim on her interest and she had virtually ignored me. As we would be working together, not to mention fellow brides-maids, she would presumably have to notice my existence, but I wasn't looking forward to it.

I confided some of my misgivings to Russell, who was philo-sophical. With a track record in makeover shows he was used to unpredictable behaviour and recurring disaster, and clearly took it in his stride. 'First law of television,' he reminded me. 'If it can go wrong, it will. Why worry?'

'So you don't?' I said.

'Never. The nervous twitch and palsied hands are just indications of years of inner calm.'

We got through the remaining auditions pretty briskly and I made travel arrangements for all and sundry and fixed up B&B accommodation in the village. On Tuesday, Delphi and I had another session with Maddalena Cascara, this time involving bolts of material and, worst of all, tape measures. I was appalled to see how large the measurements were for my waist and hips, though Delphi said comfortingly that they always held the tape loose. (Then she flipped when her waist came out at twenty-five.)

'You have a good figure,' Maddalena assured me. 'Womanly.'

Help! Who wants to be *womanly* nowadays? It's one step from matronly, and we all know what *that* means.

No wonder Kyle had married someone else.

By the time I flew back to Scotland on Saturday – alone since Russell was playing golf and Delphi wanted a weekend for her social life – I was back to gloom and depression. I hadn't arranged to be met, so I got an expensive taxi, and Morag welcomed me to the castle. If welcome was the word.

'I hear ye've been in London,' she said darkly.

'Yes,' I admitted, hoping this wouldn't incriminate me.

'Sod 'em!'

'I'm sorry?'

'Soddom!' she declared. 'The city o' sin and corruption. May the Lord strike them down in the midst o' their wicked ways!'

'It wasn't that much fun,' I murmured.

'Give it a rest, Morag.' Harry walked in, patted her bottom with a chutzpah which took my breath, got away with it (she looked at once shocked, disapproving, and slightly tickled) and picked up my bag. 'I'll take this. You look bushed. Bad journey?'

'Bad everything,' I sighed. He was easy to talk to, and as we went upstairs I poured out some of my woes.

'So the fair Delphinium is getting married,' he said. 'What's he like, the lucky groom-to-be?'

'A high-society rich kid,' I said. 'Very good-looking, very charming, very sweet. He dabbles in various career options without really getting anywhere and likes to hang out with the stars. He hasn't needed rehab yet so I suppose you could say he's dependable. Shit, I don't mean to sound so . . . disparaging. He's okay, really. It's just—'

'He's not up to her weight?' Harry supplied.

She isn't madly in love with him. But I couldn't say that. 'Mm.'

'How come you two are such friends? You're a nice girl, and Delphinium is a self-centred ego on legs. Pretty good legs, but doesn't she know it.'

'Are butlers supposed to talk like this?' I retorted.

He grinned the irrepressible grin. 'Probably not.'

'There's a lot more to Delphi than that,' I told him. 'Don't judge her on externals – underneath, she's a really loyal friend and a good person. We grew up together. My mother died and my dad used to leave me with the Dacres when he went away for work. Delphi's father ran off not long after. Everyone said he was an attractive rogue, but I thought he was a total bastard. Delphi adored him, but after he left he hardly even bothered to write to her.'

'That,' said Harry, 'explains a lot. She demands the adulation of all around her in an attempt to make up for it.'

'She doesn't *demand adulation*,' I said indignantly. 'She just enjoys being a star. Who wouldn't? And she's incredibly generous and loving to the people she cares for. You're just determined to dislike her.'

'She's very lucky to have you,' Harry said. 'I'd better get

back to butlering. How about some tea, or do you want to have a zizz?'

'Tea would be great,' I said.

'Cedric's made some fabulous coffee cake . . .'

'God, no. Not with my waistline.'

'Don't be silly.'

That evening, I sat down to dinner with Crusty, Mortimer Sparrow and Nigel. Ash was eating in the Dirk and Sporran for local background and HG was out visiting some other celebrity who had a mansion within driving distance. Dorian was probably communing with the Internet: he wasn't a great one for sit-down dinners.

'I'm off tomorrow,' Crusty told me. 'After that, you're on your own. Keep the team together – don't be afraid to crack the whip. You're the one in charge. Call me if the manure starts to fly.'

'We'll give her plenty of back-up,' Mortimer said. 'She knows she can rely on us.'

Delphi was wrong about him, I decided. He might be a bit of a lech, but he was kind at heart. He was looking at me with the glow of kindliness in his eyes – and it couldn't be lust, not with my waistline. (Twenty-seven inches, according to Maddalena.) The thought of being without Crusty's support scared me rigid, but perhaps with the help of Morty's kindness and Russell's inner calm I would get by.

To cement good relations, I sat with Mortimer over a brandy after the others had gone to bed.

'How did you get interested in gardens?' I asked. It was a conversational gambit: I knew quite well that he'd been an all-purpose TV presenter who'd gone in for gardening because there was an opening.

'Always was, always was,' he said expansively. 'It's the English thing, isn't it? The French have cuisine, the Italians have art,

but we have gardens.' It was plainly a line he'd used before.
'When I was a kid in a suburban semi in Bristol I had my own
little patch out the back. Grew snapdragons – lovely things.
Antirrhinum, to give them their proper name – but I prefer
'snapdragon'. Much more evocative. I used to like pushing my
finger into the flower and feeling the petals close over it.' His
smile invested the image with sexual undertones, but that
might have been my imagination. I hoped so. I wasn't feeling
up to sex, even in an undertone. 'I like to get close to nature.
Nowadays we're surrounded by technology, even here.
Plumbing, central heating, electricity, computers. It's all man-
made, artificial. We need to reconnect with the natural world.
We're all too busy to get out into the wide open spaces, but a
garden is a little piece of nature on your doorstep.'

'What about decking?' I said. 'All gardening shows used to
promote decking, but that's hardly natural.'

'I've gone beyond decking,' Mortimer said, rather as Picasso
might have declared he had outgrown his Blue Period. 'Actually,
I'm into the meadow garden now: wild flowers, tall grasses, a
stream winding through. We're going to do something like that
along the edge of the loch. It should make a great contrast to
the formality of the maze and the more contrived layout of
the cultivated areas.'

I made appreciative noises.

'Of course, my interests cover a much wider spectrum than
just gardening,' Mortimer continued, happily swigging brandy.
'I'm working on a book right now.'

'A gardening book?' I enquired.

'No, no. I've already done several of those. This is a novel.'
Oh dear. Delphi had told me Nigel was doing a piece of historical faction. Now Mortimer . . . 'It's the story of a TV presenter: attractive, successful, young middle age. He meets this girl
in her early twenties – a brilliant mind, stunningly beautiful.

She becomes completely obsessed with him. He's married, but she has no scruples, she's determined to seduce him. He struggles to resist her but his marriage has gone stale and he feels alienated from his children: the temptation is too much. They go away for a week of passionate sex – or possibly a fortnight, I haven't decided. Then his daughter takes an overdose and he realises he must sacrifice his happiness and return to his family. In the end, the girl kills herself because he has abandoned her.'

He stopped, obviously awaiting applause. 'It sounds wonderful,' I said.

'Ransome Harber have already paid me a six-figure advance for it. I'm looking forward to writing the sex scenes – but perhaps I need to do some more research.'

Bugger.

As soon as it was diplomatically possible I put down my brandy, excused myself on the grounds of jet-lag – 'London to Glasgow?' Mortimer queried – and bolted to my room.

Delphi and Russell returned on Monday with Alex and the other actors. Brie, who had little to do but stand around looking tragic – Russell hoped it wouldn't be beyond her range – was due a couple of days later. Wardrobe supplied costumes which Nigel declared were from the wrong period, Delphi complained her neckline wasn't sufficiently low-cut and then, when it had been altered, decided it was too revealing, one of the extras inadvertently quoted *Macbeth*, causing a universal panic attack, and another fell down the steps when we were filming in the oldest part of the castle and declared he had seen a ghost. Ash proved unexpectedly helpful here, listening politely to a melodramatic account of the incident and pointing out that the dead, if they are still around, have little power compared to the living. 'A draught – a whisper – a transparent form – what harm can they do you? The dead are ineffectual: it is our fears which give them strength.'

'The show is cursed,' maintained the injured actor, but the conviction was gone from his voice, and he sounded merely petulant.

'Can't you do an exorcism?' asked Wardrobe.

'I'm not a priest,' Ash said. 'But why? If there are ghosts, they aren't in the way.'

'Something *pushed* me down the steps . . .'

'Lay off the Scotch,' Ash said. 'I saw your hip flask.'

As Russell said later, 'Nothing gets past *him*. I hadn't noticed the hip flask.'

'Elf eyes,' I said.

Matters were further complicated by the presence of Fenris, whom Alex had insisted on bringing with him. The puppy was so traumatised by the journey and the change of location that he crapped on several of the Basilisk's rugs, twice rushed on to the set when we were filming, and insisted on leaping into Alex's arms every time Elton and Sting appeared, from which vantage point he would do a volte-face and bark aggressively at them until forcibly muzzled. The two German shepherds, having checked him out with a thorough sniff, paid him no further attention, but Alex was convinced they were out to devour him and wouldn't let Fenny out of his sight.

'Maybe we could turn him into a sporran,' Russell muttered savagely after a third canine invasion made it necessary to reshoot yet another scene.

'He just wants to join in,' Alex said. 'Hey, why *don't* we put him in the show? He's awfully clever, aren't you, sugarpoop? – and I bet Alasdair McGoogle had a dog.'

'He had several,' I said. 'There's a portrait of him with a couple in one of the galleries. Lurchers.'

'Dramatic licence?' said Delphi.

Nigel persisted in hanging around in historical-expert mode, all too often having fresh inspirations, leaving Mortimer to take charge in the garden. When we first arrived, Auld Andrew had been heard to make various remarks in broad Scots about the currse of television and city types who thocht they knew aboot gardening and so on, but Mortimer made friendly if faintly patronising overtures and, thanks to the language barrier and his own native insensitivity, had no idea he was being repulsed. Improbable though it seemed, they bonded; once Auld Andrew realised he might actually appear on the small screen, holding forth on matters horticultural (hopefully with subtitles), his objections vanished. The television was no longer currsed; he even deigned to give advice, matching Mortimer's patronage with a regal condescension that way outclassed him. In between, both of them enjoyed criticising the youthful labourers, though only Auld Andrew was allowed to tell Young Andrew when he was in error.

In the midst of all this HG moved like a king among his courtiers, a rather informal, hail-fellow-well-met sort of king who would frequently join in the digging, uproot a weed or plant a bulb, while Auld Andrew looked on with disapproval at this disruption of the natural order of things, and Mortimer surveyed him with the indulgence of a mentor for a favoured protégé who has stepped a little out of line. HG's part in the historical scenes would be shot later – Wardrobe was still working on his costume, which would be a symphony in tartan and dead badger – so to date he had stayed away from the acting.

He was a thoughtful host, but as the place filled up he showed a tendency to retreat into a private sanctum, dining alone and only putting in occasional appearances to liaise with his guests. I didn't blame him: a houseful of strangers was no joke, even if the house was a castle with more rooms than you could count and an efficient (if colourful) staff to look after them. I'd done some research on him over Easter, trawling the Internet for details of his past, trying to fill in the background so I could have a better understanding of the man I saw daily but didn't feel I knew at all. There were web pages galore, books, newspaper articles, even an autobiography – *Call Me God* – with the ghostwriter credited in smaller print alongside HG himself. As most ghosts get no credit at all, I was favourably impressed. I rang a friend who's a rock enthusiast, knocked him sideways by mentioning my current job and location, and borrowed videos and DVDs of HG's concerts, going right back to the days of the Fallen Angels. I wouldn't have time to watch half of them, but I could skip through, getting a taste of his work.

Comparing the concerts with filmed interviews, I realised he was one of those performers who only come alive on stage (and, presumably, at certain wild parties). Offstage, he was quiet, articulate even when stoned, betraying his alter ego only in rare moments, usually when drunk. But once in front of a live audience, with reeling lights and the throb of the music, his inner demon was unleashed: he became manic, electrifying, dripping with sweat, vibrating with sex appeal – more than mortal, less than human. A god, maybe, but pagan, feral – a god of crude passion and the dark. In the sixties he looked fresh-faced and rather clean under the daringly shaggy haircut; by the seventies his cheeks had begun to hollow, his hair was longer, his clothes tousled, his jeans tighter in the crotch. Come the eighties there were deep lines in his face beneath the gloss of perspiration, and the theatre lights showed his eyes both hooded above and puffy below. In interviews he slurred his words, and failed to meet the gaze of the camera. Then, as the century turned, it was comeback time. Under the ripped T-shirt his chest was fleshless, a web of rib and sinew that twitched in response to the plucking of his fingers, as if the twang of the guitar strings flowed throughout his whole body. His arms were all knobs of bone and knots of muscle; his hips were too lean for the clinging leather trousers, and the bulge in his groin looked like the only spare flesh he possessed. On talk shows it was clear he had gone beyond wildness, recovering the quiet of his youth in the calm of age. This was the Hot God I had met, but now, having seen the film excerpts from his life, I could glimpse the spectres of time and tide in his face. What was it Ash had said? Something about how the ghosts are inside us, not the dead but the living.

We all carry our own ghosts, I thought. Bits of our past selves whom we can never be free of.

HG's private life had been nearly as public as his performances. There had been the inevitable early marriage which had gone with fame and fortune: a little investigation revealed that the wife had used her divorce settlement to train as a lawyer, had remarried, and HG's first son had taken his stepfather's name. His second marriage, to the actress Maggie Molloy, an Irish redhead with as much temper as temperament, had been the stuff of legend. There were two daughters of the union, Melisanda Moonshadow and Cedilla Stardust, both evidently named by their mother under the influence of hallucinatory drugs. (That was the only possible excuse.) Once asked by a journalist if she realised Cedilla was a form of punctuation, she replied airily that she didn't care, she was too dyslexic to punctuate and had chosen it because she liked the sound. She died in a car accident when she was barely thirty, out of her mind on LSD. HG was said to be heartbroken and didn't marry again for at least a year.

After that came the first of the models, Romany Leighton, a brunette a foot taller than her husband who streaked through his life in a mere six months, reputedly costing him five million in alimony. Deciding marriage was an expensive hobby, he refrained for a while, instead parading a succession of girl-friends in the public eye, each blonder and leggier than the last. He ventured into matrimony again with Tyndall Fiske, Dorian's mother, a relationship which ended with her in an obscure American cult and him in rehab. When he emerged it was the turn of Basilisa Ramón – the Basilisk – a Spanish model famed for doing her own stunts in a succession of daring car ads. She had balanced on the bonnet along a twisty mountain road, steered with one foot while painting her nails, and tossed the driver out with a judo-throw in order to slip into the driving seat herself – and all this while wearing nothing but a leopard-print bikini and five-inch gold stilettos. Her marriage to HG had so far lasted six years, perhaps because he was tired of divorce, more probably because they spent a lot of time apart. She had a reputation for rapacity unequalled by any woman since Imelda Marcos, and columnists opined that if they ever did split up, he would be lucky to come out of it with a tent, let alone a castle.

But I didn't think that was the reason he continued to put up with her. Watching him one evening when he joined us for a drink after dinner, I thought he looked bone-weary, world-weary, far older than his years. He stuck with Basilisa the way he stuck with Dunblair, if with less affection, because he'd had enough of drama and changes; he just wanted to settle down.

He made me think of a poem by Lord Byron:

> *So we'll go no more a-roving*
> *So late into the night,*
> *Though the heart be still as loving,*
> *And the moon be still as bright.*

I couldn't remember the rest, though there was something about 'We'll go no more a-roving By the light of the moon', but I felt it said everything about HG's state of mind. He was a pirate retired from a life of blood and swashbuckle, an adventurer who would have no more adventures, a Casanova who had hung up his – well, whatever he had to hang up – and relaxed into restful celibacy. All HG wanted, after decades of chaotic rockstardom, was to linger quietly in his garden.

Which made it pretty idiotic to call in a TV makeover team, I reflected. But that's celebrity thinking. A normal person would go out and buy a seed catalogue; a celeb summoned Mortimer Sparrow and Delphinium Dacres. HG wasn't really dumb: he just couldn't kick the thought processes of a lifetime.

It was his tragic flaw, I concluded, and, as with all tragic flaws, only trouble could come of it.

Delphinium

I thought working with Alex would be a ball; I was wrong. The problem was, he'd never done a regular job in his life. I'm rich, successful and famous, but I didn't get there without hard work (well, sometimes); Alex has just had the easy life handed to him on a plate. He evolves wonderful plans but never gets round to making them happen, he has business lunches that never produce any business, he plays at being a model, actor, impresario without ever staying the course. The pressure was on with the historical scenes – we needed to get them done quickly so we could pay off the extras and get back to the garden – but Alex was magnificently unaware of pressure. He fussed over Fenny when he should have been rehearsing, routinely got his lines wrong ('They aren't that good; what does it matter if I alter a few words?'), fiddled with his costume, adding out-of-period accessories, ignored direction when it didn't suit him. I mean, I argue with Russell occasionally, but that's different: I'm a professional. I know what I'm talking about. Alex isn't, and doesn't. I got pissed off with him, Russell got pissed off with him – he pissed everyone off. Probably because of that, our sexual chemistry wasn't working the way it should. But then, with Fenny around we never managed to have sex any more.

In the bedroom, Alex said the Basilisk's décor was 'total pants', but later declared the fertility goddesses reminded him of his nanny, and started dancing around naked with a devil-mask over his crotch. He wanted to shag on the zebra-skin rug, claiming it made him feel animal, but I preferred the comfort of the bed, so we had a row instead. Not a screaming row, just a bicker, but we'd had too many bickers lately. Alex was letting me down, spoiling my lovely scheme of how things should work out, and it was really getting to me.

Then Brie arrived.

Brie *adored* the castle, *loved* the décor, gushed over HG at the first opportunity. 'It's so exciting the way you've done it up,' she told him (I hadn't explained to her about Basilisa). 'Most of these places are really dull, all stodgy paintings of people's ancestors and ornaments on every table and that old-fashioned furniture that's always so bloody uncomfortable. Frankly, I can't see why anyone should rave about antiques just because they're old. New stuff is much more fun. I think the castle is fabulous. The purple gallery, the African bedroom, the Indian room where I am – it's all so cool.'

HG responded by treating Brie rather as if she were an entertaining child, an attitude she mistook for encouragement. Later, he disappeared off to have dinner on his own. Several of the crew were already claiming there was a priest's hole or a dungeon where he hid when he wanted to get away from us all.

Acting-wise, as I'd guessed, Brie had very little to do, her only lines being in the short scene when Alex relinquishes her, when she had to say: 'If you're going to leave me for yon Sassenach hussy, Alasdair McGoogle, may the curse of all the powers o' night rest upon both ye and her!' Whether her original character had ever said anything of the kind we didn't know, but Russell thought it would be dramatic to throw in a curse and altered Nigel's script accordingly. (He altered Nigel's script whenever he got the opportunity, on principle.) Unfortunately, Brie couldn't do a Scots accent, and when we gave her a crash course of conversation with Morag to get her attuned, she really upset the old fruitbat, telling her: '*Do* shut up, you silly cow. Everyone knows that religious stuff is a load of horseshit.'

In the end, Russell sneakily decided to record someone else's voice when she had gone, without telling her anything about it. Ten to one Brie wouldn't notice.

The one part of my plan that did seem to work out was the bit about improving relations between Brie and Alex.

Initially they refused to air-kiss or even shake hands, treating each other as if they were mutually poisonous. Unlike Alex, Brie *was* capable of concentrating on work, but she had so little to do, and was so bad at it when she did, that her efforts were immaterial. Once her scene was out of the way she was at a loose end, and wound up thrown into Alex's company because he was her only available kindred spirit. The rest of us were professionals with jobs to do, and HG, after the first evening, preferred to be reclusive in his dungeon. Brie was happy to drool over Fenny provided he didn't crap anywhere near her, and by the second day she and Alex were getting together to bitch up media acquaintances and share scandal about the other 'stars' in *Celebrity Murder Island*, some of which Alex had watched. He still said, behind her back, that she was common, and refused to concede she might actually be quite pretty, but he admitted she could be 'amusing' and said grudgingly that it was okay for her to be my second bridesmaid. While I was filming the scene when I had to grope my way through a computerised reconstruction of the maze before vanishing into the dark for ever, he and Brie were hanging out, whispering and giggling a lot. When Fenny was found to have peed on Russell's discarded jacket, I was sure it was at their instigation – Alex looked innocent, Brie smothered laughter. I'd forgotten that Alex's sense of humour, like some of his other qualities, had never really grown up.

I removed Fenny from their vicinity, leaving him in the custody of Jules in the hope that Elton and Sting, once he got used to them, would provide better role models. Roo calmed Russell and promised to get the jacket cleaned, which dealt with the matter, but it left a sort of residue of bad feeling, like dregs in a wine glass.

Alex also enjoyed playing on the nerves of the more highly strung extras (minor actors often have more temperament than stars, to compensate for their lack of success). He removed a claymore from the castle weaponry and left it in their allocated dressing room, lavishly stained with stage blood. More blood was splashed all over the floor, the walls, and people's street clothing, reducing one woman to hysterics. She claimed, not for the first time, that the programme was jinxed, while one of her mates cried, 'We're all doomed!', if only because someone had to.

Brie thought that was funny too.

Roo didn't.

In a display of uncharacteristic toughness she took Alex on one side and spoke to him very quietly and at some length, only releasing her stranglehold on his shirt-collar when she had completely finished. The expression on her face showed quite clearly that murder *was* one of the future options.

Afterwards, Alex complained, 'I'm not sure I like your friend Roo any more. She's getting awfully stuffy. Why do all these people take themselves so seriously?'

'We're trying to make a TV series,' I said. 'We have to take it seriously.'

'Well, I don't think I want stuffy Roo as one of your bridesmaids. She's been acting so uptight lately . . .'

'I don't care what you think!' I snarled. 'It's my wedding, and I'll do what I bloody well like!' What with pressure of work, and pressure of Alex, my tolerance levels were right down.

'Can't we get rid of those two?' Russell grumbled the next day, eying Alex and Brie with distaste. 'We don't need them for shooting any more.'

But we couldn't. I'd rashly promised them both they could remain at Dunblair till we'd finished the re-enactment scenes, and there was no way they'd pass up the prestige of a stay with Hot God (even if he was absent for most of it) for so much as an hour. Which meant, since we still had to do the razing of the computerised maze (Alex looking brooding in the background) and all the bits with HG himself, that we were stuck with them for at least another week, maybe a fortnight.

'I do love Alex,' I told Roo, 'but working with him was a mistake. He just isn't *focused*. Anyway, I'm afraid he's a bit bored up here. He's used to the big city lifestyle with clubs and restaurants and parties all the time. I think he expected this set-up to be much more glamorous, what with HG being such a big star. There isn't enough here for him to do.'

'Walking?' Roo suggested. 'Deer-stalking? Feeding the sporrans? Fishing for monsters in the loch?'

'He likes watching television,' I said, 'but HG doesn't have very many channels. There's only twenty or so. It seems a bit strange to me: he doesn't even have UK Old Gold or Sky B-Movies 3.'

'Extraordinary,' said Roo.

'At least Alex is getting on with Brie . . .'

'I noticed.'

'He doesn't *really* like her all that much,' I explained. 'He said last night she was a natural-born Essex girl with a giggle like a tap with hiccups, but he's sort of forced into her company at the moment, so they've had to bond. They've both got plenty of mutual friends they can enjoy being nasty about. It keeps him entertained. He's just a child at heart.' It was that sweetness and simplicity, that touch of playground innocence (under the sophistication and the taste for wearing my thongs) which I'd always loved in him – wasn't it?

'He needs plenty of toys,' Roo deduced.

'I thought you liked him?' Until Dunblair, Alex and Roo had always got on.

'Sort of,' Roo said. 'I *do* like children. But I prefer them to be less than four feet high.'

And then: 'Are you *sure* you're in love with him?'

'Of course I am. I'm going to marry him, aren't I? I wouldn't marry someone I didn't love. You can't expect people to be perfect all the time. You know your problem? You're too idealistic. You think someone's going to come along like . . . like Mr Darcy, all handsome and strong and silent, but real life isn't like that. Real life means falling in love with a real person, somebody who'll care for you and make you happy, but who has faults that you have to put up with.'

'I was in love with Kyle,' Roo said quietly. 'He was a real person. With faults.'

'Yes, but . . . he didn't make you happy, did he?'

She had no answer to that.

What with all the hassle, I hadn't had much time to concentrate on getting close to Elizabeth Courtney, or figure out what had actually happened to her. Apparently, after her disappearance Alasdair had been so heartbroken he had destroyed nearly all the pictures of her, unable to bear the anguish of looking on her face again, but Nigel had unearthed a surviving portrait from one of the storerooms and hung it in the hall. Elizabeth wasn't quite what I'd expected – not really beautiful at all, with a long, rather horsey face – but the more I looked at the picture the more sympathetic I found her. She seemed to be smiling, or maybe her mouth was naturally turned up at the corners, and her eyes were lovely, narrow but very bright, full of light and laughter. There was strength in her face, too, the courage and determination to go against the crowd. She didn't look like someone who should have died tragically.

Meeting her gaze, I said, 'I'll find out the truth. I promise.'

I'd come in from filming and was standing in the hallway, still in costume, talking to a portrait, when I heard a voice behind me.

'Are you busy, Miss Dacres?'

That bloody butler. Ideal butlers are supposed to move silently, performing their duties so unobtrusively that you are hardly aware of their presence, but as Winkworth had no other butlerish qualities it seemed unreasonable that he should be capable of such noiseless movement. I felt stupid, but had no intention of showing it.

'What is it?' I asked coldly.

'Telephone call for you.' He passed me a cordless handset.

Mobiles worked erratically in the castle, and you weren't meant to carry them during shooting (Alex did, but he had no signal so it didn't matter), so I'd left the landline number for anyone who wanted to contact me.

'Hello?' I said to the receiver.

'Delph?'

'*Pan?*'

It was my sister.

We weren't big on regular calls and sibling chit-chat, so I was surprised. At the last count she'd been back in Paris, sharing a flat with some friends on the Ile St Louis. They'd set up their own label, a sort of counter-culture coûture, basse more than haute; Pan was designing as well as modelling. It was the kind of thing that would have had much more of a following in London – the French are too elegant for grunge – but Pan was pig-headed and liked living in Paris. I sometimes suspected it was because she was more comfortable at a distance from me.

'Where are you?' I asked.

'Café Valjean. How are the wedding plans?' She sounded unusually hesitant. And it wasn't like her to call about any plans of mine.

'Hectic. Are you coming?'

"Spect so. *Encore de bière, s'il v' plaît*. Look, I have to talk to you.'

'Where did you get this number?'

'Mum. I talked to her too. She wasn't much bothered, but she said I should tell you.'

'Tell me what?' Pan's conversation was always confusing – she spoke the way she thought, leaping from one subject to the next like a jumping bean – but it was unlike her to skirt round an issue.

145

'Dad turned up the other day.'

'What?' Just for a second, I felt *pale* – not just pale-cheeked but pale inside, in my stomach, a horrible draining sensation, as if all my Self was oozing away.

I said stupidly, 'Whose dad?'

'Ours, of course.' He'd left when she was a baby. She had no recollection of him at all. No childhood loss, no fantasies unfulfilled. Pan was far too pragmatic to waste affection on someone who wasn't there. 'He turned up here in Paris.'

'Why?'

'To see me. Or so he said.'

The twinge of jealousy I experienced was automatic. Pointless.

'He's fallen out with his other daughter – what was her name?'

'Natalie.'

'That's right. Anyway, she seems to have got sick of playing his adoring baby girl and buggered off with some bloke he doesn't approve of – too poor, too rich, too good-looking, whatever. Apparently, she'd been lying to him – Dad – for ages, saying she'd given the guy up when she hadn't, sneaking off to see him on the quiet. Dad went on and on about her duplicity, and how she'd betrayed his trust—'

'Good,' I said. His turn.

'Too right. So he shows up here, out of the blue, starts coming the loving dad with me, wanting to take me out, buy me pretty clothes, all that shit. I told him, I don't do pretty clothes. I dress how I like and that's that. He's going on about how beautiful I am, and how he wants to make it up to me, take me to live with him on the Côte d'Azur. I say no thanks. I mean, I'm twenty-five. Much too old to be Daddy's girl – even if I'd ever had a proper daddy. Are you still there?'

'Yeah.'

'Then he says, do I have a boyfriend? I say no, I just shag around. He didn't like that at all – *Merci, Luc, c'est parfait* – really fucked up my chances.'

'Did he ask about me? Or . . . or Mummy?'

'Nope. I said, he must want to know Mum's okay, send his love, but he said not really, his first marriage was long over, there was nothing left to send love to. Then he said I could send his love if it made me happy. Too generous. He's a total prat. If I've got any of his genes I'm going to have them surgically removed.'

'Did you say so?' I said, knowing Pan.

'Later.'

'What about . . . me? Did he—'

'I said if he wanted a beautiful daughter he should try you. I said you'd remember him, and you're much prettier than me, and successful and everything, but he wasn't interested. He said you're too old, you didn't need a daddy any more. I told him you were getting married, you might want him to give you away – well, you might have – but he just brushed it aside. He wants a doll, not a daughter. A doll who never grows up. So I threw my drink over him – it was champagne, we were in La Coupole – and he was shocked, because it was so expensive. *Quel connard. Then* I said about having his genes removed.'

'What happened next?' I was having trouble keeping my voice normal.

'I walked out. No – I forgot. He said I couldn't be *his* daughter after all. I was such a monster, Mummy must have shagged someone else. I said I wished it was true, I *really* wished it was true, but she wouldn't have, because she was decent and honourable and other things he wouldn't understand. The waiter arrived with the main course, some sort of tournedos in sauce, and I emptied that over him too. Then I walked out.'

If there's one talent Pan and I have in common, it's our ability to make a scene. I knew I'd appreciate it later, but I still had that awful draining sensation inside.

'Did you tell Mummy all this?' I asked.

'I toned it down a bit. I didn't want to hurt her. After all, she was married to the prick, even if it was years ago.' Pan hadn't had the same scruples about me. But then, she probably didn't think it would affect me, and I was damned if I was going to give myself away. 'The thing is, she said I should tell you, in case he got in touch. I don't think he will, after what he said, but you never know. And you're pretty easy to find. Mum says there's been things in the papers about the new series you're doing. Are you really staying in a castle with Hot God? What's he like? Has he got fat?'

'Thin.' I would've enthused about him, but I couldn't find the words. My brain had got stuck.

'I met one of his daughters a couple of years ago,' Pan volunteered. 'Dilly – Dilly Stardust. I think that really *was* her name. She was coked out of her mind, except she didn't have much of a mind to be coked out of. I bet Hot God's a shit father too, but he can't be as bad as ours. He's the arse to end all arses. Thank God he buggered off.'

'Yeah . . . Look, thanks for filling me in. I must go now – work. If Dad turns up, I'll . . . set the minders on him. Don't suppose he will, though.'

'You'd better hope not.'

'Don't forget the wedding, okay?'

''Kay.'

I rang off. Winkworth emerged from the shadows to take the phone from me. Actually there weren't many shadows – the front door was open and it was still daylight – but he emerged anyway, and I realised he must have been there all the time.

'Were you listening?' I demanded. 'Were you listening to my private conversation?'

'Yes,' he said with disconcerting bluntness. 'I could deny it, but I won't. Not that it told me much. You look upset, though. Can I get you a drink, or some tranks, or a spliff, or whatever you take when your universe doesn't go according to plan?'

'I'd like a *cup of tea*!' I stormed, relieved to find a visible target for pent-up emotion. 'And I'd like it still better if you started behaving like a real butler, and not eavesdropping, or being impertinent, or poking your nose in things which are none of your business, or—'

'Why shouldn't I eavesdrop?' he retorted. 'I might be one of those sinister butlers like in period whodunnits, learning everyone's secrets and blackmailing them. They were real butlers too. Remember, *the butler did it*.'

'I'll *bet* you did it,' I said, 'whatever it was. Only you're not sinister – you're not that good. You're just a creep. If I thought HG would sack you I'd tell him—'

'He won't. Not on your say-so. Sorry.' Infuriatingly he was grinning again.

'I wouldn't want to inconvenience him!' I said haughtily. 'Unlike you, I'm much too considerate!'

'About that tea, where would you like it? Downstairs, or in your room?'

'In my room! Immediately!'

I swept up the stairs, tripping over my skirt on the bottom steps. I would have fallen if Winkworth hadn't caught my arm.

'Piss off!' I said by way of thanks, kilted up my dress about a yard, and ran up the staircase towards sanctuary.

By the time Winkworth tapped on my door with the tea tray, I was out of my costume, wrapped in a bathrobe and feeling slightly better. I wasn't sure why.

'Feeling any better?' he asked.

'Mind your own business.' I had dropped any pretence at politeness.

'Obviously you are. That was almost a normal tone of voice. Rude – but that's normal too.'

'I'm only rude when offered provocation,' I said with what I hoped was quiet dignity. I kept trying to do quiet dignity with Winkworth, but it didn't work the way it should.

'It's my job to offer provocation,' he said. 'I try to be a perfect butler and provide whatever's required. You evidently needed a good yell, so I gave you an excuse. Now you've got it out of your system. You should thank me.'

'*Thank* you?'

'Well done. Keep practising, and you might actually achieve good manners.'

'I have *extremely* good manners—'

'I know. You're just selective about applying them. Let's change the subject. When's the wedding?'

'Summer,' I said. 'July the sixteenth. Not that it's anything to do with you.' Why the hell was I even discussing it?

'No, but I can't help wondering why you're marrying that useless twerp. You're arrogant and ill-mannered, but you're a smart girl in your way — not exactly intellectual, but quite bright — and I'm sure there are sterling qualities in there somewhere. You could do a lot better for yourself than a spoiled little rich boy with no talent, no brains, and probably no balls to boot.'

'How DARE you?'

'You need a man with balls. But I don't suppose you've ever had the nerve to go for one. You feel safer with the wimpy types whom you can boss around.'

'Alex isn't a wimp,' I raged, 'and I DON'T boss him around, and if you ever speak to me again except to say "*Yes, ma'am*" and "*No, ma'am*" YOU won't have any balls either, because I'll cut them off and fry them on a spit! Clear?'

'You don't fry things on a spit, you roast them—'

'I can fry things on a spit if I want to, and believe me, when it's your balls on the fire you won't be in a position to quibble! Now get out, and don't . . . and don't . . .'

'Don't ever darken your door again?'

'Exactly!'

He went, leaving me burning all over, ablaze with outrage, fury, embarrassment . . . with I didn't know what. No one had spoken to me like that in years, if ever. Not even Ben Garvin, who was definitely a man's idea of someone with balls, who was offhand when I got angry, and stayed cool when I was hot. He'd dumped me, coolly, offhandly – I didn't want to think about it – saying we were too young, and he had his life to get on with. My first and last mistake. Alex was sweet and loving and sensitive (after a fashion); he couldn't help it if he was spoilt. A bit moody at times, a bit difficult – but who wanted an easy guy? And he *did* have balls; I knew that personally. He just wasn't the kind of macho yob whom someone like Winkworth would consider worthy of respect.

And Winkworth was the bloody *butler*, for heaven's sake. What did his opinions matter?

This was ridiculous.

'I don't believe he's a butler at all,' I said to Roo later. I'd told her about my telephone conversation with Pan and Winkworth being a pain, but I hadn't gone into details. It was too shaming, having a run-in with a servant. 'I think he's up to something.'

'Like what?' said Roo.

'He might be a tabloid hack working undercover to get the lowdown on HG. Or on us.' The crew had come back from the Dirk and Sporran with a rumour of journos in the village sniffing around for a story. 'How long has he been here?'

'I don't know.'

'I bet it isn't long,' I said confidently. 'He's got an agenda, I'm sure of it. We should check him out.'

'I'm sure HG checked before he employed him,' Roo said. 'He wouldn't take a butler without masses of references.'

'Well, even if he *is* genuine, he's still up to no good,' I averred. 'He's probably collecting material for a book. All these butlers and nannies and people sell their stories in the end.'

Roo considered the suggestion seriously for a minute. 'It won't be much of a book, then,' she said eventually. 'HG seems to lead a pretty quiet life now. All the fun and games are in his past.'

She had a point, but I wasn't prepared to concede. 'Winkworth wouldn't have known that till he got here,' I reasoned. 'And he could still dish the dirt on *me*.'

Roo giggled. 'Then you'd better behave perfectly, hadn't you? Big Butler Is Watching You.'

'Not funny,' I said.

I thought I might feel uncomfortable at dinner when Winkworth came round to pour the wine, but when our eyes met he winked at me and indignation eclipsed any awkwardness.

'Remember,' I whispered in passing as I left the dining room, 'your balls – spit-fried.'

'You've got to get your hands on them first,' he responded, *sotto voce*.

I blushed – I couldn't help it. I hadn't blushed in a decade, but I could *feel* the blush, a hot red tide, flowing over my cheeks, right up to my forehead. I grabbed Alex's arm and walked out with my face turned affectionately into his shoulder, hoping no one had noticed.

One day, I was going to get Winkworth fired. Preferably out of a cannon.

Ruth

I thought the likelihood of Harry being an undercover hack remote in the extreme, but since Delphi seemed to have a bee in her bonnet about him – and vice versa, come to think of it – I decided it wouldn't hurt to ask a few innocent questions. Delphi was exuding stress at the moment: anything to put her mind at rest.

I got lucky, catching HG having a pre-dinner drink with Nigel before anyone else arrived. Nigel wouldn't cramp my style: he's one of those people who's so focused on his own interests that extraneous conversation flows over him. HG looked quite pleased to see me, which was flattering, and since Harry wasn't around he got me a G and T himself.

'Thanks,' I said, and, seizing the opportunity, 'Where's Harry?'

'Somewhere. I don't like the staff under my feet all the time, so I can't complain if they don't hang about. You seem to get on with them all – even Cedric, I hear.'

'They're great,' I said. 'Harry's a bit unconventional for a butler, though.' As if I would have known, my previous experience of butlers being nil. 'Has he been with you long?'

'About six or eight months. He's got attitude, but I like that. He came to me with glowing references – five years with the

Earl of Grantchester, two with Sir Gordon Chisholm, owner of the Manson Trust. I must admit, I expected him to be more Old School – but I like him better the way he is. I want good service, but this isn't a ducal residence. Don't need to surround myself with stuffed shirts saying *yessir, nossir, three bags full sir* all the time.'

'From what I've read, that's in the best tradition of Dunblair,' Nigel said. 'Some of the lairds ruled with a rod of iron, but if they were unjust the locals wouldn't take it lying down. It wasn't unheard of for the incumbent priest to have a go at the laird from the pulpit, and once a band of tenants actually marched on the castle and camped outside the door to make their landlord hear their complaints.'

'And did he?' HG asked.

'Eventually. But he shot one man dead, another got him in the leg, and two went to gaol before talks got under way.'

HG and I both laughed, and Nigel allowed himself the satisfied smile of someone who has scored a double, being erudite and witty at the same time.

Then Morty came in, followed shortly by the others, and HG bowed himself out to go and dine somewhere away from the crowd. I noticed Brie looked annoyed, but she turned her conversation on Alex – they seemed to be getting very chummy – and paid little attention to anyone else for the rest of the evening.

'I asked about Harry,' I told Delphi in an aside. 'He's been here just over half a year – too long for an undercover hack, I'd have thought. Anyway, his track record includes an earl and a baronet.'

'Fake,' Delphi hissed. 'How do we know they exist?'

'I don't know about the Earl of Grantchester,' I said, 'but Sir Gordon Chisholm of the Manson Trust definitely exists.'

'Forged, then.'

'Difficult. HG's bound to have contacted the referees.'

Delphi looked frustrated and turned away, her notice claimed by Nigel just as Harry himself walked in to announce dinner.

I found myself sitting between Mortimer, who was still determined to find me sympathetic, and Ash, who wasn't. Morty began to talk about the weather, which had shown signs of spring that day, and how we ought to do some filming of work in the garden while the sun shone, and Ash informed me coolly that if we weren't using the old hall he was going to perform some tests there, measuring temperature changes and other factors relating to unexplained phenomena.

'So if you record a sudden chill,' I said, 'that proves there's a ghost around?'

'Of course not.' Ash chose to ignore my sceptical tone. 'Evidence is never conclusive, but it can be suggestive. Besides, the public like the scientific approach, even though it's largely irrelevant to genuine manifestations. People like your viewers feel much less credulous believing in something if there's physical proof on offer.'

'That seems logical to me.'

'Ghosts have nothing to do with *logic*. That's the trouble: you don't trust your own feelings. You'll believe in a thermometer which tells you it's getting colder, or a glitch in the earth's magnetic field, when you should have more faith in instinct and intuition. We were given those qualities to use them: unlike scientific knowledge, we've refined them over several millennia, yet we persist in doubting ourselves. We're a species of one idea. We've discovered science, and now we want it to explain everything. Stupid.'

'But you go along with it,' I said. 'After all, you've brought your thermometer.'

He shrugged. 'It's part of my job. Just not the important part.'

'So the ghost-buster's going into action,' Alex said from across the table. 'Does that mean there'll be fluorescent green slime-monsters crawling out of the woodwork playing the bagpipes?'

'I think it's really exciting,' Brie said. 'The castle feels, like, *so* creepy – all that death and tragedy and stuff in the past, you can sort of sense it. Ash is right: you have to go with your intuition. I'm a very intuitive person about things like that.'

At this point an idea presented itself to me, so diabolical I could feel the smile spreading on the inside of my face.

'We don't really need you two tomorrow,' I said to Brie and Alex. 'Perhaps you'd like to help Ash with his experiments? I'm sure he could use some assistance.'

'Brilliant!' Alex said instantly. 'I saw the movie when I was a kid: I've wanted to be a ghost-buster ever since. We'll get the castle spooks by the short and curlies – if they *have* short and curlies.'

'I work alone,' Ash said. If there had been a thermometer anywhere in his vicinity the mercury would have dropped out of sight.

'No man is an island,' I declared. 'Ask not for whom the bell tolls. We none of us walk alone.'

'I said, I *work* alone . . .'

'We'll do whatever you say,' Brie promised him. 'I know we'll be a big help. I've always been really sensitive to the super-natural.'

'There you are,' Alex said. 'Brie's sensitive, I'm a ghost-buster, *and* we'll have Fenny. He's such a clever puppy, I bet he can sniff out any spooks. Can't you, honey-poo-poo?' The dog, who was sitting in his lap being fed morsels of unsuitable food, peered hopefully over the edge of the table.

For the first time since I'd met him, Ash was losing his cool. 'I honestly don't think—'

'I've got you *three* helpers for the day,' I said brightly, assuming an expression of shining innocence. 'Isn't that great? You were talking about the importance of intuition – I'm sure Brie will be invaluable. And animals are much more tuned in to the paranormal than people.' Hadn't he told me something of the kind once?

'Maybe.' Ash spoke with a suggestion of clenched teeth. 'However . . .'

But Alex and Brie, oblivious to his reaction, began to make enthusiastic plans. Watching Ash, I allowed the smile to transfer itself to the outside of my face. He might be able to handle teenage poltergeists and phantoms from the dark side of human nature, but I'd teach him to mess with me. In the cutthroat world of TV makeover shows, I was learning fast how to play dirty.

Thanks to my plot, the next day's filming was relatively trouble-free. Even Delphi, out of period costume and back in presenter mode, seemed more relaxed, the only hitch occurring when she discovered her Matthew Williamson jacket was trimmed in real fur not fake. 'I didn't know!' she wailed. 'My image is supposed to be eco-friendly! I'll have to find something else to wear –' this could take hours – 'and do the shoot again.'

'It's rabbit,' I said desperately. 'You said it's okay if it's rabbit.'

'It's awfully fluffy for rabbit . . .'

'You get long-haired rabbits. It's probably angora. You've heard the phrase *fluffy bunny*, haven't you?' The fur didn't look at all rabbitty, but I had no intention of scrapping our morning's work.

Russell came over to join in, looking irritated, met my gaze and backed off tactfully.

'Supposing viewers don't realise,' Delphi was saying. 'I've

got a reputation to maintain. Perhaps we could put something in the credits. "*Miss Dacres will only wear fur that has been . . . has been environmentally approved, such as sheepskin or rabbit. She does not wear endangered species or . . . or animals killed for their skin.*"

I was well aware that some rabbits are bred, and killed, for their fur, but didn't say so. I was too busy visualising the lawsuit when Matthew Williamson objected to having his mink or chinchilla or whatever it was libelled as bunny. You walk a tightrope with environmental ethics, and it's all too easy to fall off.

'We can do something like that,' I lied.

In the evening, when work was over, I fled to the kitchen to recuperate. It had become my regular retreat: Cedric's quixotic unpleasantness meant the rest of the team avoided it, and I could always get a cup of tea, a quick snack (I invariably missed lunch) or alcoholic refreshment as required. This was a cup of tea day, with fruit soda bread on the side.

I swallowed violently when Ash came in, scalding my larynx. At the sight of me, his slim mouth clamped into a tight line and his elf-eyes glittered.

(I learned later he too used the kitchen as a haven, being on Cedric's shortlist of approved visitors, though normally earlier in the day.)

'I hope you're pleased with yourself,' he all but snarled at me. Elves don't snarl, but he came close. 'Thanks to you, today was a total waste of time.'

'Rather yours than mine,' I said cheerfully.

'You employed those two: they're your responsibility. You had no right to palm them off on me.'

'We're all supposed to be working together. If you were more of a team player—'

'Well, I'm not. I'm not part of your team, in case you've forgotten. I work alone.'

I was getting sick of that phrase. 'Who do you think you are – Garbo?' I blazed. 'You're in a castle full of people, and you vant to be alern – is that it? So do I, but I've got a job to do, just like everybody here. We can't afford to go around being supercool and above it all. You said I have no compassion, but you're the one who goes around despising people, thinking you're too grand and lofty to work with anyone else. It's easy to meddle with the dead – they can't answer back. If you had any humanity, any . . . any real *kindness*, you wouldn't act like we're all dirt.' I was being unfair, but I didn't care. I didn't care what he thought any more.

'Dear me,' said Cedric. 'Aren't we in a tizz?'

Neither of us paid him any attention. Ash was frowning slightly. 'Did I say that?'

'Say what?'

'That you had no compassion.'

'Something like it. I don't remember the precise words. But if you think I give a damn what you said—'

'I'm sorry.' His gaze met mine. 'That was unkind, and untrue. You do a difficult job and it seems to me you show a lot of patience with people who don't always deserve it. More patience than I possess. I don't know if that counts as compassion, but I shouldn't have judged you when I hardly knew you. Sorry.'

'Oh. Oh well – all right then.' An apology you don't expect, from someone who doesn't seem the apologising kind, is always disconcerting.

'But I still think that was an excessive revenge, dumping those two airheads on me.'

'How about a cuppa?' Cedric said. 'If you've done having a go at each other. Or a drink. Looks to me like you need alcohol.'

'Tea's fine,' said Ash. 'Thanks.'

'Much better with a slug of Scotch in it.'

'Just tea.'

'Alex is okay really,' I said, feeling obliged to defend Delphi's future husband. 'He's just not very . . . he's not used to a work situation.'

'He has the mentality of a fifteen-year-old,' Ash said cuttingly. 'An immature fifteen-year-old. As for Brie—'

'Didn't her intuition come in handy?' I couldn't resist it. 'I was so sure it would.'

'Oh, she intuited all over the place. Sinister vibes, past sorrows, hatred and murder – you name it, she sensed it. Towards the end, she even claimed she saw something – a shape in the shadows. She got quite worked up about it. It was growing dark, the hall was pretty gloomy: it was obviously apparition time. At least it means I won't be saddled with her tomorrow. She managed to scare herself so much she's through with intuition for a while.'

'Bugger,' I said. 'The trouble is, neither of them have enough to do, and as they're both staying here they're permanently in the way.'

'They could walk the dog,' Ash suggested. 'It would do them all good. And we're surrounded by beautiful countryside.'

'I don't think they're countryside people,' I said.

'You got to be careful out walking,' Cedric interjected. 'The mountains can be dangerous if you ain't got a guide. Rough going, unpredictable weather – fogs and bogs, bogs and fogs. Jules and Sandy been up here a lot longer than me, they said two people got lost once, few years ago. One bloke fell in the mist, broke his leg. His mate went for help. The search party found the leg-break, got him out in the end, but the other – he vanished for good. They reckon he went into the loch. It's treacherous going round some of the shoreline. Creeks and things. Or a bog got him.'

'People always seem to be disappearing round here,' I remarked. 'If it isn't the maze, it's the bogs.'

'Sounds good to me,' Ash said, dreamily contemplating the middle distance. 'Let's send Alex and the bimbo for a stroll.'

Cedric and I both laughed.

Chapter 6:
The Basilisk Effect

Delphinium

I'd been so preoccupied with my wedding plans and the problems thrown up by the series that I'd hardly given a thought to promoting Roo's love life. When I'd originally proposed her involvement in *The Lost Maze* I'd hoped there would be some talent for her, someone to take her mind off Kyle Muldoon. Nigel was far too unattractive to fit the bill, Morty was just a standard lech, Russell had been faithfully married for umpteen years, HG, for all his glamour, was way too old, spotty Dorian (though less spotty now) was way too young, the natives were too native, and the psychic researcher, though ravishing in a slant-eyed, pixy-faced way, was far too pretty to be heterosexual. There remained the crew, including the Terrible Trio of sparks, cameraman, and sound, Mick, Dick and Nick, any extras who showed promise, and those locals on the civilised side of Scottish. It wasn't an inspiring selection, and I couldn't help thinking it was just as well none of them were queuing up, since nobody came up to the mark.

I suppose because I had so much on my mind it took me a while to realise I was wrong, at least about the queue. Though Nigel was fascinated by my dramatic imagination, I'd begun to notice a glint in Morty's eye which had formerly glinted at me; Dorian, when home from school, was always dragging Roo off to confide his teenage woes; and even HG, when he emerged from seclusion, seemed to gravitate to her side. Mick, Dick and Nick were overheard speculating on her sexual talents, and Russell revealed that conversation in the Dirk and Sporran often turned on who she was shagging, and whether it was any of those present.

'You think you've got sex appeal,' Russell said to me, taking advantage of long association to get, frankly, much too personal, 'but you lack the one quality which makes any woman irresistible. Ruthie, on the other hand, has it in abundance.'

'What's that?' I obliged.

'She's a wonderful listener. We men are simple, self-centred, egotistical creatures: we love talking about ourselves. Any woman prepared to listen is going to have admirers clustering round her like wasps round a jam jar.'

He may have had a point, but I still think tits beat ears in the sex-appeal stakes any day of the week.

Anyway, being a good listener can get you into no end of trouble. There was Roo, providing a sympathetic audience to several inappropriate men, who sooner or later were going to take it the wrong way. Worst of all, I discovered she had taken to hanging out in the kitchen with the gays, and that was the thin end of the wedge. Before she knew it, she'd be a full-time fag hag, falling for men who were sexually out of bounds and having a child with some guy who wanted to give her his sperm in a teaspoon. Once she started down that route, she'd never have a normal relationship again.

I know it's trendy to have a gay male friend (I've got a couple), but I don't believe in overdoing it. Some women maintain it's like having a male girlfriend, but I don't go with that: a guy is always a guy, even if you change the middle letter. No matter how camp they sound, how interested they are in clothes and handbags and other men, there'll always be testosterone in there somewhere. And

163

testosterone is sneaky stuff. Even the nicest men have double standards, an inability to resist temptation, and a tendency to lie when
they don't like the shape of the truth. Different sexual orientation
doesn't change a thing. If a guy is really a girl inside, he'll have the
op.

I'd tried to discourage Roo from spending too much time with
Cedric and Ash, but I wasn't sure I was getting anywhere. Like I said,
Roo can be really obstinate about all the wrong things. At least Ash
wasn't her type, otherwise I'd have worried she was developing an
unrequited passion. Plenty of women at Dunblair did. The two village
girls who came in to do the cleaning could be seen to swoon as he
walked past, neurotic female extras tried to intrigue him with stories
of ghost sightings, Makeup and Wardrobe fluttered when he was
around. Brie, normally unimpressed by anyone without a celebrity
profile, spent a day helping him take the temperature of the old hall
and, according to Alex, who was there too, trying to intrigue him with
her ghost-spotting skills. It wasn't just his bone structure that hooked
them: he had the cool green gaze of an absinthe cocktail and the
aloof, disinterested manner of an elf at a football match. He wasn't
camp, but his looks, combined with a total indifference to all women
except (presumably) dead ones, gave him away. Besides, I know a
gay when I see one. I'm never wrong.

Roo's love life would have to wait for more promising material, I
decided.

Meanwhile, I still wasn't convinced that Winkworth was the genuine
article. I could hire a private detective to check his background, but
I had no idea how you found a private detective to hire (Yellow
Pages?), and anyhow, it felt like overkill. After all, he wasn't *my* butler.
Inspiration came to me in the bath. HG must have got him through
an agency, and all these agencies were bound to know each other,
the way people in the same field always do.

I rang the one in London through which I'd got Anna Maria. The
woman who runs it knows me well, so she was eager to oblige.

'I'll ask around,' she said. 'Give me a couple of days.'

We'd done all the historical scenes except the ones with HG by the time she got back to me.

'James Henry Winkworth,' she said. 'He's with Acme Domestics. *Very* posh. One of the directors is an ex of mine, so I got all the gen. Winkworth's been with an earl, a lord, and an industry baronet. Hot God, I suppose, counts as royalty. Meedja royalty, anyway. He pays better than the others. Winkworth had a choice when he took the job – he's very sought-after. Could have gone to another aristo, or there was an American agency chasing him for a film producer in California. With that kind of pull, he must be the Admirable Crichton.'

I hadn't a clue who *he* was, but in any case, I didn't believe it.

'I don't care,' I said. 'This guy's no Jeeves, honestly. Maybe . . . maybe they paid off the real Winkworth and sent in a substitute.'

'They?'

'The tabloids. Whoever. Do you have a description of him?'

'About six foot, medium build, fair hair, grey eyes. Works out.'

There was a gym at Dunblair – I'd used it twice so far – but I had no way of knowing if Winkworth frequented it.

'I'll swear he's only five eleven,' I said.

'So he lied about his height. Men do sometimes: it's an ego thing. They'll add an inch on paper.'

'Yes,' I said, 'but usually on a different part of the body.'

She laughed. 'He's got a wife and two kids, if that's any help. Have you seen them?'

'*What?*' The possibility that Winkworth might be married had never occurred to me. He didn't *act* married. The idea unsettled me, for some reason. He didn't give off a married vibe. 'He can't have. He lives in, and I'm sure he's not hiding them anywhere. They'd be around – kids always are. I mean . . .'

'Perhaps he's left them in London. His home address is in Kensington. HG might have specified no family, though it would be unusual. Or perhaps Winkworth's got divorced.'

My sudden jumpiness steadied. 'I don't believe any of it,' I said. 'He's a fake – he's got to be. The only thing is how to prove it.'

The next step, obviously, was to search his room. That's what heroines always do in thrillers. But I didn't know where his room *was*, it was almost certain to be locked, and even if I could get in, supposing he found me there? What on earth would I say? The thought of it made my blood run cold – or rather hot, anticipating embarrassment. I'd need to steal a key (there must be master keys somewhere) and take someone to act as a lookout. In short, I'd need Roo.

'You have to be joking,' she said.

'He's a fraud,' I reiterated. 'I know he is. My agency contact says he has a wife and two kids, but if so, where are they? Besides, Winkworth's never been married – whoever he is.'

'How do you know?'

'He doesn't have that stressed look that men get when they're worrying about teenage daughters and school grades and paying the maintenance and all that. Anyhow, I just know.'

'Did your contact get you another address for him – apart from here, I mean?' Roo said.

'Kensington. I wrote it down somewhere.'

'You could ask someone to go round there, I suppose. If you must go on with this. It's becoming an obsession with you – a sort of paranoia. You've got to stop . . . well, fantasising about Harry. He's a nice guy, he's a butler. That's all.'

'I'm not *fantasising* about him! He could be a crook, in with some gang planning a robbery – the man on the inside. He could be—'

'He could be the Akond of Swat. Listen, Delphi, I'm not going to start playing detective with you and get caught snooping in Harry's underwear drawers. You can't do things like that. I think the atmosphere of this place is getting to you – all those mysterious disappearances and murders and things. Your imagination's doing overtime.'

'Winkworth's attitude isn't a figment of my imagination! All we have to do is steal – *borrow* – the key, and then you keep watch while I—'

'*No.*'

'You can't let me down,' I said, shocked. 'When we were kids, you always helped – whatever I planned.'

'We're not kids any more,' Roo said unhappily.

Since she was being so stubborn, I decided I should take her advice and get someone to go round to Winkworth's Kensington address. I wasn't sure whom I could trust, but in the end I asked Anna Maria, telling her I was trying to trace the wife of a friend and assuming an air of dismissive hauteur when she questioned me. 'Be discreet,' I ordered. 'I can't tell you what's going on; I just need to know if Mrs Winkworth's there.'

But she wasn't. Anna Maria reported back that the house was let but the lessee was unresponsive to her enquiries and would say little about the owners except that they were away. All of which did nothing to allay my suspicions.

And every time I saw Winkworth, which was much too often, even the hint of his grin set my nerves tingling with remembered indignation.

We were shooting the scenes with HG over the next couple of days. Wardrobe had pulled out all the stops and he looked spectacular in an outfit patched together from bits of animal pelt and the McGoogle tartan, festooned with assorted weapons, stained with stage blood, his long hair gelled into wildness and his piratical features enhanced with greasepaint versions of sweat and grime. The effect was sort of Braveheart meets Conan the Barbarian. HG's short and fairly skinny, but somehow, once in costume and in front of the camera, he seemed to *grow*, in some intangible way, switching on his aura, becoming larger than life. It wasn't that he was a great actor – he was just the only person you wanted to look at in the whole room. I don't know what they call that quality; it isn't charisma, because if you've got that, you've got it all the time. More like presence, if presence is something you can activate at the touch of a button in your subconscious. It went away as soon as the camera stopped rolling, and suddenly he looked shrunken and tired, just an elderly guy in bizarre fancy dress. Maybe that's what aged him, I thought: not the drugs and the drink but the presence, that magical energy that possesses and expands and surrounds him, a magnetic field that, in a concert, could knock out a crowd of thousands.

Like the Force in *Star Wars*. If he wanted to, I bet HG could use his presence to control people's thoughts, when he's on stage anyway. After all, he's made audiences think he's a star for more than forty years.

That evening he sat down to dinner with us, looking haggard and wrinkly but still sort of lit up, more alive than usual in the aftermath of performance. The Force wasn't with him any more, I concluded, but there was a little bit of glitter left over, in his eyes, his voice, his manner. In his heyday he must have been amazing, not just a megastar but a real god: the übergod of rock superfame. Like Elvis and Bacchus and the Pope all rolled into one.

I was sitting next to him. Brie tried to muscle in, but I was determined and I'm bigger than she is. Mindful of Russell's comment, I thought I'd try being a good listener, as a result of which dinner took longer than usual, or at any rate *felt* longer, though of course it was a big thrill to have HG beside me talking about the old days and so on. It was rather less of a thrill when Morty, who was opposite, began to go on about *his* youth, when he'd played bass guitar in a band called the Weeds (or something like that). This is what it's like to be Roo, I told myself, smiling and saying, 'How fascinating,' in all the right places. By the time Morty had finished the saga of his (brief) musical career, I'd decided it was just too much hassle. Being a good listener may make you irresistible, but it simply isn't worth it. In future, I was going to stick to a push-up bra.

We'd just finished dessert when it happened. Footsteps outside – clinky footsteps, the unmistakable sound of very high heels on an echoing floor. The door was flung open the way someone flings a door open when they are going to make an Entrance, rather than merely coming in. An icy blast invaded the room, the sort you get with the arrival of Banquo's ghost or Jacob Marley, except in this case it was because the three doors through to the front had all been flung wide and left that way. The woman who entered so dramatically didn't look at all ghostly. She wore embossed silver thigh boots and a pink mink jacket, with bits of brown flesh showing in between. She was at least five foot ten (plus four inches for the boots), with the kind of good looks that seem to have been soused in preservative just a little too long: plumped-up pout, complexion of moisturised leather, eyes a fraction too small, cheekbones a fraction too large. And big hair. *Enormous* hair. Once it might have been dark, but now it was coffee beige with vanilla streaks, moussed out into a mane worthy of a fashion-conscious lion, with waves and curls and shaggy bits over her forehead. As she must have been travelling all day, she had either brought a portable hairdresser or was wearing enough hairspray to hold the style in a tornado.

She could only be Basilisa Ramón.

The mere sight of her explained the magenta sheepskin, the devil-mask, the fertility goddess bedposts. Everyone stared at her in glazed horror, pretty much as if she *was* Jacob Marley. Except HG, who appeared inscrutable. He must, I thought, have a skin of rhinoceros hide and balls of reinforced concrete. I mean, when your wife looks like a cross between Ivana Trump and a high-class drag act, how many men could remain inscrutable about it?

'Who are these people?' she demanded. 'They are from television, no? Why you not tell me you make television here? You are *mi marido*, you make television, but I have to read about it in *la prensa amarilla*. It is *asqueroso*! If there is television, of course they will want me. I am big star of television, I have many fans—'

'I did tell you,' HG said quietly. 'I told you we were redoing the garden. You've never been very interested in gardening.'

How he said that with a straight face I don't know. Behind Basilisa, I saw Harry, who caught my eye and rolled his. For once, I bit back a smile.

'You tell me about garden but not about *la televisión*,' Basilisa reiterated. 'You know I—'

'I told you there might be a feature. I didn't know how things would develop.' To his credit, HG managed to interrupt her without sounding as if he was interrupting – a major diplomatic achievement. And he lied so well even I almost believed him. 'Why don't you join us for a drink, meet everybody, then we can talk about it.'

Everybody blenched in anticipation.

'I go to my room,' Basilisa announced, retrieving the initiative. 'I get changed. *Then* I have a drink and *then* we talk.'

She swept from the room in triumph, though there was nothing in particular to be triumphant about. But she was clearly the sort of person who favoured the triumphant exit as much as the dramatic entrance. I wondered if she ever went in or out of a room normally.

As she retreated, I could hear her tossing orders over her shoulder. Harry – *Winkworth* – followed her, presumably picking them up. I bet he behaves like a proper butler with her, I thought. It should have annoyed me, but it didn't.

Ruth

The arrival of Basilisa was the one thing that could have made everyone appreciate Alex and Brie. Alex might be a spoiled child who had never grown up, but, bar the practical jokes, he was quite a nice spoilt child, who responded well to threats of being horribly murdered if he didn't behave himself. Brie was a bad actress but at least she wasn't trying to hog the lime-light.

Basilisa was a nightmare.

She wanted to star in the historical scenes, she wanted to pose in the reconstructed maze, she wanted us to film her efforts at interior design. 'This is makeover show, no? I know all about makeover. When I come to Dunblair it is – how you say? – *andrajoso*, old-fashioned, boring, boring. Furniture, curtains, carpets – all dark, all dull. I change everything. I bring colour, *vitalidad*. You will make film of my *transformación*, you will show everyone I am not just a beautiful woman, I am great artist, great imagination. What you mean, your show is just about garden? *Estúpida*, who wants to go outside in Scotland? Is cold, is grey, is rain all the time. Who cares about garden? You want to film here, you film my rooms. Garden not important. You film what I say, or you leave.'

The manure was flying – it was time to call Crusty. But I

didn't. I've been shot at in Kosovo, I told myself (even if the sniper had been aiming elsewhere); I've been haunted in Surrey; if I can't handle this, I can't handle anything. I had a private conversation with HG and then deployed the crew to spend a day shooting Basilisa in her various interiors.

'We're wasting *time*,' Russell muttered, his rather lugubrious face becoming actively moribund. 'Not to mention the cost.'

'HG's covering it,' I whispered. 'I arranged it with him.'

'Clever girl. All the same—'

'It's a nuisance, but it's not as if we're going to use it. HG asked to keep the film afterwards. I suppose he doesn't want it turning up on one of those celebrity hatchet-jobs on *ITV Scandal*.'

'Probably needs it for his divorce,' Russell said.

The real trouble started with Basilisa's determination to appear in the historical scenes. Initially she elected to play the murdered wife of HG's laird, a choice many of us thought deeply significant. ('Perhaps he'll take the hint,' Russell said.) We were forced to remove the actress who had been given the role, causing issues with the union and a threatened strike by all the minor roles. We then had to re-employ the actress in question on the realisation that Basilisa couldn't do an English accent, let alone a Scots one, and we would therefore need another vocal stand-in. Like Brie, Basilisa was not informed of this. Meanwhile those of the cast who had actually struck had to be routed out of the Dirk and Sporran, along with several crew members who had come out in sympathy. The electrician, Mick, was found to be, as Russell put it, spark out, after an excess of sympathetic Laphroaig, and the cameraman, Dick – all too well named – had got his hands on some quality Leb and was useless for the rest of the day. By the time I had calmed everyone who needed calming and Russell had rallied the troops, we all wound up back in the pub – even

Alex, Brie, Delphi and Ash – in a rare display of team spirit, the spirit in question being mostly single malt.

There's nothing like a common enemy to turn lesser enemies into bosom friends.

'If you try to fob the Basilisk off on me,' Ash said with uncharacteristic heat, 'there will be another ghost on the castle roster. A Spanish one.'

'Couldn't you arrange for her to be haunted?' I said wistfully.

'She wouldn't notice. There are some people who are so self-centred, so oblivious to everything around them, that phantoms simply bounce off them. The only atmosphere Basilisa's aware of is the one inside her head.'

'No intuition,' said Brie. 'I can tell.'

'She's an Insensitive,' I supplied.

'You said it,' murmured Ash. Under stress, he was becoming a lot more human. He was even drinking beer, an improbable drink for an elf.

The pub was named after the landlord and barman, Angus McSporran and Dirk McTeith, who had been on a roll ever since the TV crowd hit town. Now, they were more than ready to join in the fun, relating tales of the Basilisk's unpopularity in the village, through which she was prone to drive, much too fast, in the Ferrari, splashing old ladies with mud, flattening sheep, and narrowly missing innocent children. Apparently she had once had a run-in with a bull (no doubt her Spanish blood taking over), where both sides had threatened legal action after the bull was severely bruised and the Ferrari gored. Maids working at the castle had been terrorised or summarily dismissed for trivial offences; even Dougal McDougall had been fired for aggressive dourness, though reinstated later the same day after HG made it clear he was outside Basilisa's jurisdiction. Local opinion was largely in HG's

favour – 'We call him the Laird noo, though only tae his face,'
Angus said. 'He dinna say so, but he's muckle keen on it' –
but his wife, it was felt, was suitable material for the ducking
stool and burning at the stake. (The Scots are old-fashioned,
and don't really believe in divorce.)

'Mebbe, when the accurrsed maze is replanted, ye could lose
her in it,' Dirk said.

'No chance,' said Delphi. 'She'd be too busy carpeting it in
lilac fur and installing decorative totem poles at every inter-
section.' Although Alex was to hand in fiancé mode, she
appeared to be hitting it off unexpectedly well with Dirk, who
was rather good-looking in a brawny, Scottish way.

The evening slid comfortably downhill. We missed dinner,
dining off crisps and sandwiches stuffed with what might have
been haggis, none of which did much to soak up the alcohol.
By closing time, we were on the toasts, drinking not just to
the downfall of the Basilisk – 'Anyone got a magic sword?':
Russell – but anything else that came to mind. Alex and
Delphi's marriage, Brie's breast implants, the Atkins Diet, the
F-you Diet, independence for Scotland, the success of the local
football team (Dinnaguigle), the failure of the rival team
(Midloathsome), Shakespeare, Robbie Burrns, Robbie
Williams, and Fenris the bichon.

(As far as I can recall, the proposers of the toasts were, in
order: Dirk's girlfriend, Nick the sound recordist, Brie, Russell,
Dougal McDougall, assorted locals, more assorted locals, the
reinstated actress, Angus McSporran, Brie again, and Alex.)

Afterwards, I remember noticing that two of the villagers (I
assumed they were villagers) had accents which didn't quite
match and joined in rather too fervently with all the wrong
toasts, but we were all too far gone to pay any attention.

By the time those of us based at Dunblair came to stagger
the mile and a half homewards, the problem of Basilisa Ramón

had dwindled to a mere joke, to be laughed over and forgotten. We had that group high that you can only get after confronting trouble together and overcoming it, a feeling normally associated with wartime scenarios like the Resistance and the Blitz. The enemy had been outfaced and outjockeyed; we were the tops.

Which goes to show how wrong you can be.

The first intimation of disaster came when I tottered down to the dining room the following day, half an hour after shooting was due to start, feeble apology at the ready. But there was no one to apologise to. The only occupant of the room was the Basilisk herself, sitting at the table, simultaneously drinking black coffee, smoking a black cheroot, and painting her nails black. Well, crimson-black anyway. She wore an eau de Nil negligee trimmed in pink swansdown, the sort of thing Ginger Rogers might have carried off in a thirties film, provided it was in monochrome. First thing in the morning on top of a bad hangover it was not a pleasant sight. I sank into a chair, feeling slightly queasy. Harry, who had evidently been hovering in the vicinity, looked me over thoughtfully and said, 'Don't touch the coffee: I'll bring another pot. Time for the *really* strong stuff, I think.'

'It is good you are here,' Basilisa said, surveying me with a distaste which was almost certainly unfair. My complexion might be pale green (I could feel it), but at least it matched the negligee. 'I have an announcement to make.'

I mumbled something which she took for encouragement. Not that she needed any.

'Last night, I read the script. *El papel* I play, it is not enough important. I think I play someone else.' My stomach shrank in horror. 'The big part, it is Eleezabet Courtnee. I am going to play that.'

If I had had the forethought to eat more the previous evening, I would have thrown up on the spot.

Wild ideas spun through my lurching brain. We could film Basilisa as Elizabeth secretly, without Delphi knowing, then bin the lot afterwards. But it would never work, even if HG agreed to pay for it: it would take far too long. We had the garden to get on with, and the chances of keeping it from Delphi were nil. Oh de nil. Or Russell and I could try to find a way to convey to Basilisa, tactfully, that she was completely unsuited to playing a nineteenth-century English heiress. Or . . .

At that moment Morty came in, wearing a glow of good health that made me suspect he'd been at the make-up long before shooting. He gave me a rather familiar pat on the shoulder and greeted Basilisa with an enthusiasm which might or might not have been insincere. He'd been in the pub the previous night with the rest of us, drinking to her undoing, but instinct told me he was a sail-trimmer who would go with the prevailing wind. Or hurricane.

Equally, he might have felt her Amazonian good looks outweighed the minor flaws in her personality.

'*Buenos días,*' she said. 'I am telling Senora Rooth –' that was how my name came out – 'today we must start again to film *la historia del castillo*. I am to play Eleezabet. Is best part, so I play it. I am great actress. You fire whoever have it before.'

Morty's mouth opened and shut, fishlike. 'Yerse,' he said at last, achieving what passed for a smile. 'I'm sure you'll be . . . very good. Very good. Great idea, isn't it, Ruth?'

I glared at him. With eyes undoubtedly bloodshot in my pale green face, the effect must have been horrifying. 'I don't think . . .'

The advent of Harry with extra-strong coffee created a timely interruption.

Russell was the next to hear the good news. Almost as soon

as he came in Basilisa seized on him to discuss *her* motivation
in the role, if not Elizabeth's – 'In Spain, I am already big star.
Now, I will be big star on English TV too' – and Morty took
the opportunity for a low-voiced conversation with me.
Whether I wanted one or not.

'I can see you don't like it,' he said, perceptively, 'but
honestly, Delphinium's not that good an actress. Basilisa can't
be worse – she might be better, and she looks terrific.'

'So does Delphi,' I snapped back, 'and she may not be Cate
Blanchett, but she's a damn sight more convincing as an
English heiress than Carmen Miranda here. She also happens
to be nearer the right age – a *lot* nearer.'

'You try telling that to HG,' Morty said. 'He may find her
a handful, but he always gives her what she wants, in case you
haven't noticed. I reckon once they're in the bedroom she
knows exactly how to get her own way. They say she has a
tongue longer than a sea serpent and enough suction for a
turbocharged vacuum cleaner.'

'If you're thinking of finding out,' I hissed savagely, 'never
mind her married state – you'd be safer having oral sex with
a rattlesnake.'

'Delphinium may be your friend, but you're a fool if you go
out on a limb for her,' Morty persisted. I remembered she had
brushed him off, a long time ago – but he was the type who
nursed grudges. And hell hath no fury like a TV presenter
scorned. 'Don't expect John Beard-Trenchard to support you:
he'll go with HG all the way. If you want to keep your job you'll
back Basilisa, whatever your private feelings.' He added, with
an air of reasonableness that made my palm itch to hit him:
'After all, Delphinium will still be swanning around in the
garden. Losing the acting role is no big deal for her.'

What I might have said I don't know. The coffee was kicking in, my head was clearing, and all my most irrational brain

cells were going into action. He was right in a way: Delphi would still star as co-presenter, she wasn't a brilliant actress, and the part of Elizabeth Courtney would probably do little for her career. But that wasn't the point. (She'd also got me my current job, but that wasn't it either.) What mattered was that she was my friend. Friends stick together, regardless of cold logic. Friendship always comes first.

I felt my temper rising to breakpoint, then the door opened and I swallowed my anger unexpressed.

Delphi walked in.

It took her about two minutes to assimilate the latest developments.

'You want – to – play – Elizabeth – Courtney?' she said to Basilisa, spelling it out, her rigid self-control somehow a grim warning of what might happen when, and if, that control should shatter. 'That's out of the question. We've already shot those scenes, and *I* starred in them.'

'*You?* But you are just *jardinera*. You cannot play great acting part. We shoot them again.'

The rage that flooded through Delphi seemed to make her grow several inches in height. Whatever hangover she might have had melted in its heat: her eyes flashed hazard warning lights, her hair crackled, her very teeth appeared to lengthen. To anyone who knew these signs, there were two courses of action to take: 1. remove all breakables from her vicinity, and/or 2. get under the table.

'Now would be a good time to duck,' I told Morty sweetly.

But Basilisa was no pussycat, and she had all the muscle of a rock-star empire behind her . . .

Delphi didn't care. When she really lost it, Delphi didn't care about anything. 'I am an actress, a presenter and an all-round star!' she declared. 'All *you've* ever done is jump in and out of a moving sports car while varnishing your toenails –

not exactly Oscar-winning stuff. You couldn't act tragic if your hair extensions were pulled out! As for your playing Elizabeth Courtney – we could dub your voice over the top, but we couldn't dub your face. Elizabeth was twenty-six – no plastic surgeon could rise to the challenge! And if we put you in period costume you'd look like a . . . like a transvestite matador! We might let you do a small part because you're HG's wife, but you as Elizabeth Courtney – we'd be laughed off the screen!'

'Beach!' Basilisa screeched incomprehensibly (it took me a moment to realise she meant *Beetch!*). She leaped to her feet. Delphi's tall, but she was taller, much taller. Even her *slippers* had four-inch heels. 'You forget, you are in *my* house. In *mi casa*, *I* am the only star! *I* decide! You leave now – you leave without your clothes, without anything. I throw you out myself!' She seized Delphi's shoulders in what looked like a grip of steel. She was a strong woman, plainly athletic and very fit – the sleeves of the negligee fell back to reveal arms like Arnold Schwarzenegger. Russell laid an ineffectual hand on her by way of restraint.

'Try it!' Delphi snarled.

(There was a lot of snarling at Dunblair. Probably the ghosts in the atmosphere taking over.)

Unfortunately, there was no half-grapefruit to hand, not even a bowl of cornflakes. She picked up the nearest cup of coffee and threw it at her opponent, splattering the eau de Nil silk and brown-leather cleavage. Luckily for Basilisa, it was cold. The Spaniard produced a string of what must be oaths in her native language, shaking Delphi violently. Delphi retaliated with a kick which knocked her opponent off her stiletto heels, twisting her ankle in the process. As Basilisa lurched sideways she started to scream for HG.

'My husband is biggest star in the world – he see you never work again – no *tele*, no *jardín*, no *actriz*, *nada*! We have lawyers, we have *influencia* – your career is *terminada* – you starve in the streets –'

She yanked Delphi towards her, landing a vicious blow on her breast. Delphi yelped with pain and doubled over, then sank her teeth in her enemy's arm. Russell, Morty and I all moved to intervene – it was getting nasty – falling over each other and proving generally useless. Behind me, I heard Harry's voice: 'This is fun, but it's gone on long enough. You two –' this to the guys – 'grab Bazza. I'll handle Delphinium.' He wrapped his arms around Delphi and pulled her back; a mouthful of Basilisa's flesh appeared to come with her. There was blood running down the pale green silk, blood round Delphi's lips.

'She is evil – she is *vampiresa* – *caníbal*!' Basilisa accused, not without some justification. 'Look what she do to me – look what she do! I sue for *millions*!'

'She was worried about starving on the streets,' I said. 'She wanted to get a good meal in first.'

'Beach!' Basilisa howled. 'You are beach too! You fired, you all fired! We find new producer, new director –'

'What the fuck is going on?'

It was HG.

He didn't exactly take charge; rather, taking charge was thrust upon him. Basilisa, hastily released by Russell and Morty, clung to him and burst into unlikely tears. Between sobs, explanations came pouring out – demands for Delphi's instant expulsion, for the role of Elizabeth Courtney, for legal action against all and sundry and major surgery to save her arm.

'If you persuade Crusty to cast *her* as Elizabeth,' Delphi said, having been unhanded by Harry, 'I'm quitting anyway. It's a breach of my contract – or if it isn't, it should be. I won't stand for it.'

'If she goes, I go,' I said. 'And if you had any decency –' this to the other two – 'you'd back me up.'

'Consider yourself backed,' said Russell.

Morty – the prat – didn't say anything, merely looking doubt-ful.

Basilisa was now weeping into HG's shoulder, a major feat since she was several inches taller than him, even without her heels. He concentrated on soothing her, speaking in passable Spanish, before reverting to English to explain that although she would have been wonderful as Elizabeth Courtney, those scenes had, alas, already been shot, and there simply wasn't time to do them again. He was relying on her to support him in the alternative role . . .

Basilisa's tears evaporated at the speed of light.

'*Support* you? Why should I support you when you don't support me? Why do you not throw her out immediately? You are in love with her, no? Why else do you back another woman – *una desconocida* – against your own wife?'

'Don't be ridiculous.'

'You know I do not approve divorce – *soy católica* – so you think you can betray me with this whore, and I will say nothing, I will suffer in *silencio*! *Bastardo*! You are wrong. *Never* will I be silent! I will tell the world how she seduced you, how she stole your love from me. No – do not touch me. I go now to call my *publicista*. You –' she turned back to Delphi – 'remember, I make promise. You are *terminada* – you will never work again.'

Delphi, at a loss for a sufficiently devastating retort, yawned in her face.

Basilisa would have swept from the room, but her ankle slightly impeded her progress, lending an element of hobble to the sweep.

'I'll deal with her,' HG assured us when she had gone. 'She's a little temperamental, that's all.'

'Really,' I said, not bothering to remove the dryness from my voice. 'She *attacked* Delphi.' I decided to disregard the coffee-throwing incident. 'I mean, physically attacked her. Are you all right?' This to Delphi.

'That was a nasty blow you took,' Harry said. 'Maybe I should have a look at it.'

'No!' Delphi jumped like the proverbial startled hare when he laid a hand on her shoulder. 'You're a butler, not a doctor, and this is my boob we're talking about. Anyway, it's just a bit bruised.'

'I'll get you some arnica,' Harry offered, unperturbed. 'Don't worry: you can rub it in yourself.'

'What I really need is to wash my mouth out. I mean, I *bit* her. I've probably got blood poisoning – her blood must be pure strychnine.'

We'd got past caring that HG was still there. Iconic super-stardom stops being quite so impressive when you see it every day.

'Look after her,' he told Harry, and went out, at a guess to talk to Basilisa, though what he was going to say I had no idea. He hadn't taken her part, but in the face of her overweening ego I couldn't see him taking ours.

'We could all be out of a job,' I said, meaning Delphi, Russell and me.

'I doubt it,' Harry said. 'You're forgetting something. HG mayn't make a lot of noise about it – he doesn't need to – but he's been king of the heap nearly all his life: he's used to doing exactly what he wants. Much more used to it than the Basilisk. He'll let her have her own way when it doesn't interfere with his, but not otherwise. Right now, he's really into developing the garden. You're all part of that. He won't let anyone upset his plans.'

'I hope you're right,' Russell said. 'I've got a wife and kids to support. The *grande geste* is all very well, but I much prefer not having to live up to my principles.'

Once the crew turned up and Delphi had had time to recover from whatever she might have ingested when biting Basilisa, we spent the rest of the day in the garden filming, though I was privately apprehensive and aware it might prove to be a waste of time. After all, if Basilisa put the kibosh on the show, HG could always go ahead with someone else. In the world of TV gardening, Mortimer and Delphi weren't the only game in town. Belatedly I tried to phone Crusty, but his mobile wasn't answering and both office and home numbers gave me a machine. I left a message asking him to call back, hoping I wouldn't have bad news.

Improbable versions of the Fun-Fight at the OK Castle were circulating somehow, almost before anyone had arrived to circulate them. I was constantly being asked for information or corroboration: was it true that Delphi had pulled out Basilisa's hair extensions, run her through with the claymore, torn off her negligee to reveal the extra nipple she used for suckling her familiar? As a result Delphi enjoyed a rare surge in popularity, becoming a heroine to actors who had formerly deplored her using her celebrity status to snitch the best role. I didn't pass on the fact that the Basilisk wanted to terminate the whole project; but that leaked out too.

'Why're we still rolling?' Dick demanded. 'No point if the show's folding. We could be in the pub.'

'HG will sort things out,' I said. 'We have to trust him.'

'*I* heard,' said Nick, 'that Bazza gives billion-dollar head.' He'd obviously been talking to Morty. 'HG won't have a prayer. Nor will we.'

'With all those groupies and things, HG's probably had more

head than . . . than Philip Treacy!' Delphi declared. 'At his age, he ought to be blasé about it.'

'Exactly,' I said. 'He's old enough not to be thinking with his dick any more.'

'Did you know you can have an erection after death?' Mick remarked brightly. 'I think it's a side effect of rigor mortis.'

'I don't *want* to know,' I said.

The castle staff, alienated by Basilisa over a long period, were particularly attentive to Delphi, even Morag offering what passed for approbation, in her own special way. 'The Lord be wi' ye!' she declaimed. 'Ye ha' defied the deil, and spat in the face o' yon Jezebel.' ('I didn't think of that,' Delphi murmured.) 'For all your vanity and sin, ye ha' done God's work.'

'Let's hope he sees it that way,' I said, unable to resist the pun.

HG put in an appearance around four, looking more than usually world-weary.

'I've discussed the situation with Basilisa,' he said. 'She was pretty upset. You must understand, she's rather like an over-grown kid.' Not *another* one. 'She's used to being the centre of attention, the one the party's all about. It's very difficult for her to adjust to taking second place, especially in her own home.'

'Has she?' I said bluntly. 'Adjusted, I mean.'

'Mm. She knows how much the garden means to me.' How much? I wondered. I was prepared to bet it had cost him in diamonds, at the very least. Basilisa wasn't the type to skimp on the price. 'Of course, she still wants to be part of the project. I said you might consider keeping her in the role of my wife, provided she's ready to take direction.' Harry was right, I thought, my respect for HG going up in leaps and bounds. 'She hadn't appreciated what a very good team you are. I explained that even with the prestige of my name, we couldn't get the same high-profile coverage with anyone else. She doesn't spend much time in the UK, you see.'

'Of course,' I said, mesmerised. His tactics were inspired.

'She wanted a change of producer,' he continued, 'but I said you were the best. Basilisa's used to having the best – of everything.'

I swallowed, stunned by the vision of myself up there with Peter Bazalgette and Verity Lambert.

'However, she has been rather distressed by the incident of the – er – bite on her arm.' My spine stiffened; flattery wasn't going to get him anywhere on this. 'It took me some time to persuade her that sacking Delphinium wasn't an option. She wants compensation and a written apology, but I pointed out that Miss Dacres' injuries were worse than hers—'

'Absolutely,' I said. 'I mean, they *were*. Basilisa punched her in the breast, and she doesn't have silicon to protect her.'

HG allowed himself the flicker of a smile. 'I'm sure of it. Anyway, now Basilisa understands I'm not involved with Delphinium, she will be more . . . flexible. Compensation, naturally, is out of the question – the offence is far too serious for mere money to make a difference. As for the apology, I told her it would have to be deferred until shooting is completed. Then we'll see. Basilisa realises the importance of maintaining good relations with your team.'

'She hasn't any good relations to maintain,' I said.

'Go along with me here,' HG said, switching out of diplomatic mode. 'I'm not going to end in the divorce courts because of a TV programme. I don't mind looking like a bastard, but I'm buggered if I'm going to look like a fool.'

'I hadn't thought of that,' I said, disarmed by this sudden frankness. 'It must be tough, having an image like yours to live up to.'

'It is. My image, as you call it, has survived a lot of shit, but it would never outlast my being dumped over a makeover show.'

'You could always pretend you were having an affair with Delphinium after all,' I suggested.

'I'd rather have one with you.' Hell. He really was *very* charming when he chose to be. 'I'm giving up viragos in future.'

'Delphi will never apologise,' I said, 'and frankly, I don't see why she should. Basilisa got physical first. Delphi was just defending herself.' With a vengeance.

'Like I said, the apology's deferred. Let's finish the job in hand and then we can sort out the fine detail. When my garden looks the way I want . . .'

'All right,' I conceded. I didn't really need to be back on the breadline. 'But how do we keep the peace in the meantime?'

'It's a large castle. Basilisa will behave, now her position has been made clear.' I couldn't help speculating exactly what that position was. 'It's up to you to manage Delphinium.'

I nodded, concealing inner qualms. Delphi might not demand Basilisa's head on a platter, but she wasn't going to be in the mood for self-restraint.

'As for mealtimes,' he concluded, 'I'll see Basilisa eats with me, not in the main dining room. That should simplify matters. Deal?' He extended his hand, his smile making wicked little wrinkles at the corner of his eyes. He might be old, short and string-and-sinew thin, but he was still a knockout. I succumbed to the handshake and found myself smiling in return.

'Deal,' I said.

('HG's got quite a thing for you,' Russell said later. 'Better watch out, or you'll top the Basilisk's hit list.')

Once HG had gone I was pounced on by everyone to find out what had happened, what was happening, and, if possible, what would happen next. I said we were all still in work (cheers), Basilisa would play HG's wife (boos), and the object was to carry on as usual (silence).

'What about Delphi?' Alex protested, putting his arm around her in a protective gesture. He had evidently decided to constitute himself her champion, even though he was a little late on the scene. 'That dago bitch actually *assaulted* her. We should be suing for compensation.'

'Basilisa wants compensation too,' I said, 'so they cancel each other out.'

'Compensation is for wimps!' Delphi pronounced, discarding Alex's arm. 'The point is, I can't work with her – even at a distance. None of us can. The laird's wife was supposed to be a braw Scottish lassie, whatever that means. Basilisa looks about as Scottish as a plate of cold tapas. She makes nonsense of the whole historical thing.'

'That isn't your problem,' I said. 'Look—'

'What d'you mean, it *isn't my problem*? *I*'m the star of this show, *I* got you your job—'

'You recommended me, yes, but—'

'*I got you the job*,' Delphi's voice was shrilling at danger point, 'and now you're letting me down!'

'No she isn't,' Russell interceded with a gallant disregard for his own safety, '*you're* letting *her* down. You may have helped her to get the job in the first place, but she's kept it on her own merits – and she put herself on the line for you earlier today, in case you've forgotten. The least you can do is back her up now.'

'Well, *excuse* me,' Alex said, 'but I think Delphi's just a little more important to this programme than Roo—'

'*Do* shut up!' snapped Delphi, rounding on him with a capriciousness that was extreme, even for her. 'This isn't about whether Roo's more important than me or any of that shit, it's about bloody Basilisa. She hit me, she tried to pinch the role of Elizabeth Courtney, and she's probably poisoned me as well, but I'm supposed to just *overlook* it?'

'Yes,' I said, screwing my courage to the sticking point, 'you are. I was employed to get this series made, and that's what I intend to do. I'm sorry if you think I'm letting you down, but I'm not going to let Crusty down by forcing HG to welsh on us, and I'm not going to let everyone else down by putting them all out of work. I never said so, but I always knew working with you was a mistake. I love you, but you're every bit as selfish and thoughtless as Basilisa, and if you did me a favour it was only because you expected me to be your yes-woman. Well, I won't. I'm going to do this job my way, and if you don't like it you can lump it.'

'Roo . . .' Under her screen make-up Delphi was almost white. I'd never spoken to her like that in my life. Maybe it was long overdue, but it didn't make me feel good. 'You . . . you *traitress*! I got you that job when you were totally suicidal, and now – I'm quitting this programme, I'm quitting right this *second*, and that will destroy you with Crusty and anyone else who matters! You'll never get work as a producer again!'

'You sound *exactly* like the Basilisk!' I said, fighting an idiotic urge to burst into tears. 'Next thing you'll be calling me a beach!'

'Beach!' Delphi screamed. 'Beach and superbeach!' She stormed off, brushing Alex aside like a mosquito, leaving me trembling and inwardly wretched.

Ten minutes later Crusty rang. I answered my mobile so promptly I didn't have time to register the caller's number. 'Hello?'

'You left a couple of messages for me,' Crusty said. 'Got a problem?'

'N-no. No, of course not. It's just . . . HG's wife Basilisa's turned up, back from the Caribbean. She wants to play a minor role . . .'

'Make sure it stays minor,' Crusty said. 'She'll be all wrong, but never mind. Bit of the price for doing the series. HG likes to keep her sweet. Wouldn't fancy her myself, but he's a rock star: they go for that type. Should have thought he'd be happier with someone a bit less . . . Still, she's hot stuff. Or so they say.' Perhaps he had the same sources as Morty.

'Thing is,' Crusty went on, 'she can be a bit of a drama queen, Latin temperament and all that. Handle her tactfully.'

'I'll do my best,' I said.

'Good girl,' said Crusty (he'd never heard of sexism). 'Knew I could rely on you.'

Everyone knows they can rely on me, I thought bitterly. If there's a gene for reliability, I've got it. But that's my problem.

When we had finished for the day, I retreated to the kitchen. Ash was there too, but I was past caring.

'Alcohol,' I told Cedric without preamble.

'I gather it's been quite a day,' Ash said with his usual understatement.

'*I* heard the two she-demons came to blows,' Cedric said with relish. 'Must've been worth seeing.'

'If you like blood sports,' I said. 'And Delphi isn't a she-demon. She's just a little . . . hot-tempered.'

'Heard *you* had a set-to with her as well,' Cedric said. 'Flounced off in a huff and hasn't been seen since. Doing a good job, aren't you?' He handed me a strong smell of whisky with a small glass half full of golden liquid in its wake.

'Your spies are everywhere,' I said moodily. I took a gulp of the whisky, which wasn't a good idea. It slipped smoothly down my throat and exploded. Heat coursed through me; my cheeks flamed.

'Not really a whisky drinker, are you?' Cedric commented brightly.

'Take it gently,' Ash advised. 'You look pretty upset.'

'I *hate* arguing with Delphi,' I said when I got my voice back. 'I hardly ever do. And I said things . . .'

'True things?' Ash asked.

'Umm. Sort of.'

'I see. Those are the worst. It doesn't matter what you call someone if it isn't true because it doesn't hurt. Only the truth hurts.'

'Do you have to be quite so . . .'

'Truthful?'

We were sitting opposite each other, eye to eye. He smiled; I smiled. I couldn't help it. Suddenly, Cedric wasn't there.

Only of course he was.

'You two having a Moment?' he said in his most disagreeable voice.

Ash ignored him. 'Sometimes, the true things have to be said, no matter how painful they are,' he continued. 'You can't go on bottling them up for ever. Maybe you needed to clear the air. Maybe she needed to hear them. Have you ever worked with her before?'

'No. I really didn't want to. She's been my best friend all my life, but . . . I was afraid of the pressure we'd be under, afraid of . . . this. Now it's happened. I've said things that can't be unsaid.' I stared down into the depths of the whisky. It didn't help.

'Then say new things. Go to her. Make it up. Making up isn't difficult once you get started. It's the starting that takes nerve.'

'I never apologise,' Cedric volunteered. ''Pologising is a weakness. You go through life saying sorry all the time you're just asking to be trodden on. Sorry for this, sorry for that, sorry for existing—'

The speech was all too familiar. 'Oh shut up,' I said. 'Why don't you get your teeth fixed? You've got a smile like an orc.'

It really was my day to upset *everyone*.

It was about half an hour before dinner and I was standing outside Delphi's door, two large whiskies to the good (or bad) and still feeling trembly inside. I knew Delphi was in there because I'd run into Alex on my way up.

'I wouldn't if I were you,' he said. 'She's so miffy she's snapping everyone's head off. I'm not even allowed in to have a shower. Oh, and I don't think you're Miss Bridesmaid-of-Honour any more – in fact, I bet you're right off the invitation list.'

He sounded positively spiteful about it, but perhaps that was his concept of loyalty.

I said, 'Thanks,' I don't know why – a verbal reflex – and went up anyway.

The heat of the whisky evaporated at the door. I'd refused to apologise to Cedric on the grounds that apologising was a weakness, but somehow Ash had smoothed things over, though I'd left Cedric peering in a hand mirror (he kept one in the kitchen) and contemplating cosmetic dentistry. Now all I had to do was knock, say sorry, make up . . .

Supposing she wouldn't? Supposing I'd lost my best friend for good?

I stood there, trapped by my own hesitancy, waiting for my knuckles to tap on the door panel all by themselves. Then I heard the rattle of the key. The handle turned. I hadn't knocked, but the door opened.

'Roo!' Delphi said. 'I was . . . I was coming to find you . . .'

'I came to find you—'

'I'm so sorry,' she began.

'I'm so sorry—'

'I've been awful—'

'No, *I*'ve been awful—'

'You're trying so hard to make a go of things, inspite of Basilisa and . . . and people, and I made it worse for you . . .'

'No, no – I should've supported you – I *do* support you – you were quite right to bite her, except you could have gone for the jugular . . .'

'I'll do better next time!'

'I'm sorry I called you selfish . . .'

'I'm sorry I called you a beach . . .'

We hugged, made up, said sorry all over again.

'I *am* selfish sometimes,' Delphi said candidly. 'I'll try not to be, but I can't always help it. After all, if *I* didn't think of me first, nobody else would.'

'Alex?' I said.

'Don't be silly. Alex is selfish too. It's another thing we have in common. That's why we're so well suited.'

I couldn't find an answer to that, much as I wanted to.

'You're the only truly unselfish person I know,' Delphi said, 'and that's why I worry about you. You need a bit of selfishness to survive. Unselfish people are always last in the queue at the great checkout of life.'

'I'll bear that in mind,' I said.

'I want you to be at the front,' Delphi persisted. 'With me.'

We went down to dinner together – late, since Delphi insisted I change – and I had time to tell her in detail about my conversation with HG, and how kind he'd been.

'He's got a thing for you,' Delphi declared. 'It's on account of your being a good listener and all that. Hot God has the hots for you – wow! Wow and triple wow. It ought to be me, but I don't mind because I'm *not* a good listener and, anyway, I'm going to marry Alex. It's a pity he's so old – HG, I mean. I don't suppose you could . . . ?'

192

'He's drop-dead attractive, but no, I couldn't. Even if he was twenty years younger I couldn't. The thought of getting involved with a huge international rock star would scare me shitless. Anyway, he's married to the Basilisk, in case you've forgotten.'

Delphi waved that aside. 'A detail. He's long overdue for divorce. D'you really think he's attractive? You ought to go for it – marry him. Even if he's dead in ten years, you'll be a fabulously wealthy widow. You'll be forty-two, but that's no age nowadays, and, anyway, you'd be able to afford amazing plastic surgery. Honestly, Roo, you should give it a try. I'm being very unselfish about this, too – marrying HG would make you a much bigger star than me.'

'I appreciate your unselfishness,' I said, 'but I can't.'

'Your trouble is, you have no ambition. You only want to marry sleazy ne'er-do-wells like Kyle Muldoon . . .'

'Actually,' I said, on a note of self-discovery, 'I haven't thought about Kyle in ages.'

'You haven't? Okay, who *are* you thinking about?'

'Nobody,' I said hastily. 'I haven't the time. All I think about is work.'

'I don't believe you. Everybody thinks about *somebody* . . .'

'We're late for dinner. Come on.'

In the dining room, Alex looked surprised to see Delphi and me back on good terms.

'You don't understand girls,' Delphi said tolerantly. 'You guys think we have shallow relationships that fall apart as soon as a man comes into the equation, but we aren't like that. It's male friendships which are superficial – based on getting pissed together and talking about football or cricket and sharing confidences like, *Cor, look at the tits on her!* Girl friendships go deep – we talk about deep stuff. Not just our love lives, but philosophy and fashion and things.'

Jemma Harvey

'Girls get pissed together too,' Alex retorted, sounding faintly aggrieved.

'Occasionally, but that isn't the *point* of girlfriends. The point is to talk. Getting pissed is just the icing on the cake. Whereas for guys, getting pissed is pretty much the whole deal.'

'That's nonsense,' Alex said, still disposed to argue the toss. 'Everyone knows male bonding is much more serious. There aren't any famous examples of female friends; there are lots of them with guys. Think of the Three Musketeers.'

'I always thought they were gay,' Delphi said. 'Didn't one of them become a monk in the end? That *proves* it.'

At dinner, I sat next to Ash – I often did – wanting to check that Cedric had forgiven me for the remark about his dental care. ('Probably,' Ash said. 'If there's no arsenic in the soup, we'll know he's all right.') I'd expected Morty to be rather subdued after the way he'd chickened out on us earlier, but he chatted away as usual, apparently unaware that he had done anything to be ashamed of. But then, I reflected, sail-trimmers are like that: they think their attitude to life, honour and friend-ship is sheer pragmatism, and as such comprehensible and even admirable. Either that, or Morty was just naturally brazen.

'Well, here we are again,' Russell said cheerily, 'one big happy family.' At times like this, you can overdo the irony. 'Let's hope now we can finish the series with no more melo-drama.'

That definitely came under the heading of Famous Last Words.

Delphinium

Having made it up with Roo, I was in the sort of warm, loving mood where I wanted the world to be right with everyone, so when we went to bed I snuggled up to Alex, determined to get our sex life back on track. Somehow, since he'd come to the castle, I'd been too tired, or he'd been too peevy, or Fenny had been in the way, whatever – but we hadn't had full sex even once. Fenny tried to join in as usual, wagging his tail and burrowing between us with his nose, but I deposited him on the floor, telling him to *stay* so firmly that he got the message. I'd kept my underwear on – Alex liked to remove my bra himself and play with it, probably a fetish dating back to babyhood and some breast-feeding incident when his mother got her lingerie in a twist. We got cosy and I went down on him, though I didn't have a feather to give him the ultimate thrill. Then suddenly, out of the blue, he said, 'I don't know why you were so anxious to patch things up with Roo.'

I stopped what I was doing immediately. You can't have a row with your mouth full. 'What?'

'I thought you'd changed your mind about her – having her as your bridesmaid and all that.'

'She's my best friend – she always has been. I'm not going to *change my mind* about her just because we had a falling-out. Friends fall out, and in again, all the time: it doesn't mean a thing. What's got into you? You used to like her.'

'I *have* changed my mind, okay? She's got so bossy up here, ordering everyone about. I don't want her at my wedding.'

I opened my mouth to say it was *my* wedding, not his, and shut it again. It *would* be my wedding, naturally – I'd made all the arrangements, and, anyhow, the groom isn't important: weddings are always about the bride. But I couldn't tell him that. Instead, disdaining defensive tactics, I went on the attack, reviving the subject of Darius Fitzlightly and other pals of his whom I didn't go for. Sex was forgotten and Fenny, detecting a change in the ambience, jumped back on the bed and began to bark. Alex muzzled him, swearing, I accused him of cruelty to dogs, and the quarrel degenerated into general silliness.

In the end I got up, snatched my dressing gown – for the record, a particularly gorgeous man's one in embossed velvet with a quilted silk lining – and went out, slamming the door pointedly behind me. Being solid oak, and heavy, it slammed with a thud that would have done credit to the door of a dungeon. I stormed off, though I had no real idea where I was going to storm *to*. The castle was dark and very quiet; assorted electric lighting only served to emphasise the shadows. In the dimness, Basilisa's décor was oddly reassuring: it was difficult to imagine a phantom in Highland kit would deign to promenade in front of a Dali lip sofa and purple cushions. Still, I was glad I didn't believe in ghosts. Atmosphere and communing with Elizabeth's memory I could go with, but a skeleton in tartan, possibly playing the bagpipes, was an idiotic idea.

I went downstairs, aiming vaguely for the drawing room and the chance of a drink. In the hall, I couldn't find the light switch – the staff normally dealt with turning lights on and off – and I had to feel my way, but I knew it well enough by now to reach my goal without toe-stubbing or colliding with furniture. Suddenly, a face emerged from the gloom ahead of me – a pale, alien face with cold slanting eyes, a dark fall of hair, high cheekbones catching a glimmer of light from somewhere or nowhere.

'Shit!' I said, my heart jumping despite all my native scepticism.

'Delphinium?' It was Ash.

'What are you doing? Can't you put the bloody light on?'

'I'm testing for physical signs of the supernatural. It's something that works better in the dark.' He found a switch and light flooded the hall. There was a kind of camera on a side table, and various bits of technology scattered around.

'Imbecile!' I said furiously. I don't like being scared, especially when it isn't necessary. 'I thought *you* were a ghost – except I don't believe in them. I might have taken you for a burglar and attacked you.'

'I don't think you should attack more than one person per day,' Ash said with a faint – a very faint – hint of a smile. He doesn't do smiling much.

'It would have been self-defence,' I said, 'like with Basilisa. What *is* all this stuff? Do you seriously expect to get a picture of a hooded figure clanking chains and going *Woo*?'

'The camera's a control. You activated it when you got near enough; there's an infrared flash. The object is to prove the hall's empty while I run the tape.' He indicated another gadget resembling a tape recorder.

'What's that for?' I wasn't very interested; the question was a reflex.

'An experiment. It's supposed to pick up sounds we can't hear – voices from the past, the whispers of the dead. It may work; it may not. Researchers have claimed success with it from time to time. I like to explore all possibilities.' He'd switched the machine off while we were talking. 'You're up late. Are you all right?'

'I couldn't sleep,' I said. 'I came down to get a drink or something.' I'd had a half-formed project of waking up Harry to order tea or cocoa, because, after all, waiting on people was his job, but I didn't want to do it with Ash there.

We went into the drawing room and he opened the drinks cabinet. 'I'm guessing you're not keen on Scotch?'

197

'No. Gin and tonic.' There was a small fridge adjacent to the cabinet for mixers, champagne and anything else that required chilling, concealed behind a walnut door. 'Lots of tonic.'

While he poured, I asked, 'Do you *really* believe in ghosts? Not just memories – real spirits that come back after death?'

He threw me a swift, sharp look. 'I keep hoping. *My* mother claimed to remember former lives, though she was as high as a kite much of the time. She was no historian, yet some of her recollections chimed perfectly with factual records – I researched them later. My grandmother had the Sight; my great-aunt was a medium. It's in the family. I have . . . curiosity. I believe there are other worlds which touch on ours, but I'm always looking for more evidence. After all, it's the ultimate question, isn't it? What happens next?'

'D'you think there are actual ghosts here?' I asked. Perhaps I should add him to my list of useful gays. At least he was different.

'I . . . yes.' He handed me my drink. 'The atmosphere in Dunblair is rather overcrowded – too many people, too many tensions – but when I'm alone, I feel something. A consciousness, or more than one. Brooding – malice – guilt. An urge to communicate. But it may all be in my imagination.'

'I've felt something too,' I said, suddenly eager. 'Playing Elizabeth Courtney, I've sort of got close to her. When I look at her portrait, it seems almost . . . alive. We have to find out what happened to her – how she died.'

'A whodunnit,' Ash said. 'Maybe ghosts want justice, or some kind of exoneration. Have you tried the standard detective approach? Who benefited from her death?' As he spoke, he took a beer from the fridge and flipped off the cap with a can-opener.

I sat down for a minute.

'The husband, of course,' I said. 'He inherited a fortune. But he was broken-hearted and went off to Africa and died tragically, so it didn't do him much good. Indirectly . . . his family, I suppose. The mother and the long-lost cousin, especially the cousin. He got the castle *and* the money in the end. But he was on another continent when Elizabeth died.'

'What about the other woman – the one Alasdair abandoned? Lately played by your friend Brie.'

Did I see him wince at the thought?

'I *like* that idea,' I said. 'Revenge is always good. *And* she married the cousin in the end, so she got the castle and Elizabeth's money too, though she couldn't have known things would work out that way.'

'Pity the cousin was abroad for the murder,' Ash said. 'Otherwise they could have planned it together.'

'Maybe he wasn't,' I said slowly. 'Maybe he was here . . . in disguise. Alasdair was with him when he died – some tropical fever. Supposing *that* was murder, too? Out in the wild somewhere, it would've been really easy to cover it up. He didn't dare claim his inheritance until the mother was dead, but after that he had a clear field. Come home, get the castle and the dosh, marry the girl – they were in cahoots all along.'

'It's a theory,' Ash said. 'Talk to Nigel. There might be some documentary evidence on the cousin's movements. We don't even know his name, do we?'

'I'll find out.'

I was sure I was right – or almost sure. It all fitted so well – *if* the cousin had been in Scotland. Thinking about the mystery, I headed back upstairs, leaving Ash to his experiments. (I must discourage Roo from spending time with him. For a gay guy, he acted awfully straight.)

I lingered in the purple gallery to finish my drink. The lip sofa wasn't very comfortable, but there was a chair on the same lines, shaped like a yawning mouth with a cushiony red tongue lolling out. I sat down in it, tucking my feet under me; it encased me like a large squishy bowl. Thanks to the central heating, the room was warm; a lamp at my side cast a soft pinkish glow. I set down my glass on a low table and curled up, letting my imagination drift back into the past. At some point, I fell asleep.

I dreamed.

We all have dreams which seem to mean something from time to time. I had a recurring one after my father left, where I was in a crowded room, trying to reach him, calling out, but he never heard me, never saw me – he just went on talking, and the people got in my way until I was pushed out of the room, on my own. There was another version where I was following him down the street: he walked and I ran, but I never caught up. The dreams stopped after I visited him in the South of France. Anyway, *this* dream must have come from my conversation with Ash, an idea that got into my subconscious and took over. It was the kind where you don't know you're dreaming, which makes it very vivid and frightening, though I wasn't sure what there was to be afraid of.

I was in the gallery, but Basilisa's décor had gone. Instead there were dingy paintings, heavy curtains, hulks of furniture that looked as if no one had moved them for centuries. My chair was no longer squishy: the upholstery was worn, coarse against my skin. There was very little light. At the far end of the room, two people were talking. A man and a woman. The man had his back to me: he looked tall and dark, but under those conditions, anyone would. He was wearing a long coat with a shoulder-cape, or maybe it was a cloak; I couldn't be sure which. The woman was much shorter. She held a candle. Mostly, his body screened her from my sight, but at one stage she moved, or he did, and I saw her face. She was very young – not a woman but a girl, seventeen or so. Young enough for it not to matter that she wasn't wearing make-up. Her face was beautiful, in a full-lipped, sensuous sort of way; she had very dark brows and lashes, dark hair (I think), cheeks flushed with natural colour. Her expression was eager, nervous, desperate, bold . . .

They were talking about committing a murder.

I don't recall many of the words, just the tone of their voices: hers all breathy and panting, his low-pitched, even, urgent. I didn't catch the name of the victim, or the method of killing – only a sense of conspiracy, a stolen meeting, hugger-mugger, intent on crime. They were lovers, I knew that, though they never kissed, never touched. Lovers planning to kill. A slow dread crept over me, a cold, paralysing feeling, like you're supposed to get in the presence of evil. And evil was present, evil was *them* – the shadowy form of the man, the girl, young, so young, with her vivid, passionate face.

I woke abruptly, shivering in spite of the warmth, started out of the chair. But the gallery was empty. I made myself relax and leave without haste to show I wasn't scared. There was nobody there, but I had to prove it to myself. The dread still hung on, left over from the dream. It was irrational, of course; the couple were just phantoms of my imagination, the by-product of my talk with Ash. The McGoogle cousin and the girl Alasdair had jilted . . . It seemed to make sense, or half-sense, but I couldn't be sure. (That was love in her face, first love, the Juliet syndrome – not the drive for revenge.)

I decided to discuss it with Roo in the morning. The next day was Sunday, and Sunday was our day off. Plenty of time to talk.

Back at my door I opened it without trying to be quiet, but Alex didn't stir. Fenny leaped off the quilt and rushed to greet me, and I shed my dressing gown and got into bed, snuggling up to the puppy instead of my fiancé.

Thankfully, I had no more dreams.

Chapter 7: Rescue Party

Delphinium

I gatecrashed Roo's bedroom in the morning to tell her about my dream. I wanted to discuss it *now*, I couldn't wait, though her reception of it was sceptical. 'It was probably just your imagination doing overtime,' she said. 'Still, we should tell Ash about it. Analysing dreams is bound to be one of his skills.'

Ash, however, was really interested.

'Our conversation beforehand must have stimulated your subconscious,' he said, 'but that doesn't mean the dream was a lie. Your state of mind might have made you more receptive to an echo from the past. Do you remember any of their actual words?'

'She was saying something about . . . they must do it quickly. Not later than tomorrow night. Then I think he repeated "*Tomorrow night*" . . . I didn't catch any more.'

'Are you *sure* it was murder they were planning?' Roo queried doubtfully.

'Of course I'm sure. It wasn't what they said – I just *knew*. You know how you do in dreams. Besides, there was this feeling of *evil* . . .'

'And you think it was Elizabeth Courtney they were plotting to kill?' Ash persisted. I hesitated. 'There've been a lot of murders here in the past. You have plenty to choose from.'

'What were their clothes like?' Roo said. 'Assuming you were dreaming with historical accuracy, that should help us to date it.'

'It was too dark to tell,' I explained. 'Long. He had a coat or cloak; she was in a long dress. Full skirt, tight waist. Could have been Victorian.'

'If it *was* Elizabeth's murder they were planning, you think the girl had to be her rival – Alasdair's ex?' Ash said thoughtfully.

'Yes. Do we know her name?'

'Iona Craig.' This was Nigel, joining in. Despite his lack of sex appeal, his historical expertise might come in useful. I wasn't certain how he would react to my dream, but he put it down to my dramatic flair and went along with the rest of us.

'She looked awfully young,' I said. 'Sixteen or seventeen. Would that fit the facts?'

'It does indeed,' Nigel said. 'Iona was barely seventeen when Alasdair deserted her for Elizabeth. We have no pictures of her at that age, but there's a portrait done after her marriage to the laird about eight years later. It's in the main drawing room. You've probably seen it.'

'I don't notice things like that,' I said. 'Even if I did, I wouldn't have known who it was.'

'It's possible to absorb details without realising it,' Nigel said, sounding maddeningly pompous. 'You may have known more than you thought you knew.' And, to Ash, 'Wouldn't you agree? After all, mediums and other supposed psychics depend on the clues people inadvertently let fall to give the impression of telepathic awareness. Their target rarely appreciates how much she, or he, has given away. This could be a similar effect, in reverse. Delphinium may not realise how much she has assimilated.'

Ash was non-committal. 'Let's take a look at the picture.'

It was just one gloomy Victorian portrait among many, the kind of thing you see in old houses, when the artist isn't famous enough for it to be worth selling. I'd seen it before, but *without* seeing it, if you know what I mean. Its subject was light years apart from the girl in my dream – the girl with her breathlessness and her beauty and her

203

suppressed passion. Nonetheless, there was a sort of likeness: the colouring, the shape of the face, the fullness of the mouth, set now in the demure lines the painter considered suitable for her age and station. It was less than ten years later, but she looked all lady-of-the-manor, the kind of person you could imagine in church on a Sunday, or sitting at the head of the table being charming to her husband's friends. It was the same woman, I was sure – the girl I had dreamed, the conspirator, the murderess. But I didn't think my subconscious could have invented the girl after half noticing the picture even if I'd known who it was. The portrait was dull; the girl in my dream, whatever else she might have been, hadn't looked dull at all.

'What about the man?' Roo said. 'Is there a painting of Alasdair's cousin – *if* it was him?'

'I only saw his back,' I pointed out. 'Even if a picture exists, it wouldn't mean a thing to me.'

These enigmatic dreams can be very irritating. They never give you enough information.

'There are a couple of pictures of Archie McGoogle,' Nigel told us. 'He bore a strong resemblance to his cousin Alasdair, though he was older and not so handsome. Of course, living in Africa had had its effect on him: he was sallow and weather-beaten and had survived various fevers, including malaria. One of the pictures is in the old hall now.'

We trooped after him, feeling investigative, although, as I said, Archie's image wouldn't convey much.

There were two paintings side by side. The smaller one showed Alasdair, looking quite young and very good-looking (for a portrait), despite the sideburns that made him resemble someone out of an old seventies TV series. He had light brown hair, blue eyes, a cleft in his chin worthy of the Douglas family (I remarked on this and said there might be a connection, since Douglas is a Scottish name, but Roo said they made it up and they're Jewish like everyone else in Hollywood). Next to him Archie McGoogle, painted when he became the Laird, had the faded yellow complexion of last year's tan, greying hair, the same blue eyes though slightly lighter (possibly an effect of the tan), a flourishing moustache, and a sporran on his chin which passed for a beard. The Victorians, of course, were big on beards; I think it had to do with the British Empire, and the men having to be so macho. Male-dominated societies always do beards: it's because all guys hate shaving, and in a social system where they have the edge they don't feel they have to placate the women. (The Romans were generally clean-shaven, but then, half of them were gay.)

You'd think in a nation ruled by a woman the girls would have got more of a look-in. Fat chance. These mad female supreme rulers all like to surround themselves with men: it's a perk of the job. Elizabeth I had Raleigh and Drake and the one she executed by accident (Essex boy?) and the one played by Joseph Fiennes in the film. Victoria had various prime ministers like Gladstone and Disraeli and that Scottish guy who was her butler or pool cleaner or something. Maggie Thatcher had the Tory party. (Elizabeth II's different, but she isn't really a supreme ruler so she doesn't count.) Put a woman at the top, and the testosterone count of the whole country goes up. Instead of becoming more sensitive and caring, men become more . . . well, *male*. Maybe it's some kind of reaction. Female leader equals macho society. Strange but true.

I thought of mentioning this to Nigel, as it's the sort of concept he would be bound to go for, but decided against it. It would only lead the conversation round to sex again.

Anyway, Nigel was really hitting his stride, showing us even more dreary pix of past McGoogles, and explaining their relationships to each other and whatever dirty deeds they had deeded. One of them was Lady Mary McGoogle, Alasdair's tragic mother, dressed tragically in black from the day her daughter-in-law disappeared. Somebody should have told her unrelieved black is very unflattering for the older woman. But it was probably Victoria's fault: she set the trend. Another thing about female supreme rulers is they never have any fashion sense. Elizabeth I went in for those spangly stand-up collars and vast skirts that seem to be made from upholstery; Victoria wore the crinoline and the bustle (how *did* you sit down in a bustle?); Maggie Thatcher had shoulder pads and big hairspray. The supreme-ruler gene obviously comes hand in hand with another labelled fashion accident. Of course, if you're supreme-rulering, no one's going to tell you you look a twit, for fear of being decapitated.

When the lecture tour was over we got back to Elizabeth's murder and the big issue of whodunnit.

'If it was Iona,' Nigel insisted, 'the motive had to be revenge. Elizabeth stole the man she loved. Remember, he was also the local laird: it would have been a very good match for her, by the standards of the day. Her family were respectable but their social status was lower than the McGoogles and they had no money to speak of.'

'Then why was Lady Mary so keen on the marriage?' Roo said. 'You'd think she'd prefer her son getting off with an heiress like Elizabeth. You said the McGoogles weren't rich.'

'No, they weren't. But you're forgetting that Lady Mary was a woman of her time. She'd been brought up in the strict Christian ideology of the Scottish Presbyterian Church. She believed Alasdair was committed to Iona, even though there had been no formal engagement, and contemporary morality was inflexible. Alasdair's attachment to Iona was known and accepted; for him to back off, as he did, was considered extremely dishonourable. Records show some local dignitaries actually cut him, though they seem to have changed their minds when invited to his wedding with Elizabeth. Her fortune might have helped to reinstate him in their eyes, I suspect.'

'What happened to it when she died?' Roo asked. 'If no body was found, could Alasdair inherit?'

'Her money passed to him on their marriage: that was the law of the time,' Nigel responded. 'But he had little chance to enjoy it – he went off to Africa almost immediately. Lady Mary seems to have left it virtually untouched. In the end, Archie inherited it, with the title, the castle and all.'

'And Iona married the lot,' I said. 'Where *was* Archie at the time of Alasdair's wedding?'

'In Africa. There's no doubt of that, I assure you. He was suppressing a native uprising – the kind of thing that went down very well with the Victorians, though it would have been frowned upon by us. It was a particularly bloody insurrection, even by African standards; we have the documents to prove it. There's no way he could have been back in Scotland, even supposing a relationship between him and Iona, and there's no evidence of one. I suspect your dream took an assortment of facts and mixed them up. Dreams are not noted for their accuracy.'

I gave him a *very* cold shoulder. I can't stand it when these academic types turn patronising and superior.

Besides, the re-enactment scenes were nearly all finished now, so I didn't have to be charming any more.

'He could be right,' Roo said later. 'Your dream doesn't really fit in with the chain of events, does it? You obviously got Alasdair's love for Elizabeth confused with his connection to Iona. After all, it *was* just a dream. Dreams do muddle things.'

'It wasn't that *kind* of dream,' I said, though I was beginning to doubt myself. 'It was so . . . *real*.'

And, to Ash, 'What do *you* think?'

'Most dreams, like most ghosts, come from the dark places of the mind. How far they could be subject to an outside influence I don't know. The past is always with us, but . . .'

He was plainly hedging his bets. For a psychic researcher, he seemed rather cautious about believing in things.

But then, I don't believe in ghosts either. In daylight, the impression of my dream was fading, and I wondered, reluctantly, if Nigel might be right. I must have seen Iona's picture many times in a not-noticing sort of way; perhaps I'd heard him or HG say it was her. The rest could have come from a confusion in my imagination. I wasn't going to go around talking about my intuition or any of that bullshit; I'd leave that to Brie.

I took the opportunity to remove Roo from Ash's company (in case she was enjoying it) and take her into the dining room for a late breakfast.

Brie was in there, drinking something that looked like her own urine – camomile tea? – and eating a boiled egg with no marmite soldiers. Her latest diet. Yuk.

She was talking to Dorian because there was no one else around. Or rather, listening, in a sort of catatonic trance, while he explained the details of some computer game he'd invented. Brie, too, was obviously having a go at being a good listener, and was finding it even more heavy going than me. At least I'd had HG to practise on; the thought of doing it with Dorian was truly scary.

It must be very hard for HG, having a nerd for a son. I mean, at an age when he should have been cutting his first album and generally treading in his father's footsteps, he was *designing software*. Too embarrassing.

Brie looked up thankfully as we sat down. 'What've you guys been doing?' she asked.

'Checking up on the castle ghosts,' said Roo.

I hadn't wanted to mention it. I knew Brie would start intuiting as soon as the subject came up.

She did.

'Have you figured out what it was that I saw the other evening? It was like, this looming *shape*, just standing there, in the darkest part of the hall. It was only there for a second, but I saw it quite clearly—'

'Man or woman?' I said, helping myself to coffee. I knew an urge to upstage her with my dream, but I didn't want to sound all New-Age phoney about it.

'I don't know. I told you, it was just this *shape* . . .'

'Well, *what* shape?'

'I couldn't tell; it was dark. The shape was dark and the hall was dark and the evening was getting dark . . .'

'Then how could you see it?'

Dorian interrupted, which was probably just as well. The business of the dream was making me twitchy and suddenly I wanted all the ghost stuff to be nonsense. 'That actress woman saw something too; she said it was a man in Highland dress – but then, she *would* say that. And Morag's seen things.'

'Awful old hag.' Brie shuddered. 'In her case, it was probably DTs. That sort always drinks on the quiet.'

'She thinks strong drink is an instrument of the devil,' Dorian said. 'Except for whisky.'

Roo stood up abruptly, leaving her coffee untouched. 'I'm going for a walk,' she announced. 'I need some air.'

'You'd better be careful,' Dorian said. 'It can be dangerous if the mist comes down. I'll come with you. We can ask Dougal about the weather.'

That's what happens if you're a good listener. You get saddled with people who want to be listened to. Roo and Dorian went off together, and I took the opportunity to pump Brie about Ash.

'He's gay,' she said. 'He's got to be. One, he's absolutely beautiful, in a gay sort of way, and two, he never made even a flicker of a pass at me.'

My feelings exactly.

It was a strange sort of day and, though I didn't know it, about to get a lot stranger. Sundays are always a little weird when you're on location, because you feel you ought to be working and you're not, and at Dunblair there wasn't much to do. Alex had found a small room with a large TV screen and ensconced himself on the sofa in front of it, cuddling Fenny and saying he didn't feel well, so I went to the bedroom to paint my nails and do some serious thinking, though I wasn't certain what about. The disappearance of Elizabeth Courtney, Roo's love life (lack of), the niggling fact that Alex and I *still* hadn't had sex since he came to Dunblair. I decided to have some tea so I could order Winkworth about, but when I picked up the phone (all the bedrooms had one, like a hotel) a broad Scots accent told me he wasn't available.

'It's his day oot,' said the accent, possibly Dougal. 'And Morag's i' the kirk. One of the girrls is here tae cover for them. If there's something ye were wanting, I daresay ye could ask her.'

'Tell her to bring me some tea,' I said. 'Earl Grey.' I didn't really want it, but the germ of an idea had come to me, and I needed to talk to the girl.

When the tea arrived, it tasted more like PG Tips, stewed rather than brewed, dark and strong and bitter. But I didn't complain.

'Winkworth took my shoe to be mended,' I said, improvising. 'The heel came off. D'you know what he's done with it?'

The girl – Margaret, I think her name was – looked dumb. It wasn't difficult.

'Perhaps it's in his room,' I said. 'Could you look?'

'I'm no siccar . . .'

'I'll come with you,' I said. 'I know what it looks like.'

Fortunately, it didn't occur to her to point out that Winkworth would be unlikely to keep many women's shoes in his room. Although you never know with some guys . . .

Once we had found the room (but not the shoe), I dismissed her. 'Don't worry about it,' I said airily. 'I'll ask him myself.'

When I was sure Margaret had gone, I slipped back along the corridor and went in. It was a good thing doors weren't kept locked at Dunblair. I was slightly nervous – in detective thrillers, whenever the heroine goes to search a suspect's room, they're guaranteed to turn up in the middle. 'He's out,' I reassured myself. 'I've got plenty of time.' I didn't really know what I was looking for, or where to start, but it's customary to open drawers, so I did. It was a large room, lacking the Basilisk touch, comfortable and, for a man, fairly tidy. The drawers contained the usual things you find in men's drawers: socks, sweaters, boxer shorts. (Why do men always have so many socks? I swear they have more than women have tights or stockings.) In the cupboard, shirts, jeans, jackets, a couple of suits, a few ties. Owing to the informal lifestyle obtaining at Dunblair, he didn't normally wear a tie. In the shoe rack, mostly outdoor footwear and trainers. No pyjamas anywhere (he obviously slept naked or in his boxers), but a burgundy towelling bathrobe hung on the door to the en suite. In the bathroom, toothpaste, razor, Hugo Boss eau de cologne. In short, everything you would expect.

'This is boring,' I said out loud. 'Why isn't there any personal stuff?'

There were a couple of books by the bed: a Michael Marshall thriller and a book on Middle Eastern politics by someone called Adel Darwish who, from the jacket shot, appeared to be male. Also *Private Eye* and *The Economist*. What butler reads *Private Eye* and *The Economist*? He ought to have a trade publication, *Butling Weekly* or something. And the *Mail*, or the *Sun*, or . . .

Why wasn't there any personal stuff?

No diary, no address book, no laptop. (Presumably he carried his mobile with him, since there was a recharger plugged in at the wall.) No photographs. If he had a wife and two kids, there should be pictures. I *knew* he wasn't married . . .

Even so, there ought to be photographs of *somebody*. His mother, his sister, himself in school uniform, himself as a child with pet gerbil/kitten/tarantula. We all keep those photos, even the embarrassing ones. I've got my best PR shots framed at the mews, plus snaps of me with every famous person I've ever met, ready to include them in my autobiography, but back at my own flat there's a pin-up board with all the family ones. Me as a baby, Pan as a baby, Roo and me as kids on the beach, Roo and me in fancy dress, Mummy in the garden with assorted dogs and children, my grandparents, an aunt, some cousins. Me in a leather jacket on Ben Garvin's motorbike. Roo and me, respectively sixteen and eighteen, dolled up for a party. Me at drama college, as Juliet. Roo's graduation. I've even got some old sepia pictures of relatives long deceased, in the cloche hats and dropped waists of the 1920s, or in one case an Edwardian tea gown.

Winkworth had none. Very, very suspicious. I couldn't wait to tell Roo.

I found the briefcase under the bed. It was one of those multisectioned efforts with an optional shoulder strap, quality leather, unmistakably expensive. Not at all appropriate for a butler, I decided. And it was heavy, suggesting technology inside. The missing laptop.

It was also locked.

A fictional detective would know how to pick the lock, but I hadn't a clue. You were supposed to use a hairpin, only I'd never worn a hairpin in my life, and I wouldn't know what to do with it if I had. Or a nail file (I had those, though not on me). But this lock didn't look easily picked. It was much too efficient a lock for the requirements of a mere butler.

'I *knew* he was a fraud,' I said, feeling vindicated. A genuine butler would have *Butling Weekly* at his bedside, and pictures of his sweet, white-haired old mother in Surbiton, and the laptop on the desk, open for all the world to see. He wouldn't have a briefcase hidden furtively under the bed, with a lock on it that would have defeated James Bond . . .

I heard the footsteps just in time. (Thank God the corridor was uncarpeted.) I shoved the briefcase out of sight and, reduced to desperation, dived after it. Happily the bed was well off the floor and there was a frill screening me from view. I lifted it enough to see feet – girl's feet, in pink trainers. Margaret? I hadn't noticed her footwear, but pink trainers seemed likely. They padded towards the bathroom, did something meaningful there – changing the towels? – then returned towards the door and departed.

I wriggled out, feeling horribly shaky, waited a minute or two, and left.

Roo wasn't around, so I sent her a text. 'Serched Ws rm. Defnitly fake. Tell u al latr.' Then I hung about, feeling impatient. I'm not good at waiting.

Roo got back around lunchtime.

'What have you done?' she demanded, panicking unnecessarily. 'You can't go around searching people's bedrooms just because you don't get on. It's . . . it's invasion of privacy.'

'He's invading our privacy,' I said, 'by pretending to be a butler when he isn't. Anyway, there's no point in flapping over something I've already done.'

'What did you find?'

'It's what I *didn't* find,' I said, and told her all about it.

'It's odd,' she conceded, 'but it isn't conclusive. Maybe the family photos are in the attic of his house in Kensington. Maybe his wife has them. She could have left him, and taken the children *and* the pictures. Or maybe they're in his briefcase.'

'Rubbish,' I said. 'People don't keep personal pix in a locked briefcase . . . unless they're actually incriminating. Perhaps he really *is* planning to rob the place, and the pictures show him with notorious Mafiosi.'

'You're getting carried away,' Roo said. 'Harry isn't the criminal type. He's just—'

'He's up to *something*,' I declared. 'We have to find out what. HG will be very grateful.'

'There's nothing else we can do.'

'Yes there is. We can open that case.'

'Lock-picking isn't one of my talents,' Roo said. 'Nor yours. So—'

'There's a gun room here somewhere. We could shoot the lock off.'

'You know, I don't need mousse or hair gel,' Roo remarked. 'With you around, my hair stands on end by itself. Of course we can't *shoot the lock off*. For one thing, it would be awfully noticeable afterwards. Not to mention the noise involved.'

I waved aside *afterwards*. 'Once we know the truth about him, it won't signify.'

'Supposing the truth is that he's just a normal butler? It isn't a crime to lock your briefcase, particularly with people like you around.'

'You can't keep changing your position,' I said. 'You've admitted it's odd about the photos. It might be far-fetched to suggest he's a crook, but he *is* likely to be an undercover reporter.'

'Which reminds me—'

'Anything he's written will be on the computer, which is why he's locked it away. We can get Dorian to hack in and retrieve it. He's pretty keen on you.'

'Don't,' Roo said, with a shudder. 'He tried to kiss me today. He says he likes older women – it's not as if I'm *that* old, either – and we have a connection, and I really understand him. I should never have let him show me his computer game.'

I burst out laughing. 'That's what comes of being a good listener. I *knew* I was right to give it a miss.'

'Anyhow, never mind about Dorian – or Harry. We've got a real problem to sort out. We heard this morning that there are a couple of journos in the village. They were in the pub the other night, only I didn't realise. They're flashing cheque books and trying to get the inside story on your row with the Basilisk.'

'It doesn't matter if they do,' I said. 'I won.'

'It *does* matter. If anything got into the gutter press, HG would hate it, and you can't blame him. Basilisa *is* his wife, after all. And without HG we have no series.'

'There's nothing we can do,' I said. 'You're not used to working with celebs, are you? We have the paparazzi on our tails all the time;

it goes with the territory. We can always leak them something about my wedding to keep them happy.'

'I think they'd prefer the fight,' Roo said. 'Violence beats romance in the popularity stakes, any day.'

Ruth

Sunday was usually a quiet day, time to have a lie-in and do nothing, a vital oasis of calm in the chaos of the working week. There was little to show that this Sunday was going to be any different, no forewarning of the drama that was to come. I lost my lie-in to Delphi's dream-phantoms, my solitary walk to Dorian's determination to keep me company. HG, he told me, had taken Basilisa away for a day or so to placate her, visiting an exclusive hotel with designer cuisine, deluxe indoor pool and spa, beauty therapy (for the Basilisk) and golf (for HG). The thought of having to work with her again appalled me, but that was my job, I would do it if it killed me, and in the meantime I tried to clear my mind of worry and anticipation and enjoy my day off. I was succeeding so well that Dorian's amorous advances went unnoticed until he flung his arms round me and attempted to eat my face.

'What the hell—'

'You know how I feel – you must do,' he said as I struggled to push him away. 'You've always been so . . . I mean, no one else *understands* like you do. I can tell you anything . . .'

'I'm much too old for you!'

'I like older women. Older women are cool. I've met lots of girls, of course – I've been out with lots of girls—'

'Of course.'

'– but I'm too mature for the young ones. I didn't fancy Basilisa, but she had the right idea. I need someone really *adult*, someone compatible who can enter into my interests. You and I would be perfect together. Besides, I've got much more sexual energy than older guys. Men peak at eighteen – I'm nearly at my peak. Women peak at twenty-five. We'd be ideal in bed – both almost at our peaks. We could have such great sex—'

'I'm not feeling very peaky right now,' I said hastily. 'Dorian, pull yourself together. I – just don't think of you that way. It's very sweet of you to—'

'I'm not *sweet*!' I'd got him in the ego – and I was trying to be nice. Fatal. 'I'm a *man*, not some cuddly little boy! If we were in ancient Rome I could've been a centurion by now. Did I tell you how many hits I had on my website last year? I'm much smarter than my dad. I know he likes you, but he's *really* old – he's so old it's obscene – and anyway, there's my step-mother. You *can't* fancy dad – can you?'

'No, of course not, but—'

'There you are!' He grabbed me again, lips homing in on mine. I saw to it they missed. 'Ruth – you're so special . . .'

'No I'm not! I mean, I do like you, but I can't – I don't – oh, for God's sake cut it out! I really don't need this . . .'

He drew back, looking hurt. The kicked-puppy effect. 'I thought we . . . had a connection.'

'Well, we haven't,' I snapped. We'd walked towards the village, since weather-prophet Dougal McDougall had said the day would turn foggy, and wandering round the loch might be dangerous. The Dirk and Sporran loomed up ahead, the inn sign swaying slightly in the wind. It showed a warrior in full Highland regalia, wielding his dirk and flaunting his sporran. It was Angus, I suspected, who had the questionable sense of humour. 'We're going into the pub. You aren't having any alcohol because you're too young, but I'm going to get a coffee and a cheese sandwich. Okay?'

'I have alcohol *frequently*. I'm not a baby.'

'Under law you're too young. End of story. Are you coming with me or not?'

We went into the pub, which was when Dirk filled me in on the roving journalists. Coffee was a sophisticated development for a bar in the wilds of Scotland, but Angus, ever shrewd, had extended his repertoire for the benefit of his new clientele. He was even talking of a cappuccino machine. I added lots of milk – it was on the bitter side – and fished for more information about the two hacks.

'Do you know what paper they're from?'

'The *Mail* – the *Mirror* – no, the *Scoop*.' Dirk shrugged. 'They've been going round the village axing questions – ay, and offering folks money too. O' course, nae decent body would ha' a word to say to 'em, but there'll always be one or two for whom money talks, e'en in Lochnabu.'

'You're very loyal to HG,' I said doubtfully, 'considering he isn't really the Laird.'

'Ay well, he's been guid for business. He employs folk, spends money – he built the new school, for the kids under eleven. He supports us, we support him. We never had a laird as did sae muckle for the community.'

Well done HG, I thought. Open-handed *and* clever. 'Can you keep an eye on the journalists?' I asked. 'There's no way to get rid of them, but it would be something to know what they're up to.' They weren't really my problem, but there were enough pitfalls ahead, visible or otherwise, without adding tabloid scandal.

'Mebbe there's a way,' Dirk said, looking pensive, but I didn't take him seriously.

I should have done.

I walked back to the castle with Dorian in a silence that was constrained on his part and abstracted on mine – my thoughts were elsewhere. Getting Delphi's text so horrified me I even forgot about the rogue journos, at least for a short while.

It was evening before they were recalled to my attention.

Delphi and I were in the dining room enjoying pre-dinner drinks with Mortimer and Nigel. (Actually, they were *pre*-pre-dinner drinks; on Sundays, we started early.) When I say *'enjoying'*, we were enjoying the drinks, even if we had mixed feelings about some of the company. Ash hadn't showed up yet, Russell was last heard of heading for the bath, Alex (according to Delphi) was feeling off-colour, and Brie had appropriated the maid Basilisa brought back from Mande Susu and was having her toenails pedicured, her chakras re-energised, and so on. We were discussing Elizabeth Courtney, as usual, with Morty advancing a new theory that she'd had a fall, knocking her head and suffering from concussion, and had then wandered too close to the lake, slipped in and drowned.

'Unlikely,' Nigel said. 'The body would have turned up. After drowning, gases are produced in the corpse which cause it to float. I'm not well up on the forensic details –' he had already made it clear he knew more than the rest of us – 'but I can assure you, if someone dies in the water the body has to be weighted to make it sink. Hence the – er – concrete boots favoured by gangsters.'

'So if she went into the lake,' Delphi said, 'she had help. Someone put her there, and made sure she stayed on the bottom.'

'I must say,' I said, 'I think it would be difficult for anybody to disappear as completely as she did by accident.'

Morty looked as damped as his ego would allow, although the disparagement of his idea wasn't personal. At least, not in my case. Delphi had never liked him and Nigel, I surmised, saw him as competition in the TV fame stakes.

In short, it was a normal evening: overcurrents of polite disagreement, undercurrents of rivalry and nastiness. Being stuck on location with colleagues for far too long, even if the location is a luxury castle, is invariably detrimental to working relationships. Things were sliding gradually downhill.

Then Harry came in, with Ash on his heels, and everything changed.

I think I said, 'What's wrong?' because it was so obvious something was.

'The two hacks from the *Scoop* have gone walkabout,' Harry said.

'You mean they're spying on us?' Delphi demanded, looking round as if she expected to see eyes peering from the portraits, or a telescopic lens poking between the curtains.

'That was probably the idea. They wanted to find a way into the castle grounds and someone in the village seems to have sent them to the far end of the loch. The terrain there is dangerous, there's a mist come down, and they haven't got back. We're sending out search parties led by anyone who knows the area well enough.' He was already booted and jacketed; so, surprisingly, was Ash.

I remembered Dirk's expression earlier in the day, and my own idle phrase: *There's no way to get rid of them.* Suddenly, I felt like a murderess. 'Oh God . . .'

'What is it?' Ash said, detecting more than normal horror in my face.

'I think it might be my fault,' I said, stammering a rapid explanation. The others treated it with the contempt it probably deserved – 'I thought Delphinium was the one into self-dramatisation' from Harry – but I still felt a relentless panic knotting in my stomach.

'I'm coming with you,' I said.

'Don't be silly.' Delphi added her voice to the general disapproval. '*You* don't know the area. And it's dark and cold out there.'

'For once,' Harry said, 'I agree. You'd just be in the way. We're covering one section of the grounds with Young Andrew; Jules and Sandy are doing the other with Dougal McDougall and the dogs. Dirk and Angus are leading search parties round the village in case the buggers turned back. Sit down, finish your drink, eat your dinner. This is a job for the men.'

Oops. I saw Delphi bristle. While prepared to exploit her femininity whenever it suited her, she didn't react well to assertions of gender superiority. Harry was topping up a hip flask from a bottle of single malt; Ash turned to me and said, 'He's right, you know. There's nothing you can do.'

'Why are *you* going?' Morty asked on a faintly scornful note.

'I do rock climbing. It might come in handy.' He really was full of surprises.

'Wait for me,' I said. 'I won't be in the way – that's bullshit. You need all the back up you can get. I do first aid.'

'So do I,' said Ash and Harry in chorus, but I was already out of the room.

Delphi followed. 'If you're going, I'm going,' she said, a typical volte-face. 'A job for the men, indeed! Huh, huh and triple huh!'

'Anyway,' I said, 'we have eyes and ears. That's what's needed. Don't forget your torch.' We all had them in case of power cuts, or for walking back from the village in the dark.

As we approached our rooms, Fenny came rushing out to greet Delphi, curly tail wagging furiously. He'd evidently decided to abandon master for mistress. It wasn't a good move on his part.

'We'll take him!' she declared, struck with sudden inspiration. 'Elton and Sting have gone with the other group – we ought to have a dog too. And I'm sure he has bloodhound in him somewhere.'

'He's a pedigree bichon! Delphi—'

'Spiritually,' she insisted, 'he's a bloodhound.'

I dived into my bedroom and dragged on boots and Barber at warp speed in the hope that if I got downstairs fast enough, Delphi – and Fenny – might be left behind. I knew the hope was vain, of course. When you wanted her to hurry, Delphi would take an hour to get ready; but should you want her to delay, she was guaranteed to be with you in minutes. She emerged even as I closed my door, wearing fashion wellies patterned in raised gold swirls and a Vivienne Westwood jacket – a safer bet than Matthew Williamson on the faux fur issue – that appeared to have been patched together from a combination of leather and dead Wookie. The impression was vaguely reminiscent of a barbarian warrior-maiden in a sword-and-sorcery epic, only with less cleavage on view.

'Is that . . . suitable?' I faltered.

'Just because I'm joining a search party,' Delphi said, 'it doesn't mean I have to dress like a rescue worker in an earthquake. Besides, it keeps me warm.'

I didn't attempt further protest.

We found Harry, Ash and Young Andrew waiting in the hall. (Harry had correctly guessed that if they didn't wait we'd try to follow, and probably get lost ourselves.)

'You're not – bringing – that – dog!' Harry expostulated, seeing Fenny under Delphi's arm.

(Men don't expostulate much nowadays, it's a little archaic, but Delphi has that effect on people.)

'Of course I am,' she said at her most irritatingly reasonable. 'There are two people lost out there, maybe injured: he can sniff them out. Like a St Bernard. I'm training him to attack journalists, but I'm sure he'll get the difference.'

Ash succumbed to a smile; Harry looked murderous.

'If he's a nuisance,' he said, 'I'll throw him in the loch. Can he walk, or do you carry him?'

Delphi set the dog down, hooking the lead on to his collar. 'Do we have an item of their clothing for him to pick up the scent?' she enquired, ignoring his sarcasm.

'Airhead,' Harry snorted.

On which note, we filed out into the dusk.

Though spring was officially here, it grew dark early – we were a long way north – and the last of the daylight was fading rapidly from the rim of the sky. The air was cold and growing colder. A white mist lay along the borders of the loch, looking as if a cloud had drifted down and wrapped itself like an ermine stole around the shoreline. Twilight gleamed faintly on the open water. The dim slopes of the nearer mountains rose out of the mist like a fairy country that floats above an unattainable horizon. The castle was still clear, but the fog crept closer even as we stood there. We all switched on our torches. The beams didn't show much except the ground immediately before us, but made the evening darker. Harry was having a word with Young Andrew. 'Come on,' he said to Delphi and me, 'since you insist on coming.'

His attitude was more than justified. We weren't going to do any good. I was there from a hazy sense of guilt, relic of my conversation with Dirk that morning, Delphi out of sheer pig-headedness. Or maybe it was that neither of us wanted to spend the rest of the night waiting for news, with only Nigel and Morty for company. Fenny scurried along happily, checking out passing smells, obviously believing the whole exercise was entirely for his benefit.

A wall marked the boundary of the garden and the transition to the uncultivated grounds. On the eastern side of the loch there were fields running down almost to the water where

HG let local farmers graze their livestock, but here on the west the terrain was steeper and wooded. We went through the gate, latching it behind us, and began to follow a rough track that meandered between the trees. I'd often meant to explore this way, but work had left me little leisure and somehow when Sunday came around I was always too tired – or too lazy – for serious walking. Stupid, I thought. I'd been a footstep away from beautiful countryside and now when I got to investigate it was in darkness and fog. *Nacht und Nebel.* The allusion made me shiver. That was what the Nazis called it, when people were arrested and made to vanish without a trace, so even their nearest and dearest would never know what had happened to them. I didn't like the idea of tabloid hacks on the prowl, but I hadn't meant the villagers to dispose of them for good.

I was overreacting on the guilt issue, I know. But in Scotland in the dark, even the flimsiest spectres can grow huge, acquiring claws and teeth.

Harry was up ahead with Young Andrew, followed by Ash, then Delphi and me. Although we kept close together, we didn't talk much. Harry and Young Andrew paused from time to time to consult.

'Is he looking for tracks?' Delphi whispered during one brief halt, referring presumably to the guide. 'You know: broken twigs, footprints, that sort of thing.'

'He's not Aragorn,' I whispered back. The vision of Young Andrew as Strider, listening, ear to the ground, for the rumour of distant feet, made me stifle a giggle.

After a short exchange about our route, they went on. We trailed after them.

The mist had closed in and beyond the torch beams was a grey, formless world. At Ash's suggestion we used only one between us, saving the battery on the other since we had no idea how long we'd be out. Harry and Young Andrew also shared. Ash, no doubt accustomed to working in the dark, kept his switched off most of the time, following the two leaders without a stumble. Tree roots sprawled across the path like knobbled snakes, ready to trip the unwary, and the occasional low branch brushed my face with twiggy fingers, but our pace was slow and such hazards were a minor factor. There seemed to be little undergrowth and the trees grew some way apart. We couldn't see far to either side; I knew the lake was on our left, quite close by, but the night was windless and the sleeping water made no sound. Once, there was a kind of slither and a soft splash a short distance away – we all jumped – but according to Young Andrew's unruffled mumble it was only a small animal.

I found myself muttering the traditional prayer Jennifer had taught us in childhood:

> *From ghoulies and ghosties and long-legged beasties*
> *And things that go bump in the night,*
> *Good Lord, defend us.*

Delphi had always thought *long-legged beasties* meant spiders, of which she was terrified. I had marked reservations about *ghoulies*. But in the gloom it was all too easy to imagine a dripping head rising from a dim swirl of water, serpentine neck extended, or grey shaggy shapes flickering between the trees, trailing bits of shroud. I found myself wishing I'd never seen *The Blair Witch Project* or *The Evil Dead*. Woods in daylight are beautiful places, with the sun-spatter coming through the leaves and the piping of invisible birds, but by night they change, becoming shadow-forests haunted by our darkest fears. A few thousand years ago our ancestors trod lightly through such woods, in dread of nocturnal hunters: the wolf, the bear, the sabre-toothed tiger. And then there were the demons of our own invention, the blood-drinkers of nightmare and legend: the vampire and the werewolf, Grendel and his mother, the Ringwraith and the Grey King . . .

'Should we call out?' Delphi asked. 'They might be nearby and not know we're here.'

'Good idea,' Harry conceded.

Every so often we called, paused, listened, called again. No answer. The ground grew more rugged, making walking harder. The damp of the mist and the chill of the night began to eat into me. Discomfort took the edge off my fears, but I had no intention of complaining: I wasn't giving the men the chance to act superior.

'Aren't you c-cold?' I said to Delphi, keeping my voice low.

'Not really. This jacket is amazingly warm.'

It would be. My supposedly practical and weatherproof Barber wasn't doing the job at all. But then, I only had a light sweater underneath.

'Your teeth are chattering,' Ash said, passing me his scarf. It was long and wide and felt like cashmere. 'Tuck that inside your jacket and wrap it round you. It'll help.'

'Thanks.'

I saw the turn of Delphi's head as she glanced towards me, but I couldn't distinguish her expression.

Fenny created a diversion by stopping to growl, and then bark, but whatever it was must have fled. There was a growing murmur up ahead, like the rush of water.

'That'd be the Cawdron,' Young Andrew said, in response to a question from Ash. 'We maun go careful here. Mony folks ha' slippit in wi'out seeing the edge i' the dark.'

'What's the Cauldron?' Delphi asked.

'It's a pool,' Harry explained. 'There's a stream flowing into the loch via a couple of short falls and it's scooped out the Cauldron among the rocks. It isn't very wide or deep but the water swirls around like a whirlpool and the drop into it is about fifteen feet. If you missed your footing and went in you could easily be knocked out and drown.'

We went forward cautiously. The murmur swelled to a roar, but fog and darkness alter your perceptions and it was hard to judge how close we were. Harry and Young Andrew halted suddenly, and the rest of us came up beside them, Delphi picking up Fenny in case he attempted to leap over the edge. The earth thinned to rock and a chasm opened at our feet, a roughly circular pit perhaps ten yards across at the widest point. Foam gleamed on the fall that poured down from above; the torch beams glanced along the steep sides enclosing the pool. Below, the water seethed and bubbled, spilling over another, shorter fall through an opening in the rocks down to the loch. Crawling plants trailed over the lip of the ravine; a stunted shrub clung to the further edge, root filaments webbing the rock face like a wispy growth of beard. My torchlight skittered downwards and arced along the rim of the pool. At one point the rock didn't drop sheer into the water – perhaps the level was low – and there was an exposed sliver of earth or stone, a snarl of tangled stems. And something else, something white, hooked on the claws of the plant.

A shoe.

To be exact, a white canvas trainer. It was impossible to be certain in the torch-glimmer, but it didn't look as if it had been there long. Bits of it were still clean enough to gleam in the probing light.

Harry said: 'Shit.'

'Has anyone called the police yet?' I said, stating the obvious.

'Yeah,' he said, 'but the professionals won't come looking till morning. You've got to be a local to risk a search at night.' He added, after a pause: 'Does anyone know if those hacks wore trainers?'

No one knew.

'I could climb down and take a look at it,' Ash offered, discarding his jacket, which was padded and bulky.

'In the dark?' Harry sounded scathing. 'Don't be idiotic.'

'It isn't far, and there are plenty of handholds. If a couple of you keep your torches fixed on the rock I can do it. By day, it would be nothing.'

'It's much too dangerous,' I said.

'You're crazy.' Delphi.

But he had already handed me the jacket and was making his way round the edge, following the oval of his own torch-light. 'You can cross above the fall,' Harry said. 'They've put stepping stones in the stream.'

'I see them . . .'

The ray of the torch crossed the water in three short bounds, then zigzagged along the far side of the pit, pausing every so often to dart down towards the pool. Right above the shoe it stopped, and went out.

'Harry . . . Ruth . . . can you focus here?'

We did our best to comply. They were good torches, sending two distorted oblongs of radiance flickering across the rocks, but the shadows played tricks, shrinking into every crevice or stretching out like a spear behind each tiny notch of stone. It was impossible to tell rock-knuckle from twig-finger, or what was solid from what would snap.

'This is bloody stupid,' Harry said as Ash lowered himself over the edge. 'For God's sake be careful.'

'I have a bad feeling about this,' Delphi announced in the language of *Star Wars*.

Young Andrew muttered something in Scots too broad to understand.

I didn't say anything at all. My breath stuck in my chest; I moved the torch beam to instruction, desperate not to let my hand shake. There are some instants in your life when you exist totally in the moment: there is no past, no future, only Now. A Now so powerful that it excludes all thought. The moment when he says 'I love you' (or 'It's over'); the peak of orgasm; the zing of fear. The best moments, the worst moments.

This was one of the worst.

Ash moved down the rock with the agility of Legolas, only slower. Much slower. There was a second when his foothold slipped – he seemed to be hanging on by his fingertips – then he retrieved his position and was somehow back on track. Harry said, 'Fuck.' I breathed again, but not much.

At the bottom Ash turned round carefully, steadying himself against the wall of the ravine. Then he dropped to a crouch and felt his way over stone and plant-tangle, reaching for the shoe. I could see the surge of the water over his ankles, buffeting his legs. As he grabbed the trainer, trying to yank it free – the laces must have been caught – he almost went in.

'Don't do that!' Delphi begged. *'Please.'*

'It's okay. There's nothing else here, I'm pretty sure.' He was fiddling with the laces, tying them together to loop round his arm.

'How many shoes did he expect to find?' Delphi said.

'He means there's no body,' Harry said tersely.

'Oh . . .'

We trained the torch beams on to the rock face again, and there was a further hideous interlude while Ash climbed back up. He was quicker than on the descent, and didn't slip, but even when he reached the top it was a few seconds before my heart started beating again and normal service was resumed. A sudden lightning-flash of awareness streaked through my brain: *If anything had happened to him . . .*

I didn't take it further. Not then, not later. There was too much else to think about, and *further* was a place I wasn't ready to go. But the lightning had flashed, and it wouldn't quite go out.

Guided by Young Andrew, we skirted the pit and crossed the stream (not difficult: it was narrow and the stepping-stones were broad and flat) to join Ash. A torchlit examination of the shoe didn't tell us much, except that it had belonged to a man with size nine feet.

'Not worn much,' Harry deduced.

'How do you work that out?' I asked.

'It doesn't pong.'

Delphi insisted on encouraging Fenny to sniff it. 'Then he can track down its wearer!' she said brilliantly.

'The smell might've washed off in the pool,' I said.

'It's not that wet,' said Ash. 'The wearer could have gone into the pool, but the shoe didn't. It's only damp from splash-back.'

'Could a body be swept away over the lower fall?' Harry asked Young Andrew.

'In the winter months maybe, if it wasna froze. But there's no muckle water tae gang over it the noo,' Andrew responded inscrutably.

But Harry had been living at Dunblair for over half a year, and his ear was attuned to the native brogue. 'Good,' he said. 'We'll keep going.' And to Delphi: 'Better get that bloodhound of yours on the trail.'

'No need to sneer,' Delphi snapped. 'He's more of a blood-hound than . . . than you are a butler any day.'

'I wasn't sneering,' Harry said. 'I have absolute faith in him. Anyway, I'm an extremely good butler. I give satisfaction, as the saying goes, whoever I'm with.'

'You're a fake,' Delphi said, ignoring my elbow in her ribs. Possibly she couldn't feel it through the layers of Wookie.

'And if you come up with one more sexual innuendo, I'll – I'll –'

'What sexual innuendo? Don't tell me you're one of those deluded women who think they're so beautiful every man they meet must be after them. So sorry, Miss Dacres, but your fan mail hasn't exactly been piling up on the doormat—'

'My fan mail,' Delphi said, her voice rising, 'is dealt with by my fan club, in London, where my PA – where *several* people – spend *hours* answering it. And I'm *not* deluded, because I'm marrying an incredibly handsome, gorgeous, *rich* young man who adores me and who—'

Who is currently back at the castle watching TV while the rest of us are trekking through the woods in the dark in search of stray journalists.

I didn't say it, Delphi didn't say it. The words hung in the air, unsaid.

Then Delphi walked into a bush.

'Look where you're going,' Harry said, taking her arm and steering her back on to the path.

'I think you're part of a criminal plot,' she resumed in a low voice. 'A butler should be more like Jeeves, or—'

'Jeeves was a valet.'

'Or Batman's Alfred—'

'You can call me Alfred,' Harry said, 'if it makes you happy.'

I managed to kick Delphi on the shins – in a minute she'd be telling him she'd searched his room – and she subsided, switching her attention to encouraging Fenny.

'Does HG's property extend much further?' I asked, fishing for a viable change of subject.

'All round the loch,' Harry replied. 'He's got about twenty-five thousand acres. It's a big estate.'

'Do we go on till we bump into the search party coming the other way?'

'We go on till I can get a signal on my mobile and report finding the shoe,' Harry said. 'After that, we'll see. We can't scramble about in the woods all night. Still, it really depends on Andy here. What do you think?'

Unnerved by the mantle of responsibility which had settled so suddenly on his shoulders, Young Andrew was silent for some time. 'I'm clemmed,' he volunteered at last.

'What's clemmed?' Delphi hissed in my ear.

'No idea,' I said.

'Hungry,' Ash explained briefly. We'd all missed dinner.

'Good point,' Harry said. 'We won't go much further. It'll take a while to get back, anyway. We could try the other path higher up the slope.'

'It's no safe the nicht,' Young Andrew demurred. The thought of food had evidently had an effect on him. 'It's mortal steep, that way.'

'All right then, we'll retrace our steps. But we should try calling again first.'

We called – 'Hello? Hello? Anyone there? Can you hear us?' – feeling slightly stupid, the way you do when you're yelling for someone and you don't even know their name. Our shouts fell flat, absorbed and deadened by the mist-wall all around us. Fenny barked in support – he had a big bark for such a small dog – but it sounded little more than a yap in the vastness of the fogbound night. Then we stood silent, listening. Hearing nothing. Fenny barked again. Harry tried his mobile in vain.

'We'd better go back,' he said.

'Wait a minute,' Delphi said. Fenny was pulling on the leash, tugging her forward and barking madly. 'I think he's on to something.'

'Probably a dead rabbit,' Harry retorted.

Delphi let the dog drag her off the track, veering towards

the lake, the torch wavering in her left hand. The four of us trooped after her.

'Careful!' Harry admonished. 'There's uneven ground here and it gets boggy. You might slip.' He took the torch from her, holding it steady and gripping her arm to support her.

'Can you hear anything?' she demanded. 'I thought I—'

'Of course I can't hear anything with that bloody dog making such a racket!'

They were going too fast for the terrain and inevitably she skidded, or he skidded, and they both slithered several yards, winding up in a heap halfway to the loch while Fenny, released from bondage, shot off along the bank, trailing his lead.

'Are you okay?' I called out as Ash, Young Andrew and I approached more slowly.

I couldn't see who was on top of whom, but I heard Delphi say, '*Do* you mind?' and 'Keep your hands to yourself!' during the disentanglement process. Then she got up, protesting almost tearfully, 'Of course I'm not okay! I'm *covered* in mud and this is a nine-hundred-pound jacket and it's utterly ruined—'

'I told you not to wear it—'

'Don't you *dare* say *I told you so* – and I've just been pawed by a sex-crazed fake butler and – where's Fenny?'

Fenny, some distance ahead, had evidently stopped and was barking more enthusiastically than ever. And beyond the bark, there were voices.

'Shut up, you little bugger! – Watch out, it could be savage. – Perhaps it's with a search party. – It's a fucking lapdog, you moron! Search parties have Alsatians and bloodhounds.'

'He's not a lapdog!' Delphi yelled indignantly. 'He's a bichon frisee!'

'He's a hero,' Harry said, smothering laughter.

We'd found the missing hacks after all.

It was the usual sort of story. Eager for a closer look at Dunblair, they had borrowed a ladder (from Dirk – very suspicious) and climbed over the wall that bordered HG's property. It was a long jump down and one of them had slightly twisted his ankle on landing. Then they'd tried to make their way round the loch towards the castle, falling into a bog in the process, stumbling over tree roots, and aggravating the twisted ankle until it became a sprain and its owner was virtually incapacitated. His associate tried to help him, supporting him as he hobbled, staying close to the lakeside for fear of getting lost in the fog. Inevitably they'd fallen again, the ankle was agony, the mist thickened, their mobiles wouldn't work and evening found them without a torch, left with no choice but to wait for rescue.

Neither of them, incidentally, had lost a shoe.

They hailed us with more indignation than relief, apparently feeling that their plight was all our fault anyway, since we'd made their job impossible by refusing to leak snippets of scandal, bitch up our colleagues on the record, or give interviews detailing ex-lovers' penis size (or lack of it) and sexual performance. Such uncooperative behaviour had driven them to today's exploit and their subsequent predicament.

'You've got a story now,' Ash pointed out. 'Your own.'

But the tabloid-reading public have only a limited interest in hacks with ankle sprains, though the two of them agreed rather disconsolately that something could be made of Delphi's participation. (Delphi, who was deeply annoyed by their reception of Fenny, looked partly mollified.) They were even more pissed off when Harry explained they would have to wait some time for a full rescue, since we would have to return to base and send a boat and stretcher crew for the injured man.

'What about Hot God's helicopter?' he demanded between gulps from Harry's hip flask. 'Can't he airlift me out of here?'

'He hasn't got one,' Harry said brightly. 'Sorry. He has a private plane but he keeps it at Inverness airport. It wouldn't be any use here.'

Then the other man decided he didn't want to wait with his chum, causing a further deterioration in the situation. Eventually he was persuaded to stay – Harry gave him the hip flask – with Young Andrew to keep them both company, while the rest of us headed back to the castle. Harry knew the way well enough for our return.

'It should have been me who stayed,' he said, 'but I'd probably have pushed either or both of them in the loch.'

'It should have been me,' said Ash, 'but I'm better with the dead.'

'It should've been me,' I said. 'This was my fault all along.'

'It wasn't going to be me,' said Delphi. 'I've been a heroine but I'm not going to be a martyr.'

So we left Young Andrew to his fate.

'I wonder whose trainer it was?' I said.

'We may never know,' said Harry.

(In fact, we discovered later it belonged to one of the village lads currently helping in the garden. He'd gone for a stroll in the woods above the Cauldron with a local girl, removed various items of clothing including his shoes – though not, of course, his socks: men never do – and a trainer had been kicked away in the excitement, falling over the edge. As it was far too early in the year for such outdoor activities by the time we located him he had a bad cold, a splinter in his foot, and – interestingly – a black eye. The identity of his partner was never established, but one of the maids had skinned knuckles and an air of quiet satisfaction for the next several days.)

By the time we got back to the castle we were all cold, famished and desperate for a drink.

'I'd better go with the boat party,' Harry said with resignation. 'Make sure Cedric keeps plenty of hot food ready for Young Andy and me when we get back. Remember, he's clemmed; he may just have eaten those journalists by the time we get there.'

'I hope so,' I said.

'Not *both* of them,' said Delphi. 'I want a big picture of Fenny and me on the front page of the *Scoop*, saying what a great bloodhound he is. After all, he was the one who found them.'

We went into the entrance hall, pulled off boots and jackets – 'I'll *never* get this clean!': Delphi on the Wookie – and were greeted by a welcoming party of Russell, Morag and Cedric, who appeared from the direction of the kitchen with a tray of hot toddies and assurances of dinner whenever we were ready.

'You should have given me a shout,' Russell said. 'I'd have come with you.'

'You were in the bath,' I pointed out.

He went off with Harry to sort out the final stage of the rescue, and Delphi, Ash and I, flushed from the abrupt transition to central heating and hot whisky, went into the drawing room to find the others. Morag told us HG and Basilisa were away for the night; Dorian was in his lair; Brie, we learned later, had gone to bed early with a face pack. Morty and Nigel turned to us with mild interest – 'Did you find them?' – and Alex was on the sofa talking to a man I'd never seen before. An elderly man with silver-streaked hair and a face in which the collapsed remnants of good looks still lingered, like left-over guests after an all-night party. At a second glance, something about him was faintly – very faintly – familiar. Alex looked up, saw Delphi, said automatically, 'What *have* you been doing?' and didn't wait for the answer.

'Look who's here!' he went on. 'Why haven't I met him before? You never even talk about him and I think he's fabby. We're best friends already. He's going to come to our wedding and give you away. Isn't it fantastico?'

Delphi dropped her glass. The whisky-glow drained from her cheeks, leaving her so white I thought she would faint.

'Hello,' she said in a voice that was almost unrecognisable.

Then I realised who it was.

Her father.

Chapter 8: Petting Party

Delphinium

There he was, sitting on a sofa in the Relatively Normal Drawing Room, drinking HG's liquor, all nose-to-nosey with Alex. My father. Just for a minute, I got that awful draining sensation again, when everything seems to be oozing out of you and you have no strength, no power, no control. I told myself it was sheer surprise. I hadn't forgotten about the call from Pan, but I'd simply never expected him to head my way. He's running out of daughters, I thought. I'm the last resort. Scraping the barrel. The dregs in the wine glass. Natalie's gone, Pan's not interested, he's stuck with me. I'm too old and not pretty enough for his taste, but he can have fun giving me away.

He used to call me Princess, when I was four feet tall and had dark blonde curls to my waist. (Well, mouse blonde, and it wasn't far to my waist in those days.) He'd read me stories, or tell me stories – I'm sure he did, though I can't remember any of them – and play records for me, and teach me the words of old songs. He was the one who liked me to have pretty clothes, adult fashions in miniature, who encouraged my childish vanity and an inclination to dress up. He once gave me my grandmother's pearls to wear to a party – I can't have been more than eight – though Mummy was furious when she found out, saying I might have lost or damaged them. She was right, too, I thought with hindsight. He'd taught me from infancy how important it was to be pretty, because only the pretty are popular and loved; how I must have admirers and boyfriends when I grew up, and marry a prince like all true princesses. I called him Daddy then, and for years after he left I dreamed of my daddy, and cried and cried over the end of *The Railway Children*, when Jenny Agutter runs down the platform with the fumes from the steam train billowing around her, calling out, 'Daddy! My Daddy!'

I couldn't call him Daddy now. I couldn't call him anything. I let him kiss my cheek and sat in an adjacent chair while he told me how much he approved of my chosen prince, and called Roo to mind with the mechanical charm he reserved for people who didn't interest him. He'd never thought her much of a friend for me, I realised: too quiet, too timid, a fraction too low down the social scale. It's strange, the things you pick up instinctively which don't make it to your conscious mind sometimes for decades. He said he was looking forward to meeting Brie – whose social origins clearly didn't matter since she was famous and sexy, and joined Alex in wedding talk. The assumption that he would give the bride away was made without my being consulted. I didn't contradict him. I wanted him to go – I certainly didn't want him at my wedding – but my brain was temporarily numb. I felt trapped by the ease with which he'd re-entered my life, by his expectations, his charm. Pan didn't seem to have made a dent in his assurance; he was confident of a welcome and Alex, at least, had provided one.

'Roddy's staying in the village,' Alex said. That's my father's name: Rodney St John Dacres. Rodney 'Call me Roddy' Dacres. The landlord of the Sportsman's Rest in Little Pygford still asks after him, if I'm unwise enough to go in there. 'Seen Roddy lately? Good chap, Roddy. Bloody good golfer. What a one for the ladies!'

'I told him he must come here,' Alex was saying. 'I asked Morag to prepare a room for him, but she just went off muttering something religious. Sour-faced old cow.' And to Roo: 'Can you sort it out with HG tomorrow?'

'This isn't a hotel,' she said, plainly daunted. 'Mr Dacres – Roddy – hasn't anything to do with the show. I don't think . . .'

Alex protested, but my father was too busy being charming to push. 'I wouldn't dream of imposing,' he declared. 'Of course I'd like to meet Hot God – what do you call him? HG? Yes, I'd like to meet him, whenever he's around. He used to have a place in Antibes, not far from me. Didn't spend much time there, though. Sold it to a retired dictator a few years back – lovely chap, three wives at least, gives wonderful parties. Only the best champagne. I went to a reception over here just last week, a cousin of the royals: the champers was very inferior stuff. These African rulers may be black, but they have a lot more style than our chaps, I'm afraid.'

'That's because our chaps don't defraud and exploit their subjects to pay for it,' Roo said tartly.

'Dear me. Quite a Commie, isn't she?' my father said with an air of good-humoured tolerance. 'Glad it's still fashionable for young people to be idealistic. You'll grow out of it all too soon. I know women: when you get engaged, you won't want to check his principles, just the size of the diamond.'

I stared at him in growing horror. No one's been called a Commie since the Berlin Wall came down; it's so dated as to be really embarrassing. He was also clearly both racist and sexist, though prepared to be broad-minded in the cause of displaying charm and drinking good champagne. Suddenly, I worried that I might be like him – not that I'm racist or anything, but I *am* a material girl and I do like my Bolly and Cristalle. I reminded myself that as HG didn't care for champers, I'd been deprived for weeks without becoming embittered, and had just voluntarily spent three hours trudging through cold muddy woods on a mission of mercy. That made me feel good about myself again. Perhaps I'm not totally materialistic after all.

My father was still on the subject of HG. 'I'm sure we'll get along,' he said. 'Friends in common. And of course we're very much of an age.'

'You look a lot better on it than he does,' Alex said.

My father accepted the compliment as his due, despite an automatic disclaimer. I suppose it was true. But it's difficult to know what your parents actually look like; you can't see them with genuine detachment. I'd never discussed him with Alex, so I couldn't blame him for letting himself be charmed, but I wanted to get him away from there, to make him *understand* – to have him back on my side. Not my father's. I couldn't bear seeing them together, nose-to-nosey, isn't-this-cosy, father/son-in-law bonding. Normally I can handle any situation, but my brain was still refusing to function and I groped in vain for an exit strategy.

It was Roo who did it for me. Wonderful Roo. (I'll never call her a beach again, no matter what.)

'Delphi and I need to eat,' she said. 'I think dinner's waiting for us. Why don't you get some rest and we'll see you tomorrow? We've got an early start in the morning so we'll be crashing out straight after dinner.'

Alex said he'd stay and have another drink with my father while we adjourned to the dining room, but at least Roo had got me out of there. Ash, who had been chatting with Morty and Nigel, came with us. My father said he wouldn't leave till we'd finished.

'I'm a night owl,' he reminded me. 'Anyway, can't go without kissing my little girl goodnight.'

'I'm hardly a little girl,' I said. 'I'm thirty-four.' I don't usually announce it to the world, but just then I wanted to sound very mature.

'You'll always be my little girl,' he said.

At dinner, Ash was amazingly tactful and didn't ask any awkward questions. Gays are always so sensitive. The food was gorgeous, a wild-rabbit casserole with wine and damsons and spices ('The inside of your other jacket,' Roo said), but although I'd been starving when we got back, somehow I couldn't eat it. Cedric served us himself, since the drama of the search had thrown everyone out of sync.

'You don't look good,' he told me. (He definitely isn't the sort of gay I want for a friend.) 'Face like whey. Too late for extra blusher – you need to eat up. Food'll put some colour in your cheeks.'

'She's tired,' Roo said hastily, 'and she's had a bit of a shock, what with her father turning up out of the blue.'

'On bad terms, are you?' Absent-mindedly, or so I assumed, he pulled out a chair and sat down beside me. 'Can't stand my old man, never could. When I came out he tried to take his belt to me. I was twenty-two. I got it off him and gave him a wallop round the ear. "I'd love some bloke to give me a whipping," I told him, "but not you, ducks." We ain't spoken since.' He filled a glass from the decanter on the table and took a mouthful. 'That how it was between you and your dad?'

I saw Roo sucking her cheeks in, and bit back a sharp reply. 'Not exactly.'

'So what's wrong with my casserole then?'

'Nothing,' I said. 'It's lovely. I'm just . . . not hungry.'

He gave me a weasely look. 'Up the spout, are you?'

'I *beg* your pardon?'

'Leave her alone,' Ash interceded. 'She's had a tough day. We all have. It was a long, cold walk, and even though we located our quarry in the end, they didn't seem to be very grateful.'

'Those sleazemongers are all the same,' Cedric said. 'Load of wankers.'

Harry – I mean Winkworth – walked in partway through the meal. Cedric got him a plate and sat him down with us, but by then I was too shattered and stressed to object. It was a disorganised kind of evening; no doubt that was why we were eating with the staff.

'Did Operation Tabloid-Rescue go all right?' Roo asked.

'Just. If you allow for the fuss they made. Oh, and they took the opportunity to make me an offer for my story.'

'What story?' I said with an upsurge of hostility.

'Any story. HG – you – you and HG – you and Mortimer Sparrow

242

– your bust-up with Basilisa – your bust-up with Mortimer – your bust-up with Alex. Whatever.'

'Did you go for it?'

'Not this time. They wouldn't meet my price.'

'Creep,' I said. I must have sounded half-hearted, because he looked up from his plate to study me closely.

'I gather your father's turned up,' he said eventually. 'Alex asked Morag to prepare a room for him, but I'm afraid we can't do that. Aside from the fact that it's Morag's day of rest – the Sabbath is sacred to her – we'd need HG's permission to put up another guest. I'll ask him when he gets back tomorrow, if you like.'

'No!' I said. 'I mean . . . it really isn't necessary. I'm sure my father will be fine in the village.'

Harry's regard grew thoughtful. 'You haven't seen him in a while, have you?'

'Quite a while,' I answered evasively.

'Morag said he and Alex appeared to be pretty good friends.'

'They've only just met,' said Roo. 'They bonded.'

Harry hmmed in response, polished off his wild rabbit and accepted an offer of Scotch from Cedric.

I decided things had gone far enough. 'If this is turning into a staff piss-up, I think I'm in the way,' I said as grandly as I could manage, which, under the circumstances, wasn't very grandly at all. 'I'm going to bed.'

'Me too,' said Roo with a smile which didn't even attempt to be grand. 'Thanks, Cedric. Night, Harry . . . Ash.'

'Goodnight,' Ash said.

'Night,' from Harry. And to me: 'You were a sport today, Dacres; you really were.'

'It'll get me some good publicity,' I said on a defiant note.

How dare he call me a sport? As if I were some jolly-hockey-sticks type who went around being hearty and clapping people on the back. And *Dacres*??!!

In the hall, Roo said, 'You look zonked. Why don't you go up to bed now and I'll make your excuses to your father?'

I hugged her with real gratitude. 'I don't know what to do about him,' I said.

'We'll think of something,' she responded. 'Tomorrow.'

When I got to my bedroom I found Fenny, exhausted by his stint as a bloodhound, curled up asleep on the tiger-print duvet. I wanted a bath, but I couldn't even be bothered to wash my face. I undressed and tumbled into the bed beside him, unconscious in minutes.

I dreamed I was back in the gallery with the conspirators, but when the man turned round it was my father, and I knew the person they were planning to kill was me.

I woke in the morning to the sensation of Alex nuzzling my breasts. It should have been enjoyable, but with the presence of my father looming over me (not literally, but in the immediate future), I felt far too tense for sex. Haltingly, I tried to convey to Alex the real nature of my (non-existent) relationship with my long-absent parent. But I didn't want to go into details – it would mean exposing myself too much, showing myself as weak and vulnerable instead of the strong, successful person I knew I really was. Alex needed my strength to lean on, my success as a substitute for his own idle dabbling; he wouldn't be able to cope if I became helpless and needy. So all I could say was that my father had gone out of my life when I was ten and I didn't want him back.

'He treated my mother appallingly,' I said, 'and he never bothered about Pan at all. He had another child and didn't even tell us. Now he's fallen out with her so he's getting back in touch with me to try and fill the gap.'

'You're not being fair,' Alex said. 'Roddy told me about Natalie. He said *she* filled the gap in his life after he lost *you*. Your mother wouldn't let him visit you – she told him he wasn't even to write.'

'Rubbish,' I said. 'She's not like that.'

'She was mad at him for running off with someone else. She used you – you and Pan – to hurt him. Mothers do that sometimes. It's sort of understandable. I mean, he broke her heart and punctured her ego all in one go – but that's ancient history now. He's your dad: you've got to give him a chance. He's a great guy. I really like him.'

'I don't,' I said, more bluntly than I intended. He'd twisted everything for Alex's benefit, but he didn't fool me. I know my mother. She'd never tried to set me against him; she'd even made excuses for him from time to time. '*I expect he's busy. I'm sure he'll come and see you soon. He's got to sort out his financial affairs from France now.*' He'd always been 'in business' in a vague sort of way, dabbling in the markets, playing with stocks and shares. Another dabbler.

Mummy would never have used me as a marital weapon, or Pan. She wasn't an adoring parent, but her principles were unshakable.

'I want him out of here,' I said. 'Today.'

'I don't know what's happened to you lately, Delphi,' Alex complained. 'You used to have more heart. This is your dad we're talking about, for heaven's sake. He just wants to make it up to you for all those years apart. You're obviously a bit jelly of Natalie, but you shouldn't be so . . . vindictive. It's not like you. Roddy's a charmer. He's got a lot more charm than your mum, frankly. You'd love him to bits if you let yourself.'

'I don't need his charm,' I said. 'I've got mine.'

'I haven't noticed much of it since I got here,' Alex said nastily.

'Look, I want him to leave, and that's it.' I was all out of reasons, operating on instinct. I'd been expecting Alex to support me, to be sympathetic and understanding. I hadn't given him much to understand, but I thought he would stick by me no matter what. His defection hurt.

Too many things hurt right now.

'You can't send him away,' Alex said. 'Think what the press'll make of it.'

'Why should they make anything of it?'

'Come off it, Delphi, you know they will. Your estranged father tries to patch things up with you, but you turn him away because you're hanging out with an international rock star. It's a hot story. One interview with him in the *Mail* or the *Scoop* and your name will be mud.'

'He wouldn't,' I said. 'He couldn't be so . . .'

Treacherous.

A man who'd dumped his wife and daughters without a qualm had no problem with treachery.

'Why not?' said Alex. 'You're the one who's treating him like shit.'

'He wouldn't even think of it. He's a bastard, but not that kind of a bastard.' I was clinging to a forlorn hope, and I knew it.

But I wasn't prepared for Alex's response.

'He already *has* thought of it.'

'*What?*'

'Well, he asked where you were last night, and I told him about the missing journalists. I can't think what came over you, going to look for them, but anyway . . . He said maybe they'd like to talk to him.'

'So all this crap you've been spouting about father-daughter relationships is just . . . crap! What he really wants is to blackmail me—'

'No . . . no,' Alex floundered. 'He wasn't threatening, he was just . . . thinking aloud. He might give a wonderful interview about you. But if you boot him out, he might . . . You see?'

I saw.

If I wasn't going to tell Alex the whole story about me and my father, I certainly wasn't going to tell the papers. Whereas he would paint a picture of himself as a lovable rogue, trying to build bridges with a long-lost daughter, shut out of Celebrity Castle because I was too busy being famous to want to see him. It was all right for Pan, who had no public profile to live up to, but I was caught in the trap of my own success. And as far as I could see, there was nothing I could do about it.

'He's a loose cannon,' I told Roo over coffee. 'If I send him away – if I say I don't want him at my wedding – he'll head straight for the pub, pal up with those bloody journalists, and then I'm cooked. And it won't be just me. He'll have a go at Mummy too; maybe even Pan. Perhaps if I offered him money . . . ?'

'Why should you?' Roo said indignantly. 'Besides, does he need it? He seems to be fairly comfortably off. Does he – did he – ever work?'

'Inherited income,' I said briefly. 'He just plays around with it. I think he's played around quite profitably sometimes. I gather his second wife left him a packet, too. I don't know for sure, but that was a Savile Row suit he was wearing yesterday, and the sweater under it was cashmere. And his watch is a Rolex.'

'Bugger,' said Roo. 'Still, if you started paying him off you'd never stop. Best not to start. We'll come up with something.'

We spent the day filming in what was to be the meadow garden, planting a range of wild flowers which might not have managed to take root on their own. Russell had wanted to do the last of the historical scenes, but HG and Basilisa didn't get back till late afternoon so they would have to wait. I didn't witness their return, but flying rumours said they were not on good terms and she was turning people to stone with a single glance.

'I thought that was Medusa,' Roo said.

'Basilisks are similar to gorgons,' Russell explained. 'They can kill with a look. Know your Harry Potter.'

Wardrobe had set to work cleaning the mud off my Vivienne Westwood, and in the meantime I was wearing a cloud-pink lambskin with fuchsia embroidery which I'd picked up at Maddalena's. I liked it so much I'd even contemplated paying for it. Normally, pink suits me (I have warm complexion tones), but Dick the cameraman said I was looking washed out, and even Russell suggested a touch more blusher.

'You're supposed to exude a healthy outdoor glow,' he said. 'Makeover shows are all about the relationship between the environment and the soul of the person in it. Beautiful environment equals beautiful soul. It's a load of bollocks, of course, but we have to go with it. Actually, all a garden really does is up your stress levels over the weeding.' Russell lives in a terraced house in Camden with a paved patio, two terracotta urns, and a hanging basket beside the back door.

He's thinking of getting rid of the basket.

'I'm sorry my soul isn't beautiful enough for you!' I blazed. 'Could you get me a new bulb for my bloody outdoor glow?'

I threw a tantrum, but only a small one. Generally, blowing up in all directions makes me feel better, purging my spirit of all the bad stuff that builds up inside – little tensions, frustrations, irritations, slowly accumulating into one big explosive lump. Then boom! I go up like a mini volcano, and after that I feel light and cleansed and happy and in love with the whole world. But the hovering presence of my father couldn't be exploded away. He was there at lunchtime, sharing a sofa with Alex again, flirting with Brie in an avuncular sort of way, there in the evening, talking golf with HG, flattering Basilisa. The female toreador and I swapped glares but didn't speak. She at least seemed to be impervious to my father's charm, as she was to everything else outside the range of her self-interest.

'It is too much!' I overheard her saying to HG. 'First, I have to put up with the *jardinera*, who has the manners of a pig and the temper of a mad bull. Now, it is *su padre*. Next, it will be *toda la familia*. This is *mi casa*. It is a situation *insoportable*! Why do you not make the *viejo* leave? He is disgusting. He look at me with the eyes of *lujuria* – the eyes of lust – though he is so old he cannot have used his deek for many years.'

'The same age as me,' HG said evenly.

For an instant Basilisa faltered, then she steam-rollered on. 'He seem older,' she declared.

'I'll bear that in mind.' HG's voice had an edge I hadn't heard before. Maybe nor had the Basilisk. I wondered, hopefully, if he was reaching the limit of his tolerance.

They went off to dinner in HG's private dungeon and I found a minute to repeat the conversation to Roo.

'Do you think we could use the Basilisk to get rid of my father?' I speculated.

'Maybe,' Roo said. 'Provided she doesn't twig that's what you want.'

'We need a plan,' I said.

I was beginning to feel like myself again.

The following morning I came down to breakfast early. I don't usually do anything early, it's against my creed; if you don't have your sleep, you get tired, and you look like hell, and you don't have that glow that Russell was on about. Early rising is incredibly bad for your health. But I can do it if it's really important. Besides, I'd gone to bed around ten-thirty to avoid a late-night session with my father, so I was awake well before eight. Alex had evidently stayed up drinking; he barely stirred when I wriggled out from under the duvet, dislodging Fenny in transit, and headed for the bathroom. (We really must have sex soon, but somehow the more I thought about it the less I wanted it. It was weird, like Hamlet: '. . . *the native hue of lust Gets sicklied o'er with the pale cast of thought*.' I would have worried I was becoming frigid, not to mention getting saggy tits, if I hadn't had so many other things to worry about.)

Downstairs, as I had hoped, I found the dining room empty except for the servants. Well, *one* servant. I sat down, requested coffee.

'Winkworth,' I said, 'I need your help.'

He leaned against the table beside me, arms folded, a little too close for comfort. But I wasn't going to snub him right now.

'I thought you decided I wasn't a real butler,' he said. 'You can hardly trust me to help you if I'm a fraud.'

'That's exactly why you're the person I need,' I said. 'You're naturally devious and underhand. The thing is, I have to get rid of my father—'

'I don't do murder.'

'Stop being stupid. I don't want to *murder* him, I just want him to leave. That's what he's good at. Why is it people only walk out when you don't want them to? When you're desperate for them to go, they stay and stay.'

'Are you desperate?' Harry asked.

I nodded. He didn't push me on the personal stuff. He just said: 'Why don't you tell him yourself?'

'He might go to the press,' I explained. 'You can imagine the head-lines. '*GARDENING DIVA DELPHINIUM DUMPS DAD*'. You know the kind of thing. It would be awful.'

'Would he do that?'

'Yep. He's sort of hinted to Alex already.'

'What do you want me to do about it?'

'Basilisa doesn't like him. I thought, if HG invited him to stay here, she might have a temperament and start screeching and force him to leave. He's got nothing to do with the show, so he wouldn't be able to come back to Dunblair. He'd have no option but to quit the area.'

'And you want me to talk to HG?'

I nodded again. 'On account of your natural deviosity. I thought you could handle it.'

'Maybe,' he said. 'It depends.'

'On what?'

'What's in it for me.'

'There doesn't have to be anything in it for you,' I objected. 'You're a butler. It's your job to sort out awkward domestic tangles.'

'What *have* you been reading? Anyway, according to you I'm a fraud, so . . .'

'Yes, but you're *pretending* to be a butler, so you can still buttle. Jeeves would have done it.'

'I keep telling you,' Harry said, 'Jeeves was a valet.'

'*Alfred* would have done it.'

'All Alfred had to do was polish the Batmobile and iron Robin's tights – or possibly vice versa. No one ever asked him to outwit Catwoman's mother or spike the Ovaltine for the Penguin's dad. Deviosity wasn't in the job description. So I repeat, what's in it for me?'

'A very large tip?' I suggested viciously.

He considered for a minute. 'Only if I get to specify the precise amount and the nature of the currency.'

For a wild moment I had visions of him demanding South African rand to be lodged in a Swiss bank account. 'What the hell . . .'

'You can afford it. You're a C-list celeb, after all.'

'C-list? *C-list*?' I got to my feet, bringing us almost nose to nose. (Almost – he's taller than me.) 'I refuse to respond to provocation. I'm definitely B-list: we both know that. If you can't handle my parent problem, forget the whole thing.'

Harry grinned that maddening grin. 'Calm down. You haven't heard my price.'

'I don't think I want to.'

'All I'm asking is a kiss.'

I stared at him. I was so stunned I couldn't say anything at all.

'One kiss. With tongues. Duration: minimum two minutes. Oh, and half before, half after. That's the usual arrangement with dodgy deals of this kind.'

I found my voice again, though my nervous system was spinning out of control and I had an extraordinary feeling that the floor heaved beneath my feet. 'I am *not* going to kiss you! I don't go around kissing the butler—'

'Fake butler.'

'I don't kiss fake butlers either! I am never, *ever*—'

'You want me to get rid of Roddy, that's my price. Deal?'

'Absolutely not! I don't believe you can do it, anyway.' I meant, get my father away from Scotland. Not kiss me.

'Of course I can,' he said.

I should have backed off – we were still too close for comfort, too close for safety. I shouldn't have hesitated. He caught my arms and twisted them behind my back, holding them with one hand. I suppose I struggled; I don't remember. He was stronger than I expected. He took my face in his other hand – I must have tried to turn away. The grin was gone; his expression was somehow intent. I thought: he's not even good-looking. Not like Alex . . .

He kissed me.

I don't know why I opened my mouth – probably to protest – but it was *very* bad timing. His tongue went in and it pressed all the wrong buttons: it was terrifying, intimate, halfway to sex. His body was clamped against me and the biggest erection I'd ever felt was pressing into my groin. Just for a second I lost it completely. It was like when I was fourteen and Ben Garvin kissed me for the first time, only worse. Much worse. My whole body was sliding out of control, melting into him, melding into him . . .

It must have been well over the allotted time when he drew back . . .

Several heartbeats before he let me go.

'That was something else,' he said. 'Mm. Definitely . . . something else.'

'I didn't agree to you kissing me!' I fumed, groping for indignation, outrage, life-saving fury. 'It's eight-thirty in the morning! You can't – you can't maul me about at *breakfast* . . .'

'Sorry. I'll remember to collect the second instalment later in the day.'

'You haven't done anything to collect on! We don't have a deal – we *never* had a deal. And if you lay so much as a finger on me again, I'll sue you for assault – I'll tell HG – I'll—'

'You could tell Alex.'

That was below the belt. Alex in the grip of protective rage, Alex on the warpath doubling a fist in Harry's face . . . the fantasy was beyond the reach of imagination.

'I don't need Alex,' I declared. 'I'll deal with you myself.'

'So we do have a deal?'

That, of course, was the moment when we heard voices outside, and Russell came in, followed by Roo.

'You're up early,' she said, gazing at me in faint surprise.

'I . . . I had something to sort out.' I didn't look at Harry. 'Anyway, I went to bed early.'

'I noticed,' said Russell. 'It isn't natural. Are those scrambled eggs? Good. Roo tells me we've had the *Scoop* on the line already. They want to come and take some pix this morning. They'll want you too, Harry. Also Young Andrew and Ash.'

'I don't need PR,' Harry said, disconcerted.

'Don't worry, you can stay in the background. Delphinium'll see to that.'

'I'm afraid I'm a bit busy . . .'

'No, no,' I said, relishing his discomfiture. 'You led the rescue party. You have to be there.' Latching on to the chance of a small revenge, I radiated sweetness and generosity. Russell looked startled, Harry both annoyed and faintly appreciative of my tactics. 'I won't do it without you,' I announced.

It didn't occur to me to wonder why Harry should be quite so camera-shy. It should have done.

Ruth

We spent most of the morning posing for pictures against the background of Dunblair castle, while the surviving journalist from the *Scoop* took notes about our expedition. Young Andrew was both tickled and uncomfortable at being included, making him more inarticulate than usual (especially since Auld Andrew came along to supervise). Ash was bored and increasingly impatient, Harry curiously reluctant to be involved at all. Delphi enjoyed herself hugely, thrusting Fenny into the limelight and evidently determined to make Harry take his share. I had no idea what she was up to, but in the end he said curtly: 'If that's enough, I'm off. I need to talk to HG about something,' shooting Delphi a look which totally bewildered me. The *Scoop* fished for HG's participation, but in vain.

In fact, he was doing the final re-enactment scenes with Basilisa, well out of range of Delphi and me. I was so relieved I allowed myself to be inveigled into the front row of the publicity shots without complaint, although in the main I hate being photographed. I was itching to ask Delphi what she was up to, but we didn't get the chance for a private word. She seemed to have got her glow back with a vengeance, though perhaps it was more glitter than glow, a kind of diabolical sparkle that made me deeply suspicious.

At lunchtime, I began to have an inkling of the truth.

Roddy Dacres was present, being chummy with everyone, acting as if he was part of the scenery instead of somebody whose only claim to be there was a tenuous relationship with his daughter. He had a strangely mesmeric effect on the company: he was so much at ease, so sure he belonged that no one had the nerve – or the effrontery – to question him. Even HG, putting in an appearance in the wake of his acting success, seemed to accept him at his own valuation. They'd talked golf and mutual friends (none, but Roddy stretched a few acquaintances) the previous day; now, to my amazement, I heard HG actually proposing that Roddy should stay in the castle, 'Join the crowd – much more convenient than being stuck in the village.' I glanced at Delphi, expecting to see raw horror in her face. But she seemed preoccupied, and was looking beyond HG to the door.

None of us had noticed Basilisa. For once, she had made an unobtrusive entrance, following on the heels of Harry, who was at his most butlerish. It took about five seconds for the entrance to become obtrusive.

'What are you doing?' she demanded. In the heat of the moment, any concerns about the security of her marital position went out the window. 'You invite this deekhead to stay here – in *mi casa*? I will not permit – *no le dejo* – he cannot stay! First, I must have these TV people everywhere – they insult me – I am *atacada* in my own home by *una jardinera psicótica*. Then you invite *su padre* to stay here! *Ya estoy harta!* He go, or I go. Now!'

'Basilisa . . .' HG turned towards her, extending a conciliatory hand.

'And if I go, you know what I take with me? You know?'

HG slipped into Spanish, murmuring reassurance, until Basilisa was persuaded to back off, throwing repulsive glances at Roddy. Then HG reverted to him, apologising smoothly, withdrawing his invitation, and explaining that he was afraid Roddy would have to leave Dunblair for good, all in a single faultless manoeuvre. Feminine caprice was touched on, masculine fellow-feeling appealed to, but HG wasn't a superstar for nothing; without uttering an impolite word he made it very clear that Roddy was no longer welcome anywhere in the vicinity of the castle.

Bewildered by the turn of events, Roddy found himself edged towards the door before he had time to object. Eager to save face, he did his best to salvage his leftover dignity, acting as if his mild departure was a special favour to HG.

'Surprised someone like Hot God has marriage problems,' he remarked to Delphi in transit. 'Still, anything I can do to help him out. Handsome woman, Basilisa, but temperamental. I gather you upset her, Del. You should be more careful. Remember: your behaviour reflects on your old father.'

Delphi's expression tensed, but Harry snatched Roddy away before he could come up with any more comments on her filial shortcomings.

'Time to leave. Jules is waiting to escort you back to the village.'

That was quick, I thought. Much too quick. Jules was already at the door with Sting by his side; evidently he had been forewarned.

'You set that up,' I whispered to Delphi as Roddy departed, muttering something about visiting friends in Gloucestershire. 'When did you get hold of HG?'

'I didn't. I don't know him well enough to ask a favour like that.'

'Then how . . . ?'

'I asked Harry to help me – I mean Winkworth.' As he reentered the room, I saw him catch her eye with the familiar incorrigible grin. To my surprise, considering he'd just bailed her out of a serious dilemma, she didn't respond in kind.

'At least he must be in your good books for once,' I said, 'whatever your suspicions of him.'

'No,' Delphi said baldly.

'What d'you mean, no?'

'I think I've just swapped one problem for another. I can't talk about it now, though. Tell you later.' She was looking very thoughtful – generally an alarming prospect – but this didn't look like the kind of thought that preceded a brainwave, more the sort where you're thinking about something unpleasant or disturbing. As her biggest bugbear had just walked out of the door, I wondered what could be bothering her. I resolved to find out when the first opportunity offered, but work absorbed my attention for the rest of the afternoon, and Delphi, between filming with bog asphodel and some rather attractive tasselled grasses, rushed off to telephone Jennifer about her ex and return calls from Maddalena on the sacred subject of The Dress.

As we'd finally finished the historical scenes, the actors, extras and so on were due to depart the following day. (Alex and Brie were leaving a day later in acknowledgement of their superior status.) Inevitably, that meant a party. An impromptu, let's-do-the-show-right-here sort of party, with last-minute catering by Cedric and large quantities of booze imported from the pub by Dirk and Angus. As they clearly felt themselves to be honorary members of the team, they stayed to help, though I wasn't sure what they were helping with. Probably eating and drinking. One of the actresses (the ghost-spotter) had a birthday (we were too tactful to enquire which), and HG donated a crate of champagne, despite his dislike of the drink, and allowed himself to be persuaded to sing 'Happy Birthday' to her. He did it in a low-key style which went down well – with everyone except Dorian.

'They'll ask him to sing again now,' he said despondently. 'They always do. He'll act modest and say no, and they'll beg him and then he will. He'll sing that awful stuff from the sixties and seventies and dance about and everything – sometimes he goes on for hours. I can't stand it.'

'It mayn't be your kind of music,' I said, 'but most people love it. He's a great star. I would've thought you'd be proud of him.'

'I *am* proud of him,' Dorian said awkwardly, 'sort of. It's just . . .'

'I bet your schoolfriends think he's cool.'

Dorian shuddered. 'No they don't. We were at this do once – someone's sister's wedding – and Joshua Kensington-Gore was there, and Dad was singing, and I went into the kitchen and there was Josh doing a piss-take, sticking his pelvis out with a frying pan for a guitar, and the others were all standing round laughing and laughing. When they saw me they went quiet, like, *really* embarrassed, and I tried to hit Josh, but he's bigger than me, and back at school he'd keep doing it – the pelvic wiggle thing – whenever I was around, and all his mates would be sniggering . . . I can't tell Dad. I mean, *he* thinks he's cool – of course I can't tell him. But I *wish* he wouldn't sing. I sometimes pray he'll be ill and lose his voice for good.'

'Oh dear.' I sat down beside him on the settle. We were in the great hall, which had, among other things, superb acoustics. HG, as predicted, was just launching into 'Get Down and Get Dirty', Number One in 1968, with a backing tape filling in for the Fallen Angels and a lot of audience participation. 'Right, where do I start? First of all, imitation really is the sincerest form of flattery. If your dad wasn't a superstar, if he couldn't sing, couldn't wiggle, and did nothing to justify his existence but juggle his share options, your classmates wouldn't take the piss. One of the penalties of success is that it spawns envy, and people who are envious do everything they can to denigrate what you do. Stars are always a target. In a sense, it's fair enough – too much idolisation is bad for them. But it can be hard on their families. Your schoolfriends are jealous – not so much of your dad, but of *you*, because of him.'

'Yeah, yeah. Heard that one before. Look, Josh's dad makes millions in the City *and* he's an Olympic-standard skier. When they have parties there he's so cool he doesn't even come. He's usually off on business trips. Josh gets left on his own, like for *days*, with just the servants, and they're not allowed to tell him off or anything. I mean, Harry's okay, but if Dad's away I have to do what he says. It's like Dad thinks I can't be responsible for myself. Josh's parents let him do what he likes.'

'That explains a lot,' I said. 'Listen: your dad loves you. He's made a lot of mistakes in his life and he doesn't want you to repeat them. Sounds to me like Josh's parents don't give a damn – and you can bet he knows it. He may act like he thinks he's the coolest, ordering the servants about and partying while his dad's away, but inside he feels lonely and unloved. No wonder he's crawling with jealousy of you. Your dad's a big star *and* he cares for you. That must be gall and wormwood to poor Joshua.'

'You don't understand,' Dorian persisted. 'I thought you did, but you don't. Josh doesn't care about that stuff. He says his dad trusts him, lets him be his own boss. My dad doesn't trust me with squat.'

Suddenly, I'd had enough. 'You know what?' I said. 'I *do* understand. Worst luck. I've heard all the clichés before. I've *been* sixteen, so has your dad, so has everyone else in this room. But you haven't been thirty-two, or forty-four, or fifty-nine, or sixty-seven. You've got years and years of understanding lying ahead of you, if you've got the brains for it. Right now you're shut up in your little sixteen-year-old world – you and your pal Joshua – and you think that's all there is. It's like locking yourself in your bedroom and saying there's no universe outside. Josh is obviously a dumb schmuck, but I thought you were brighter than that. You're the guy who designs computer games, after all. Wake up and look around you. Being sixteen isn't the only game in town.'

Dorian's mouth had fallen open, but after a minute he remembered to shut it again. He was looking at me with a mixture of resentment, shock, and – just possibly – a germ of new thought. I didn't really care. I was done with being sympathetic.

'Now I'm going to listen to your dad,' I stated, 'and admire his pelvic wiggle, because he's just about the best in the world at what he does, and I feel bloody lucky to have the chance to see – and hear – him. Enjoy your sulk.'

I got up, grabbed a drink, and made my way towards the fireplace, where HG was singing 'Caramel Eyes', the slow-motion smooch from the late seventies. We still dance to it now, wrapped around someone or other at the tag-end of a party. He didn't have a mike – he didn't need one – but if he missed it as an accessory, a beer bottle in one hand did the trick. Once, he broke off to dance with the birthday actress for a few beats, occasioning scattered applause from several people in the crowd. When he saw me his smile changed, wrinkling at his eyes, becoming somehow more intimate. He came towards me, turning the song into a personal serenade. (Thank God Basilisa wasn't around.) When he finished there was more clapping, some of which, to my amazement, seemed to be directed at me. I couldn't think why.

'Three cheers,' said Russell. 'You're doing a great job.'

'You're the best,' said Delphi. 'Wasn't I right about this project?'

To my surprise, I found myself thinking that she was. No one on *Behind the News* had ever expressed impromptu appreciation – unless you counted the hypocrisy of my leaving party. Nor had any of the exposés led to my being serenaded by a rock star. I'd missed out on promotion and been upstaged by a pair of legs called Cheryl (or Cherie), I'd been shagged and bagged by Kyle Muldoon, and at the end of it I was left out in the cold with no job, no fella, and a set of broken crystal glasses. Now, here I was in a romantic Scottish castle, being appreciated and serenaded. I would have been pretty idiotic if I hadn't been having a good time.

HG returned to his station by the fireplace, and the next old favourite ('Rockabye Lula', around 1970 I think). When he had done a second encore, by popular request, he bowed out, excusing himself from both the singing and the party, leaving us with the state-of-the-art sound system and Dirk McTeith's services as DJ. Several people were dancing, or at least throwing themselves about in bizarre contortions, mainly out of sync with the music. I realised that if I was becoming a dance critic I must be far too sober, and started putting beer on top of the champagne. On the floor, there were couples likely and unlikely. Nigel appeared to be dancing with Cedric, though that was probably an accident of positioning; Brie danced variously with Nick, Dick and Mick; Delphi and Alex swayed gracefully in unison – at any rate, Alex was graceful, whereas Delphi seemed slightly distracted, as if she was concentrating on something else. Eventually, she trod on his foot, he switched his attention to the Dom Pérignon, and Delphi transferred her sway to Morty with an absent-minded air, as if barely conscious of her partner's identity.

'Do you dance?' asked a voice beside me.

Ash.

'Sometimes,' I said. 'I'm not very good at it.'

'Nor am I,' he responded. 'Come on.'

He separated me from my beer, circled me with an arm, and propelled me effortlessly between the other dancers. No gyrations, just the two of us moving in rhythm with each other and occasionally with the music. Lazy dancing, gentle and slow. An embrace in motion . . .

I decided I'd never felt so comfortable on the dance floor with anybody. Not cheek-to-cheek or crotch-to-crotch, just a leisurely stroll in someone's arms. Ash's arms. I found myself seeing him as if for the first time, the way you do with a person when you hit that turning point, the moment of choice, the teeter on the cusp of fate. Seeing the slant of his cheekbones, the not-quite-pointed ears, the serious mouth. He was so beautiful – but I'd never gone for beautiful men. I'd gone for men like Kyle Muldoon, stubble-chinned and macho and crudely sexy. Men who had the obvious masculinity that I'd always mistaken for strength.

But Ash is far stronger than Kyle, I thought. He had the strength of principle, and kindness. He might fall out of love, but he would always treat people with respect; he would never tell lies from cowardice or convenience, never be indifferent to another person's pain. In short, he was the type of man that most women could only dream about.

Only I hadn't dreamed about him. Armoured in my broken heart, I'd been hostile to his beauty, resented his qualities, derided his chosen career. I didn't know when things had changed, or how he'd sneaked under my guard. And I had no idea if he knew it.

He drew me a little closer, our bodies touched – not in passion but in rhythm, in perfect accord. We're only dancing, I told myself. Only dancing.

Oh shit . . .

When we took a break to get back to drinking, he started

asking me the questions he'd never asked, the routine life-story stuff, except with Ash it didn't seem routine. I found myself telling him about Kyle, and quitting *Behind the News*, and even my disastrous leaving party. He laughed out loud when I described smashing the glassware. It felt strange to be pouring my heart out; except with Delphi, I'd always been the listener. I'd certainly never dumped my woes on Kyle. Though he would occasionally ask the right questions, he paid no attention to the answers. I thought: Ash is a good listener, he's sympathetic, like me and not like me. Not murmuring a prompt or interpolating with a verbal nudge the way I would have done, but using the ease of his silence, the gravitas of his expression, the sudden warmth in those cool, cool eyes. It perturbed me a little, as if he was using my own qualities against me. But I knew really that was nonsense. I recall thinking, somewhere around my third – or fourth – or possibly fifth – beer: I'm always going to remember this evening. The haphazard party, and being appreciated, and Ash. Especially Ash.

I was getting dangerously carried away.

At some point Delphi came over to tell me she was going to bed. 'I've got to go to London tomorrow for a fitting with Maddalena,' she said. 'You can manage without me for a day, can't you? I'll be back Thursday morning. Vanessa's booked me on early flights.' Vanessa was Delphi's PA, a latterday Sloan of effortless efficiency who worked on a part-time basis for a string of media celebs who didn't need an assistant full-time.

'All right,' I said. 'But you must get back quickly. We're laying out the maze before the end of the week.'

'Promise,' she said, giving me a kiss and casting a rather hostile glance at Ash. I still wanted the background details of her plot with Harry, but it was obviously going to have to wait.

The party was winding down now, the way such parties do.

There was no bar to close, no shortage of booze, but party-fatigue was kicking in, and the post-filming high was declining into the low of imminent goodbyes and unemployment. The tempo of the songs got slower, and the last of the celebrants malingered over their drinks, bemoaning their lot, or whatever else they wanted to bemoan. Cedric approached, plainly drunk, and asked Ash to dance.

'One dance,' he said. 'The last dance. One perfect fucking moment to carry in my 'eart till I die. Ruthie here won't mind, will you?'

I minded. I minded the end of my tête-à-tête with Ash, but I couldn't say so. Ash got up, giving me a smile that might have meant something, and might have meant nothing. Then he was dancing, the same leisurely stroll he had danced with me, arms latched loosely around Cedric's neck. They talked – seemed close – even intimate. I didn't think Ash was gay, but suddenly I wasn't sure – I wasn't sure of anything any more. Would a straight guy have danced like that with another man, chatting with him so carelessly, so comfortably? Wouldn't a straight guy have worried that anyone watching might have leaped to the wrong conclusions? But Ash wasn't worried – he wasn't the type. Gay or straight, he wouldn't have cared what anyone thought.

He doesn't care what *I* think, I realised.

I tried not to watch him, letting my gaze roam over the other malingerers: the birthday actress, now sunk in alcoholic gloom, admitting to Angus how awful it was to be forty-nine (I learned later she was fifty-five); Dirk and Morty, competing for the attention of one of the researchers; the actor with the hip-flask problem, now asleep in a chair. Alex and Brie were doing a slow shuffle in the dance floor area; Brie was leaning into him wearing a vacant expression which matched her dress, most of which wasn't there. She was much shorter than Alex and they looked slightly awkward, the way dancers do when there's a big height discrepancy. Ash and Cedric appeared far more graceful . . .

I mustn't watch, I mustn't *mind*, I mustn't think whatever I was thinking. I got up and left the hall, gravitating instinctively to the drawing room in search of a slug of something anaesthetic. Like chloroform. I could hear music playing, something I didn't recognise, a woman's voice singing in a foreign language or no language at all, sounding faintly Oriental, faintly operatic. In the doorway, I hesitated. HG was stretched out on the sofa, whisky glass in hand, listening with his eyes shut. Apart from the fact that his mouth was closed, he might have been asleep. I drew back, not wanting to intrude, but I must have made a slight noise. He opened his eyes and smiled at me.

'You're busy,' I said. 'I didn't mean . . .'

'Come in.'

He unpeeled himself from the sofa, offered me a drink.

'What's the music?' I asked.

'It's a new Arthur Brown CD, made with some Tibetan singer who had to flee from the Chinese. You wouldn't remember Arthur; before your time. I knew him in the late sixties when he became a star. He left the business but we kept in touch, in a distant sort of way. Now, he's making a comeback.' The next track switched to something which was recognisably rock. I found myself accepting a vintage Armagnac which swirled around the bottom of a brandy bubble with the lazy smoothness of golden syrup.

'I saw you talking to Dorian earlier,' HG continued. 'He seems to like you.'

Too much, I thought with a twinge, but I didn't say it.

'It's a difficult age, sixteen. Kids nowadays seem to have so many pressures: exam pressure, peer pressure, lifestyle pressure. The urge to conform is always strongest in your teens. And the urge to rebel. You need to be exactly like all the other teenagers and you need to be against anyone older. It's a formula. Mind you, Dorian's very clever. Much brighter than me. I've got O and A levels, though I don't advertise the fact. Bad for my image. But Dorian – he's a maths genius, good at physics and chemistry, brilliant with computers. I suppose he's a bit of a geek, but—'

'You must be very proud of him,' I said.

'Mm. We seem to get along. Of course, he doesn't much care for Basilisa, but then children never do like a stepmother, do they? They started off all right – believe it or not, she was great with him, but when he hit thirteen or fourteen things went downhill. Teen trauma. Like I said, the difficult age. Mel and Dilly, my daughters, were much worse. But I was a lot younger then and dealing with my own problems, and they'd lost Maggie when they were kids. They've sorted themselves out pretty well now. I think Dorian'll be all right.'

'I'm sure he will.'

'I'd like him to go to Oxbridge; he's got the brains for it. He's been on half-term this week, but he shuts himself up with the computer all the time. I used to think he was download-ing porn – natural enough, at that age – so I got the machine monitored. Apparently, he's designed some game or other, has his own website.' HG sounded mildly stunned, as if his son had trekked into the Amazon jungle or composed a symphony for Martians. 'He does porn, but not much. Bit worrying, really. Can't be healthy, immersing himself in all that techno stuff. He ought to be more interested in girls.'

'I expect he is,' I said, reeling at the idea of a father who felt his son needed more pornography in his life. 'But he wouldn't necessarily tell you, would he?'

'Suppose not. Still, when I was sixteen that was all I thought about. And seventeen – eighteen – nineteen . . . you get the picture. I only wanted to play in a band because that was how you got the girls.'

'Did it work?' I asked, unable to resist.

He gave a rueful kind of half laugh. 'Much too well. Although . . . well, apart from Maggie, I never really met the right one. Basilisa was wonderful to begin with – so much fire and vitality, I thought she would keep me young, but these days it just wears me out. Now, I want the quiet life. Just to potter between here and the island, stay out of the spotlight, spend time with my favourite people. Fix up the garden, indulge in a few luxuries – just like anyone else my age.'

Absolutely, I thought. Fix up the garden, get in a TV crew to help, pop off to your own island every so often. Just like anyone else.

Celebrities, even the nicest ones, really do live in their own universe.

'You'll go no more a-roving,' I said, meaning spiritually, not geographically.

'You know Byron.' He looked pleased.

> *'For the sword outwears its sheath*
> *And the soul outwears the breast,*
> *And the heart must pause to breathe*
> *And love itself have rest.*
>
> *Though the night was made for loving*
> *And the day returns too soon,*
> *Yet we'll go no more a-roving*
> *By the light of the moon.*

'Yes, that's me. My song. Clever of you to realise. You're a very perceptive person; I've noticed that.' He changed the CD for some kind of jazz – the sound of a late-night bar when they're putting the chairs on the tables and drinking the last drink and the sax player just won't go home.

'I'm writing a novel,' HG went on, with an air of originality. 'I feel I've got to that period in my life when I've got something to say and, at last, the time to say it. So I thought I'd give it a go.'

There was an expectant pause.

'About a rock star?' I said.

'Not exactly. About a . . . musician. He has one or two hits, then declines into obscurity. His wife leaves him, his whole life becomes a pattern of constant failure and frustration. If it's autobiographical, then the hero represents my alter ego. The me that I might have been without success. He's a failure, but he has friends – a close-knit group of eccentrics who are always loyal to him. Then he meets a girl.'

'Of course,' I said absent-mindedly.

'Of course?'

'Well, there wouldn't be any story if he didn't,' I improvised.

'You said it. Anyhow, she's young, beautiful, caring. The quiet type. They fall deeply in love. Through her, he starts to rebuild his world. But she grew up in a housing estate on the edge of an area of industrial pollution, and she contracts leukaemia. Ironically, the company responsible for the pollution is owned by an old associate of Jordan's – my hero. Thirty years ago, this executive was a bright young whiz-kid with a record company, the company which catapulted Jordan to brief stardom then dropped him cold. He's become totally corrupted by his own success. Jordan's a failure, but his ideals have stayed pure. The girl dies tragically –'

'They always do,' I murmured, but HG didn't register the remark.

'– and he writes a song about it, a great song. It's a huge

international hit and he becomes a star again. But fame destroys him. He's estranged from his old friends, and at the end he finds he's thrown back together with the man whose corruption and indifference led to his girlfriend's death.'

'Does he kill himself?' I asked.

'I'm not sure. I haven't decided.' He relieved me of my glass, which had emptied itself into my system without my noticing, and replenished it. 'You know, you're the only person I've told about this. Apart from my agent and publisher, of course.'

'I'm . . . privileged,' I stammered.

'Nonsense,' he said gently. 'You're just . . . a *very* nice girl.' As he returned my glass, his hand closed over mine. The light was dim, softening his face into timelessness. I saw there all the ghosts of his past: the fresh young star, the jaded cynic, the junkie – the ageing comeback kid, the retired pirate, the weary Casanova. *We'll go no more a-roving* . . . A superstar who dreamed of failure because it was a place he'd never been, a man with, perhaps, deep uncertainties buried beneath the life-long insulation of super-status. And someone who got a book contract to write about them, and a TV programme to replant his flower beds, had his own island to get away from it all, his own castle in which to ponder life's little ironies. I smiled – I couldn't help it.

He kissed me.

A slow sort of kiss, lingering, not unpleasant. A kiss that was very sure of its welcome.

I found myself thinking, not '*I'm kissing Hot God*', but '*I'm kissing a man of sixty-seven*'. What was the line? '*Of more than twice her years, seam'd with a hundred scars* . . .' Elaine on Lancelot, I think.

It was enjoyable enough for me not to call a halt. HG put

my glass down on the cabinet, slid his arms round me and drew me closer, all without breaking mouth contact. He really was a *very* smooth operator.

Then the inevitable happened. There were two doors to the drawing room, one open, one closed. Ash appeared in the open one – and stopped dead on the threshold. His beautiful face went white and still.

The other door was flung back with familiar impetuosity. 'Where are you?' Basilisa demanded. 'Darrling—'

She, too, stopped dead, even as I detached myself from HG's embrace. A range of expressions chased themselves across her face at lightning speed. Her eyes widened, narrowed, glittered; her lips parted, closed, thinned to a line, opened on a scream. The activity of her eyebrows was limited by Botox, but her massive hair, sleep-tousled, seemed to curl into snakes. And hiss.

'So!' she cried. '*So!* It is not just that *puta de jardinera*, it is this – this – *cabrona* – this *zorra*! She is not even very pretty, but you don't care, no? As long as she smile at you, as long as she is willing! You cannot keep your *polla* in your pocket for five minutes! You are like all men – you follow your deek anywhere with a *coña*!'

'It was just a kiss,' HG said, looking amazingly unruffled. 'She's a nice girl: she listens. You could learn from her.'

That was reckless provocation. '*Hijo de puta!*' Basilisa raged. '*Cabrón! Gilipollas!* Hole of the arse! I divorce you – I divorce you a thousand times – and I take *everything*! I take the island, I take the castle, I send the bulldozer to smash your precious *jardino* into a desert of earth! Always I am faithful, I am good wife, I suffer in silence when you leave me on Mande Susu, I suffer when I must live in Scotland, which is so cold and *bárbaro*. I suffer when you not let me redecorate this room, though it is so ugly – old-fashioned – boring boring. You are old man but I give you my youth, my beauty, my *fieldad*, and in return I suffer suffer!'

'You weren't that faithful,' I said involuntarily. 'You tried to seduce Dorian.'

For a second her anger hiccupped, then, typically, she swept on. 'He lie, he is *estúpido*, he is *niño*, I never touch him—'

'We'll leave Dorian out of this,' HG said, throwing me a sharp look. 'As I know about your former personal trainer, and my major domo on the island, and Dirk McTeith last winter, that will be quite enough. I've had a PI firm collecting the evidence for some time. We should be able to settle things quietly.'

'Never!' Basilisa shrieked. 'You lie – they lie – you pay them to lie! I tell the judge – I tell the press – I tell *la prensa amarilla* – how you treat me like sheet, how you make me suffer. I ruin you! I tell them how you go with the *jardinera*, with this *puta*, with everyone except your *esposa* – how you are no good in bed any more, how your deek it is limp limp limp—'

'You can't have it both ways,' HG said. 'Either I'm impotent or I'm shagging around. The two don't go together.'

'I say what I like!' Basilisa declared, disregarding logic. 'I say you never go down on me, you give me no *orgasmo*, you have limp deek—'

Glancing at Ash, I essayed a smile of complicity. A smile that was supposed to say, 'This is nothing to do with me. I was just in the wrong place at the wrong time. Aren't they ridiculous?' On reflection, that was a lot to say with one smile, so it's hardly surprising it didn't work. Ash, like Queen Victoria, was plainly Not Amused.

'I don't go down on you,' HG was saying crushingly, 'because you haven't had your Brazilian redone in months. I don't like oral sex with a gorilla. It's enough to give anyone a limp deek.'

271

'I think,' I whispered, sidling towards the door, 'I'm going to bed. Er – excuse me?'

I hoped for a word with Ash, a chance to explain, though I wasn't sure what or how, but he swung on his heel and vanished.

'*Hija de puta!*' Basilisa said to me by way of goodnight. '*Perra!*'

'Don't worry,' HG said. 'We'll talk in the morning.' And to the Basilisk: '*Perra* yourself. Don't blame poor Ruth because I find her sweetness and good manners a relief after years of living with a loud-mouthed slut.'

They were clearly all set for a long session. I bolted.

Upstairs, I thought of tapping on Delphi's door to tell her everything, but Alex would be there, and, anyway, she was probably asleep. She had an early start the next day.

It would have to wait.

I dived into my own room, shut the door against the world. Slowly I took off my make-up and got into bed. My brain was fizzing with a chaos of images – me and Ash dancing, Ash and Cedric, HG and the kiss, Basilisa's rage and horror, Ash, still and silent in the open doorway. I kept trying to sort out what I felt, what Ash felt, what was really going on, but every time I attempted to put a good spin on it my thoughts spun off on their own, taking me somewhere I didn't want to be. I couldn't relax, let alone sleep. I read, watched television, struggled my way through the long, dark wakefulness of the night.

Some time around five or six I went to the window and opened it, inhaling the cool dampness of the air from the loch. Faint and far off I heard the eerie moaning of the bagpipes, which was odd, because bagpipes don't usually sound eerie. They sound like a tuba with indigestion. It seemed a strange hour for someone to be practising, but no doubt it helped maintain the castle's reputation for haunting.

I left the window open a crack since the room felt airless and overheated, and went back to bed. Curiously lulled by the gentle wailing of an instrument played by the Scots in battle to terrorise the enemy, I finally fell asleep.

Chapter 9:
Catastrophe Castle

Delphinium

The next day, Roo came to breakfast in her glasses, in a vain attempt to hide the black smudges under her eyes. Since Harry (and HG) had routed my father, I was avoiding a tête-à-tête with him, so I didn't go downstairs until she was up. Alex, as usual, was still sleeping.

'What happened last night after I left?' I demanded. 'You seemed to be getting very friendly with Ash.' He's not her type at all, besides being gay, but it really worried me.

'Yes,' she said. 'That wasn't the problem,' and out came the whole story about HG, and the kiss, and the showdown with Basilisa.

'Fantastic!' I said gleefully. 'You've actually sparked off what will be *the* celebrity divorce of the year! You'll be famous, in all the papers—'

'I don't want to be famous and in all the papers, and I didn't spark it off. I was a . . . a symptom, not a cause. From the sound of things, HG's been planning it for months, possibly years. I assume he hoped to get through the TV series first, that's all.'

'I wish I'd been there,' I sighed, wistfully. 'That *would* be the night I go to bed early and miss all the fun.'

'If you'd been there,' Roo pointed out, 'HG wouldn't have kissed me.'

'I suppose not. What was it like? Is he a good kisser?' I was a little bit green, but only a little. After all, I'm marrying Alex.

(Let's not think about Harry.)

'I think so,' Roo said, evidently reluctant to tell, if not to kiss. 'It was . . . nice. Not earth-shaking, but sort of pleasant. The thing is, you can't help being distracted by who you're kissing.'

'I know,' I said. 'Robbie Williams kissed me once, at the fag-end of a party. Same thing. Except HG is older, and an icon.' I added, generously, 'I've never kissed an icon.'

Roo gave a sudden tired grin. 'You can do it in any Russian church.'

'Are you going to be all right?' I pursued. 'I mean, left here with Basilisa on the warpath. She'll be out for your blood, and you're not as good in fights as me. I wish I wasn't going to London. Only there's the dress, and I said I'd see Mummy . . .'

'I'll be fine. I don't need my hand held, honestly.'

The others started trickling in, all looking more or less hungover, followed by Harry with reinforcements of coffee and scrambled eggs. Everyone except Roo and I pounced on them. Word had obviously not yet got around about the scene the previous night, so I didn't mention it. Gossip would begin percolating soon enough.

'Does anyone in the castle play the bagpipes?' Roo asked Harry.

'Dougal McDougall. Why?'

'I thought I heard him practising, really early in the morning. Filling in for the phantom with a quick skirl along the battlements.'

'I doubt it,' Harry said. 'He overdid the Scotch last night. He was out for the count. You must have dreamed it.'

Roo looked startled, and only remembered when it was too late to ask what was going on with me and Harry.

'Nothing,' I said. 'I have to go now.' I was damned if I was going to admit to being kissed by the butler when she'd been kissed by Hot

God. It was all the wrong way round, I decided. I mean, I do generous, but I don't go looking for humiliation.

Outside, Sandy was loading my bags into a silver Porsche. For once, I wasn't taking much – an overnight bag and some clothes I was bored of and wanted to leave at the mews. I hugged Roo very tight, feeling a weird flash of panic, I didn't know why.

'Take care. Don't work too hard. Stay out of Basilisa's way – she's going to be like a tigress on the prowl. What did you say she called you?'

'I'm not sure,' Roo said. 'It was in Spanish.'

I got into the car and we drove off at breakneck speed, since I was, of course, late. As the castle and lake disappeared I had another odd rush of anxiety, like a presage of disaster.

'You will look after Roo, won't you?' I said to Sandy. 'She's – um – fallen out with your mistress. Your future ex-mistress, to be precise.'

Sandy digested this. 'Future ex,' he repeated. 'Know that for a fact, do you?'

'Pretty much.'

'Good. It's been a long time coming. Don't you worry about your friend. She's a good girl. We'll see she's okay.'

I got to the airport just in time, raced through the check-in and boarded in first class. The flight was efficiently brief. In London, I took a taxi into town, dumped my bags at the mews, and met my mother for a late lunch at the Ivy.

Mummy is magnificently unaware of all London restaurants except the ones that were there when she was young. The Ivy may be the ultimate celebrity hangout where you eat to be seen, but to her it's just a place with nice food where she and my father (or whoever) used to go thirty years ago. She ordered onion tart because she always does, and rack of lamb. Mummy doesn't do diets.

She's wide rather than fat, broad-shouldered and broad-hipped, supple from much bending. Earth-mother tits, arms like a gladiator. Her face has a gardener's tan, her grey-fair hair is always pinned up in an untidy fashion with a crooked butterfly clip. As she was in London, she'd honoured the occasion with a daub of make-up: face powder that was too pale, mascara that was too dark, lipstick that didn't fit her mouth. She wore a loose dress and jacket which co-ordinated mostly by accident and the embroidered pashmina I'd given her four or five years ago. In addition, she had odd earrings, one necklace set with garnets and another with a yellow sapphire pendant, and an assortment of rings which had survived decades of grubbing in flowerbeds. I'd tried occasionally to smarten her up, since she's good-looking in an older, country-mum, don't-give-a-damn sort of way, but although she would conscientiously wear anything I gave her (*vide* the pashmina) it never made any difference to the overall impression.

She brought my father into the conversation casually, without hesitation or awkwardness. Instead of the husband who'd deserted her and her children, leaving his own parents to offer the financial support he should have supplied, he might have been a rather tiresome distant relative who had turned up out of the blue to make a nuisance of himself. A relative with a blood-is-thicker-than-water claim on her which she acknowledged out of duty or mere habit.

'He phoned me,' she said, 'after he left Dunblair. He doesn't change, you know. He expected me to sympathise because his daughters had rejected him. Said Pan was an ugly overgrown brat with no manners – what *did* she say to him? – and either I'd played him false or made a real mess of her upbringing. I said I was afraid it was the second option; it's tough being a single parent. So he went on about how hard it had been for him, after Véronique died. Poor sod, he obviously adored Natalie, and she must have played him like a fish, till she chucked him back in the pond for good.'

'How can you be sorry for him?' I said. It was a question I'd never asked before.

She smiled. 'Look at him now, getting older and not liking it, lonely and sad, chasing his own tail trying to find someone to love him. It's a pathetic picture. Poor old Roddy. He was so charming once – till I saw beneath the surface. Charm, the real thing, comes from the heart; his was only skin-deep. He's weak, superficial, not too bright. I used to worry you might turn out like him, though you're a lot smarter, but fortunately you've got less charm, more depth. Glad about that.'

'Thanks,' I said tartly. Mummy's never been one to lavish praise on her daughters.

'I'm your mother; I'm not here to massage your ego. You're pretty successful these days – you can find plenty of people to do that.'

'Did – father – say I'd rejected him too?' I resumed.

'Not precisely, but he's decided it was your fault he had to leave Dunblair. I gather you fell out with the Spanish woman – HG's latest wife. Not surprised: John says she's a nightmare. Basilisa the Basilisk. Roddy went on and on about how he'd really hit it off with HG, how matey they were getting, how your tactlessness messed up every-thing. Said he was thinking of having a chat with the papers about you – apparently he's been approached by a couple of hacks – but I turned him off the idea.'

'How?'

'Pointed out he'd upset HG, might lay himself open to legal action. Also said the press had been in touch with me. He didn't like that at all.'

'*Have* they?' I asked, shocked.

'Of course not, but they might have been. Anyway, there are two sides to the story and he knows it. He's almost sure I wouldn't sell mine – but not quite. He manages to like himself most of the time without too much effort, but there are moments when an inkling of the truth gets through. He can't deal with that. The possibility of being confronted with himself in the national press really scares him.' She took a mouthful of Pomerol. 'Still, we don't want to go there. Once the mud-slinging starts, everyone gets dirty. It wouldn't do you any good, in the public eye or in private. He's your father, after all. You have to put up with him.'

278

'He wants to give me away at the wedding,' I said.

'Would it matter if he did?'

Yes. But I didn't say it – not to Mummy. Not now.

'These big weddings are all about the show, not the real relationship. Excluding Roddy seems a bit petty. Besides, who else would you ask?'

'I haven't decided,' I said, as if there was a short list of possibles. There wasn't.

'There you are. It doesn't make any odds. Alex won't mind, will he? Roddy evidently approves of him, so I infer they got along.'

'Sort of.' I didn't want to admit how betrayed I felt by Alex's attitude.

'No harm in it then. Give Roddy the chance to be pleased with himself. It doesn't happen much any more. He's a part of you, Delphi, however you feel about him.'

'I'd like to have his genes surgically removed,' I said with sudden violence. 'That's what Pan told him. Good for her.'

'Don't be silly.' My mother was unruffled. 'You're you because of him. If he hadn't left, maybe you'd have grown up more like Natalie, spoilt and manipulative. In a way, his weakness has helped to make your strength. You should keep that in mind.'

I was pleased she thought me strong. I've never been sure how my mother sees me and it's always made me a little uncomfortable. All the same, I wasn't prepared to make concessions over the wedding. I said, 'All right, but I still don't want him giving me away. I'm not his to give.'

I'd been so absorbed, I hadn't noticed the eyes on our table. Then a leading columnist wandered over, all smiles, probably fishing.

'How are things at Dunblair?' he asked. 'I hear there's been some trouble between you and Basilisa Ramón.'

'Idle gossip,' I said sweetly. 'You shouldn't believe all that you hear.'

When he'd gone, I filled Mummy in on the forthcoming divorce. (In a whisper, which must have maddened neighbouring diners.) She expressed mild interest.

'He's one of the greats, Hot God,' she said. 'You wouldn't under-stand: you're too young. Nowadays, pop stars are all packaging. The record companies find someone with the voice and the looks and mould them to fit the market. In the sixties, the stars made them-selves. They didn't fit the mould; they broke it. No one cared what they looked like. Mind you, Hot God had sex appeal. I saw him twice in those days, three times later on. He had so much sex appeal I wet my pants.'

Mothers aren't supposed to say things like that. I tried not to be shocked.

'Do you still think he has?' I enquired tentatively.

'Lord yes,' she said. 'Buckets of it.'

I suggested she came with me to see the Dress, but she declined: she was having tea in Harvey Nick's to talk to an old friend about azaleas. I got to Maddalena's by half three and, on an impulse, called Vanessa to see if I could grab a flight back to Scotland the same evening. She called back twenty minutes later to report that I was booked on a flight to Glasgow with a chauffeured car to get me to Dunblair. I would surprise everyone, I thought. I'd get another night with Alex before he left and be ready to shoot first thing in the morn-ing. First thing for me, anyway.

'You want to rush back to your lover,' Maddalena said. 'That is romance. Something has happened between you – *posso vederlo*. There is a new sparkle about you. When you first come to me, it is all about the marriage, but not the love. Now, it is *in verità l'amore*. How I envy you! To have both the perfect wedding and the perfect man – it happen to so few of us.'

'Yes,' I said, 'Alex is pretty perfect.' In view of recent events, I couldn't think what she meant about the extra sparkle, but maybe it was just reflected off the Dress.

It looked incredible. My breasts swelled from the bodice, my leg nudged at the gap in the skirt. In multiple mirrors I saw the silk streaming out behind me, flowing into the train, and the glitter of iridescent embroidery (still incomplete) which made me look like a May queen dressed in snow blossom and sewn with rainbows. This was front-page stuff. I'd decided I wouldn't sell exclusives: I wanted to be a headline in every tabloid. Maybe even the broadsheets – after all, the *Telegraph* is always featuring pictures of Liz Hurley . . .

Alex would be stunned at the sight of me.

'It's fabulous,' I told Maddalena. 'Totally fabulous. You're a genius.'

'Of course.' She accepted my praise as her due. 'We need to take it in a little *qui*, to finish the embroidery *là* . . . Also I must see your friends for the dresses of the bridesmaids. Brie de Meaux, and the lovely Ruth.'

'Brie'll be back in town tomorrow. I'll get Roo down here as soon as I can.'

'It is *molto importante*. Everything must be wonderful.'

'It will be,' I said, pirouetting in the Dress again – as much as you can pirouette with a ten-foot train behind you. 'It will be.'

By eight, I was back in the air on my way to Glasgow. The flight was slightly delayed so it was nearly ten when I got into the chauffeur-driven car and relaxed thankfully in the relative comfort of the back seat. It was a far longer drive to Dunblair than from Inverness, but with luck I would sleep on the road. I closed my eyes and did my best to close my mind, with only moderate success. Too many thoughts kept intruding: my father, Harry, even Elizabeth Courtney and the mystery I still had to unravel. I rehearsed conversations, envisaged scenarios. At some point I must have dropped off because when I awoke there was a full moon beyond the window and a vista of trees that parted to show the loch and the moon-shimmer on the water.

Home, I thought automatically. After all, the castle had been my home for months.

A startled Jules, on night duty, admitted us through the electronic gates. At the castle, he was there to let me in. Everyone else seemed to be in bed. I dumped my overnight bag, declined offers of tea or alcohol, and made my way upstairs to my room.

In the corridor, a small white tornado encircled my legs and resolved itself into Fenny, who must somehow have got shut out. I was surprised, because although the first flush of Alex's adoration had worn off, he still liked to sleep with the dog on top of the duvet. He must have gone to bed completely blotto, I deduced, unless he had decided to go home early since I wasn't there, which would be extremely irritating. But no – Alex had no PA to book flights for him; he invariably used Vanessa, and she would have told me. (Alex never did anything himself if he could find someone else to do it for him.) Anyway, I was confident he wouldn't rush away from Dunblair any sooner than he had to.

I opened the bedroom door very quietly. The curtains were drawn back and the moon shone in through the window, so it wasn't pitch dark. As my eyes adjusted I could see the bed was occupied. I picked up Fenny and stole softly across the room. Dimly, I made out the disorder of the pillows and the double hunching of the duvet. And two heads resting there.

Two heads.

One was Alex. The other had a long spill of hair sprawled across the pillow, colourless in the moonlight. But I knew who it was without colour. Brie.

Just for a second I remember thinking: he's sleeping on the wrong side. He always sleeps on the left . . .

Stupid little thoughts that you think because you don't want to think the big thoughts – the thoughts that are going to destroy your life.

Then along came that awful draining sensation, only worse than ever before – total weakness, almost faintness, as if my body didn't belong to me, *I* didn't belong to me. Delphinium Dacres, Delphinium the star, beautiful and successful and beloved, didn't exist any more. My spirit shrank away to nothing; I just stood there, utterly silent, as lost and ineffectual as one of the castle ghosts.

My fiancé was in bed with my best friend (my *official* best friend). The ultimate cliché. I should have made a scene. I should have made the scene to end all scenes. I should have screamed and ranted and thrown a tantrum of nuclear dimensions. I couldn't speak, could hardly breathe. Somehow, I backed towards the door, still clutching Fenny. (Of course – they'd thrown him out so they could have sex without interruption.) In the passage I pulled the door to behind me, closing it with a shaking hand. I didn't know what to do, where to go. Tremors started to rack me; I held on to Fenny as if he was the only warm thing in the world.

Then there were footsteps. Harry. Harry bending over me, looking concerned because I was sitting on the floor.

'Delphinium . . . Delphi . . . Jules told me you were back. I thought you might need something. You're ill . . .'

He was lifting me to my feet, putting his arms around me, not in desire but support. I let him. I didn't care. 'What's the matter?' His face was all changed, not smug or taunting but sort of softened. As if he was really worried about me.

'Al . . . Alex.' My voice stumbled on the name. I couldn't lie, not to save my life, not even to save my face. 'In bed. With . . . Brie.' The words stuck in my throat.

Harry said: 'Oh *shit*,' as if he meant it. His arms tightened around me and suddenly I was glad of them, glad he was there, squeezing me and Fenny against his chest. I didn't think I could have stood up without him.

'He's an arsehole,' he said presently. 'He always was. And she's a cheap little bimbo on the make. They suit each other. You have to make allowances for the attraction of identicals.'

Alex had called her a bimbo, back in the days when he couldn't stand her. Cheap, *ordinaire*, on the make. And now he was fucking her . . .

'What d'you want to do?' Harry said. 'I can throw them out for you – all the way out, if you like. It would be a pleasure.'

'Roo,' I said. 'I want Roo.'

'Okay.' He scooped me up in his arms, holding me huddled against him with Fenny on top. At Roo's door he set me down, leaving an arm round me in case I fell. Then he knocked, calling her name. No response. He knocked and called again. After a minute or two the door opened and Roo's face appeared in the gap, sleepy-eyed and squinting because she'd forgotten to put on her specs.

'Yes?' And then: '*Delphi?* You're back early . . .'

'Look after her,' Harry said, pushing me gently into the room. 'She's had a bad shock.'

'What is it? What's wrong?'

'Alex . . .' I tried to say it again. Failed.

'What's he done?' Roo must have switched on the table lamp when she got up. She led me to the bed, sat me down, stroked my hair back off my forehead. 'He hasn't . . . ?'

'In bed with Brie,' Harry said tersely. Filling in for me.

'Oh God, no. Delphi – oh Delphi –'

'I don't think she's up to doing anything about it right now,' Harry went on. 'I found her on the floor outside her room, hanging on to the dog like a child with a favourite teddy. Can you keep her here for tonight?'

'Of course.' Roo was already unzipping my boots.

'I'm going to fix some tea. I'll be back in a minute.'

I was in bed when he returned. He gave me the tea himself: it was sweet, which I hate, and had a familiar peat-bog tang which didn't belong to Earl Grey.

'I don't take sugar,' I said. 'It's fattening. Or whisky.'

'You'll take both and like it,' he ordered. 'Never mind about your figure. Sugar's good for shock, and the whisky will help you sleep. Specially if you're not used to it.'

'He's right,' Roo said. And to Harry: 'Thank you. If I could afford a butler, I'd want you.'

He laughed the kind of laugh people give when something isn't funny. Later, I'd remember it. 'Try to get some sleep, both of you. Call me in the morning, before you come down. Then we'll decide what to do.'

'Thanks,' I said, as he got up to leave. It was the first time I'd ever really thanked him.

When he'd gone, I lay down with Fenny in my arms. Roo got in beside me. I didn't talk or cry. After what seemed like hours the whisky took effect and I slipped into an uneasy sleep, riddled with ugly dreams.

Ruth

I faced that Wednesday with a hangover and a sense of impending doom. Of course, the two could well be connected: a hangover *feels* like a sense of impending doom, transmuted into nausea and headache and a mouth like the inside of a kettle, both gritty and furry. At some point I would have to face HG, possibly Basilisa – and Ash. Not to mention work.

Once Delphi had gone, I despatched the actors and others involved in the re-enactment to the airport and got back to the garden. It was time for final decisions about the location of the maze, with Morty, Russell and Nigel all putting forward different theories. As our resident expert, Nigel's opinion had more weight, but Morty claimed years of horticultural experience had given him a 'gut feel' for such things, and Russell said (fortunately only in an aside) that as neither of them could find their backsides with both hands, sorting out the maze was clearly beyond them. HG was naturally included in our confabulations, and, although we could hardly discuss anything personal in front of the others, he gave me that special smile (the one with the eye-wrinkles) and a murmur of reassurance, though I wasn't certain about what.

In the late morning there was a huge flap when Basilisa left, taking the cream-coloured Ferrari and followed by Sandy in the Range Rover loaded down with even more suitcases than Delphi boasted.

'That's just her hand baggage,' Harry explained. 'The rest goes later, in a fleet of container lorries.'

There was much excitement and surprise among the team – much raising of eyebrows and lowering of voices – since no one but me had seen it coming.

'I go to Glasgow Hilton,' Basilisa had announced to HG. 'You pay. Then I contact *mis abogados*. You pay, and pay. I buy *casa nueva*, maybe Chelsea. You pay, and pay, and pay. You cannot treat me like this. I make you pay in *sangre*, in the blood of your heart. You will see!'

'Not under English law,' HG retorted with the hint of a grin.

Basilisa, however, did not deign to hear him; it might have spoiled her exit. She drove off in convoy leaving a furore of speculation in her wake. Happily, it didn't occur to anyone that I might be involved, and only Russell remarked that I had very little to say for myself on the subject. 'Does that mean we cut her out of the historical scenes?' he said. 'If she and HG are splitting up, she may not wish to be part of the show any more.'

'After we went to all that trouble,' I moaned, as horrific possibilities rose before me. Basilisa getting an injunction to stop the show because she was in it, Basilisa getting an injunction to stop the show because she *wasn't* in it . . .

'Plus,' Russell said, determined to plumb the depths of gloom, 'HG may not want her included now.'

'Don't,' I said faintly.

'*She'll* want to be in it,' Morty said. 'It's *television*.' As if that was a clincher.

With Basilisa, it probably was.

'Do we know what happened?' Nigel enquired, as if discussing an intriguing incident from history. 'I assume from prior events that Delphinium was involved in some capacity.

Were her charms the catalyst for this occurrence? Could that be why she decided to leave this morning? Some sort of connection is indicated. Ruth, you must know what happened.'

'Haven't a clue,' I said. 'Delphi's back tomorrow, anyway. She only went to London to try on her wedding dress. I think that's more important to her than anything Basilisa gets up to.'

'A likely story,' said Morty.

'Actually,' I snapped, 'it's so bloody likely it's true.' But my little spurt of rage didn't convince anyone. Rumours multiplied and spread; at lunch, Alex and Brie joined in, the latter also determined to attribute Basilisa's departure to Delphi; by the afternoon newspapers were ringing up on every number they had. Presumably, the uninjured hack from the *Scoop* was still around and had seen the cavalcade pass through the village, or Basilisa had called them herself. Or both. I didn't see Ash till the evening, but although he must have heard what people were saying he didn't make any attempt to contradict it, merely giving me a cold look and the briefest of greetings when we met.

I didn't venture down to the kitchen; I was too afraid of finding Ash cheek-by-jowl with Cedric, looking more than just friendly. His coldness *might* mean he liked me and resented HG kissing me, but it might mean something completely different. I'd obviously made a total fool of myself; there was no need to make it worse.

Nobody had the nerve to ask HG what had really happened. The staff looked discreetly cheerful about the change in their circumstances. Morag was heard to mutter something about 'the depairture o' the ungodly', and Sandy, when back from Glasgow, was seen to toss one of Basilisa's shoes to Elton with the command: 'Kill!' I saw Dorian only for a minute: he appeared pleased about his stepmother's exit but, with the perception that often accompanies unrequited passion, regarded me with a suspicious eye. Neither he nor his father came into dinner, and I escaped early, crashing out by ten, too tired for secret misery to keep me from sleep.

Until Harry woke me around one, knocking on my door, and Delphi, white and shaking, tottered into my room.

Delphinium

That was the worst awakening of my life. It was one of those morning-after awakenings that I'd sworn never to do again – never, since Ben Garvin left me, and I'd had a week – two weeks – of waking up like that. There are a few seconds before recollection kicks in, when you think everything's all right, and then it all comes flooding back. The warmth and security has gone from your life; you're cold and empty and alone. And this time, there were so many things to do, so many arrangements to make and unmake. I had to call Maddalena about the Dress – the dress I would never wear. I was still lying down and tears overflowed at the thought, trickling down my temples into my ears. It's not a good idea to cry lying down. I sat up to do it more comfortably and found myself sniffing back the tears, too empty to give way.

But first and foremost there was Alex – Alex and Brie in my bed. I had to do something about that. Now.

I wasn't angry – there wasn't any room for anger in that awful hollow coldness – but I wanted to be, I needed to be. Anger is heat and fire and life, the blood-rush that courses through your body, eclipsing grief and hurt. I took the tiny spark in my heart and blew on it, fanning it with images, fancies, fantasies. Not those two heads on the pillow, dimly visible in the moonlight, while I slunk away like an intruder, unwanted and unseen – that was too much even to remember. Instead, I let imagination take over, inventing scenarios, focusing repeatedly on the one central fact. Alex and Brie. Alex and Brie. *Alex and Brie . . .*

I swung my legs out of bed. Roo rolled over and blinked at me.

'Delphi? Are you okay?'

'Can I borrow your toothbrush? Mine's in my room.'

'Sure.'

I went into the bathroom and cleaned my teeth with savage energy, until my mouth foamed like a rabid dog. I can confront the world with an unwashed face but not with yellow teeth. Then I wrapped myself in Roo's bathrobe and went back into the bedroom. Fenny, who had settled on top of the duvet in the hollow between me and Roo, was just beginning to wake up. He'd need a run outside to pee – something Alex usually delegated to one of the maids.

'I called Harry,' Roo said. 'He's bringing tea.'

'Good. Can you hold Fenny for me and ask Harry to see he gets a run?'

'Where are you going?'

'To deal with Alex.'

But when I opened the bedroom door, Harry was already there. If he'd gloated or grinned that infuriating grin, I might have been embarrassed by the memory of the previous night and furious at my own embarrassment. But he was just there. On my side.

'Time to throw them out?'

'Yeah.'

'Jules has got a car ready; he can take them both. What with Basilisa yesterday and all those excess actors, it really is chucking-out time at Dunblair. I'll come with you.'

'I can manage,' I said.

'I'm coming anyway. You may need back-up.'

I was grateful, though I didn't show it. I'd stoked up the anger but it still wasn't hot enough, and part of me was dreading going into my room, seeing them together. *Them*. They weren't people any more, they weren't individuals – just Them. An entity of deceit and betrayal. I wouldn't have admitted the dread to anyone, not even Roo – after all, I was supposed to be Delphinium Dacres, the gardening diva with the superstar temperament and the superstar temper – but I thought Harry guessed.

He said, 'Just one minute,' and went into Roo's room to pick up her phone and give some orders. I waited. When he emerged, I went to my bedroom door and walked straight in.

They were at it. Brie was on top – Alex always liked that – and bouncing up and down like a kid on a pogo stick. She was wearing the devil-mask from the wall, holding it in position with one hand. Although the rest of her bounced, her tits didn't: the implants kept them rigid and virtually immobile. Alex was making the groany noises he always made just before coming, so that for a second it hurt me unbearably – and then the anger rushed back, a great scorching flame of it, and I began to scream.

'Get off him – get out of here – get out both of you – get out – get out – get out!' I'd meant to come up with something more pungent, but anger, real anger, isn't original.

Brie stopped bouncing, shed the mask, and looked stunned – appalled – uncomfortable – and then her expression settled into a kind of vague resentment tinged with something that was almost satisfaction, an expression that told me everything I needed to know about our so-called friendship. I may not have loved her the way I loved Roo, but I'd done what I could to help her – *I* was the one who had brought her to Scotland – and my rage hotted up a few more degrees.

Alex, meanwhile, looked . . . well, the only way a man can look when caught by his fiancée shagging another woman. I didn't need to see his dick to imagine its collapse. Embarrassment fought with horror in his face and just about won. 'Delphi!' he cried. 'My God, Delphi – I didn't expect . . . I didn't know . . . you don't understand . . .' It took several seconds for him to detach himself from her, and Brie, still exuding a faint sense of triumph, didn't give him any help. 'This isn't the way it looks,' he went on, defying credibility.

'It isn't?' I retorted, slightly calmed by his panic. 'It looks like sex, but tell me it's something else. Miniature golf, perhaps? Tiddlywinks?'

'She came on to me,' Alex insisted desperately. 'I was pissed, and she just *threw* herself – I mean, she was here in the bed when I—'

'Liar!' said Brie, groping for her clothing, which seemed to have made its way under the bed. 'You were the one who suggested it. Go up first, you said, wait for me—'

'I don't care who did what,' I interrupted, snatching the dress from her grasp. 'I don't care if it was *rape*!' I meant, if Brie had raped Alex – Alex wasn't the aggressive type. 'You get out – both of you – *now*! No clothes – just as you are! NOW!'

'Give me that dress!' Brie's air of triumph disappeared. 'I'm not going anywhere till I—'

'Delphi! You don't mean it! I love you – we're getting married . . .' Alex stood up, clutching the duvet round his hips. (This can be done with a sheet but should not be attempted with a duvet. It's overkill.)

'Not any more!' Not without a pang, I tugged off the ring and hurled it at him. 'You can take this, but that's all! No clothes – no bedding – you go as you are!'

Alex scrabbled on the floor for the ring (the diamond was seriously valuable) still trying to preserve what modesty he had left with the duvet. Brie grabbed her dress and tried to wrench it from my hands. Amazingly, it didn't rip.

Harry's voice rose above the furore, sounding very level and calm and, for once, exactly like a perfect butler. 'Ladies and – er – gentleman, no fighting please. Miss de Meaux, Mr Russo – I'm afraid I have to insist that you leave. Immediately. The bedding belongs here; your clothes will follow you. There's a car waiting outside.'

'I'm not going like this!' Brie objected. 'How dare you! I won't be ordered about by a *servant*!'

These arrivistes are always so vulgar.

'Bloody cheek,' Alex said. 'Look here, this is . . . is . . . a private affair, and none of your business, so—'

'Everything that happens in the castle is my business,' Harry said, 'by authority, in case you've forgotten, of the owner. Now, *sir*, let me relieve you of that. You really can't walk out with the bed linen, you know. It's extremely bad manners.'

'I won't—'

Sandy materialised in the background with Elton and Sting. On cue, one of the dogs growled.

'You can't do this,' Brie almost begged, gazing from me to Harry to the dogs and back again.

'Yes we can,' I said.

'I'll tell the press . . .'

'Tell 'em,' I said. The tabloid coverage was going to be a blood-bath. There was nothing I could do to stop that.

And, from Harry: 'Perhaps you'd like pictures?'

They left – naked, protesting, with Sandy and the dogs on their heels and Harry in the rear. I leaned out of the window. Naked, they got into the car. 'Leave them in the village,' Harry told Jules. 'At the pub. Then you'd better come back for their clothes.'

'You can't do this!' Alex fumed. 'It's – it's – assault.'

'Actually it isn't,' said Harry. 'I would never hit a man with no clothes on. Be glad of that.'

'I don't want to go to the village!' Brie declared. 'I want to go to the airport.'

'If you like,' Harry said obligingly. 'I'm not sure they'll let you on the plane like that. Of course, it would make the security checks very simple . . .'

Sandy got in the front with Jules, and they drove off.

I went back to the bed, picked up the devil-mask. I'd always hated it. It was part of the Basilisk effect – but Basilisa had gone. I put it on the floor and stamped on it, hard. The papier mâché cracked and scrunched underfoot. I stamped on it again and again in a sudden outpouring of pent-up violence. When Harry came in with Roo, I was sitting on the edge of the bed, hugging myself. The mask was in fragments.

Harry nudged them with his toe. 'Feel better for that?'

'Not much.'

'Go back to Ruth's room. I'll bring you some tea and sort out Alex's stuff.'

'Can you – can you change the bedding?'

'Mm.'

'Could you throw this lot away, or put it in the back of a cupboard? I don't want to sleep where . . .'

'I'll arrange something.'

Back in Roo's room, she said, 'D'you want to take the day off work? We can manage without you, if you feel it's too much. I'll see to it.'

'No,' I said. 'No, that would be silly. I have to get on, do things. I can't just sit around. But I'll need some time to make phone calls. Cancel stuff. You know.'

'I'll give you a hand,' Roo said.

'Thanks.'

The worst wasn't over, I knew that. Not by a long shot. The worst was out there, waiting to hit the news-stands. Soon, the journalists would be circling, then the feeding frenzy would begin.

The downside of being a celebrity. For the first time ever, I almost wished I was on the Z-list.

That day, everyone was busy laying out the maze – marking out pathways, arguing over how wide they should be, trying to decide what was an opening, what was hedge. I left them to it and sat down with the telephone, starting with my mother, who took the news in her stride and offered to call any relatives on the guest list, including Pan. (We didn't mention my father.) Then it was the company who owned the castle in Kent, the caterers, the florist. And Maddalena.

'*Cara*,' she said, 'I am so sorry. *Ovviamente* he was wrong for you. That Brie, she is nothing but a little *puttana*. All the same, it is strange how you have that sparkle, when you come yesterday. Maybe you are in love with *un altro*, and you don't yet know it. You want I keep the dress for you, just in case?'

'No,' I said. 'I mean, there isn't anyone. Honestly. You'd better ditch the dress. I couldn't wear it now. Bill me.'

'*Non è necessario*. I sell to someone else. Unless you want I burn it?'

''Course not. But . . . when you sell it . . . you won't say it was made for me, will you?' I hated the idea of someone crowing that they'd been married in my discarded wedding dress.

Maddalena reassured me, sounding shocked that I should suspect her of such vulgarity. 'I do not boast of my *clienti*,' she said. 'Why should I? Everyone come to me anyway. *Allora*, what do we do with the bridesmaid dresses? *Fortunatamente*, I haven't yet made up the one for Brie – I did not have her size. But the dress for Ruth, it is nearly ready.'

'Finish it,' I said. 'We'll give it to her anyway. I'll pay. She never has any decent dresses.' I could tell her it was completed already and would simply go in the bin if she didn't take it.

'*Benissime*,' she said. 'She will look wonderful. Always it is wise to make something good from bad situation. Do not worry, *cara*, all will be well. You are young and beautiful. All will be well with you. *Magari*, as we say in Italy.'

'What does that mean?' I asked.

'Like "maybe",' she said, 'only more so.'

Magari. It sounded to me like she was hedging her bets.

Finally, I contacted Vanessa and Anna Maria (she had the spare key to Alex's place) with instructions to go round to the mews and remove anything which was, or might be, mine. This included all female clothing, all jewellery, half a crate of Bolly, my post, Fenny's basket, food bowl, and other canine accessories, and the new megascreen TV, which I'd paid for. Also the limited edition Hockney print which I'd given Alex for his last birthday, all the good CDs, any book with words of more than two syllables . . .

'Don't worry,' Vanessa said. 'I get the picture. Anna Maria and I can take care of it.'

Back at work, everyone was extra nice to me – in their way. Nigel was patronisingly kind, Morty avuncular, Russell bracing. ('You're well rid of him. Do we have to cut him and Brie from the scenes, as well as Basilisa? The end result is going to look like a patchwork quilt with holes in it.') The camera crew, who sometimes took the piss – 'Show us your good side, Delphi!', 'Bit more cleavage' etc. – refrained. HG, who was around a lot to follow the progress of the maze, said to me, 'Both of us in the shit, huh?'

I'd almost forgotten about his divorce (we weren't really cutting Basilisa from the historical scenes: too complicated). The thought of the double scandal hanging over Dunblair made me blench.

'The press'll go berserk,' I said, visualising waves of paparazzi assaulting the perimeter wall with grappling hooks and rope ladders. Still, they might decide the two stories were connected and couple my name with HG, which would at least salvage my public pride, even if it didn't heal my damaged heart.

'This is a castle,' HG said. 'We can stand a long siege.'

'Unless war breaks out or there's another royal divorce, we may have to,' Russell said. 'On second thoughts, scratch out the war. It'd never make the tabloids.'

Later in the day, I had to switch my mobile off since someone (probably Brie) had leaked the number to a contact at the *Daily Mail*. She and Basilisa were presumably signing up with Max Clifford even now. By evening, reports were coming in from the village of a massive influx of journalists wielding tape recorders, mikes, hand-held movie cameras and so on. Apparently, every resident was giving interviews about Basilisa's unpopularity, if not her mating habits. They knew little about Brie and Alex but, according to Angus (our man on the inside), most decided to improvise, embellishing our night in the pub until Brie was alleged to have done a striptease while Alex tried to seduce at least a dozen local lasses. Meanwhile, Jules and Sandy got creative, patrolling the estate armed with paint guns, which they fired at anything resembling a telescopic lens. As a result, two red deer wound up a good deal redder, and several perfectly harmless birds turned into robins.

I recalled the good publicity of the rescue – it seemed a lifetime ago – and stiffened my upper lip in anticipation of the next day's papers. I'd never had a really bad press. But I'd risen too fast and too far; the new series, and my wedding, had been too widely hyped; the vultures were out there, or possibly it was the sharks, circling their prey, sharpening their teeth and their talons, doing whatever it is sharks and vultures do before they zoom in and pounce. However you saw them, I was going to be dinner.

'It'll be *awful*,' I told Roo. 'They'll make me look like a bitch or a loser or both, and then it'll be the turn of the female columnists, dripping venom and being sorry for me, all in the same paragraph. I think it's time I committed sooty. Oh God, I'm *single*! I hadn't realised . . . I've *never* been single. When Ben Garvin left there was David Tennison, waiting in the wings. But now I've got *no one*. What am I going to do?'

'Get off with Nigel?' Roo suggested.

'Definitely not funny.'

On my way to my room to change I stopped in the entrance hall. There was the picture of Elizabeth Courtney, so positioned that a shaft of light from an upper window fell directly on her face. It struck me suddenly that it must have been moved; previously it had hung right above the stairs, in shadow unless the electric light was on. Now, someone had shifted it a little to the left, so the evening sun lit up the portrait with a sort of golden softness. I wondered who had moved it – it must have been difficult: its new location wasn't easily accessible – and why. I must ask Harry.

Elizabeth looked very warm and alive in that sunset glow. Too real to be just a picture. Too vital, too modern, to have lived and died in the fusty Victorian age, wearing whalebone corsets and embroidering samplers and doing the other things women did in those days to pass the time. She didn't look to me like a natural embroiderer, not her. And once again I felt her there, not just the portrait but the person, as close as my own thoughts. She'd never been betrayed and left in solitary singledom, she'd been wealthy and sought-after and beloved – but in that moment she seemed as near to me as a friend, an intimate, understanding presence. Trying to comfort me, trying to say something – but was it something about me or something about her? She'd been sought-after and beloved, until she vanished into the lost maze, never to be seen again. The maze we were reconstructing – the maze that would soon be as large as life and twice as expensive. I shivered, though not at the cost.

The dread of my dream in the gallery had faded, and so had the vivid impression it had left behind, but if it really was an echo from the past – Elizabeth's past – the two conspirators had hated her, hated her happiness and her bright energy . . . Or had they? I concentrated, struggling to remember them – Iona Craig and another. I'd sensed evil in the atmosphere, but not hate; I couldn't be sure but I thought the killing had been, from their point of view, an ugly necessity, part of a ruthless plan with an unknown object. There had been passion in Iona's face – the dark side of love. Whatever drove her, it wasn't revenge.

But we were talking dreams here. Dreams and ghosts. Nothing tangible.

The facts were that Archie McGoogle, my prime suspect, had an unbreakable alibi: he was suppressing natives at the time, on another continent. Iona's lover, if she had one, must have been a local lad, but how he fitted in or who he was I couldn't guess.

Suddenly I wondered who would have inherited the castle if Archie hadn't returned. Perhaps there was a bastard son of Alasdair's father waiting to emerge from obscurity, only for some reason he kept quiet. Perhaps Iona was pregnant by Alasdair, and that made it imperative for Elizabeth to be removed. Only she must have lost the baby, and then . . .

Too many perhaps. And Elizabeth's spirit at my shoulder, telling me something I couldn't hear.

I went slowly upstairs to change for dinner.

Ruth

There wasn't much I could do for Delphi, but I phoned Crusty
to warn him that a wave of dubious publicity was about to
sweep the board in the gutter press. An innocuous series on
gardening was going to be elevated to top TV scandal, whether
we liked it or not. I expected Crusty to be appalled; after all,
he was an old-fashioned English gentleman to whom the public
washing of dirty linen must be deeply distasteful. I'd forgotten two things: he was also a successful producer, and it wasn't
his linen. He took the news of the debacle philosophically –
so philosophically that I realised during the course of our
conversation that he, at least, had never lost sight of the ball.

'Good thing about HG,' he said. 'Never thought Basilisa was
really his type. Thing is your type changes as you get older,
but it can take you a while to find out. Delphinium okay?'

'She will be,' I said.

'Didn't really know Russo. More money than brains, I always
thought. Bit of a lightweight but no harm in him. Oh well,
she'll get over it. Plenty more like that around. She mixed up
with HG?'

'No, but I'm sure that's what the papers will say.'

'Inevitable,' Crusty agreed. 'She's pretty; he's a superstar.
Tabloids'll have them both engaged by the end of the week.

Won't hurt. We've got Russo, the model and the Basilisk all on film for the programme, right?'

'Yes. In the historical bits.'

'Pity we can't bring the show out this week. We'd have better ratings than *Big Brother*. Latest I've heard, we're in the schedules next autumn. Have to see if we can manage a little nugget for the press then, won't we? Something to nudge their memory.'

'Umm . . .'

'Nothing for you to worry about. Keep everyone focused on the garden: that's the main thing. The press – that's just sound and fury. Blow over in a few days. Unless . . . nothing else likely to crawl out of the woodwork, I suppose?'

I reviewed the line-up: Morty, Nigel, Russell . . . None of them had a spouse on location. 'No,' I said. 'There are no more couples available for divorce at the moment.'

'There you are, then. You're in Dunblair: paparazzi may be on the doorstep, but the doorstep's well outside. HG's people will keep them at a distance: they're used to it. Ignore the headlines. Should be all out of scandals by now.'

'I think so,' I said.

There are times when you can almost hear the Fates laughing.

I desperately wanted to talk to Ash, but I couldn't think what to say, or how to say it. He'd agreed to expound on camera about ghosts in general and Dunblair ghosts in particular, and he came across very well – not just because of the light on his cheekbones (though that helped). He could have his own series, I thought, but he probably wouldn't want to. He didn't have the TV mentality. In any case, he undoubtedly saw the supernatural as too sensitive a subject for what he would term crass exploitation.

'Memories linger on in the atmosphere,' he said. 'We pick

up on them as feelings, what you might call vibes, even apparitions. They are like echoes of the past still reverberating long after the event. The evidence for actual spirits is more debatable. We live in a world that has little faith in the afterlife; many people doubt the existence of the soul. Even if we *do* have souls, we cannot know if they endure: logic suggests haunting a place after death would be a form of immortal cul-de-sac. The religions might claim it would be a punishment for wrongdoing in life; popular fiction generally favours the concept of unfinished business. The two theories are not incompatible. Both see phantoms as bound to this world by something they cannot leave behind, whether crime or tragedy or the need for justice.

'I suspect that some spirits do remain with us, but the evidence for it is unscientific. Spirits are outside science. It is unreasonable to expect manifestations of the metaphysical to be measurable in physical terms. There are indications – temperature changes are the most common – but for the ghost-hunter, feelings are the best guide. Dunblair has many echoes from the past: most old buildings do. But I believe there may also be spirits here, trapped in this world by some great need that has outlasted life.'

'He could be a bit less airy-fairy,' Russell muttered. 'People aren't interested in theory; they want to get down to the nitty-gritty. The clanking chains and the skirl of ghostly bagpipes.'

'Not . . . necessarily,' I said. I hadn't told Ash, or anyone, about the bagpipes. 'Anyway, he's supposed to be airy-fairy. It goes with the job. You can't expect a psychic researcher to be down-to-earth.'

'At least he's articulate as well as pretty. We'd never get away with it if it wasn't for that.'

Ash went on – more reluctantly, I thought – to talk about what other people claimed to have seen, heard and felt. HG did his part, relaxed as always, giving his own view of the atmospherics at Dunblair, and just for fun we persuaded Morag to do a bit of doom-and-gloom, propounding the legend that the reconstruction of the maze would wake the spectres of all who had died in it. She was far and away the most effective, if only because she obviously had no doubts.

We were probably going to chop up the pieces and intersperse them with the castle's history, the garden, and everything else – the patchwork quilt.

'This is a makeover show with a difference,' Russell remarked. 'I've dealt with dry rot and death-watch beetle, poor topsoil, poor bottom soil and woodworm in the decking, but I must admit I've never had spooks before.'

'Look on the bright side,' I said. 'We haven't found a skeleton yet.' Only the dog, which didn't count.

'There is that.'

Ash was being so aloof he didn't come in to dinner, and Delphi, still in shock at her single state, had rather too much to drink and had to be helped to her room by Harry and me.

'I don't like it,' I said. 'She never gets this drunk.'

'It won't hurt her,' Harry said. 'Just the once. What about cocaine?'

'She doesn't do that much either. Delphi likes to be in control.' She got pissed sometimes in her teens, but who didn't? I was the one whose self-control went down the drain whenever it got the chance.

'It figures,' Harry said. 'And now her life's got away from her and she doesn't know how to get it back. Might do her good.'

'I don't suppose you'll tell me what happened when you and HG got rid of Roddy? I know Delphi was pretty uptight about something – something to do with you.'

'We had a deal,' Harry said, with only a hint of the grin. 'She owes me. But I wasn't planning to collect right now.'

'What deal?' I said suspiciously.

'Confidential.'

He wouldn't say any more.

With all the talk of ghosts I went to bed feeling spooked and lay awake for a long while with my ears on the stretch, though I didn't hear the bagpipes again. The castle breathed softly in its sleep, its joints shifting and creaking arthritically from time to time. There was the sigh of a draught, the rustle of a curtain. I thought of Delphi's dream – the plotters in the gallery – and the ghost of Alasdair McGoogle roaming the castle corridors in search of the bride he had lost. When I drifted over the borders of sleep I saw the maze pirouetting on Nigel's computer screen, while a Lara Croft action-girl from one of Dorian's games dodged down the pathways, pursued by Cedric and his orc-band. Then I was in the garden, and the maze was real, and the hedges were sprouting before my eyes, growing taller and darker by the second. There were snufflings and groanings among the roots as Morag's spectres came to life. I saw the back of a female figure running towards the heart of the maze, her stiff silk skirts swishing around her. I knew somehow it was Elizabeth Courtney, wearing Delphi's wedding dress. I followed her, but she kept disappearing round corners the way people do in dreams, and I couldn't catch up. Then I reached the heart of the maze, and there was a statue in rusted iron with a gigantic phallus, and Elizabeth was rushing towards it. I saw the phallus was really a claymore, dripping with stage blood, and I called out a warning, and she turned round, but she had no face, only a skull.

I woke abruptly and sat up, groping for the light switch to chase away the shadows that crowded round my bed.

* * *

'D'you want to see the papers?' Harry said at breakfast. 'HG ordered them all, so we could check for anything actionable. His lawyers read them too, but he likes to run an eye over them himself. It's the recipe as usual. They haven't actually said that there's anything between HG and Delphinium, but the hints are dropping like flies. Basilisa seems to have given at least three exclusives claiming she caught him in flagrante delicto with almost every girl on the team.'

'Does she say he has a limp deek?' I enquired absent-mindedly, my gaze focusing on the *Express* with the headline 'HOT GOD'S HOTBED OF SCANDAL'.

'No, but their legal advisers may have expurgated it,' Harry said. 'So . . . when did you hear her say that?'

'I witnessed their final showdown,' I said, disregarding the shrewdness of his scrutiny. 'Or part of it.'

'Should think it would be difficult to shag around with a limp deek.'

'That's what he said.'

Delphi was still in bed; my knock on her door had elicited only a tragic demand for coffee. Russell joined me, leafing through the papers. 'BREAKOVER SHOW,' declared the *Sun*. 'Hot God Marriage On Compost Heap. DD Wedding Off: Fiancé Alex and Best Friend Brie.' The tabloids often called Delphi 'DD' for the sake of brevity. 'FLOWER POWER!' cried the *Mirror* with something approaching wit, beside a picture of HG on the beach at Mande Susu looking like an ageing hippy. (Presumably one of Basilisa's.) 'Makeover Show Blamed For Rock Star's Marital Bustup.' 'CATASTROPHE CASTLE,' alliterated the *Scoop*. 'BROKEN MARRIAGE; CANCELLED WEDDING,' juxtaposed the *Mail*. 'The Lost Maze of Relationships,' said the *Guardian* (inside pages). 'Come into the Garden, Gawd,' quipped a misguided wag in the *Telegraph*. 'Hot God's Fifth Wife Demands Divorce,' the *Indy* said pedantically. (We all tried counting on our fingers to see if they'd got the number right.)

It went on and on.

'It's the cringe-making attempts at humour that really get you in the gut,' Russell said. 'Still, it gives people a change from tsunamis and suicide bombers.'

'True enough,' Harry said. 'It's the cream cake in a diet of rare steak and greens. It's high in cholesterol and puts on weight, but everybody likes cake best.'

'Crusty thinks it won't hurt the show,' I said.

'Good God, no,' Russell responded. 'The only trouble is, we're peaking too early. By the time the show hits the screens HG could have notched up two more divorces and Delphi married a minor viscount with a fortune in sugar and half a dozen brain cells. We need to keep something in reserve. D'you have a story you can leak at the right moment, Ruthie?'

He gave me a canny look – he was much too acute at times – but I managed a light answer. At least the only people looking at me that way were him and Harry. HG's slight penchant for me had evidently made an impression with the observant, even though Basilisa seemed to have omitted it from her various interviews. She probably didn't want to reveal that the final straw had been catching her husband kissing a total nonentity.

'I know you hate the idea,' Delphi said when she surfaced, 'but you could sell your story for *millions*. I wouldn't mind, truly I wouldn't. Right now, I'm getting the credit for something that was nothing to do with me. It's an improvement on "Delphinium Dumped!" or whatever they would've said, *but* . . .'

'You can have the credit, if that's the right word,' I said. 'I don't want it. Get your make-up on; we need to do some work.'

Delphi shuddered. 'I can't face the camera,' she announced. 'I look like hell, I feel like hell, life is hell.'

'Don't be wet,' Harry said, supplying a third cup of coffee. 'It doesn't suit you.'

In the garden, we were doing more digging than filming. (That's the royal 'we', since I didn't actually dig.) Nigel & Co. had agreed on the centre of the maze and Young Andrew and another local lad were excavating there, since HG's new statue was to include a water feature which would require underground pipes. About three feet down they struck stone. Not rock, but the smooth face of a man-made slab. Clearing the soil away, an area was revealed about four feet by six, with a hinged section at one end obviously designed to be raised. The hinges had rusted as rain had seeped through the earth, and the stone was very heavy, so it was some time before it was possible to lift it.

'Of course!' Nigel said in a state of great excitement. 'You've heard of a priest's hole? It was a kind of secret room installed in many old houses during the Civil War, so runaway clerics could hide from Cromwell's men . . .'

'We know that,' Morty said irritably.

'This has to be the same type of thing, only underground. These stones are very old. Who knows why it was built originally – no doubt for some nefarious purpose – but at a guess Bonnie Prince Charlie hid here while British soldiers scouring the maze were picked off one by one by the Laird's henchmen.' Only Nigel could use the word '*nefarious*' in ordinary conversation. He always talked as if he were narrating one of the more dramatic history programmes; it could have been force of habit, or maybe he spoke that way from infancy. Probably the latter. 'It's been buried deeper over time, but when in use it would have been concealed by the plinth of the statue, with only a thin layer of soil to cover the trapdoor. On a dark night, of course, even the soil wouldn't be necessary. This was the secret of the maze: people would go in, "disappear" . . .' he drew the punctuation marks in mid air – 'and leave later when everyone had ceased to look for them.'

'They'd need help,' Russell opined. We still hadn't raised the trapdoor. HG had taken over and was directing operations.

'Yes, but . . . why would Elizabeth do that?' Delphi said. 'Why hide at all? She wasn't a fugitive. She was madly in love – she'd just got married.'

'We don't know if she *did* hide,' I said, feeling a strange sense of disquiet.

'We're there,' HG said as Young Andrew levered the trap-door open.

There was a dark cavity below, out of reach of the daylight. In the frenzy of anticipation, no one had thought to get a torch, and we had to wait while somebody ran to fetch one. Then HG dropped to his knees by the hole and shone it down into the blackness.

I couldn't see much – Nigel, Morty and Delphi took up most of the space round HG. But I didn't need to.

'Dear God,' he said. 'There's a skeleton in there. And it looks as if it's wearing a dress.'

Chapter 10:
The Butler Did It

Ruth

I didn't realise, but if you find a skeleton in your garden, no matter how old it may be, the first thing you have to do is contact the police. HG's name meant we actually got a super-intendent, a red-haired Glaswegian whose cheerful references to 'muddurr' reminded me irresistibly of *Taggart*. Incredibly, the centre of the maze became a crime scene, with yellow tape to discourage intruders and people dressed from head to foot in white plastic tramping around looking for clues. The pathol-ogist, however, soon confirmed that the *corpus delicti* was some one hundred and thirty years old, at which point the Law lost interest and a forensic archaeologist took over. Nigel, practi-cally shivering with enthusiasm, put on a spiritual deerstalker and set about detecting the crime – if crime it was. Delphi, rather to my surprise, appropriated the role of Dr Watson.

'We need him,' she said to me. 'He *is* an expert, after all. It's Elizabeth: we all know that. But how did she get there, and why?'

'You look upset,' I said stupidly. Finding a skeleton is always upsetting – or so I assume; I haven't found many – but Delphi seemed to be suppressing real distress.

'I feel . . . like I knew her. Like she was a friend.'

'She died over a century ago. Before your mother was born. Before your *grandmother* was born.'

'That doesn't change things. I said we had to solve the mystery, didn't I? Well, now we've got a body. That's a start. They can get DNA from a skeleton, can't they? No matter how old it is.'

'I think so,' I said. 'But what would they have to compare it with?'

Overhearing, Nigel chipped in. 'There may be modern descendants of the Courtneys,' he said. 'Remember, Elizabeth went into society under the aegis of her aunt and uncle, the aunt being her father's sister. Their name was, I believe, Dagworthy. He was untitled but well connected – a bishop in the family – so they shouldn't be difficult to trace. And the name is uncommon. If we can locate a latter-day Dagworthy who will agree to give a DNA sample, we can confirm that the remains are those of Elizabeth Courtney.'

'That would be great,' Delphi said, flashing a quick ray of charm in his direction. 'We know it's her, but it ought to be official. I wonder . . .'

'You wonder what?' I prompted. She had that glint that Delphi always gets when inspiration comes along.

'If we could speed things up a bit. There are all those journalists hanging around. Why don't we give them something to do?'

So the hacks got a story, if not the story they came for. They already knew about the skeleton, of course; someone in the police must have tipped them off. But Nigel organised an impromptu press conference in the pub where he ran through the history of Elizabeth Courtney, her romantic marriage and tragic disappearance, explained that the corpse was believed to be hers, and requested help in tracing modern-day relations for a comparison of DNA. Russell, Morty and I were there for back-up; for obvious reasons, Delphi and HG weren't present. There was a hail of questions about the forthcoming divorce, the aborted wedding and all concerned in them, but Nigel rose above the mêlée and even managed to engage his audience's attention over a mystery that happened two centuries ago. My respect for him increased dramatically.

'Was Elizabeth murdered?' several people asked, temporarily distracted from more recent shenanigans at Dunblair.

'As yet we don't know,' Nigel said. 'The remains are amazingly well preserved thanks to the dry atmosphere in the underground chamber. It is completely lined with stone, watertight and virtually airtight; there were holes bored in the trapdoor to admit oxygen, but they were very small and blocked with impacted earth. However, we do not believe Elizabeth suffocated. Her position, laid on her back with her arms at her sides, doesn't show any indication of trauma. She may well have been dead when she was placed there. We have to wait for the results of the autopsy; it's possible that may give us some clues as to how she died.'

'If she died by violence, surely it must be obvious,' someone said.

'Not necessarily,' Nigel pursued. 'Remember, after so long the flesh and internal organs have rotted away. What we have left is a skeleton with some mummified skin and the remnants of female clothing. Stabbing or shooting might mark the bones and a head wound would damage the skull, but something like, say, strangulation would leave little or no evidence behind. Of course, the dress may be helpful; it really is in extraordinarily good condition. It is worth noting that this body is almost exactly contemporary with the ones in the catacombs at Palermo, which can be seen today as skeletal corpses fully dressed in their original clothes.'

This piece of erudition silenced everyone for a moment or two, since nobody knew anything about skeletons at Palermo. ('Where the hell's that?' I heard one man asking in an aside. 'Italy – I think,' said his colleague.)

Afterwards, back in the relative security of Dunblair, we found Fenny had treed a photographer who'd sneaked in over the wall and was growling menacingly every time he attempted to come down from his perch. Jules and Sandy finally conde-scended to rescue him and escort him off the premises – 'He'll say it was a Dobermann,' Harry guessed – and the rest of us went in to dinner, eager to discuss our discovery and all its implications. Ash joined us, though his icy mood didn't seem to have thawed out, and even Dorian was there, allowing himself to give way to schoolboy enthusiasm at the gruesome nature of what we had unearthed. This, it was clear, would definitely boost his status at Gordonstoun. Anybody could be the son of a rock star, but digging up a corpse was *really cool*.

'Can I see it?' he demanded. 'Does it look, like, all green-ish and manky?'

'It's a she,' Delphi snapped.

'Brown, not green,' HG said. 'And not manky. More dry and shrivelled. It's in the laboratory at the moment. The forensics people have to do a lot of tests.'

'When they've finished with her,' Delphi said, 'we should see she gets a proper burial. With a vicar and everything. She was bound to be a Christian; people were in those days. If we could do that, and solve the mystery, maybe her spirit could move on. Don't you think so?'

The question was addressed to Ash, who came down from whatever plateau he was on to look faintly intrigued.

'Possibly,' he said. 'Religion was very important to the Victorians. It's something she would have wanted, I suppose.'

'Can't you – er – commune with her spirit?' Morty suggested

with a sarcasm that was presumably meant to be subtle. 'You're the psychic, aren't you?'

'I'm a researcher, not a medium,' Ash said, failing to rise to the taunt.

Delphi, who thought any communing with Elizabeth should be done by her, said: 'Will they give us back the body?'

'Good question,' said HG. 'Who does it belong to – apart from its original owner? As it's on my land, it might be me, or so I imagine. Unless any of her sister's descendants want to claim it. Formal burial is an idea, but I'm not sure where.'

'The local churchyard?' Russell said.

'Iona Craig, later McGoogle, is interred there in the family vault,' Nigel pointed out. 'If she *was* involved in Elizabeth's death, I doubt her victim would want to spend eternity lying beside her.'

'Bloody right,' Delphi said warmly. She and Nigel were showing dangerous signs of bonding over this. 'Maybe we could boot Iona out.'

'We have to prove she dunnit first,' I said.

After dinner I hung around, hoping for a chance to talk to Ash, but other people monopolised him and when I *did* get the opportunity I couldn't think of a conversation starter. He left without so much as a goodnight, and I found myself thrown together with HG, who wrinkled his eyes at me.

'Sorry about the row the other night,' he said. 'I didn't mean anyone else to get caught in the crossfire. At least you've been left out of the publicity. I had someone drop a hint to the press – off the record – about Delphinium and me. Under the circumstances it probably wasn't necessary, but it doesn't hurt to give them a nudge.'

'Did you ask her?' I said.

'No.' He lifted an eyebrow. 'She's a bright girl on the make. It can only be good for her image.'

'Maybe,' I said, 'but you should have asked.' I still liked him – I couldn't help it – but he had the classic arrogance of the megastar and the slight contempt the ultra-famous feel, not so much for the fan in the street, as for those rather less famous than themselves.

'In that case, I must apologise,' he said, with a trace element of irony.

'Not to me,' I responded. 'To Delphi.'

I turned my shoulder and moved away, and it was only on the way up to bed that it occurred to me I'd just snubbed Hot God, one of the biggest rock icons of all time. Would he mind? Would he cancel the show? Would he be amused/offended/disgusted/enraged? I lay awake worrying about it for what seemed like an age.

It was only the next day that I realised from his attitude, which hadn't changed, that snubs were plainly so rare in his life he hadn't even noticed it.

Delphinium

It is a truth universally acknowledged that a single woman, whatever her income, is sad, sad, sad. I think it was Jane Austen who said something of the kind, ages ago (people are always quoting it), but although this is the twenty-first century and we've emancipated ourselves out of the kitchen and into the office, the studio and the boardroom, it's still true. To get away with being single you've got to be frightfully eccentric, or Germaine Greer, or both. Otherwise, to be thirtysomething and single, no matter how glamorous you are, is just to look as if you can't get a man. The coolest women are the ones who are married to one husband and then pinch someone else's before they've finished with the first one. It's the kind of thing that soft-hearted, principled girls, like Roo, would never do, but society doesn't admire soft hearts and principles. Society admires success – man-grabbing, man-holding success. And the worst of it is, it isn't the men who are doing the admiring – men like soft-hearted singles: it gives them a better chance of a shag – it's *the other women*. It's women who eye their single girlfriends askance, and talk of them in pitying murmurs, and don't invite them to dinner parties (unless there's someone really boring to pair them off with). That's where all our emancipation has got us. We aren't in contention with the male sex any more – we're too busy being our own worst enemies.

Take Tasha Blaggard (known in the trade as Trasha), queen of the crap-show hostesses. I met her once at an awards ceremony. When she wants to put down the competition, the clincher she utters about her rivals is always that they *aren't married*. And she's supposed to be a classic example of successful modern womanhood. Or Princess Di, the ultimate end-of-twentieth-century heroine. She made a career of being single and having unhappy affairs and making everyone sorry for her, but *she was married to a prince*. If she'd been single and unmarried, no one would have paid any attention.

And now here I was. Single. Totally, devastatingly single. With not even the glimmer of a suitable man on the horizon. Roo was breaking up superstar marriages and being pursued by half the men in the place, and I was going to bed alone, unloved, unlusted-after. I wasn't jealous of Roo because I love her so much and I *want* men to pursue and appreciate her, but I couldn't help minding a bit. I mean, I'd always been the beautiful one with a string of guys in pursuit, and now we'd swapped roles. I minded, and I didn't like myself for minding. I knew it was nasty and mean-spirited, so the end of it was I felt worse than ever.

And in bed there was no Alex to cuddle up to, which was . . . well, bearable. After all, I had Fenny. And the great thing about Fenny was that I didn't have to deal with his little moods, or put up with his tiresome friends (*vide* Darius Fitzlightly), or feel anxious because I wasn't having sex with him. Of course, he didn't have a gorgeous mews house, and a high-society profile, and . . . But there was no point in dwelling on all that. The catch was, I'd been madly in love with Alex, we were supposed to be getting married, and now my heart was broken and what I really needed was someone to pick up the pieces and stick them back together again. But this was Dunblair, and though the castle was full of men, there was nobody who fitted my requirements.

Besides, far too many of them were Scottish.

So there we were. The paparazzi were besieging the castle. The press were having a field day. And then, on top of everything else, we found the skeleton.

I knew at once it was Elizabeth Courtney.

Roo was right: even if she'd lived to be old she'd still have died nearly a century ago; but I cared about that, too, really cared, with a sort of sharp angry pain at the thought of her. The pathologists took lots of photographs and then had to bring the skeleton out in pieces because the trapdoor was too small to lift it through intact. They reassembled it on a board like a kind of stretcher before taking it to the laboratory for an autopsy. I was impressed you had to have an autopsy, even after so long. That made it sound as if her murder *mattered*, even though a hundred and thirty years had gone by: she was still a victim and someone would be held to account for what had been done to her.

I thought the bones would be white, but they were brown, with shrunken brown stuff clinging to them which the woman from forensics said was skin. The dress, too, was brown and papery round the edges, but in places you could see the original pattern, embroidered flowers on a background that might have been cream or white. She was a bride, I thought; it was her bridal gown. It reminded me, spookily, of my own unworn wedding dress.

Because Elizabeth was lying on her back, her mouth had fallen open – death, apparently, would have slackened her jaw muscles – but it looked horribly like she was screaming. A brownish skull with empty eye sockets and lipless jaws, screaming and screaming in its underground prison . . .

I shivered. Nigel, who was beside me, said, 'I can see this has really gripped your imagination. That's great: I'm going to need your input.'

He was being patronising again, but I ignored it. Maybe it was just his unfortunate manner.

'We *have* to find out who did this,' I said.

318

'Forensic analysis should give us some idea of the cause of death,' Nigel offered.

'They didn't . . .' I stammered in sudden horror . . . 'they didn't put her in there – *alive*?'

'I don't think so. Her position looked fairly relaxed. If she'd been trapped in there she would have attempted to get out, there would have been indications . . .'

I breathed again. It was bad enough to see that hideous skull, thinking of the woman in the portrait, vital and glowing with the sunset golden on her face. Worse still if she had died in abject terror, struggling to escape her subterranean prison . . .

The police cordoned off that part of the garden and that was really all we could do for the day.

'Does this sort of thing happen often in garden makeover shows?' Roo asked me. 'I mean – what else have you dug up?'

'We found some coins once,' I said. 'Roman, I think. And dead pets. But this is my first human skeleton.'

'I was beginning to worry,' said Roo. 'I've worked in the Balkans in the aftermath of war, I've been in an earthquake zone, covered inefficiency and corruption in famine relief and checked out an environmental disaster, but I've never seen anything as catastrophic as everyday life at Dunblair. To think I was afraid this job would be dull.'

Up yours, Kyle Muldoon, I thought with a tiny flicker of satisfaction. Roo, like me, might still be single, but at least she was having fun.

At dinner, I had my brainwave about giving Elizabeth Christian burial when the forensic archaeologist had finished with her. I thought it was something she would want, something that might help her spirit to find peace after all those years of being shut in a kind of stone coffin in the no-man's-land of the vanished maze. People used to think Christian burial was important; I know, I've seen lots of old movies. Personally, I don't care about the Christian stuff so much, but I want a huge funeral with lots of celebrities and people crying (and absolutely amazing flowers) but not, of course, for an *awfully* long time.

Anyway, Roo called Crusty with a progress report and we decided to take the weekend off until we'd got more info on the skeleton. Morty made plans to go away for a couple of days (good), as did Russell, who'd hardly seen his family since we started the series. I felt depressed all over again because I couldn't fly off to see Alex. I hadn't even been invited to a glamorous party. Mind you, with my mobile switched off most of the time that wasn't surprising. It cut out the nagging journos and the drip, drip of sympathy from friends who wanted to hear every detail of my plight, but if there was someone eager to ask me to a wonderful party where I would meet a wonderful guy it cut that out too.

I went up to bed around ten-thirty – far too early, but there wasn't much night life at Dunblair, unless you counted the ghosts. I thought I was tired – I hadn't been sleeping too well lately – but in bed I found myself thinking about Elizabeth, and the skeleton, and the whole murder mystery thing, until I was so creeped out that I had to sit up and switch on the light. Basilisa's horrible décor surrounded me, thankfully minus the devil-mask, but I was so used to it I barely reacted any more. That's the danger of bad taste. It's insidious – or do I mean invidious? It sneaks up on you and takes over and in the end you don't even notice it's there. Working on a makeover show is a good thing because it's supposed to be about making the world more beautiful, though I have serious doubts about Laurence Lloodwelling-Boredom. After one or two series these interior people go slightly off the rails, if you ask me.

It was nearly half-eleven now and I couldn't sleep, so I picked up the phone – Morag answered – and ordered tea. I was more or less prepared for it to arrive with Harry, but he'd been so nice to me lately I wasn't worrying about it.

Presently, there was a tap on the door and he came in. No tea.

Just a tray with several bottles, alcoholic ones, and two brandy bubbles. *Two*. I was suddenly aware that I ought to be wearing a bedjacket. I've never owned a bedjacket in my life, naturally, but I remember my mother having one, a sort of fluffy angora thing which tied across her bosom with pink ribbon. I suspect somebody knitted it for her. Mummy will actually wear the things people knit for her, unfortunately. (First rule of fashion: never, *ever* wear anything anyone has made for you, no matter how much you care for the person – unless they're a leading couturier, of course.) Anyway, all I had on was a pair of men's pyjamas I'd bought for Alex but liked too much to give him, thank heaven. They weren't indecent, but they *were* sexy.

And there was the alcohol and *two* glasses . . .

'Where's my tea?' I demanded.

'I thought you needed a nightcap,' Harry said. 'I recommend the brandy, but I brought Cointreau, Grand Marnier, or Glayva if you'd rather have something sweeter.'

It wasn't such a bad idea, really. Except for the second glass.

'What's Glayva?' I asked.

'A Scottish liqueur. Made from whisky and honey.'

'I'll stick with brandy.' I don't really like it all that much, but those sweet drinks all taste like medicine to me.

Harry poured my drink and one for himself.

'I didn't ask you to join me,' I said tartly.

'I won't if you don't want me to. I thought you might like someone to talk to, that's all.'

He wasn't grinning, or being impertinent, or eying up my tits. He had the kind of expression which in a guy with a different type of aura might have passed for sensitive. And he hadn't mentioned anything about collecting on the second half of the kiss. Perhaps he didn't fancy me any more, now I was single. Perhaps he was the sort of guy who only fancied women who were fancied by other men, and when they didn't, he didn't either. Perhaps no one would ever fancy me again . . .

'Okay,' I said.

'Can I sit down?'

I didn't want him looming over me.

'Okay,' I said again.

He moved Fenny and sat down. On the bed. I'd expected him to pull up a chair and I was disconcerted.

'You looked pretty unhappy after finding that skeleton today,' he said gently. 'Of course, finding a skeleton is distressing for anybody, but you seem to mind a lot about Elizabeth Courtney.'

Suddenly, I was very very wary.

'You're being sensitive, aren't you?' I accused. 'You're *deliberately* being sensitive. Trying to get under my guard.'

The flicker of a grin returned. 'Is it working?'

'No – yes! You're sitting on my bed and we're drinking HG's liquor. How does he feel about that?'

'He won't notice as long as I don't overdo it.'

'I think it's a cheek.'

'Perks of being a butler.'

I didn't say he was a fraud. I'd done that one to death. I took a mouthful of the brandy and it slithered gently down my throat, evaporating into heat somewhere beneath my ribs. 'Well, all right then,' I conceded, though I wasn't sure what I was conceding. 'But I want you to know that *I* know . . .'

'You know what?'

'What you're up to.' Whatever that was. 'You've been incredibly kind to me lately, but I know it's just a sneaky attempt to . . . to . . . Look, I'm not going to start saying you're my rock or anything like that, okay?'

Harry grimaced. 'I have no desire to be anyone's rock, thank you. I don't do rock. I'm not *your* butler, anyway. I wouldn't be your butler if it was the last job in the world and you were offering me a six-figure salary.'

'Why not?' I said indignantly.

'Because it's against the Secret Code of Butlers to make a pass at your employer.'

'Are you making a pass?' I demanded, wanting clarity.

'In a minute. Don't rush me.' He polished off his drink in one long swallow.

'*In a minute?*'

'You're a believer in instant gratification, aren't you?' He took the glass from my unresisting hand and set it down on the table. 'When you want something, you want it *now*.'

Belatedly, I tried to summon up some coolth. Failed. 'If what you're after is the half-kiss I owe you . . .'

'I was going to start with that.'

And then he was kissing me, really *thorough* kissing, deep and hungry – his tongue in my mouth, his hand on my breast – sliding under my pyjama top, cupping the curve of my flesh, massaging my nipple between finger and thumb. His touch sent a lance of feeling right down between my legs and I was melting again, my whole body melting, dissolving towards a single knot of exquisite tension. The spot marked X . . .

I was in *serious* trouble. I was on a bobsleigh-ride careering downhill to destruction – but I didn't care.

Then Harry drew back and started pulling off his clothes. He was much bigger than Alex, not taller but bigger, probably a few pounds overweight, with rolling muscles and sandy hair on his arms and a diamond-shaped patch of hair beneath his pecs. Alex had been slim and willowy, with slim willowy muscles, hairless as a baby, always lightly tanned from the aftermath of some expensive holiday. Harry looked as if tans were for wimps who had nothing better to do with their time. His skin was skin-coloured, his body big – big was the word that got stuck in my head – big and powerful and intensely masculine.

'I can't . . .' I began. 'I mean, I won't . . .'

He was unzipping his fly; his boxers bulged with more bigness. Then he had kicked off both trousers and pants.

323

'All you have to do is say no,' he said.

Unfair. Totally, unscrupulously unfair.

'No?'

'Are you sure?'

'Um . . . no . . .'

He dumped Fenny on the floor and got into bed with me. My powers of resistance had gone wherever powers of resistance go at these times. He moved on top of me, undoing buttons, getting stuck with them the way men always do. His erection was pressing into me with only the thin silk of my PJs in between and the *big* word was filling up my thoughts until I couldn't think about anything else. I said shouldn't we have the light off but he said no, he wanted to see me, and then he was gazing at my breasts like a tiger at its dinner.

'No silicon . . .'

'It's all me.'

'God, I'm going to fuck you,' he said slowly, in a furry sort of voice that went to the X-spot like the touch of his hands. In his mouth, *fuck* wasn't a swear word, it was sexy and dirty and straight to the point. 'I'm going to fuck you like you've never been fucked before. I'm going to fuck you and fuck you and fuck you till you beg for mercy, but I won't stop, I'll fuck you deeper and deeper . . .'

I couldn't say anything any more. I just whimpered. He was tugging at my pyjama trousers and I was wriggling out of them, and *then* I felt his knob pushing at me, pushing into me – no preliminaries, no foreplay – and he was fucking me like he said, fucking me so deep, and I was helpless and melting and creaming myself at the feel of him, at the hardness and the deepness and *him*, Harry, Harry inside me, Harry inside me all night long . . .

Much later, when we came up for air, I asked him, 'Did you seriously expect this to happen when you came in with the drinks?'

'Yes. I made up my mind it would.'

The conceit of the guy! 'What if I hadn't ordered anything?' I said cunningly.

'I'd have turned up anyway. Or left it till tomorrow. No longer. My self-restraint was running out.'

'And if I'd said no?'

'You didn't.'

'I *did* – sort of.'

'You said no when I asked if you meant no,' Harry said. 'Double negative. Doesn't count. Anyhow, I knew you wouldn't.'

'How could you know that? Up till two days ago, I was supposed to be getting married.'

'Alex is a prat,' Harry said dismissively. 'You were wasted on him. I wanted you the first time I saw you, when you got out of the car and looked at me so snootily. I thought: What she needs is a good shagging. When a bloke thinks that, what he means is he intends to be the one doing it. I didn't like you at all, but I wanted you. As competition, Alex rated rather lower than Fenny.'

'I was *engaged* to him! He's rich and classy and much better-looking than you—'

'All true. Tell me, did you fuck him even *once* after he got here?'

'Well . . .' I wasn't going to give him that satisfaction. 'Yes. Yes, I did . . .'

'Liar.'

I collapsed. 'How did you know?'

'Chemistry,' Harry said briefly. 'You and I had it. You and he didn't. Simple.'

'Weren't you even a little bit jealous?' I knew I sounded peeved, and I didn't like it.

'Nothing to be jealous of.' He stroked my cheek with one finger. 'Why don't you just give in and go with the flow? Stop trying to fit me into your formulae.'

'Relationships always follow a formula,' I said. Mine did; I saw to that.

'Not the ones that matter. That's what bothers you, isn't it? No formula, no control. That's scary. Good. Be very, very scared . . .'

He started to kiss me again, but after a moment I pulled back an inch. I was still picking over everything he'd said. 'Do you like me now?' I said.

He smiled — not the grin but a smile, softer, more intimate. 'Sometimes.'

'Just *sometimes*?' I said furiously. It's difficult to be furious with someone when you're in bed with them, naked, within a few millimetres of penetration, but I did my best.

'All right. I think you're a terrific person — you're brave and loyal and generous and loving. You're also selfish and spoiled and in need of regular beating. And — yes, I like you. Right now, I like you a lot.'

'Thanks!' I snapped, trying for sarcasm. 'Well, *you* are—'

'I'm more selfish than you and less generous, or I wouldn't be here with you.' He looked oddly serious. 'I don't expect *you* to like *me*. Just enjoy the moment.'

He was nuzzling my ear — the line of my throat — the swell of my breast. Lifting it to his mouth, biting my nipple — so hard I cried out.

'Sorry . . .'

'No — it's okay. Don't stop . . .'

He bit me again, more gently — the tiger with his dinner — then worked his way down, all the way down, till he reached the X-spot.

He knew what to do when he got there.

Oh God . . . oh shit . . . oh bliss bliss bliss . . .

Oh *bloody* hell.

I woke up. It was morning — the daylight behind the curtains was a dead giveaway. I thought of *Romeo and Juliet* (I'd done the play at drama college): 'It is the nightingale and not the lark . . .' But it was no good. Morning had definitely broken and I was crashing back down to earth, face to face with reality in all its grim ghastliness. I hadn't even been pissed – the lack of hangover knocked that idea on the head. I couldn't plead mitigating drunkenness on any level: my sole glass of brandy still stood on the bedside table with half an inch of liquor in the bottom. I was responsible for my actions. The balance of my body had been disturbed, but not my mind. There was nothing between me and the Awful Truth.

I was in bed with the butler.

He lay beside me, half on his side, half on his stomach, one arm thrown across my chest. A chunky, muscly, bristly arm like that of a gingery gorilla. Oh God – could it be . . . I was into *rough trade*? You heard of cases – gorgeous upmarket women and sleazy downmarket guys. Next it would be the plumber, the gas man, one of those sexy couriers in black leather with his motorbike throbbing at the curb . . .

Oh *shit*.

Harry rolled over, still half asleep, pulling me into his arms. The melting process started all over again . . .

With an effort of will I dragged myself away and sat up, hugging the duvet against me by way of protection. Harry lay exposed in all his skin-coloured nakedness, big and solid and much too hairy for my refined taste. Part of his anatomy was far more awake than he was.

'Harry,' I said. He opened an eye. 'Winkworth – you have to go now. You should go back to your room and . . . and do whatever you have to do, and—'

'Winkworth? We have a night of wild sex and you're calling me by my surname? Well, Dacres, if that's how you feel—'

'That's *Miss* Dacres to you!' I flashed, determined to stay on top of the situation.

He glanced from his erection to me, pointedly. '*Miss* Dacres, may I . . .'

'Last night was a mistake,' I said hastily. 'It shouldn't have happened – it didn't happen – you took advantage of me when I was emotionally vulnerable and if you ever tell anyone –' dear God, the tabloids – 'I'll deny everything and I'll sue the shirt off your back and—'

'This shirt?' He held up the one he wasn't wearing.

'*Any* shirt! Just wipe that big fat grin off your face, because if you breathe a single word about this—'

'You're right about one thing,' he said, losing the grin and groping for his clothes. The erection was still in place, large as life and twice as distracting. Bugger . . .

'What?' I said.

'It *was* a mistake – possibly the biggest I've ever made.' He was watching my face, which fell. I could feel it. I stared at him. 'So . . . you don't want me to come back tonight, then?'

'No! Absolutely not.' What kind of game was he playing? 'Anyway, if it was such a big mistake . . .'

'It was the best mistake I've ever made,' he said. The erection was out of sight now, tucked into his trousers. 'I could make it again, no problem.' He leaned over and kissed me, mouth to mouth, no tongues. The kind of kiss that means something, though I didn't know what. 'See you later.'

When he had gone I lay down again, telling myself that as we had the day off I could go back to sleep. But it was no good. My emotions were fizzing away like a bottle of champagne in an earthquake; I felt as if the cork would fly out any minute, though whether I would laugh or cry or scream blue murder I had no idea. Under those conditions, I believe men go and play squash, or golf, or beat someone up, if they're that way inclined, but girls don't. We have a far more effective emotional outlet.

Girls' talk.

Kissing Toads

I rolled out of bed, despatched Fenny to go walkies with one of the maids, and went to wake up Roo.

Ruth

Delphi, as I may have mentioned, is not a morning person. Yet since we came to Dunblair – perhaps because she was going to bed much too early for both her health and mine – it always seemed that *she* was the one waking *me* up, especially on mornings when I was due for a lie-in. That Saturday, the pounding on my door dragged me from a sleep so deep that in the confusion of returning to consciousness I wasn't immediately sure *who* I was, let alone where. I'd locked the door out of some obscure instinct of self-preservation, but it wasn't doing me any good. The pounding was accompanied by a voice. 'Roo! *Roo*! For God's sake wake up and let me in!'

Roo. Yes, that was me. I tried hiding my head under the pillow, but the thumping still got through. In the end I surfaced, reluctantly, scrambled out of bed and staggered to the door. The lurid throw over the duvet came halfway with me, caught inexplicably round my leg. I unlocked, let Delphi in, and tottered back to bed, groping for the phone even as I subsided into the warmth of my nest.

'I *have* to talk to you,' Delphi was saying.

'I need tea – coffee – any combination,' I mumbled. 'I'll ask Harry—'

'NO!' Delphi yelled in capital letters, snatching the phone from my grasp.

'Why ever not?'

'You mustn't – you don't understand – you mustn't ask Harry for anything *ever* again. Especially not now.'

Delphi had clearly gone completely bonkers.

'Look, whatever it is you want to tell me, I'll listen much better when I've got some tea or something. Calm down and give me the phone.' Her insane panic was *really* waking me up, which is not a pleasant experience without coffee in support.

'Wait, please. The problem isn't the tea, it's Harry.'

'I thought you'd decided you liked him after all,' I said. Delphi, I knew, had always resented Harry being a normal sort of guy instead of the stone-faced fantasy butler of Georgette Heyer novels and *The Remains of the Day*. And Harry, being a normal guy, hadn't been able to resist making fun of her resentment. It all seemed harmless enough – except that there was that strange business of the 'deal' they had made to get rid of Roddy . . .

'I *don't* like him,' Delphi declared with a passion out of all proportion to the sentiment. 'I *loathe* him. He's the most disgusting excuse for a man – or a butler – I've ever met.'

'What's he done?' I said. It was too early for me to think clearly.

'It isn't so much what he's done – at least, it *is*, but . . . it's what *I've* done!' She flopped on to my bed, looking tragic. Delphi is an actress of questionable talent, but at that moment her mien – she definitely had a mien, rather than just an expression – would have done credit to a Siddons.

'Well . . . what *have* you done?' I asked.

'I – I – I shagged him,' she said, tragically.

'Uh . . . ?' I stared at her, temporarily at a loss for words.

Delphi and *Harry*???

One: although Harry is an attractive guy with an agreeable grin, he doesn't have the classic good looks or the aura of glamour that has always done it for her. Two: without being precisely a snob – okay, she's a snob, but she isn't precise about it – Delphi's taste in men runs to upper-class types with Eton accents and lots of money in the family. Even Ben Garvin, the local ne'er-do-well, had been the son of successful surgeon, and his tough-guy image (Triumph bike and leather jacket) had been paid for by Daddy. Harry was evidently intelligent and well-educated, but also indefinably blokeish – and though that said nothing about his background, it wasn't Delphi's style. Delphi's men were guys, or possibly chaps, cool and sophisticated and very, very pretty. She didn't do blokes.

'You . . . you shagged *Harry*,' I repeated, trying to visualise it and backing off hastily.

There are places where the imagination should not go.

'Yeah.'

'When? Last night?'

Delphi nodded.

'Once, or . . . ?'

'All night.' After a pause, she added: 'Not this morning, though. It took huge amounts of will power, but I pushed him away.'

'Will power . . .'

'I've got lots of will power, honestly. I'm very will-powerful. Roo, what am I going to do? How will I face him?'

'The usual way, I suppose. But . . .' I fumbled for a single question among the hundred or so that leaped to mind . . . 'how did it happen?'

'Don't ask.' She shuddered artistically.

'Well, all right, if you don't want me to . . .'

'Don't you *dare* not ask!' She relinquished the shudder, and then the whole story came pouring out. The 'deal' over Roddy, the kiss – 'I never even agreed to it! He just *forced* it on me' – how his kindness over the business with Alex had lulled her into a false sense of security. And then last night . . .

'So . . . um . . . how was it?' I asked.

Delphi looked more tragic than ever, as if smitten to the heart by some dreadful stroke of doom. 'It was fantastic,' she said wretchedly. 'It was the best sex I've ever had. It's so humiliating. First Alex cheats on me with two lumps of silicon and a brain cell, and now this. It wouldn't be so bad if it had been bad. At least I'd have felt in control of things. But I lost it completely. Roo, what's happening to us? You pull an international megastar and I shag the butler. It's all the wrong way round. I mean . . .'

I laughed. 'I know what you mean. You're right, too: we're both acting wildly out of character.'

'What do I do?' Delphi reiterated. 'How do I behave towards him? What's the – the etiquette when you've shagged the butler?'

'Tip?' I suggested.

Delphi was in such a state she insisted on shutting herself in the bathroom after I ordered tea so she wouldn't have to see Harry. However, it arrived with one of the girls, Margaret I think her name is, and Delphi reappeared afterwards looking as near sheepish as she would ever allow. 'When are you getting up?' she asked me. 'I can't go downstairs without you. I need a chaperone.'

'I thought I'd have a bath,' I said hopefully. A long one. 'Why don't you have one too?'

Eventually, we went down to the drawing room around eleven. HG was the only person there, listening to music, presumably enjoying having his home almost to himself for a day or two. However, he looked pleased to see us, smiling a welcome and turning the volume down with the remote. Delphi glanced around warily, as if waiting for Harry to pounce.

'Who's left?' I said after commenting on the quiet.

'Nigel's gone to Leicester,' HG said. 'Dorian went online last night and came up with some Dagworthys living there who're direct descendants of Elizabeth's aunt. I'm not sure how he did it, but apparently you can find out anything with the Internet these days. Much better and more efficient than leaving it to the papers, or so Dorian says. I'm the wrong generation for this sort of thing.'

'And Nigel's hot on the trail?'

'He phoned them first thing and left about an hour ago. Looks like it's just us now.'

'Where's Ash?' I said, trying to sound non-committal.

'Last seen talking to Morag. I didn't know, but evidently her mother was a Craig. I think he's sounding her out on her family history.'

'Didn't they say she was the local beauty once?' Delphi volunteered. 'I know it seems unlikely, but perhaps the Scots don't wear well. It comes of being dour all the time. Although you'd think that they'd have heard of Crème de la Mer even here.'

'Vanity is one of the seven deadly sins,' Harry said, arriving with fresh coffee. 'Morag doesn't do sin.'

'Too right,' said HG. Delphi, completely unnerved, had lapsed into silence. 'She just enjoys deploring them in everyone else. I expect that's why she works for me. I must have the whole set.'

'I can never remember what they are,' I said, feeling mischievous. 'Except for lust. I know lust is in there somewhere.'

Delphi glared at me. Harry, my target, gave me a look which said: *Touché.*

'Any news from the village?' HG asked him.

'Dirk phoned. He says three sinister strangers have arrived at the pub.'

'Lochnabu is crawling with strangers,' HG retorted. 'The not-so-gentlemen of the press. How sinister?'

'Dirk says they're *not* press,' Harry explained. 'Under the circumstances, that's sinister.'

'I could go and check them out,' I offered. 'I'd like a walk.'

('You can't leave me!' Delphi hissed.

'Don't be idiotic,' I hissed back.)

'You shouldn't,' HG said. 'The hacks will be after you like vultures as soon as you set foot outside the grounds. If you want a walk, stay on my land.'

'I'm not famous,' I argued. 'They might pester a bit but they won't mob.' I didn't feel like curtailing my activities because of the bloody press. I couldn't see why I should have the disadvantages of celebrity without even being one. 'Anyway, I want to find out about the sinister strangers.'

'Dorian can go with you,' HG said, clearly determined to look after me.

'No thanks.' I was equally determined not to have Dorian. 'I'm sure he'd rather spend time with his computer.'

'You can take Fenny,' Delphi offered, still convinced her fluffy pup was a cross between a Rottweiler and a bloodhound. 'He'll look after you – and the exercise would be good for him.'

And then Ash entered, right on cue.

'Good,' HG said, arranging matters with the careless authority of uncrowned kingship. 'You can go with Ruth. She's decided she wants to walk to the village to check on some sinister strangers at the pub. They're probably just unsuspecting tourists caught up in the scrimmage, but you never know.'

Rather surprisingly, when the situation was explained to him, Ash agreed.

I took Fenny, promising Delphi faithfully that I would return before Harry could ravish her again, and we set off.

Initially, neither of us said anything. It was a beautiful day for a walk: the sunlight on the loch sparkled like a sheet of diamonds, the woods were green with early summer and rippling with birdsong, cloud-shadows came chasing down the mountainsides, swooping across the landscape on a light breeze. Ash and I strode along side by side, playing a sort of conversational chicken, waiting to see who would crack and break the silence first. I knew it was going to be me. I may be more patient than Delphi (*mayflies* are more patient than Delphi), but I hate those kinds of games.

Only I couldn't ask the big question in my head – *Are you gay?* – because that would betray my own feelings. If he *was* gay, that would be merely embarrassing, but if he wasn't – if he didn't have similar feelings for me – I would be shamed and humiliated as well. That's what comes of living in a liberated society. Communication between the sexes becomes a total minefield.

I compromised with banality. 'Lovely weather we're having.'

Ash smiled, but not much.

'It's very beautiful here, don't you think?' I persisted.

'What's this? Pride of prospective possession?' Ash said in a flat voice.

'I *beg* your pardon?'

'You and our host seem to be on such good terms, I thought—'

'Oh, did you?' He sounded piqued. I should have been relieved, but whatever relief I felt was swallowed up in sudden anger. Not blazing anger but the sort of dagger-edged irritation which can be far more dangerous: it doesn't explode, it just saws away at you until you're in shreds. 'Yes, we're on good terms. I like him; he likes me. He kissed me. Once. That hardly constitutes a serious relationship. But, just for the record, I enjoyed it. Nobody's kissed me in ages.' (Dorian's face-eating attempt didn't count.) You didn't kiss me, I thought. I didn't say it, but I thought it so loudly he could probably hear.

'And now his wife wants a divorce,' Ash said. His tone was as bland as mine was edged. 'That was some kiss.'

'Don't be stupid. Their divorce has been on the cards for ages. He's had private detectives watching her for evidence. The kiss was nothing . . . but I'm not going to apologise for it. You're acting like I owe you an apology. Well, I don't.' There was a silence – except for the beat of our footsteps, the birdsong spilling from the trees, Fenny scuffling excitedly in a clump of nettles.

'You don't owe me anything,' Ash said.

For the first time since we had started walking I turned to look at him. He seemed too pale for the summer noon, a night creature caught in the daylight – pale and somehow bruised, overstrained, underslept. His eyes were narrowed against the sun, but ice-green gleamed in the narrows, cool as a glacier. My dagger-mood softened briefly because he looked so deadly tired . . . so defenceless. But I flinched from that glimmer of utter coldness.

'I liked you,' he went on unexpectedly. Past tense. 'Actually, I was getting to like you a lot. But that's my problem.'

'Yes, it is,' I said sharply. The dagger was back, twisting in my heart, sawing at my nervous system. It was unfair to imply I'd rejected Something Valuable when Something had never been offered. 'While I was kissing – *being kissed* – by HG, you were dancing with Cedric. Who is nuts about you. Only he didn't have a Basilisa to demand a divorce because of it.'

'*Cedric?*' Faint bewilderment furrowed Ash's brow. 'What on earth are you talking about?'

'Cedric! You *danced* with him, remember?'

'Yes, but . . . you don't think I'm gay?' His coolth was punctured; he looked, not indignant, but astonished.

'Why not? Everyone else does.'

'*Do* they? Look, Cedric's obviously gay, and Jules and Sandy, but—'

'Jules and Sandy? Really?' I was diverted for a moment.

'Of course. They've been a couple for ages. But why me?'

'Because you didn't make a pass at Delphi or Brie, you never talk about a girlfriend, you're always in the kitchen with Cedric.'

'*You're* always in the kitchen with Cedric,' Ash said. 'If I was given to thinking that way, I might assume you were in love with him. I don't . . . but I might. As for Brie and Delphi – I'd as soon make a pass at a cobra.'

'Delphi's my friend. Brie's shallow and two-faced; Delphi's not. Don't lump them together like that.'

'Sorry. I don't seem to be able to say anything right.' This time, *he* turned to gaze at *me*. 'Look, I'm not gay. I danced with Cedric because he asked me, that's all. Why not? I get gays coming on to me sometimes. It doesn't bother me. And I didn't want to hurt him by refusing. It never occurred to me you'd think . . . Is *that* why you kissed HG?'

'No,' I said. 'I told you, *he* kissed *me*. I was there. He finds me sympathetic, that's all it was. No big deal.' And then I said it. '*You* didn't kiss me, after all.'

The words hung in the air between us – a reproach, a challenge. We were standing face to face; Ash reached out, touched my cheek. But that was all.

'There's something I have to tell you,' he said in a *careful* voice, the voice people use when they're about to tiptoe over the eggshells of self-revelation.

I waited. For a second, it was as if the sun halted on its arc across the sky, and the birds ceased to sing, and my whole universe held its breath.

Then Fenny rushed over, and Ash took my arm, and we went on walking.

'I'd been with someone since I was at college,' he said. 'Neve and I were like . . . twin souls, or so I thought. So everyone said. We even looked alike.' My heart flinched at the vision of two elvish faces, side by side in unearthly harmony. Bound with a bond that was more than human. 'We have a daughter, Caitlin. She's five . . . next week. After she was born Neve didn't want to go back to work, but I didn't earn enough to support both of us. She said I should change my job, stop "messing about with the supernatural". That's how she put it. She wanted me to go and work in the City. I had a chance, an uncle of mine . . . Anyway, I wouldn't. I said we could manage. I suppose I was selfish. I love what I do, whether it's unravelling people's own hidden phantoms or tangling with the genuinely paranormal. I've always wanted so desperately to find out the truth of it all – if there really *is* a world beyond this one. Do you understand?'

'Yes,' I said. It was something we all wanted to know. And by the time we're sure, we'll have crossed the boundary beyond ever returning.

But Ash came closer to that boundary on a regular basis.

'Neve didn't,' he said. 'We started to have rows. She got a job as a PA to this merchant banker: she was making good money but sometimes it was long hours. I and a friend looked after Caitlin between us. I got so close to my daughter . . . No use talking of it. I thought Neve and I were working things out. Then, nearly a year ago, I came home from an investigation I'd been doing abroad. Budapest. There was a letter. She'd gone – Neve – she'd gone and taken Caitlin. No warning – just gone.'

'Oh God, I'm sorry . . .'

'She was with her boss – her *former* boss. He's much older, nearly fifty, very well off. She says he makes her feel secure. The thing is, he was offered a new position in the States, four months ago, heading up another company. They've gone to live in Boston. I hardly see Caitlin any more. I could have got an injunction, but Neve said if I tried to stop them it would be more selfish than ever, and I knew she was right. Neve doesn't work now; she can be with her daughter all the time. Caitlin misses me, but she's happy. She needs her mother most.' He broke off, squeezing his eyes to slits against the sun. (He really should get dark glasses.) 'Children forget so quickly. I keep thinking, soon she'll barely remember what I look like.'

I took his hand, holding it very tight. 'She can come and stay, can't she?'

'Sometimes. In the school holidays. When they're not off skiing in Vermont, or sunning themselves in Hawaii, or going to Disneyland in Florida. I can't compete with all that.'

'You don't have to,' I said. 'You're her dad. My father wasn't around much when I was a child – he was an engineer and he was always working abroad – but it was so special when he came home. Like Christmas every time.'

Ash smiled at me. Not really comforted, but trying to be. My heart turned over at the sadness in his face.

'Do you see him much?' he asked.

'Not enough. He remarried about eight years ago and they live in the West Country. It's a long way from London.'

We walked on, but slowly. We were nearly at the gate, where we would have to put Fenny on a lead and run the gauntlet of the besiegers.

'Do you and Neve get along okay now?' I said. I really wanted to know if he was still in love with her, but I couldn't ask that.

'Actually, we probably get on better. She's got what she wants, and I . . .' He sighed. 'She used to say I was like a knight on some impossible quest, looking for the Holy Grail or something else irrelevant to the modern world. She said people on quests hadn't enough time for family.'

'"*O what can ail thee, knight-at-arms,*
Alone and palely loitering?"' I quoted.

'That's me. A pale loiterer.' He picked up another line from the poem.

'"*I met a lady in the meads,*
Full beautiful – a faery's child . . ."

That was Neve. Only her heart was human. She opted for comfort and safety, not the uncertainties of the otherworld.' He put his arm around my shoulders.

'I'm no "Belle Dame Sans Merci" either,' I said a little shakily. 'I'm not pretty enough. And my heart is human too.'

'Your heart is the truest, the most loving . . .' He was looking at me again and his eyes were green but not cold, green as summer. 'You're like what's-her-name in that ballad, Tam Lin's girlfriend who saved him from the clutches of the fairy queen even though it put her in great danger. The fairies turned him into all kinds of creatures, from mouse to monster, but she held on to him, and she saved him. Would you save me?'

'As long as you didn't turn into a snake,' I said. 'I'm terrified of snakes.'

We went on walking. I thought of Elizabeth Bennet near the end of *Pride and Prejudice*, when Darcy proposes for the second time. Austen says Elizabeth rather *knew* than *felt* she was happy. That's how it was with me. Happiness like that is too big a thing to feel all at once. You have to absorb a little at a time, or it would blow your mind.

Then we reached the gate and were back in reality – or the bizarre variant on reality that currently obtained at Dunblair. I called Fenny and hooked him on to his lead. The clutch of

341

journalists encamped outside bombarded us with questions, but we said nothing and kept on going and eventually they abandoned us in the hope of more interesting prey. By the time we got to the pub the last of them was left far behind.

Ash ordered beer for him and lager for me while I whispered to Dirk in a conspiratorial voice, 'Where are they?'

'Where are who?'

'The strangers you talked about.'

'Oh – ay. I think they popped oot. Ye mun stick around a wee while; they'll be back. They dinna like tae be too lang awa' from the bar.'

So Ash and I sat down in the corner with our drinks and a bowl of water for Fenny and went back to talking about ourselves. He showed me a picture of Caitlin, who looked like a pixie, with a tiny pointy face and huge eyes. Neve, in the background, was almost as beautiful as Ash himself and didn't seem at all the type to run off with a middle-aged merchant banker. He couldn't really love me, I thought, not after her – but it was too soon to talk of love. We'd made a start.

People drifted in and out, but we paid them no attention. Then Dirk was beside me, collecting empties. 'Theer they are,' he murmured.

It was only a small bar, and the three men were leaning on most of it. One was thin and greasy-looking – you itched to drop him in the bath but suspected he would emerge looking just as greasy afterwards and leave the bathtub coated in scum. He had the sort of face that seemed to curve in upon itself as if drawn on the inside of a spoon, and spots that had never known tea tree oil. The second was heavily built with a skinhead haircut that emphasised the smallness of his cranium compared with his largeness everywhere else. But it was the third who bothered me, the moment I set eyes on him. He wore a suit, but he wore it the way a wolf might wear sheep's clothing, knowing it was good camouflage which would help him to get close to his prey. His hair was carefully styled and gelled into the windswept look at the front. But his face was all wrong. It was the face of a thug who thinks, a yob from the gutter who can use big words and knows how to twist the law every which way. It wasn't a face you wanted to get close to under any circumstances.

'D'you know their names?' I asked Dirk very quietly.

'They're staying along o' Miss McGonnagal,' he replied. 'They told her Brown, Green and White.'

'Calling themselves after colours,' Ash said. '*Reservoir Dogs*.'

'The one in the middle,' Dirk went on, meaning the suit, 'I hearrrd his mates calling him Attila.'

'I can believe it,' I said.

When he returned to the bar, Ash followed him to get a couple more drinks. I expected the threesome to leer, jeer and snicker – Ash's hair was too long and he was far too pretty to meet with their approval. The skinhead duly snickered, but Attila gave Ash a smile which was somehow worse, a civilised, faintly deprecating smile which sat on his face like compassion on the face of an alligator. Ash smiled back, coolly – he was good at that – and returned to our table with the drinks.

'Definitely not journalists,' I said. 'We should try and listen to their conversation, but without *looking* as if we're listening.'

'Why?' Ash said. 'I doubt if it'll be very interesting. I'd rather listen to you.'

But in the event, their conversation came to us.

After a brief word with Dirk, Attila approached our table, wearing an expression that was plainly meant for friendly. It made my skin crawl.

'Hope you don't mind my interrupting,' he said, pulling up a stool. He'd left the back-up at the bar. 'I hear you two are staying at the castle. Part of the visiting TV show.'

Ash looked aloof. I said guardedly, 'Yes.'

Why was Attila the Suit curious about us – or Dunblair?

'Been quite exciting over there, hasn't it?' he continued.

'Has it?' I said.

'Oh, don't worry, I'm not from the papers. Don't trust the media: they've got their own agenda. They blackout the truth, print whatever lies the government dictate – and the government's rotten through and through. But I'm sure we all agree on that.' I'm not a fan of the government, but my instinct was to disagree with Attila even if it meant supporting TB. 'Still, there are some things the press don't distort. I read about that rescue – saw you both in the photo. You found those two blokes who went missing on the mountain in the fog. Good work.'

Good work? He was acting the senior officer commending bright young recruits. It made the hackles rise on my back – and I don't even have hackles.

'The papers exaggerated,' Ash said. 'They always do. The guys weren't in any real danger, just cold and cross.' With deceptive nonchalance, he added: 'What's your interest?'

'We're just tourists, passing through.' He stretched his mouth into a smile again with the air of someone who has been practising. 'Beautiful country, Scotland. Who needs to go abroad when we've got everything right here? Britain's the best place in the world, if you ask me.'

Oh, so he was one of *those*.

'If you don't go anywhere else,' I said, 'how would you know?'

The smile stretched further, like overstrained elastic. 'Clever girl, isn't she?' he said to Ash as if I was a performing dog. Ignoring the question, he continued: 'No, I like it here. Actually, we saw a friend of ours in that photo. Working at the castle. Quite a coincidence, seeing as we were visiting these parts already. Thought we'd drop by and see him.'

'Who's that?' Ash asked. I could sense his wariness under the aloof demeanor. Or maybe it was my own I sensed.

'Harry. Harry . . . Winkworth.' Was it my imagination that he hesitated for a fraction of a second over the surname? 'The butler, the paper said. Or did they get that wrong?'

'No,' I said, doing my best to match Ash's poker face. 'He's the butler.'

Inwardly, I seethed with unanswered questions. How come someone like Attila the Suit knew *Harry*? Had Delphi been right when she claimed he was a fraud? Had—

'I see. He wasn't a butler when we knew him, but that was a while ago. He's an old friend, Harry. D'you know if he's likely to pop in here for a jar sometime soon? But of course you don't. People like you wouldn't get chummy with the servants.'

'I'm afraid not,' I said, imitating Delphi at her haughtiest. 'He's always been very helpful, but naturally I know nothing about his personal life.'

Apart from the fact that he spent last night shagging Delphinium Dacres . . .

'Of course not,' Attila repeated, smiling wider and wider, like Lewis Carroll's crocodile, only with slightly better teeth. 'But he's a good bloke. An old friend. We'd like to look him up.' He pushed back the stool, got to his feet.

As an afterthought, or so it seemed, he added the part that really chilled me.

'Don't mention you've seen us, will you? We'd like to give him a surprise.'

Chapter 11:
Laying the Ghosts

Delphinium

With my chaperone out, I retreated to my room to watch TV and paint my toenails. I usually have a pedicurist, but when I'm uptight I find it therapeutic to do it myself. I should have locked the door, but that seemed needlessly paranoid. Harry knocked and came in, uninvited, when I was halfway through my right foot.

'I didn't ring,' I said. 'You're not supposed to be here.'

I was determined to keep my cool, although I had a sneaking suspicion my subconscious had left the door unlocked, for reasons too disturbing to think about.

'I thought we should talk,' he said.

'We have nothing to talk about. And I didn't say you could sit on my bed!'

'I didn't ask permission.' He sighed – not a wistful sigh, more like exasperation. 'Come down off your high horse for a minute, will you?'

I didn't deign to answer. When I had finished applying gold spangles on to a base-coat of rosy bronze I sat back to admire the effect.

'Very pretty,' Harry said. 'Fortunately, I'm not a foot fetishist. In fact, your feet are the only part of your anatomy I can look at without getting a hard-on.'

'What's wrong with my feet?' I demanded with a show of indignation.

But Harry wasn't fooled. 'Nothing,' he said. 'They round off your ankles very nicely. But I'm more interested in what's at the other end of your legs.'

Damn. I'd walked into that one and I knew it, but I realised I didn't much care. If you allow a breach in your defences, even for just one night, you know the enemy is going to get through again sooner or later, whatever you do. It was a dull afternoon; it would pass the time. I might as well surrender to superior force . . .

(This was your fault, Roo. You should never have abandoned me.)

Harry bent over and kissed my cheek, the tip of my nose, my lips, brushed my nipple very lightly with his finger. It stiffened in response so that the lace of my bra chafed against it. Then he took my hand and carried it to his crotch, where there was already a pronounced bulge. And suddenly I wanted him in my mouth, all the bigness and the hardness of him – I wanted the power and control that you can only get with fellatio – I wanted him gasping and groaning and helpless with pleasure. The want went down between my legs with a stabbing sensation so sharp it almost hurt. Harry undid his zip and I pulled down the front of his boxers and began to suck. Happily, I'm good at multitasking. I could concentrate on sucking his dick and the growing tension in my X-spot and still remember to keep my feet off the bed so I didn't smudge my newly-applied varnish.

After a while I forgot all about that, but by then my gold spangles were dry.

Thank God for quick-drying nail polish.

'You said you wanted to talk,' I reminded him some time later. 'Or was that just an excuse?'

'No. There are things I need to— Bugger.' On the bedside table his mobile was ringing. He answered it, said 'yes' a couple of times and 'With you in a few minutes', and hung up. 'Sorry, I have to go. Technically, I'm working. I'll come back tonight . . . if you like.'

'If I don't like,' I said, 'you'll come anyway, right?'

'D'you want to be sure of that before you say no?'

I was silent, trying to find an answer that would be both witty and scathing, but would also carry the underlying message that I might not object if he were to force his attentions on me again. I was still groping for the right words when Harry gave me a quick kiss, tugged on his sweatshirt and left, with a final murmur of 'See you later'.

I got dressed again rather more slowly and went downstairs, feeling relaxed, or restored, or resigned – or a comfortable mixture of all three. So I was into rough trade. What the hell.

In the entrance hall I ran into HG.

'Tell me,' I said, remembering something I'd been meaning to ask, 'who moved that picture?'

'Which one?'

'The portrait of Elizabeth Courtney. It used to hang more to the right, but it's been moved. Now, in the late afternoon the sun falls straight on it.'

'I don't think anyone moved it,' HG said. 'Surely it was always there.'

'No – I noticed particularly. I've looked at it lots of times.'

'You must be mistaken,' HG assured me. 'No one would move it without my permission. Anyway, it's too difficult to reach.'

He continued on upstairs and I stood staring at the picture, certain I was right. I was still there when Roo and Ash came back.

I said, 'Hi,' exuding relaxability and giving Fenny a hug, but Roo didn't respond.

'Where's Harry?'

I went slightly pink – I could feel it – but neither of them seemed to notice. 'I don't know.'

'We need a word with him,' Roo explained.

In the drawing room, she picked up the in-house phone and called him.

'What's happened?' I asked. 'You look worried.'

'A bit,' Roo said. 'I'll tell you when . . . Harry!'

'What's the problem?' Harry came in, flicking me a quick glance. I felt instantly warm all over, which was ridiculous – he was having the most devastating physical effect on me, and he wasn't even really good-looking.

'There are these three men staying in the village,' Roo began. 'Dirk's sinister strangers. We saw them in the pub. They're not journalists – we didn't like the look of them at all.'

'*I* don't like the look of journalists,' I remarked.

'This lot look more like thugs,' Ash said. 'The worst kind.'

'One of them smarmed up to us,' Roo said, 'only he wasn't smarmy. It was like watching someone smarm who's read about it and knows what to do but doesn't . . . doesn't smarm from the heart.'

'*Can* you smarm from the heart?' Harry speculated.

'The thing is,' Roo said, 'he asked for you.'

Suddenly, Harry went absolutely quiet.

'Dirk told us the other two called him Attila,' Ash said. 'He didn't have the tache, but I'm afraid it suited him.'

'He had a suit,' Roo added, 'but that *didn't* suit him.'

'What's the matter?' I said. My warm feeling had been replaced by a sort of coldness, not exactly fear but the chill that comes when fear is on its way.

Harry said: 'Fuck,' and then, 'Did he say how they knew I was here?'

'They saw your picture in the paper after our search party the other night,' Ash explained.

'The Attila guy said not to tell you he'd asked about you,' Roo went on. 'He said he wanted to give you a surprise.'

'I'll bet he did.' Harry's face had a kind of tight, closed-in look which I'd never seen before.

'Are you in trouble?' Roo asked.

'You could say so.' He gazed directly at me. 'I didn't want you to find out like this,' he said. 'I wanted to tell you in my own time. I was going to earlier on, but I got . . . distracted.'

'Tell me what?' I said in a voice that came out small and scared, like a child. Had I been cheated again? had I been gullible and stupid twice in one week? Had I been fooled by the *butler*? Only somehow that part didn't matter. All that mattered was the look on Harry's face.

'You were right,' he said. 'I'm not a real butler.'

I couldn't speak. I just stared at him.

'But,' Roo said, 'but . . . how could you get this job? How could you *do* this job? For months and months . . . with nobody guessing?'

'Jim Winkworth is an old friend,' Harry said, still looking at me. 'I've stayed with him and Carrie when he was working for Gordon Chisholm. I wanted to learn about the job – it's unusual, and I'm naturally curious. All the same, I couldn't have got away with it if the regime here hadn't been so laid-back.'

'Carrie?' I said, latching on to irrelevancies.

'Jim's wife.'

The house in Kensington, the wife and kids . . .

'But why?' Roo said. 'I don't understand.'

'I needed a cover,' Harry said. 'A place to hide out. Jim had two jobs on offer – this one, and one in the States through an international agency. He was going for California – better climate than Scotland – so I took this one. On paper, I fit his description: similar height, similar colouring, no distinguishing features. It was almost a joke at first – I never thought I'd get away with it – but I suppose I got to like it, and no one found me out, so I stayed on. I knew getting sucked into your PR opportunity was a mistake.' He gave me a faint shadow of his normal grin.

'Why did you need a cover?' Roo persisted. 'What's your real job?'

Ash was frowning slightly as if struck by a new idea. 'He's a journalist,' he said. 'Aren't you?'

Harry nodded.

'No,' I whispered. Suddenly, shagging the butler was fine – the butler, the plumber, a leather-clad courier with throbbing motorbike. *Anything* but a journalist.

'Sorry,' Harry said. 'I was going to tell you.'

Roo had turned to Ash. 'How did you . . . ?'

'Attila 33,' Ash said. 'That's who that guy was. It's only just hit me.'

'Attila 33 . . .' Roo seemed to be chasing an obscure recollection.

'They're a far-right neo-Nazi group,' Ash explained. 'Named after the Hun, obviously, and . . . 1933 was when Hitler came to power, I think. Someone went undercover to investigate them, managed to join up – a year or two ago. There was an exposé, in the *Independent* as far as I recall. A couple of them were tried for murder – beating an Asian student to death. The journalist was a witness for the prosecution. He had them talking about it on tape.' He looked at Harry.

'Yep,' Harry said.

'The leader got off on a technicality. He's the one they call Attila. I'd forgotten – it's only just come back to me.'

'He had a good lawyer,' Harry said. 'Expensive. A lot of important people support these groups on the quiet.'

'And then?' Roo prompted.

'He said they'd get me. The police offered me some sort of witness protection scheme, but I didn't fancy it. I preferred to look out for myself. This –' he glanced round, shrugged – 'seemed like a good idea at the time.'

'Were you planning to do an undercover exposé on me?' HG was standing in the hall doorway. He must have been there a little while, but we hadn't noticed.

'Probably,' Harry said bluntly. 'It's not really my thing, but at least it meant I was still doing my job.'

'I read your piece in the *Indy*,' Ash said. 'They ran it over three or four days, didn't they? It was very good.'

'Peak of my career,' said Harry. 'Unfortunately, it nearly finished me too. In more ways than one.'

'That isn't my problem,' HG said. 'You can leave now. Give me a forwarding address and I'll see to it you get your final pay cheque. I guess you've earned it.'

'Okay.'

'Before you write your story, I should warn you I'll be consulting my lawyers. Journalist or not, when you came to work for me you signed a confidentiality agreement that guaranteed your loyalty and discretion—'

'Oh, shut up,' I said. Suddenly, HG didn't look like an icon any more, just an ordinary small-minded egoist who thought the world revolved around him. 'This isn't about you. I may be only a B-list celeb, but I'm the one who spent last night and . . . and part of this afternoon shagging him, and that's a much better story than anything he's got on you, so I'm first in the queue for injunctions and so on. If I'm not mad, why should you be?'

'You were the only one who suspected me,' Harry said. His face had lightened at my outburst. 'I took the piss, but you gave me a few bad moments.'

'I searched your room,' I said. 'I *knew* it was fishy there was no personal stuff – no family photos or anything – and your laptop was locked away. Nobody locks up their laptop unless they've got something to hide. I even had someone check out your London address.'

'Bloody hell,' Harry said appreciatively. 'You're in the wrong job. Have mine.'

I caught a glimpse of HG's face, which wore an expression that combined anger, intrigue and reluctant amusement. When you've got that many lines, you can do several expressions at once. But I wasn't worrying about him just then.

'These people,' I said, 'are they . . . would they try to *kill* you?'

'Possibly. Attila dropped a hint to that effect when he left court.'

I stared at him. TV is a cut-throat business, but people don't actually kill each other, though they've been known to tear up contracts, sue, throw the occasional punch, and even bite colleagues in the jugular. But a world where people threatened to kill you, and meant it, was outside my experience.

Until now.

'We'll call the police,' I said.

'You'll have a long wait,' said HG. 'They took at least an hour after we reported finding the skeleton.'

'I'll have to get out,' Harry said. 'It means driving through the village, but with luck they'll miss me.'

'Was that in one of my cars?' HG drawled.

At that point, I lost my temper completely. 'You selfish bastard! You want to talk about loyalty: where's yours? Harry hasn't just been your butler, he's been your *friend*. He's worked for you and put up with you and . . . and stood by you, and now his *life* is in danger, and all you can think about is whether he might just write a few words about you in one of the papers! You've had thousands – probably millions – of words written about you in the last four decades: what difference would a few more make? Anyway, you won't have to lend him one of your *fleet* of cars because we're going to call the police and he's going to stay here till they come. It's much too risky for him to leave – that's what this Attila lot will be expecting. If the paparazzi can't get past Jules and Sandy, then I'm sure those neo-Nazi thugs won't manage it. And,' I added, as HG opened his mouth to speak, 'you can cancel the series or demand that I'm fired or whatever – I *don't care*! Do your worst! I'm standing by Harry, and so's Roo, and Ash, and—'

'Calm down,' HG said. 'Stop turning me into the villain of the piece. I just don't like my help being taken for granted. Of course Harry must stay until the police come. Has anyone called them?'

'I'm on it,' Roo said, telephone in hand.

There followed a confused half-hour while Roo tried to convey to the Law the urgency of the situation, Harry went to his room to pack,

353

HG took over on the blower to get past reception and make high-handed demands to speak to superior officers, and beyond the windows the summer sun drew the moisture out of the ground, congealing it into a thick white mist which turned the world to a blank and hid even the loch from view.

Harry had just returned when there was a disturbance in the entrance hall – a door slamming, hasty footsteps – and Sandy walked in. In his arms was the limp bulk of one of the dogs, its cream-coloured fur damp from the mist, its head resting in the hollow of his shoulder. There was blood on Sandy's chest, more blood on the dog. Lots of blood.

'Boss,' he said, 'they got him. They got Elton. I didn't think no journo would do that. They came over the wall – three of 'em. I saw one bloke raise his arm . . . He must've had a cosh or something. He's dead, boss. Elton's dead.' His voice was hoarse and I could have sworn there were tears on his cheek.

For a minute, no one said anything. This brought the violence home to us – all the way home. And Elton had been so beautiful, so gallant and brave . . .

'It wasn't a journalist,' Ash said.

HG was bent over the dog, stroking its fur. 'This them?' he asked Harry.

'Sounds like it,' Harry said. 'Look, I'd better go. I'm just bringing trouble on everyone else.'

'No way.' I said it first, but the others followed suit. Even HG. 'This is a castle. You –' I turned to the boss – 'you said it yourself. We can withstand a siege. We've got more weapons than paint guns. There are shotguns in the gun room, and the claymore in the old hall, and some pikes, and Cedric has a couple of old-fashioned spits in the kitchen. We'll fight. There are only three of them. They won't get past us.'

Everyone was staring at me in a mixture of astonishment and horror – everyone except Harry. He had a look on his face that was both rueful and surprised, with a trace of something else I couldn't describe.

'You know, Dacres,' he said, 'you may only be a C-list celeb, but you're an A-list human being.'

'I'm a *B-list* celeb!' I retorted on a reflex.

'I think . . . no shotguns,' HG said. 'I don't really want to cap my career by being sent to prison for murder. However . . .'

Sandy put the body of the dog carefully on the floor. 'Who are these blokes,' he demanded, 'if they're not journos?'

'Attila 33,' said Roo. 'Neo-Nasties. It's a long story, but they're after Harry.'

'We'll get them,' Sandy said grimly. 'Jules and Sting are still searching the grounds. I better warn him.' He strode back through the entrance hall and out into the fog.

'Could they just walk in here?' I wanted to know. Harry nodded. 'How many entrances does this place have?'

'Too many,' Harry said. 'The front door, the door from the kitchen – the garden door from HG's private sitting room, the cellar door. Not to mention the lower windows.'

'We need to make a stand somewhere,' I declared. 'The old hall. That's where the weapons are.'

HG said, 'I'm not happy with the idea of weapons—'

'You didn't see these guys,' said Roo. 'They aren't going to be stopped because you're a big star and the police are on the way, believe me.'

Fenny had come in and was sniffing at Elton's body, making bewildered whimpering noises.

'Better get him out of here,' Harry said, distracted. 'He may be a Rottweiler at heart, but he doesn't have the physique to go with it.'

I swept him up in my arms, trying not to look at poor Elton. 'I'll shut him up in one of the bedrooms. Back in a sec.'

I went out, then halted at the foot of the stairs. It would take several minutes to get to the nearest bedroom, and I didn't want to be gone that long. Anything could happen. Besides, I *really* needed a weapon. I could just see myself as a modern-day Amazon, defying the forces of violence and thuggery. Of course, the danger of seeing yourself in a particular role is that it might inspire you to actually go for it . . .

I made my way to the old hall, still clutching Fenny. There was a sort of study beyond it which had been used as a dressing room during the re-enactment scenes; I could shut the puppy in there. In passing, I grabbed a leftover bottle of stage blood. It suggested something to me – not a plan, more a scenario. When I shut the door, Fenny barked and scratched on it, but that couldn't be helped. 'Quiet!' I ordered, dragging a chair on to the vast hearth. Fenny paid no attention to me, still barking furiously, and I did my best to pay no attention to him. I climbed up on the chair and lifted the claymore down from the chimney-piece.

Ruth

I'm not quite a stranger to violence, but that doesn't make it any easier. Once, in Bucharest, Kyle had been interviewing a kidnap-victim-turned-prostitute when some heavies showed up and we'd had to get out fast, for her sake. Another time, investigating corruption in famine relief in Africa, someone had pointed a gun at us: I still remember very clearly how it felt, staring into that little black hole, knowing that at a touch – just a *touch* – death would come out of it. But I'd never met anyone who frightened me quite as much as Attila the Suit, with his civilised clothes and his civilised smile and the visible brutality just under the skin.

And there was Elton on the floor with his head beaten in. Whoever had hit him hadn't just done it once to knock him out – they'd gone on hitting him, and hitting him, enjoying it, enjoying the violence and the blood and the act of killing . . . And now they were out there, prowling through the fog, seeking a way into the castle (there were dozens), coming for Harry, ready to crush anyone who got in their way. Delphi was brave, but she didn't understand. She thought her superstar temper – the terror of directors and researchers alike – would have an effect on people to whom all her second-rank fame meant less than nothing. HG was older but hardly wiser; he'd spent his whole life in splendid isolation. And Ash, though accustomed to the dark side of human nature, generally encountered it in the form of the supernatural, which doesn't usually come armed with a club.

But Harry knew. He was pale and tense and resolutely practical. 'I think you should all go upstairs,' he said. 'Ruth, go after Delphi – keep her out of here. This is my problem; I'll deal with it.'

'How?' Ash asked bluntly.

And from HG: 'This is my home – my castle. I'm not running away from anyone.'

'Sir—' Morag spoke, from the door through to the back. 'Have ye got a minute, sir?'

We knew instantly something was wrong. Her voice was pitched a little too high, and none of the staff *ever* called HG 'sir'.

Besides, it was much too normal a request for Morag, containing as it did no references to God or the devil.

HG said: 'Yes?'

She came in, slowly. 'These men, sir . . . They want tae see Harry.'

They were behind her. The fat skinhead had the cosh; he was slapping it on his palm like a tough guy in a film, which was such a cliché it should been funny, but nobody laughed. Then there was greaseball: he seemed to be literally trembling with anticipation, or the effort of holding his natural urges in check. And lastly Attila. Attila the Suit. When he saw Harry his smooth veneer seemed to slip sideways, so you saw something else peering out – something ancient and savage. He smiled his alligator smile, full of gleamy teeth.

There was a sharp intake of breath close by, but I didn't know if it was Harry, or Ash, or possibly me.

'Well, well,' Attila said. 'Harry – my old mate. Where *have*

you been hiding yourself? Me and the boys, we've been looking for you everywhere.'

Thump . . . thump . . . went the cosh in Skinhead's fat palm.

HG said with commendable calm: 'Get out of my house.'

Attila glanced at him as if he were a child or a pet, someone powerless and insignificant.

'This the big star? Not that big really, is he? D'you know, I
could break him with one hand? I could snap his neck like a
chicken. Maybe I should do that. Way past his best, isn't he?
Maybe it would be a kindness. Anyway, I've never killed a star.'

'If you touch me,' HG said, 'you'll go down for a *very* long
time.'

Attila laughed. '*Talks* big, don't he? He don't know about
me and the courts. Pals with all the judges, I am. Got my own
little witness protection scheme.'

(Thump . . . thump . . .)

'Let them go.' Harry spoke with evident difficulty. 'You've
got no quarrel with any of them.'

The rest of us just stood there. Frozen.

I was thinking: they'll have knives somewhere. Maybe a gun.
(Please God, not a gun.) I looked for a bulge under the suit,
but Attila seemed to be all bulges, as if the muscles were burst-
ing out of his body, straining at his clothes. Or possibly the
suit just didn't fit.

I was thinking: we have to fight.

I'd never been in a physical fight in my life.

'Nah,' Attila said. 'I'd rather let them watch. If they're good,
we'll give them a treat.' He came right up to me. 'This one
looks good. Bit small in the tit department –' he flipped my
breast with a finger – 'but really quite tasty. I love posh pussy.'

Greaseball made a noise which might have passed for a
snigger.

Beside me, I sensed Ash's tautness, though we didn't touch.

Thump . . . thump . . . went the cosh.

Seeing Attila from so close, I was nearly sure there was no gun bulge.

I was thinking: any moment now, Delphi's going to walk in. Shit . . .

Greaseball said, 'Someone brought the dog in.' He shoved Elton's body with his foot. 'Where're the minders?'

'Outside,' Attila said easily. 'Looking for us in the fog. Great stuff, fog. Keeps everyone out – and everyone in. Anyone else here we should know about?'

Cedric in the kitchen . . . Dorian upstairs . . . Delphi.

Harry said: 'No.'

'I hope you're not lying to me,' Attila said. 'I don't like liars. And your record isn't very good, is it? Pretending to be one of us, one of the team, fighting for the cause – all the time a traitor. A lying, cheating sneak working for the establishment press, betraying your own people for a load of blacks and Pakis and Jews. What d'you think you deserve, selling out your own kind?' He was unbuttoning his jacket as he spoke, pulling something out of an inside pocket. A glove. A glove which clinked. He tugged it on, flexed his fingers. Metal studs gleamed on the knuckles. 'I'll give you a clue. I didn't come here to hand you a fucking award.'

Skinhead had stopped thumping the cosh. Greaseball seemed to be wetting himself in his eagerness.

No more time for thinking.

Attila's fist moved so fast that for all the build-up Harry was caught off guard. The blow took him in the stomach, doubling him up. Then Attila grabbed him by the hair and the metal glove smacked him full in the face. Blood spurted from a dozen cuts. Ash leaped for Attila, but Greaseball knocked him sideways – I tried to get hold of his arm to pull him away from Ash but he shook me off. A knife flashed in his hand.

HG yelled: 'Stop it! The police are coming!'

Then Delphi came back.

Delphi, with the claymore gripped in both hands, the blade dripping red. Delphi, with blood daubed on her face and arms, with scarlet spatter on her clothes. Delphi, wild-eyed and mop-haired, giving off rage like an electric storm. Move over Xena, Warrior Princess. Here comes Delphinium Dacres . . .

'LEAVE HIM ALONE!' she screamed, meaning Harry.

Skinhead charged. She swung the claymore – he tried to dodge but too late. The blade ploughed along his belly, bunching his T-shirt, leaving a red stain in its wake. The end of the swing caught Greaseball in the arm, making him drop the knife. Ash and I both pounced on him and we all collapsed in a squirming heap. Meanwhile, Harry used the diversion to lunge for Attila, getting in too close for blows. HG tried to help and failed. Morag, with amazing enterprise, picked up a table lamp and smashed it down on Skinhead's skull – he subsided like a limp blancmange.

Ash said: 'Back off, Ruth, I can handle it,' while Greaseball tried to gouge out his eye.

Attila broke free of Harry's grip, flicked HG aside like a gnat. He pressed something on the glove, and tiny blades unsheathed like claws at the tip of each finger.

God knows what films he'd been watching. Probably *Enter the Dragon*.

Then Cedric arrived, hefting a spit and yelling a war cry which sounded like *Aüeeoolii*! Attila's glove was evil, but it didn't have the reach of spit or claymore. Outnumbered and outgunned, he sprinted for the door. Greaseball wriggled free and followed him. Footsteps pounded across the hall. We heard the front door open, then the fog swallowed them.

Delphi dropped the claymore and ran to Harry.

'What've you done to yourself?' he said.

'Stage blood – I'm fine – your *face* –!'

He was breathing hard and obviously in pain. Both HG and Ash had facial damage that would soon darken to bruises. Nobody cared.

When HG said, 'Everyone all right?' everyone said, 'Yes.' We all hugged each other a lot, even Morag. I think I wept a bit; I know Delphi did. Everyone said everyone else was wonderful. And meant it.

Then Morag started cleaning up Harry's face and HG called a doctor from two villages away and Delphi explained again about the stage blood and how she'd summoned Cedric on the in-house phone before making her entrance – and could someone please let Fenny out? Ash and Cedric tied up Skinhead in case he came round, using handcuffs on his wrists. ('Good thing I've got these,' Cedric said. 'Don't get to use them much up here, worst luck.') Dorian wandered into the middle of things and, once he had grasped what had happened, accused his father of deliberately excluding him, as if he'd been left out of a particularly good party. HG said his being left out was the one good thing about the whole business. I grabbed a chance to tell Dorian how brave and supercool his dad had been, concluding, 'See if Joshua Thingummy-Wotsit can match that.' We all had several restorative drinks.

Jules and Sandy came back with Sting, mortified to have missed the fight and saying they couldn't find the enemy in the fog. Weather conditions also slowed down the arrival of the police and the doctor, who finally showed up about two hours later. Harry had several stitches in his face and was escorted off by the police to make formal statements in protective custody.

'You going to write about all this?' HG said, by way of farewell.

Harry's grin was uncomfortable; his face had swollen up.

'Eventually. But don't worry: it's a wrench, but I'll leave you out. If that's what you want. I owe you that much.'

'That's what I want.'

Hesitantly, they shook hands.

'You were a good butler,' HG said. 'We'll miss you.'

Ash and I both said, 'Good luck.' There were more hugs.

Delphi said, 'Harry . . .'

Harry said, 'Delphi . . .'

And: 'You're a star. You really are.'

Then the police dragged him off to be protected and there wasn't time for any more.

The superintendent left considerably later, having collected statements from all and sundry and arrested Skinhead, who had come round and was deeply pissed off. The humiliation of being taken out by two women, one of whom was over sixty, so demoralised him that he decided his tough-guy cred was gone for good and finally pleaded guilty to everything. Our friend Taggart treated us with the mixture of suspicion and respect any cop would feel for a household which can produce an antique skeleton and a clutch of fascist thugs in the same week. He left people to assist Jules and Sandy in watching the castle in case Attila & co. came back, but there was no sign of them. We all talked things over several times and then sat down to a rather casual dinner – Cedric's equilibrium had been seriously ruffled – before heading early to bed.

'I've got Fenny,' Delphi said, 'and I'm going to lock my door. You never know: they *might* get past the police guard. In films, psychopaths always do.'

'This is real life,' I pointed out. 'Though sometimes I wonder.'

'You can stay with me,' Delphi offered, 'if you're nervous.'

'I'll be fine.'

363

'I'll take care of Ruth,' Ash said.

We were in the purple gallery at the time. Delphi, on her way out, turned on her heel, gave him a glare, said, 'Excuse me,' and dragged me to one side.

'*What are you doing?*'

'I don't see why you should have all the fun,' I said.

'ME? I mean . . .' she lowered her voice. '*Me*? You're the one who has HG trying to get off with you, and practically every guy in the place pouring out his heart to you, on account of you being such a good listener, while all I do is shag the butler – who isn't actually a butler anyway. Ash isn't remotely your type—'

'You always object to my type.'

'—*and* he's gay.'

'Then you've got nothing to worry about,' I said.

'Maybe he . . . he shops on both sides of the street. That's a situation you *don't* want to get into. Some irate ex-boyfriend could come crawling out of the woodwork and turn *really* nasty—'

'Go to bed,' I said. 'It's been a long day.'

Reluctantly, she went. 'In the morning,' she admonished, 'you tell me *everything*. Right?'

'I promise.'

Ash walked me to my door. 'She looks out for you,' he said.

'And I for her.'

'Mm. I like that.'

There was something in his tone which made me say, 'Didn't anyone ever look out for you?'

'My elder brother.' I'd opened the door. He hesitated to follow me, till I smiled.

'Where is he now?'

'He died when I was sixteen. Car accident.'

'Was that why . . . ?'

'Why I got interested in the afterlife? No. I always was.' He put his arms around me. It felt *right*, as if I'd been waiting for this for a very long time. 'Let's leave my life story for the moment. I know it all anyway, so it's dull to go through it again. You blamed me for not kissing you.'

'Not *blamed*, exactly . . .'

'I was hoping to make up for that.'

In due course, inevitably, it was morning. But it was Sunday morning, which is in a different league from other mornings. I didn't have to get up, Ash didn't have to get up. On Sundays, he assured me, well-behaved Scottish ghosts take the morning off and go to church, on account of being good Presbyterians. If Delphi knocks on my door, I thought, I *definitely* won't answer. I need to catch up on sleep.

Some of the time, we slept.

'What will HG say?' Ash asked at one point.

'HG must've dished out a hell of a lot of kisses over the years,' I said. 'He's not going to miss that one. Or want it back.'

'He's not getting it back . . .'

Eventually, we went downstairs just before lunch. Nigel had returned, very pleased with himself for having tracked down the Courtney DNA (though it would take a few days for the testing to be completed) and duly shocked by the tale of our adventures. The fog had lifted long before, and the police were still searching for Attila and Greaseball; they hadn't gone back to their rooms in the village or been seen by anyone since rushing out of the castle after the fight.

'I'm not going on a search party for *them*,' Delphi announced.

In the afternoon, she and I retired to her room, where she talked about Harry and I talked about Ash. The trade-off that's part of being female. It's like holiday snaps: you bore me with yours, I'll bore you with mine. Only if you're real best friends you don't get bored, whether it's holiday pix or men.

'Is Ash serious about you?' Delphi wanted to know. 'You're serious, I can tell. You always are.'

'Bit early to say.' I mustn't spoil the moment by worrying about the future.

Anyway, he'd already talked about things we would do back in London . . .

'What about you and Harry?'

'Oh no. No, of course not. It was just a quickie. Ships that collide in the night – and sink. That sort of thing.'

She added, belatedly, 'I don't even have his number.'

'You could call the *Indy*.'

'I'm not going chasing after him! He's not even good-looking. He's got sandy hair, and he's a bloody journalist. Can you imagine us having a high-profile celebrity wedding?'

'Aha,' I said. 'So you're thinking about marriage.'

'Don't be ridiculous.'

Later that evening, the police called to tell us they'd arrested Greaseball. He was trying to hitch a lift on the road out of Lochnabu, covered in mud and apparently very scared, though it wasn't clear what of.

We buried Elton in the garden, with Sandy reading from the ballad of Beth Gelert, though it wasn't entirely appropriate, and Dougal McDougall playing the bagpipes. (It didn't sound anything like the ones I'd heard in the wee small hours.) Delphi wept into Fenny's fur and Sting looked lost without his brother, glancing round every few minutes as if expecting him to be there. I suppose it's the same with animals as with people, only we're supposed to *understand*, though of course we didn't. HG planted a Peace rose on top of the grave.

They found Attila a couple of days later, floating in the Cauldron with his head stove in against the rocks.

'Do you believe in hell?' I asked Ash.

'No,' he said. 'But sometimes, there's justice.'

Delphinium

What did I tell you? You can never trust a gay guy – there's always testosterone in there somewhere. There was Ash acting gay (i.e. not making passes at attractive women), hanging out with a gay (Cedric), and looking so pretty he had to be gay, and suddenly he pops out of the closet and decides he's straight after all. I was concerned about Roo – I thought he might regress – and then she tells me this long saga about his ex-girlfriend running off and taking his young daughter, and how he was completely devastated by this, and that's why he'd been uninterested in women for so long. I thought it might be true, but you have to trust your instincts – Ash said so himself – so I decided to check him out. Cedric and I had bonded after I did my Amazon warrior thing, and he backed me up with the spit, so I went into the kitchen to discuss it with him.

'Is he gay? Was he gay? Has he ever been gay?' I wanted to know.

'Nah,' said Cedric. 'Straight as a plumb line. Hell of a waste. With that face, he could be pulling in droves.' He was dicing vegetables as he talked, tossing them into a large pan. There was a gorgeous smell of frying garlic. 'He fancied Ruthie right from the start; I could see that. Kept asking about her when she wasn't there. Always a giveaway. Still, I had hopes. With my charm and my looks I figured I was in with a chance.'

Cedric has all the looks and charm of a malevolent garden gnome, but I didn't say so. You should never shatter people's illusions about themselves.

'Course, Ruthie was right, it's my teeth what let me down,' he went on. 'I'm going to get them fixed. HG's giving me a fucking great bonus for routing them Narzis.'

'You had help,' I reminded him.

I thought I'd been pretty amazing the way I'd handled the situation, and I never got tired of people telling me so.

After hearing Cedric's expert opinion, all I had to do was find out the name of the magazine Ash worked for (HG told me) and pump someone there. But by the time I got his story confirmed, I knew it wasn't really necessary. Once you saw him with Roo, it became clear that Ash was that rare creature, a Nice Man. There are so few of these with sex appeal, and Roo hardly ever showed an interest in them, so it was difficult for me to believe that she had actually landed one at last.

'Marry him,' I told her, the day I presented her with the dress from Maddalena. 'You can wear this. It may not be white, but white's not your colour and you'll look ravishing in these mauvy-blue tones.'

'Don't be silly. Anyhow, I can't take it – it was meant to be for your bridesmaid.'

'You've been promoted.'

'Ash and I aren't getting married,' Roo said, adding unconvincingly: 'We've only just started seeing each other.'

'He's okay,' I said. 'I vetted him.'

'You *vetted* him?'

I explained about sounding out Cedric and talking to someone on the magazine. I wasn't sure how Roo would take it, but she became very thoughtful.

'You know your trouble?' she said. 'You're missing Harry. You miss suspecting him, and picking fights with him, and being able to ring for him any time you're bored, and—'

'Don't say it! Anyway, that's nonsense. It was just a – a casual fling – a one-night-and-an-afternoon stand. A bit of rough trade.'

'For you or for him?' Roo said, unforgivably.

Beyond the perimeters of Dunblair, the tabloid army was trickling away. The flurry of exclusives from Basilisa and Brie had run out, HG and I had primed our respective lawyers, and other scandals had come along to push us off the front pages. We said nothing about Attila 33 – that was Harry's story, and, anyway, it was all *sub jaundice*, or whatever they call it when the case is going to come to court at some point. There was an inquest on Attila, but they managed without us, bringing in a verdict of accidental death after extensive local evidence about the dangers of fog on the mountain and the Cauldron.

There were no more skeletons or sinister strangers or cheating lovers or sudden divorces. Things were getting rather dull. That was probably why I seemed to be missing Harry. I wasn't *really* missing him, I told myself: it was just a trick of the mind, a flash of creativity on the part of my underworked imagination. I threw myself into gardening, actually planting things and getting soil under my nails and grass stains on my DKNY skirt. But gardening, though physical, doesn't use up your thoughts, so I devoted every spare moment to the mystery of Elizabeth Courtney. The DNA tests came back to confirm that the skeleton was her, and Nigel in Sherlock Holmes mode expounded several theories as to how she got into the underground chamber, who put her there etc. There was no way of telling exactly how she died, but Nigel came out with long dissertations on how she *didn't* die (*not* Colonel Mustard in the Library with the Blunt Instrument – no skull damage). I listened to everything, even when he got sidetracked into talking about his novel, which now included the mysterious death of one of the characters and a plot device where the body turned up in the twenty-first century, and an academic genius was able to work out every detail of the crime. I wasn't being a good listener – well, not deliberately – but he *does* know his stuff and I thought that somewhere in the ragbag of information there might be a useful pointer. In between, I communed with the portrait – maybe it hadn't been moved; maybe it was the *sun* which had shifted, on account of summer – and painted my toenails emerald green. Not that anyone noticed. That's the awful thing about singledom. (One of the awful things.) No one notices the colour of your toenails.

(Roo says Alex was a foot-fetishist and therefore exceptional and most men never notice anything much below mid-thigh. She may have a point.)

Despite all the fresh air and digging and stuff, I didn't sleep too well. I'd heard about depression, but it had always been something that happened to other people, not to me. Now I could feel it out there, waiting for me, like this big black hole that was trying to suck me in. Once I was in there, I was afraid I'd be falling and falling into nothingness for ever. I tried to be positive, but it wasn't much use: when I was alone in the dark, all these horrible truths would come crawling out to confront me, like every bad thing in my life was marching round and round carrying a placard. I was nearly thirty-five, I'd been publicly and hideously humiliated by the man I was supposed to marry, a huge international rock star *wasn't* in love with me (despite what the papers said), and I'd had the shag of my life with a piece of rough trade whom I'd probably never see again, and I didn't want to see again, only I couldn't stop thinking about him.

There were nights when I got fixated on my father, and started worrying that Mummy was right, I was like him, maybe too like him, and I would end up like him, self-centred and alone and unloved. Then I would resolve to be kinder to him, whatever he'd done, and ask him to give me away at my wedding, only there wasn't going to be any wedding, and there was nobody to give me away *to*. When you've planned something for ages, and looked forward to it so much, it's hard to let go: your brain gets stuck.

So my thoughts went round and round in circles, and the circles would get smaller and smaller, until at last, when I was worn out, they would disappear into the dot which was sleep. I had vivid, disturbing dreams which I couldn't remember and didn't much want to, though there were moments of lucidity, not like my dream in the gallery but similar. Moments less like a dream than a glimpse into something – another life, another time. But as I said, I wondered about Elizabeth Courtney a lot, to distract me from the personal stuff, so it wasn't surprising.

I dreamed I was coming to Dunblair for the first time, driving along the private road – it was very rough, much bumpier than usual – and pulling up outside the castle. I don't remember the vehicle I was in, but I had to step down from it, not up like you do from most cars. A woman came to greet me; she had a tired, kindly face and anxious eyes. I was taken to my room. There were servants – many more servants than nowadays; I could feel them peering at me, whispering behind my back. The room was large and airy, though I couldn't help noticing the curtains were shabby and there were liver spots on the mirror. I remember thinking: I'll change all that. I went to the window, and there was the garden, sort of formal but going wild around the edges, and the loch to my left, silver under a grey sky, and rain clouds blurring the mountains.

Then I saw the maze. It wasn't a square or a rectangle, more a kind of kidney shape, so it looked organic rather than man-made, almost as if it had grown there by itself. Yet at the same time it was unnatural, the monstrosity I had always imagined it to be. The hedges were too dark and too tall, the paths were narrow and secret, and at the centre I could just make out the top of a horned statue, like some ancient demon lurking in its lair. In my dream I was afraid of it, though I didn't know why. Not the legends and the ghost stories: the dream-me was an educated woman who didn't believe in such things. I was afraid of *it*, the maze itself – the menace of the hedges and the mesh of pathways like a snare waiting to entangle its next victim. And at its heart the demon, old as sin and altogether evil.

I shivered, thought the day was mild, and made as if to draw back. That was when I noticed the girl. She was down in the garden, looking up at the window, looking at *me*. She was very young and I thought her beautiful, with raven hair hanging loose and, even at that distance, a curious intensity of expression. My dream-persona didn't know who she was, but *I* knew. Iona Craig.

The next time I found myself in the dream, I was walking in the garden, close to the loch. It was sunset, but the long rays couldn't penetrate the hedge-wall: the maze was like a blot of permanent darkness on the sunlight of my world. I was supposed to be happy – blissfully happy – but the maze was waiting for me, and I knew that one day, somehow, I would be drawn in.

The following night, or the night after, I was back in the dream again, but this time I was standing by the entrance to the maze. It was evening, and the hedges were way above my head, and the path in between was a narrow slot plunging into darkness. Someone was holding my hand, pulling me on, laughing at my fears – the girl, the girl in the garden. The dream-me knew her name but nothing more, nothing of the danger, and I let her draw me on while inside my mind the tiny little speck that was the *real* me screamed vainly in warning, *Don't go with her . . . don't go . . .* I passed into the maze, turning this way and that in her wake, until she let go my hand, running ahead – she knew every twist, every path – disappearing into the twilight. I called, but there was no answer. I was alone, trapped in the maze.

I stopped, telling myself there was nothing to fear. The hedges were too thick to force a passage through and far too high to see over, but I could find the way out, if I took my time and didn't panic. I made myself go slowly, backtracking from every dead end, trying to remember my route – first left, second left, first right. I lost all sense of direction. The maze didn't look that large from the outside, but inside it seemed enormous, an endless labyrinth of convoluted pathways with no exit and no ingress, taking me inexorably further and further inward. I didn't see the girl again. My terror grew, but I didn't know if it was the terror of the dream-me or that other me, deep inside, the one who knew what happened next. *You'll never get out . . . never get out . . .* Then the path I was on opened up and I'd reached the centre, and there was the statue, bull-horned and goat-legged, and in the growing dark I thought it moved, it was alive, and I started to scream . . . but no, someone stepped out from behind it, human not monster, and a wave of new emotion rushed through me. Sudden, overwhelming relief . . .

I woke, and felt my heart beating hard, knowing I was almost there. But the dream didn't come again.

It was Morty who suggested the séance, probably by way of having a go at Ash. Roo hadn't made any announcements and they didn't hold hands or anything, but it was generally known they were together. HG, if the rumour reached him, took it in his stride. Morty couldn't really have thought Roo's sympathy would get him anywhere, but he evidently felt upstaged. Behind Ash's back, he made references to phoneys who capitalise on superstition and credulity, clearly contrasting that with the serious role of a presenter of makeover TV. (I may have an inflated idea of my own importance, according to some people, but I know what I do isn't *serious*, just lots and lots of fun.)

Ash said he had seen few séances where participants got in touch with anything other than their own subconscious, which wasn't always an uplifting experience. Russell said séances were bullshit but it might make good TV. I didn't tell Roo, but I wasn't keen on the idea. I'd got so close to Elizabeth Courtney, dreaming myself into her head; supposing she was able to *possess* me? I don't believe in that stuff, of course, it's just for horror movies, but the castle was definitely getting to me. After Basilisa's behaviour, and the skeleton, and Attila 33, anything was possible. Ash was right: there were too many ghosts, memories or spirits, echoes of the past that lived on, or died on, never quite fading away. Being possessed would put me at the centre of the action, which is where I like to be, but I didn't fancy it at all. I might have to relive being murdered, which would *really* traumatise me.

The first hedges had been imported and were being planted in the garden. They were only three feet high, but they spooked me. My latest dream was getting much too close.

It was HG who decided us on the séance idea. 'What have we got to lose?' he said. 'If it doesn't work, never mind. I've always wanted to try something like that here.'

'Do we hire a medium?' Morty asked. 'Or can Ash roll his eyes and foam at the mouth?'

Ash rolled his eyes, but not in quite the way Morty envisaged.

He said, at his most non-committal: 'Most mediums don't like being filmed. They say it spoils the vibes.'

'I've got a ouija board,' HG said. 'Tyndall bought it ages ago in Tangiers. She was a great believer in . . . well, almost anything. She once claimed to have got in touch with Charles II.'

'*Everyone* does Charles II,' Ash said with the hint of a smile.

'Too right,' said Russell. 'Even *I've* done Charles II. Funny how no one ever bothers with Charles I.'

'He was fairly boring,' Roo said. 'No charisma, no mistresses, no head. Boring.'

'I don't like it,' I whispered to her. 'Didn't they use a ouija board in *The Exorcist*?'

'You never saw *The Exorcist*,' said Roo. 'You said it was too scary.'

'Exactly!'

But if HG wanted it to happen, then of course it did. Ash said the cameras mustn't be intrusive and ruled out TV lighting, which led to a row with the crew, but with HG's support he got his way. It was decided five of us would take part: HG, Ash, Morty, Nigel and me. But Nigel felt it would be bad for his image as an academic historian to be seen involved in a séance, and Ash said four was too few. Roo refused to go on camera, Russell declared that even ghosts needed direction, and Dorian was at school. In the end, Russell volunteered Morag, because 'she's a great character, and we need a Scots accent to get the authentic atmosphere'. Predictably, she said a ouija board was 'an instrument o' the deil', but allowed herself to be persuaded. HG's staff all saw themselves as aspiring TV stars by now. Cedric would undoubtedly have been keen to join in, but fortunately didn't find out about the project until it was too late.

We did it in the great hall for reasons of ambience, with one low-wattage lamp (at the insistence of the crew) and plenty of candles. It took me ages to make up my mind what to wear. I had clothes for swanning round the garden and clothes for swanning round the castle, but nothing suitable for a séance. Should it be clinging black with cleavage, like Fenella Fielding in *Carry On Screaming*, or something ethereal and floaty with beads? Either way, I didn't have anything that fitted the bill. (It is a curious fact, but no matter how many clothes you take with you, whether on location or on holiday, there is always one occasion where you have abolutely nothing to wear.) In the end, I settled on a compromise: velvet jeans with a baroque pattern of swirls and cherubs, and a chiffon top with droopy bits. No beads. There are lengths to which I will not go.

I had a vague recollection of playing with an improvised ouija board once with some schoolfriends, using Scrabble letters and an inverted coffee cup. Come to think of it, we got in touch with Charles II. A social guy, obviously, even when dead.

We were filming in the evening so it would be sufficiently gloomy. Roo, Nigel and Russell were there, though Russell had to promise not to interfere; Mick had gone on strike since he wasn't allowed proper lighting, Dick was pissed and Nick stoned out of his brain (or vice versa). Except for those of us taking part, no one else was allowed in. Morag wore a black dress which made her look as if she was in mourning and a heavy silver cross which Morty said, in an undervoice, she ought to turn upside down.

'This is a ouija board,' Ash reminded him, 'not satanic rites.'

We sat round the table, HG on one side of me, Morty on the other, with Morag next to HG and Ash between her and Morty. Thank God we didn't have to hold hands. Morty started the proceedings by touching my leg. I dug my nails into the back of his hand. None of it felt very supernatural.

I was co-opted to question the spirits, should any of them turn up.

I'd never seen a proper board before, and the one Tyndall Fiske had bought was a work of art, rectangular and almost four feet long with the numbers and letters in a circle and a painted eye in the centre with *yes* and *no* written above and below it. Outside the ring of letters there were the twelve signs of the zodiac, though no one knew what for, and on one side was a disfigured, rather pouty moon, and on the other a smiley sun. The lettering looked decidedly Tolkienesque, both pointy and curly, though Ash said the influence must be Arabic, since it came from Tangiers. Nigel began to talk about someone called Zorro-something (I thought he was a sort of Spanish Robin Hood) until Russell shut him up. As the board was so gorgeous, HG got one of his poshest glasses, a heavy cut-crystal whisky tumbler with lots of room on the base for five fingertips. He inverted it in the middle, the camera started rolling, and nothing happened.

Presently, nudged by HG, I asked in a suitably hollow voice, 'Is anyone there?'

'Try not to ham it up,' Russell said. 'Start again.'

'I'm not hamming! I just wanted to be in tune with the whole paranormal thing—'

'Start again.'

No lights, camera, no action. I asked the same question. 'Is anyone there?' Morty was suppressing a grin; Ash looked inscrutable. Morag, probably because of her religious training, had the right kind of frozen glare, like Mrs Danvers in *Rebecca*.

HG said, 'We may not all believe in this, but there's no point in doing it without conviction. Try to keep an open mind.'

Then the glass moved.

It moved to *no*.

'Who's taking the piss?' Morty demanded – but at least he demanded it in a hushed voice.

Ash said: 'No reason why the dead shouldn't have a sense of humour.'

Further questioning revealed a severely dyslexic spirit with an inability to keep to the point. Not surprisingly, it turned out to be Charles II.

'Perhaps it's Bonnie Prince Charlie,' Roo suggested from the sidelines. 'You know – he thinks he's Charles III, but he got the wrong number.'

The glass whizzed instantly to *yes*.

'See?' I heard Russell murmur. 'Ghosts take direction.'

He and Roo shouldn't have been talking, but everyone knew this section would be cut.

'Ask him if he hid out in the maze,' HG prompted me.

I obliged. The glass, picking up its cue, went to *yes*.

'Do you know anything about the death of Elizabeth Courtney?' I went on, deciding to cut to the chase. I didn't believe there was a spirit there at all, let alone Bonnie Prince Charlie (who was centuries too early to have known Elizabeth), but I might as well play along and ask the important questions.

The glass didn't move at all, but the silence felt suddenly tense. Then it slid from side to side, as if unable to make up its mind.

In the background, there was an audible hiccup (from Dick), and the camera stopped rolling.

Russell said: 'Bugger.' Morty gave a short laugh, HG looked exasperated. Only Morag still maintained her fixed stare, as if she was gazing into another dimension. (Or, as Nick said later: 'On some really cool stuff, man.') She spoke in a voice that would have been husky if Morag had done husk.

'*She's here.*'

'Who?' I cried. 'Who's here?'

'Camera!' hissed Russell. Dick hiccupped again. The camera jammed.

Morag didn't seem to hear me. She appeared to be talking to someone – listening to someone – who wasn't there, asking questions, repeating phrases and fragments, as if horrified by what she heard. If it was an act, it was a good one. There was no eye-rolling or mouth-frothing; her expression stayed oddly blank. What made it somehow more convincing was that her Scots accent lightened (I'd always suspected it was overdone), so she sounded quite different.

'Amends . . . ye want to make amends? . . . One evil deed . . . but such a deed . . . Ye would not give her even a single night? . . . To pay lifelong is not enough. His love wore out? But yours did not. A woman loves for aye . . . He married you . . . after all those years o' watching and waiting . . . There were others? There would be . . . but ye saw to it he could not harm you? Because ye knew . . . ye knew the truth . . . His cousin too? The wickedness of it . . . wickedness and greed . . . And ye were part of it . . . ye led her to her doom . . . All for love? Will ye tell that to the good Lord? Blood on your hands . . . for love . . . May He have mercy on your soul . . .'

She fell silent, and there were tears on her face – I saw the glitter of them in the candlelight, though her stare had not changed.

Ash said gently, 'Morag.'

She blinked, and seemed to focus on us again.

'Great show,' said Morty.

'Ha' ye finished wi' yon inferrnal game?' Morag said, indicating the board. 'I must . . . I must ha' dropped off a wee minute. I wouldna stay awake tae chat wi' the deil. Ye could talk tae demons wi'out me.'

'Actually . . .' HG said. He and Ash explained to her what had happened, while her face grew stiff again, this time in shock – disbelief – disapproval – any combination.

I got up and walked away. I needed to think. Light was dawning; facts were falling into place. Morag had evidently been communicating with her great-great-however-many-greats aunt; there were clues in the one-sided conversation, road signs pointing me in the right direction. If I could just concentrate for a moment . . .

In my head, the memory of Elizabeth Courtney said, '*Yes!*'

'I've got it!' I said, turning to the others. No one took any notice, so I said it again, louder. 'I'VE GOT IT!'

'Got what?' said Morty.

'The truth, the mystery, the secret of the maze. It came to me then – something Morag said.'

'Go on,' HG said grimly. Why grimly I don't know, but people do grim at these times. It builds up the suspense.

I was all for that.

'Iona did it,' I said, 'we know that, but not with Archie – *with Alasdair.*' Puzzled expressions met mine. 'Don't you see? *They* were the ones who were madly in love – the Romeo and Juliet syndrome, only without much opposition. Their problem was cash. The McGoogles were poor, and Elizabeth Courtney was rich. She fell for Alasdair, and he planned to marry her, and then kill her. Iona went along with it because she loved him. Like Jackie in *Death on the Nile*. She loved him "*beyond reason and beyond rectitude and beyond pity*".' I'd done a dramatisation of the book once on radio. 'Elizabeth didn't even know about the previous engagement, so Iona lured her into the maze, gave her the slip close to the centre, and Elizabeth found her own way there. And at the heart, behind the statue, was Alasdair, her new husband, her love. He put his arms round her, gave her one last false kiss –' I felt I owed it to her to get the maximum amount of drama out of the story – 'and strangled her. Then he hid the body in the chamber which, you can bet, only the McGoogles knew about. The legend was his cover story. Without a body, there was no crime – just another tragedy to add to the McGoogle family saga. It was a superstitious age, and there was no proper forensic science. The maze took the blame. Brides were always disappearing there: it was practically a tradition.'

'It sounds good so far,' Russell said, 'but then it all falls down. If he'd got away with it, why Africa?'

'What did Morag say that gave you the clue?' Roo asked.

'How did—'

'Wait!' I was still sorting it all out in my mind. 'Morag said, "*You wouldn't give her even a single night . . .*" Don't you see? Iona was passionate and possessive – she couldn't bear for Alasdair to sleep with Elizabeth even *once*. That's why they had to do it on the wedding night. Then he pretended to be grief-stricken and destroyed the maze and any plans of it *to conceal the body*. That way, even if someone heard or guessed about the underground chamber, they'd never be able to find it.'

'By George,' Russell said, in the words of Professor Higgins, 'I think she's got it.'

'It certainly fits in,' HG said. 'But then . . . Africa?'

'His mother,' Roo said, struck with the light of inspiration. 'His mother knew.'

'Of course,' said Nigel. (He hadn't said anything to date, and an *of course* was long overdue.) 'She knew he was in love with Iona – that was why she disapproved so strongly of his marrying Elizabeth. She must have sensed his moral weakness and distrusted his motives accordingly. She feared all along what her son might be capable of. When Elizabeth vanished, she would have guessed the truth and confronted him. His exile was the price of her silence. He had murdered – for nothing – and she wore black to the end of her days, not in mourning for her daughter-in-law but for her son.'

'Yes, but she must have known he would come back after her death,' Russell said prosaically.

'He died first,' HG pointed out.

'Maybe she left some sort of confession of what she knew,' Roo said. 'In the hands of her lawyer, to be opened in the event of Alasdair's return. Only when he died she destroyed it.'

'Not wanting to risk blighting the family honour,' I concluded.

'Then Archie came back, so Iona married him?' Morty sounded sceptical.

'We know that,' said HG.

'No,' I said. 'You still don't get it. It wasn't *Archie* who came back. It was *Alasdair*. Morag said: "*His cousin, too?*" In the wilds of Africa anything could happen – and it did. Alasdair killed his cousin and stole his identity. I expect he had a faithful henchman who helped him, some local chief whose life he'd saved and who thought killing relatives was the order of the day.'

'That's *so* politically incorrect,' said Russell.

'No it isn't,' I protested. 'Africa is like that – raw and primitive. Life there is cheap. I know: I read a Wilbur Smith once.' Roo stared at me. 'On holiday. Anyway,' I went on, 'he waited till *after* Lady Mary's death, then he came home. That *proves* it. Archie wouldn't have needed to wait.'

'He'd never have got away with it,' HG said. 'Someone would have recognised him.'

'He was tanned to a crisp from the sun and prematurely aged from all those African diseases,' I reminded him. 'They didn't have any drugs then. He'd probably had everything from beriberi to lesser spotted swamp fever. Also, he grew a beard. Look at the pictures: Alasdair as a young man and Archie after his return. They're awfully alike, even though they're by different artists.'

'He might have pulled it off,' Roo said. 'That was another age. Even if some of the villagers *did* guess, they wouldn't necessarily have said anything. The McGoogles were aristocrats, the most important family in the area. Archie, or Alasdair, was the Laird. Best to shut up and stay on his good side.'

'It's possible,' Nigel admitted cautiously, wary of any idea he hadn't thought of first.

'It's *obvious*,' I insisted. 'Iona married him. "*All those years of watching and waiting . . .*" He must've promised her he'd come back some day, come back and marry her – and he did. Like in "The Highwayman":

> *Look for me by moonlight,*
> *Watch for me by moonlight,*
> *I'll come to thee by moonlight,*
> *Though Hell should bar the way.*

'My grandmother told me he had the luck o' the deil, Archie McGoogle,' Morag said. 'There's only one way tae win the deil's luck. Ye mun sell your soul.'

'What happened to him?' Roo asked Nigel.

'There was a son,' Nigel said. 'He was scholarly rather than athletic, a disappointment to his father. Then there was a stillborn child, or more than one. After that, Archie lost interest in his wife. He had a roving eye and was still an attractive man, for all his weather-beaten appearance. And he was the Laird. There were women enough willing to oblige him in these parts. Iona threw herself into charitable works – she was an exemplary lady of the manor, stoic, long-suffering, always kind to the poor and needy. Whatever guilt she bore, she must have done her best to expiate it. She lived to be over ninety, and saw both her husband and her son die.'

'How?' I asked.

'The son was sickly – he died of a wasting disease. Archie had a fall from his horse. It was a black stallion called Demon, notoriously difficult to manage; Archie prided himself on mastering difficult horses. It reared and bolted just outside the castle, close to where the maze used to be. The rumour was it saw something no human eyes could see, but ghost stories, once started, have a tendency to persist. It galloped along to the loch, stumbled or something, and Archie was thrown into the water and drowned. A belated and rather inadequate punishment if he was indeed Alasdair and a murderer twice over.'

'Maybe that wasn't his punishment,' Ash said. 'Maybe his punishment – if that's the word – was to stay here, in the home he'd killed for . . . an impotent spirit bound to this place for all time. More than one person has seen a figure in Highland dress here; perhaps they weren't imagining it.'

'Brie and her intuition?' I said.

'Being empty-headed doesn't make you empty-eyed. She *might* have seen something. We think of evil as a weight, a burden on the soul. Could be that isn't just a metaphor. Evil weighs Alasdair down, holding him here – unfinished business, wrongs that can never be put right. His spirit must linger on, pointlessly, till it withers away altogether.'

'Do you really get paid for this baloney?' Morty asked.

'Why not?' said Ash. 'You get paid for yours.'

'Considering what has just happened,' Roo said, 'sneering isn't just cheap, it's stupid.'

'Oh, Morag here gave a great performance—'

'I dinna perrrform for any man,' Morag said superbly, rather as if she'd been accused of pole-dancing. 'I'm no' clear what I said, but I were Iona's image when I were a child, so my Grandma told me. She said the likeness made a bond between us. She had a picture of Iona when she were young and beautiful, but she kept it locked in a drawer, because Iona wasn't well thought of i' the kirk. She turned to heathen ways when she got old, nae doot wanting to confess and be free o' her sins.'

Heathen ways? I mouthed, visualising witchcraft and pagan rites.

'I think she means Catholicism,' Roo whispered.

'Do you still have the picture?' HG asked Morag.

'Ay, that I do. Her picture, and the box she left us, the box wi' no key. They say she gave it tae the vicar firrst, to be broke open if she died before her time, but she had a long life though none too happy, and the box came back tae her family in the end.'

'Box???' Several of us spoke more or less at once. 'She left a box?'

'Her confession!' Roo breathed. 'Like Lady Mary. Her confession she made to protect herself.'

'Of course,' said Nigel. 'If Delphi's right, Alasdair was a habitual killer. He wouldn't have hesitated to dispose of a wife he no longer loved – unless she had a hold over him.'

'Did you open the box?' HG asked.

'No,' said Morag, who was clearly superhuman. 'It were her secret, and she died in her bed. There was nae call to go opening it.'

HG paused before taking the plunge.

'Would you let us open it?' he said.

Chapter 12:
Pro-Celebrity Marriage

Ruth

We broke open the box on camera, in a moment of incredible TV drama. The real-life drama was pretty hot, too.

Sure enough, there was a letter inside. Delphi wanted to read it out on camera but we let Morag do it; that seemed more appropriate. It was written in the slanting script of the time, with long sentences and capital letters all over the place, and it went on for several pages.

'This is the True Confession of Iona Cathleen McGoogle, née Craig, being an Account of my Terrible Crime and an Indictment of the man who was my Lover and who led me into Evil. If any open and read this, after my Death, may they find it in their Heart to Forgive me, though I have done little to deserve their Forgiveness. Yet not a night now passes when I do not wish the Deed Undone, and wake in the Darkness like Lady Macbeth, to see Blood on my hands that will never wash off.

When I was but sixteen, I loved and was beloved by Alasdair McGoogle, Laird of Dunblair. We were Betrothed in secret, for he had no Money, and said he

386

would have to go to the Colonies to seek his Fortune before we could be married, and he would not have me Bound to him, though I was not unwilling to be so Bound. Then, in the summer of my seventeenth year he went to London, and wrote to me from that Capital of Empire that he had met a woman of great Wealth who was enamoured of him, and he planned to marry her, for the sake of his Family, though he would always love Me. I learned later that his Mother, who had long suspected our Attachment, was not pleased with the Match, though they were in Sore Need of Money for the Upkeep of the Estate. I thought my Heart would break, but I determined not to Stand in his Way. Eventually he returned, bringing the Heiress with him, and came privily to meet with me, unbeknownst to both his Betrothed and Lady Mary his Mother. He told me he still loved me, he loved me more than ever, and could not Live without me, but he must marry for Financial Advantage. He said he would wed the Heiress, and she would go into the Maze and vanish, like the other McGoogle Bride of long ago. Many have entered the Maze and never come out: the Legend of the Castle had taken them. At first I was shocked, and could not speak, but his Love for me overcame my Resistance, and the Danger of this Venture excited me in the most Dreadful Way, causing me to forget or abandon the Moral Precepts with which I had been brought up. Furthermore, the Heiress was an Englishwoman, older than my Beloved and not handsome, and I was so sunken in Wickedness, it was all too easy for me to see her as my Enemy, deserving of her Fate. I became involved in the Preparations for the Wedding, in order that Alasdair and I could meet in the Castle, but I was consumed with Jealousy every time I saw his Future Bride, for all her Plainness, and I made him Swear to me he would never Hold her in his Arms, never bestow on her a single Kiss. Therefore on the night of the Wedding we put our Plan into action . . .'

It went on, as I said, for several pages. Lady Mary's ultimatum, Alasdair's exile, his vow to return. Iona's Torment when she heard of his death, her Unbounded Happiness when a letter arrived six months later, unsigned, carrying the message that he still lived. And at last, beyond hope or expectation, he came back. Whether he found her changed, far removed from her seventeen-year-old loveliness, she did not say. He married her; he had no choice. She had waited faithfully for so many years, and, in any case, she knew too much. And with marriage came the final disillusionment, the realisation that the man for whom she had sacrificed her Immortal Soul no longer loved her, was perhaps incapable of loving anybody. Knowing him as she did, she wrote this confession, the only safeguard of her future.

'I would wish for Death,' she concluded, 'though that is a Sin, but it is a small Sin beside the far greater ones I have already committed. However, I cannot leave my son while he is still a child, and with such a Father, so while Life remains to me, I will do what little I can to atone. Sometimes I pray to the Soul of Elizabeth Courtney –' that was the first and only time she mentioned her victim by name – 'in whatever Paradise wherein she may dwell, that she might look down on me in the Fires of Hell, and, like the Blessed Damozel, that she may shed a tear for me, a single tear, in Sorrow and Pity for the woman who has so wronged her.'

'Do you think there is Forgiveness?' I asked Ash. After reading that document, I'd picked up the habit of speaking with capital letters.

'We have to hope so, don't we?' he responded.

HG arranged for Elizabeth's bones to be buried in the churchyard, though at the opposite end from the McGoogle family vault. There was a small service which we all attended, while the crew filmed from a tactful distance. Since we were all working on a gardening show, the flowers were exceptionally beautiful.

'Now that the mystery is solved,' Delphi said, justifiably pleased with herself for doing most of the solving, 'her spirit can move on. So can Iona Craig, with luck. I mean, I didn't like her –' we all tended to speak of them as if we knew them personally – 'but she *was* sorry for what she did, and spent years being miserable and trying to make up for it.'

'What about Alasdair?' I said. 'I suppose we're stuck with him.'

'Doesn't matter,' Delphi said generously. 'There's plenty of space. And like Ash said, he's impotent and withering away.'

'I don't think that was quite how he put it . . .'

Later on, we had a meeting, as a result of which we approached HG.

'All right,' he said. 'This looks like a serious delegation. What's the problem?'

'We don't want you to replant the maze,' Delphi said.

'Why not? That's supposed to be the whole point.'

'The mystery was the point,' Delphi said, 'though we didn't know it till we got started. Now we've solved it. Mysteries are like skeletons: you dig them up and plant over the spot and move on. That's what we need to do. Nigel says you learn from history; you don't repeat it.'

'You mean if I replant the maze I might find myself murdering Basilisa? A good idea, but I've left it too late.'

'The maze wasn't evil in itself,' I said, 'but it was used for

389

an evil purpose. It was never a place for lovers to lose themselves on a sunny afternoon; it was a snare where people could be trapped and killed. Morag says if it's replanted all the spectres will come back. She may be exaggerating – after all, we've laid a few to rest – but do you really want to spend the next ten years listening to her dire warnings?'

'I'm accustomed,' HG said.

'Besides,' Delphi said by way of a clincher, 'it doesn't fit with the rest of the garden at all. We're going for the informal look, all wild flowers and rambling shrubs and statues peeping through clouds of May blossom. Against that background the maze will be *so* out of place, you'll have to call in another gardening show to come and get rid of it.'

I agreed with her, Russell agreed with her, even Morty agreed with her; but HG remained obdurate, clinging to his pet project like a small boy with a toffee apple. It's bad for his teeth and he's covered in stickiness, but he won't give it up. We were temporarily stymied. Mini hedges were springing up in rows, looking rather silly at the moment but still suggesting the imminent arrival of Birnham Wood at High Dunsinane. Delphi tried to subvert Jules and Sandy to dig them up in the night, with the idea of blaming it on the dogs, but Sting was too well trained to be a successful suspect and Fenny had missed out on the digging gene.

'Perhaps we could arrange for something really spooky to happen,' Delphi said, 'which would put HG off. Like . . . finding all the shovels and stuff scattered across the ground one morning, covered in blood, or . . .'

'Digging up a skeleton at the heart of the maze?' I said.

'Yeah, great – oh.'

Unexpected support came from Auld Andrew, who held forth on the subject at some length in broad Scottish (or possibly braw Scottish). We didn't understand much of what he said, but the gist was clear, involving as it did much saliva-spraying use of the local 'ch', much rolling of Rs in words like 'accurrrsed', and even the occasional hint that we were all doomed. After a confrontation with him HG did appear slightly damped, but it may have been because he needed to go and wash off the spittle.

I rang Crusty. I wasn't certain he appreciated how we all felt about the maze, but he said he was coming up in a day or two and assured me: 'All be sorted out then. No need to worry,' which sounded comforting but wasn't.

'What good can *he* do?' Delphi complained. 'No one has any influence with HG. Why don't you try, Roo? You're the one he kissed. Couldn't you do it again? Ash wouldn't mind: it's in a good cause.'

'He'd better mind,' I said.

The day Crusty was due, Sandy went to meet him at the airport in a purple Rolls with the numberplate GOD 1 and a pattern of pale green swirls and bubbles which made it resemble a giant lava lamp. HG must have ordered it when he was going through his junkie phase, though that still didn't explain why he hadn't got rid of it since. Nick, who was around at the time of Sandy's departure, took one look at it and tottered away to roll himself an enormous spliff, claiming a car like that wasn't something you wanted to contemplate with a clear head.

'He once picked me up from school in it,' Dorian said, blenching at the memory. 'I was ten. I didn't think I'd ever live it down.'

Later that morning the car returned, disgorging Crusty and an unexpected extra, obviously invited for back-up. Jennifer Dacres.

I was pleased to see her, Delphi was moderately pleased to see her, Russell was daunted ('Don't we have enough oars being

shoved in already? This show is turning into a bloody trireme!'),
Morty baffled. For all her expertise, he considered her a civil-
ian who could only be a hindrance to TV professionals. Auld
Andrew instantly took a shine to her, presenting her with a
bouquet culled from the rose bushes which he considered his
personal property and actually blushing as he did so, though
it was difficult to be sure under his grizzled, wrinkled, wind-
leathered exterior. HG was welcoming and promptly took her
and Crusty on a tour of the work in progress, including the
maze. He even gave her a guided tour *inside* the castle, an
honour never accorded to anyone else, reportedly apologising
for the horrors of the Basilisk effect. Jennie is hardly a conventional style guru, with her haphazard clothing and random
jewellery, and the sun-faded hair that's always half pinned up,
half coming down, yet somehow – so Crusty told us – she
contrived, merely by being there, to emphasise the tackiness
of rooms like the purple gallery and the African bedroom. She
has class: not the stuffy, plum-in-the-mouf kind but the kind
that comes from knowing exactly who you are and where you
belong without even thinking about it.

She didn't criticise the décor, or so I heard later. She simply
remarked, 'Poor thing, she didn't have a clue, did she?', thus
putting the absent Basilisa in her place for all time.

Whether her attitude was calculated or spontaneous even
Delphi couldn't tell.

When it came to the garden, Jennie dealt with the issue at
dinner in a single nonchalant sentence, tossed carelessly to
HG over the pheasant confit. 'I expect replanting the maze
was your wife's idea, wasn't it?' she said.

Delphi's eyes narrowed at this stroke of genius.

'Just the sort of romantic notion people get when they
don't know about gardens,' Jennie went on. 'History is all
very well, provided you leave it in the past. Some of these

McGoogles were pretty dubious characters, if you ask me – always having feuds with rival clans and murdering their wives and so on. Not really gardening people. I gather one of them planted the maze as some sort of scheme to put off getting married, then a few centuries later another one burnt it down. No point in repeating the mistake just because it's historical.'

Blitzed by her quiet assurance, and the assumptions she made, HG didn't say a word.

Nigel said: 'We thought it would be in keeping with the traditions of the castle.' He still hadn't decided which side he was on.

'You don't revive a tradition if it's bad,' Jennie said unanswerably. 'Silly thing to do. The maze works fine at Hampton Court, with all those formal gardens – they've done a great job of reconstruction there – but not here in the Highlands. You want a garden that'll blend in with the landscape: rugged rockeries, wild meadows, cascading water features – all fine. But not the maze. It'll stand out like a sore thumb. Spanish, wasn't she?' Casually, she harked back to Basilisa. 'They don't understand gardening. Surprising, really: the Alhambra Palace has some of the most beautiful gardens in the world, though of course they were designed by the Moors. Anyhow, a maze here would look worse than that Dali sofa. Might as well do topiary in the shape of a penis.'

Nigel, mesmerised, murmured delicately, 'Has anyone ever . . . ?'

'Oh yes.' Jennie mentioned one of the lesser royals. Well, not *that* lesser. 'I said to him, there's a time and a place for a sense of humour. This isn't it. You make a fool of yourself on some TV game show, it's over in a night. Topiary is for ever.'

She made this questionable assertion with the confidence of someone who believed it, and a room full of TV people didn't even attempt to contradict her. Delphi looked as if she was going to say something, but I caught her eye and shook my head. Jennie's tactics were inspired.

The next day, with HG's rueful assent, we uprooted the mini hedges and put them on a bonfire.

''Tis a job well done,' Morag affirmed. 'The ghaisties can sleep in peace the noo.'

R.I.P.

A week later, we were leaving.

We'd been at Dublair so long, I felt as if I too was being uprooted. We'd be back of course, later that year and again the following spring, to film the garden as it progressed towards mature gardenhood – in autumn glory, in April bloom – but it wouldn't be the same. In retrospect, I thought muzzily, on our last drunken evening, it had been the best working experience of my life. I felt a sense of achievement, of completeness, of Angus's champagne rising to my head. I had an ongoing boyfriend, an ongoing career. Crusty had said he wanted to work with me on another project and suggested lunch in London. Back on the lunch circuit, I thought.

'I'll really miss this place,' I said to Ash.

'I can't offer you a castle,' he responded. 'I can't offer you much of anything. My house is about to be sold – it's too big and empty without Caitlin and Neve. I put it on the market after they left. I suppose I'll get a flat somewhere.'

'I've got a flat,' I said. 'Do you . . . do you want to stay with me for a bit?' I felt very tentative about it, but surely, under the circumstances, I didn't sound overeager.

'Thanks,' said Ash. 'Let's give it a try.'

For a few moments, I was so happy I couldn't speak. I didn't dare. When I sobered up, the fear would kick in. Delphi was right: I'd always been single. Single is fine. Single is having your own space, single is not needing to adapt to anyone, not needing to put up with anyone, not needing to give way to anyone. It is a truth universally acknowledged that a single woman in possession of an adequate income is *not* in want of becoming a wife. Living together: that was the plunge I'd never taken. The moment when a relationship turns from romance into reality. I might have had Kyle's socks in my drawer and his porn mags under my bed, but he'd never been there on a full-time basis. I'd said to Ash 'for a bit', but we both knew what that meant. Ash was full-time. Ash was pressing my panic button. Ash was *commitment*.

Ash was love.

Love – the real one, the big one – is the scariest thing of all, because your heart is on the line. Lose all, win all. Time to roll the dice.

(Of course, the only game at which I've ever gambled is Snakes and Ladders, when I played Delphi and Jennie for chocolate one Christmas. Jennie won.)

The party grew sentimental. In due course, HG began to sing 'Rockabye Lula'. This time, he was serenading Jennie. Presently, Nick rushed in, no doubt out of his head on something or other, claiming he had just seen a ghost in full Highland regalia. But we'd grown so used to ghosts by then no one gave a toss.

Delphi sat stroking Fenny and saying she didn't know how Sting would cope, guarding the castle without his support.

Cedric danced with Young Andrew. Cheek to cheek.

A couple of hours later as Ash and I were going up to bed, I noticed the drawing room door was half open, and there was HG, stretched on the sofa, quoting Byron.

> *'Though the night was made for loving,*
> *And the day returns too soon,*
> *Yet we'll go no more a-roving*
> *By the light of the moon.'*

I couldn't see who he was with.

I remember I woke around three or four in the morning to hear, faint and far off, the eerie music of the bagpipes.

I never found out who was playing.

We were back in London. Back in what is called, by some extraordinary error of judgement, the Real World. Mountains are real: they have stood since the Earth first emerged from the melting pot of prehistory. Lochs are real: they were made when the first rains fell. A castle, bits of which have stood for a thousand years, has at least a claim on reality. But the world of the modern media, with its ten-seconds attention span, its fifteen-minute fame, its here-today, gone-tomorrow philosophy for jobs, lovers, friends – how close to reality is that? Yet this was my world.

'The world is what you make it,' Ash said. 'The moment of the yew tree and the moment of the rose are of an equal duration.'

I don't know where he got that from.

He went back to his house to sort out his things and I settled down to deal with my post, my unpaid bills, my answering machine. I played my messages in reverse order. The most recent was from Delphi.

'Watch out. It says in *TVTalk* that Tatyana's dumped Kyle for some guy she met in Shakespeare. It's only a matter of time . . .'

The next one was from Kyle.

He came round that evening, looking unshaven and crumpled and frayed around the edges.

'I've treated you badly,' he said. 'I probably always will. But you're the one. You're my girl – for good.'

That was Kyle. Never excuse, never apologise, never give an inch. Every man for himself, and every woman for any man. Devil take the hindmost.

I'd been planning to tell him I was with someone, someone wonderful, I was in love, I was blissfully happy. I'd dreamed of rubbing his nose in it, of kicking him when he was down, the way he'd kicked me. But suddenly, it didn't matter any more.

Anyway, that isn't my style.

'Have a drink,' I said. 'You know, I'm not your girl. I never was. I'm just *a* girl. One of a long list.'

'What did you want – a virgin?'

'No. What do you want? If you need a friend, that's fine. If you need a shag, I'm sorry.'

'I need *love*—'

'To get love, you have to give it,' I said. 'You don't know how.'

Delphinium

I was back in London. For some reason, it reminded me of a line from a nursery rhyme: 'Home again, home again, jiggetty-jig'. I don't know why that stuck in my head; I'm not a nursery-rhyme person. There was something unsettling about it, maybe because it sounded so cosy. Part of a routine. *Home again, home again* . . . Was that my life: routine? My glamorous, successful, enviable life of TV stardom and celebrity parties? Alex was history, a skeleton long tidied up and filed away. Time to get out and meet a new guy. (Fenny didn't like being left alone in the evenings, but I hardened my heart. He had to learn.) According to my spies, Alex and Brie were still – just – a couple, though the scandal sheets were on the case, tracking them from club to club, from row to row. HG's split with the Basilisk had given my reputation a bit of vital spit-and-polish, but I needed to be seen with another man as soon as possible – someone upmarket and incredibly desirable.

With my phone back on, my entire social circle was on the line, wanting the inside story on me and HG. I was airy, I was casual, I was actually quite truthful. 'Honestly, darling, *nothing happened*. It's all just a fabrication by the papers. Yes, Alex *had* always been a bit jealous, but there was no reason – none at all.' The more I denied any relationship, the more credence everyone gave to the gossip. A photographer snapped me walking past Mothercare on my way to a lunch date and promptly started a rumour I was pregnant. I bought a killer cocktail dress from Maddalena and went to a string of summer parties, frequently thrown by people I didn't know who invited me in the hope that I'd bring HG. I was *the* cool guest on the social circuit, my presence required at book launches and birthday bashes, first nights and last nights, premiers and promos. Men queued to chat me up, always asking, sooner or later, about my fling with a rock icon. It was like that song in the twenties: '*I danced with the man Who danced with the girl Who danced with the Prince of Wales*'. They all wanted to shag the girl who'd shagged Hot God. And then, presumably, there would be girls who'd queue to shag *them*, because they'd shagged me, and I'd . . . and so on.

Perhaps that was why I didn't fancy any of them.

I was laughing inwardly, telling myself I was having fun, and the joke was on them, and my life wasn't routine at all. My life was one long glitterfest, and everyone wanted to be me. I'd almost managed to convince myself until, at a publishing do in the Serpentine Gallery, gazing idly through the crowd, I thought I saw Harry. A man with his face averted, fairish hair, an air of solidity about the shoulders. My heart leaped, a great big leap of hope and excitement and – yes – joy. I was having a dull conversation with a dull minor celeb who'd written a book about his trek across the Gobi Desert with nothing but a bottle of water, a packet of raisins, and a ball of string (trust me: dull). Suddenly, I wasn't bored any more. I slid effortlessly out of the conversation and made my way through the crowd, all set to say something witty, challenging, lofty yet with sexual undercurrents – though I hadn't the faintest idea what. Inspiration would come. Then the man turned round – and it wasn't Harry at all. My disappointment was so acute that someone asked me if I was feeling all right. It ought to have been Harry, I thought furiously. After all, he was a bloody journalist, and everyone knew journalists wrote books on the side. He *ought* to be at a publishing party. He should be looking for me, trying to get in touch. He was an *investigative* journalist; why didn't he investigate me?

What the hell was the matter with me?

The next night, at yet another party (early evening drinks), I met a former Olympic runner turned commentator who was good-looking, probably about B+-list, and who asked me to dinner. I said yes. He ticked the right boxes. We went to Zilli's, and I saw a gossip columnist at another table checking us out, but decided that to give her a big smile would be a bit unsubtle. The guy talked about being an Olympic runner, and asked me about Scotland, where he had once run, and in due course, inevitably, he got on to the subject of HG. Was he still attractive, even though he was so old? Had he had cosmetic surgery? Was it true he had a small dick, didn't do cunnilingus, insisted on, like, you know, the total wax? Did I still have that? He'd always really fancied shaved pussy . . .

I'd had enough.

'I'm really sorry to disappoint everybody,' I said, 'but I *didn't* shag him. I didn't want to shag him, he didn't want to shag me. He's an okay guy, Basilisa Ramón is a poisonous cow – that's reason enough for the divorce. Since you're so interested, why don't you go for *her*? I'm sick sick SICK of people who want to get off with me because I'm part of a celebrity shag-chain. Enjoy your bloody dinner: I'm leaving!'

I got up, balled my napkin, hurled it to the ground and walked out. I didn't care how it looked, or what he thought, or what the gossip columnist thought. At that moment I knew I couldn't bear to go out with him – or anyone like him – for even five minutes, let alone long-term. I stood on the Soho street feeling rage streaming from every pore and realised I needed a bolt hole, somewhere I could sit quietly, sip a drink in peace and chill. From Zilli's there was an obvious option, and ten to one the ex-runner wasn't a member; he was too new on the scene.

I walked the twenty yards or so to the Groucho Club.

The Groucho is an institution. It's been around since the mid-eighties, which makes it practically antique, though not as antique as the Garrick, of course, and there are times when it's the coolest place in town, and times when the cool people go elsewhere, but the Groucho doesn't care. It just goes on being there, and eventually the cool people come back, or different people become cool and decide to hang there, because it's comfortable. Not jazzy, not trendy, just comfortable, and somehow there's nowhere else in town where you can feel so much at ease. It's an ideal place to take the tag-end of a tantrum and unwind.

Everyone goes to the Groucho, sooner or later. *Everyone*. Actors, writers, artists, journalists.

Journalists . . .

In reception I said that if anyone asked for me, I wasn't here. They smiled and said, 'No problem.'

It was mid-evening; the downstairs bar was busy but not packed. And there he was, sitting on one of the high stools. Stocky shoulders, sandy hair. Harry. Unmistakably Harry. He was talking to some chap (thank God it wasn't a woman) and he had his back to me, but this time I was completely certain. I went to a space at the bar a couple of people along from him and waited to order. My bad temper had evaporated and my heart was beating so hard I was afraid I was visibly shaking. There's a mirror on the facing wall, ideal for making sure you look beautiful (the lighting's very sympathetic so you always do) and checking out anyone who comes in behind you. I could see Harry, intent on his conversation, but he didn't notice me.

Bugger.

The buzz of general chatter was too loud for him to hear my voice when I ordered and it looked like I could be standing there for ever, or at least until he needed to go to the loo. (He would have to walk past me for that.) I'm no good with suspense. Clutching my drink for protection, I walked over to him.

He's the butler, I told myself. The bloody butler. You can't have nerves with a *butler* . . .

'Harry,' I said.

He looked round. Smiled.

The way someone looks the first second they see you, *that's* when you know.

'Delphi,' he said. 'Delphi . . . This is Charles.' Charles and I duly acknowledged each other. 'Are you busy? Meeting someone?'

'No,' I said baldly. 'I just walked out on a dinner date. I'm fed up of people asking me about shagging Hot God.'

'I see. Did you get any dinner first? Good. Charles and I are nearly done and I haven't eaten either. Stay here, take the stool – I'll go fix up a table.' He went off to the brasserie while my heart-rate steadied and Charles, who suddenly seemed like the nicest person I'd ever met, talked about gardens – he'd just acquired one – and seemed to have no trouble not mentioning HG at all.

Then Harry came back, they finished their chat, which was journalistic in content, and we went in to dinner.

Just being next to him at the bar I was incredibly aware of him physically, as if he sparked off an electric charge all over my body. I decided he was much too relaxed. Something would have to be done about that. It was easier at the table because we were sitting opposite each other and I wasn't wondering every second which parts of my anatomy were touching – or nearly touching – which parts of his.

'So,' he said, 'what happened after I left?'

I told him. I told him about the ouija board and Morag's strange trance and how I worked out the whole truth about Elizabeth's murder and Alasdair coming back as his cousin, and then how we found the confession that confirmed it all. He was riveted and kept looking at me in a sort of warm, appreciative way which gave me a lovely glow inside. Then I told him about HG still sticking to the maze idea, and Crusty arriving with reinforcements, and how effortlessly my mother routed the opposition.

'I'd like to meet her,' he said. 'She sounds great.'

He'd like to meet my *mother*?? Does he know what he's saying?

'She's still at Dunblair,' I said. 'HG wanted more help with the garden, so she stayed on. I think she feels he needs watching, in case he suddenly decides to build a folly or something.'

Harry grinned. 'Rock stars,' he said.

'Yeah.' I found I'd picked up his grin.

'What about you?' I went on. 'You don't have a police bodyguard any more, I see.'

'Not now Attila's dead. The group just fell apart without him. The other two are heading for long gaol terms, anyway. No, it's business as usual for me.'

'More investigative stuff?'

'Various projects. Nothing undercover, though.' He added: 'You're a pretty good investigator yourself.'

'If you need a partner . . . !'

'The glamorous blonde sidekick who acts like a bimbo then shows me up at every turn?'

'That's the idea,' I said.

Main courses arrived, causing a brief diversion. I wasn't at all hungry, and apart from picking up a chip in my fingers in case I required a weapon, I left most of mine.

'New boyfriend?' Harry asked, with what I recognised as careful nonchalance.

'Not yet,' I said. 'I'm still reviewing the shortlist.' (In case he thought no one was interested in me.)

'I was going to phone you,' he said, 'but . . . er . . . the tabloids seemed to think you were pretty busy.'

So he made *me* do the work. I'd had to come into the Groucho to find him, even if it *was* by chance. Huh!

'I always tell the tabloids what I'm up to,' I snapped.

'We going to have a fight?' he said.

'Probably!'

'Then what?'

I shouldn't have let him meet my eyes. My stomach took a dive and the electric charge went straight to the X-spot. In a *restaurant* . . .

'Has there been anyone since me?' Harry asked.

'No,' I conceded. Then I went on, 'I was so traumatised by my experience with you, I've lost all interest in sex.' With anyone else.

'Really?' He let the moment linger. 'Maybe you need some therapy.'

I ignored that. 'Have you . . . has there . . .'

'No. No one since you. Lot of things to sort out.'

So he hadn't been pining for me. He just hadn't had *time* for anyone else.

'I'm sure you'll manage to accommodate someone soon,' I said coldly.

'You know, Dacres, you're dead sexy when you act snooty.'

'*Don't* call me Dacres! Just because I called you – what the hell *is* your name, anyway? It *is* Harry, isn't it?'

He laughed. 'Yeah,' he said. 'Harry Slater.'

'Slater? God, that's so . . . *plebeian*.'

'That's me. One of the plebs.' I knew he was going to say it, and he did. 'Rough trade.'

'D'you think I haven't been through all that?' I said miserably. 'Worrying that it's going to be the plumber next, or the dustman, or—'

'How can you be such an idiot,' he said, 'when you're so smart?'

'I'm not—'

'I want to fuck you. Now. Tonight. Every night. I want to fuck all the nonsense out of you. I want you in my bed, in my life. I want—'

'Yes,' I whispered.

He said: 'You're so not my type.'

'Snap.'

'I'm not going to do much for your image.'

Belatedly, I ate the chip. 'I don't care. I'm bored of it, anyway. The whole celeb thing. Been there, done that.'

Harry said, 'You won't get bored of me.'

'I know.'

We paid the bill and said the meal had been wonderful, which was true, even though we'd scarcely eaten a thing. Then we went back to my place, because I didn't like to leave Fenny too long. In the taxi, we hardly talked at all. As soon as the front door was shut we were unbuttoning, unzipping, fumbling with each other's fastenings and our own, clumsy with haste and desperation. Fenny tried to join in but Harry shut him in the living room with most of our clothes and then we were doing it, he was inside me, fucking me and fucking me, and I remember thinking, in some still quiet corner of my mind, that I would be his slave for ever, just for this. For the feel of him, his strength and his maleness, his dick in my vitals . . .

I won't ever tell him, of course.

Anyway, he probably knows.

Several months went by. I collaborated, with Nigel of all people, on the book of the garden of the lost maze. Roo was so in demand she did something for the BBC, then in the New Year she and I are going to be working with Crusty on a series about designing eco-gardens for people who want to encourage wildlife, with locations all over Europe. She seems to be settled with Ash and very happy.

Alex and Brie got engaged – it was in all the papers – and he gave her the same ring he gave me. I was furious, since I chose it and he was getting the credit for my good taste. Harry laughed and laughed.

He says he wants to marry me when we have a weekend with nothing else to do, but he won't have any guests or presents or any of the kerfuffle, because he wants to be sure I'm doing it for him and not just for the wedding.

'Can't I do it for both?' I say.

It's something we argue about when we run out of anything else.

HG's divorce went very smoothly after *her* lawyers met *his* lawyers and discovered how much dirt he had on her. Afterwards, Basilisa went to Hollywood and sank without trace.

Skinhead and Greaseball are in prison, where they are probably very happy. I know what it's like: I've seen *Porridge*. The lifestyle should suit them.

My father turned up a couple of times and I tried to be kind, in case I take after him, but Harry handled him brilliantly – friendly but firm – and since Dunblair my father is a little in awe of him. Anyhow, then he went back to the South of France and married a wealthy divorcee. She has three daughters.

I hear Cedric and Young Andrew are an item, and Jules and Sandy have two German shepherd puppies which are absolutely adorable. I'm sure Fenny will love them.

We're all going to Dunblair for Christmas.

I haven't been able to stay out of the papers as much as I expected, but it isn't my fault.

Hot God married my mother.

Being Committed

Anna Maxted

Hannah thinks you have to be insane to get married. She's content with her life – the job as a private investigator at Hound Dog Investigations, the boyfriend of five years, Jason, and the wonderful father (pity her mother is such a disaster). Besides which, she's tried marriage once before, but she ended up divorced before she was 21.

So, when the long-suffering Jason proposes, Hannah doesn't think twice about turning him down. Still, she's a little shaken when, a month later, the man has the nerve to get engaged to someone else. Is she not up to settling down? Hannah's family are convinced she blew her one chance of hooking a permanent man, and maybe – just maybe – there's something in Jason's theory that being committed means first coming to terms with your past.

Praise for Anna Maxted

'Always one to favour heroines who err on the quirky side, Hannah is her best to date – a wonderfully eccentric character who'll have you in stitches' *Glamour*

'Funny and inspiring, you'll be turning the pages 'til the small hours' *Company*

arrow books

ALSO AVAILABLE IN ARRROW

Dancing on Thorns

Rebecca Horsfall

When Jonni Kendal comes to London to pursue her dream of becoming an actress, she's young, naive, full of courage and determined to excel. Just nineteen, she's desperate to escape the narrow, parochial life her parents have planned for her.

Jean-Baptiste St. Michel is haunted by his father: the man who abandoned him as a child, the man he can hardly remember, the man he cannot forget. Driven by his determination to forge a life for himself outside of the shadow his father's famous name casts, he's ambitious, talented and dangerously attractive – but suspicious of emotional attachments.

When Michel rescues Jonni one night and takes her home, there's an immediate attraction. Jonni finds herself embraced by an exciting new world she never suspected existed, and Michel, ever wary of commitment, finds himself growing used to her presence in his life. But before he can commit to any kind of future, he must release himself from his past . . .

'The new Jilly Cooper' *Elle*

'A welcome return to the epic romance' *Good Housekeeping*

'Secrets, betrayal and friendship all play their part in this sweeping novel' *Woman & Home*

arrow books